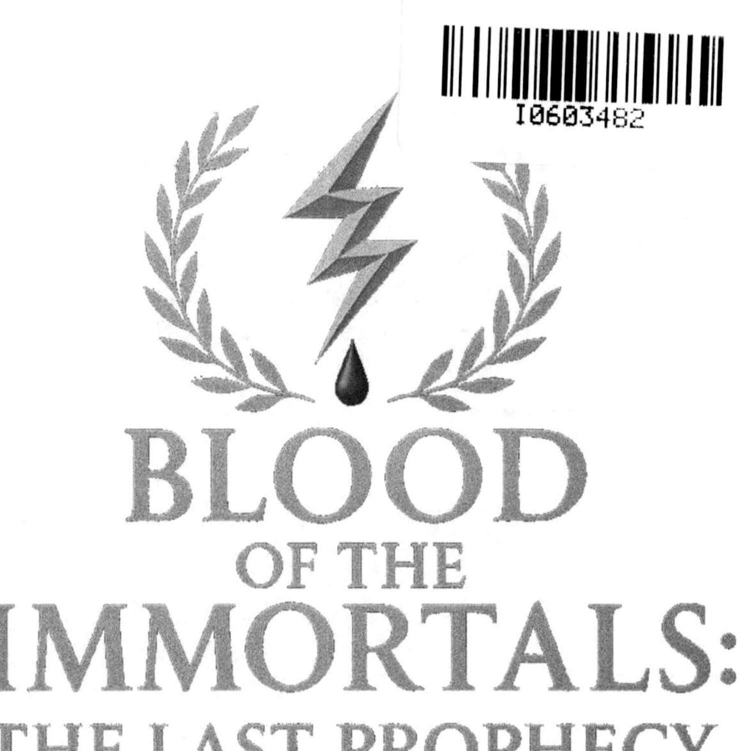

# BLOOD
## OF THE
# IMMORTALS:
## THE LAST PROPHECY

**"HISTORY IS ONLY MYTH... BUT WHEN YOU LIVE IT, YOU'LL BELIEVE IT."**

*This story was never meant to be tidy, or safe. It is a storm of fragments, chains, and choices, scattered across the world-that-was. Some will call it fantasy. Some will call it prophecy. But those who walk with me through these pages will know: the line between history and myth can quickly be erased.*

**BLOOD OF THE IMMORTALS: THE LAST PROPHECY**

# BOOK ONE: THE STORM THAT SPLIT THE SKY

William Ginn

*"For those of you who believe myth is only fantasy and not history... you're about to be awakened."*

*This is not comfort, and it is not an escape. It is a record written in stormlight and shadow, in chains and choices that will not wait for belief. Keep turning, and you will see what cannot be unseen. From this point forward, the line you thought separated story from truth will not protect you.*

This is a work of fiction. Names, characters, places, and incidents are either products of the author's imagination or used fictitiously. Any resemblance to actual persons, living or dead, or actual events is purely coincidental.

First Edition

ISBN (Paperback): 979-8-9931128-0-0

ISBN (Hardcover): 979-8-9931128-1-7

ISBN (eBook): 979-8-9931128-2-4

Published by Omen Spire Press

A Division of Omen Spire Media

Cover and interior design © 2025 by William Ginn

Fonts used: Cinzel by Natanael Gama; Garamond

Printed in the United States of America

WHEN THE HEAVENS ALIGN AND THE
STORM CONVERGES, TWELVE SHALL
WAKE FROM THE BLOOD OF GODS.
THEY WILL WALK A PATH OF
TRIALS—TORN BY LINEAGE, BROKEN BY
STRUGGLE, HUNTED BY WHAT WATCHES.
EACH WILL BEAR A MARK THAT BURNS
LIKE MEMORY; ONLY TOGETHER WILL
THEY ENDURE THE TEMPEST.
THRONES WILL TREMBLE; ALL BUT ONE
SHALL BE CLAIMED ANEW— A SEAT OF
LOVE, LEFT EMPTY, AWAITING A CHOICE
BEYOND GODS AND CHAINS.
YET THE HEART OF THE STORM WILL
DEMAND ITS PRICE: **ONE LIFE, FREELY
GIVEN**, TO BIND THE THRONES AND
SEAL THE WAY. THUS BEGINS THE
TURNING OF THE WORLD-THAT-WAS,
SPLIT AND SCATTERED, WAITING TO BE
NAMED AGAIN.

— TERM OBSCURED "THE FORGOTTEN
CHAIN" · (glyph variance noted · translation unstable

*SCHOLAR'S NOTE:* "FORGOTTEN CHAIN" APPEARS TO BE A
FIRST LANGUAGE METAPHOR FOR A FORCE THAT BINDS YET
REMAINS UNCOUNTED. NO PROPER NAME IS USED.

**The Hellenic Institute of Mythology**
Athens, Greece                                Venice, Italy

**Provenance Authentication**

The passage presented on the preceding page — now identified as *The Original Codex Fragment* — is herein authenticated by the Hellenic Institute of Mythology.

After exhaustive review, the Institute confirms that this fragment is the earliest known record in the Codex tradition. While other fragments have been uncovered across multiple excavation sites, this piece is considered the **first recovered, first translated, and first formally archived** within the Institute's vaults.

Its linguistic structure aligns with inscriptions preserved on archaic tablets found in scattered Mediterranean and Near Eastern ruins, suggesting an origin far earlier than the classical Hellenic period. The recurring references to storms, chains, and twelve figures align with motifs catalogued in other fragments, but here appear in their earliest, most unaltered form.

Scholars therefore conclude that this text represents the **original prophecy of the Codex tradition**, preserved against time and recorded for the first time in modern scholarship.

On behalf of the Institute, we affirm this provenance for the historical and mythological record.

*Dr. Eleni Makris*
Director, Hellenic Institute of Mythology
*Prof. Alexandros Stavros*
Archaeological Consultant

# PART I – THE AWAKENING



# PART II – THE GATHERING



# PART III – THE THREADS OF FATE

# PART IV – THE CITY OF GODS



# PART V – THE STORM BREAKS



# PART VI – THE RECKONING

# PART 1 – THE AWAKENING

CHAPTER 1

# THE STORM THAT SPLIT THE SKY

Halloween Night, 2025

Chicago had seen storms before, but never one that would be remembered in whispers—the night the sky itself split open. The silence after the lightning felt heavier than the thunder itself, as if the world were holding its breath. Leo thought of storms he'd seen before, but none had carried this iron taste in the air, this strange sense that the rain itself was listening.

But this wasn't weather. Later, scientists would call it an atmospheric anomaly. Survivors would call it the night the lights went out. For the first time in history, the world fell dark together—skyscrapers, deserts, oceans, mountains, all swallowed by the same silence. Months later, power grids still hadn't fully recovered. And no one could explain why.

The storm did not just split the sky—it felt as though Olympus itself exhaled. The thunder didn't just shake windows—it rumbled like chains straining beneath the world, as if each strike of lightning was a sentence of some forgotten decree.

For a heartbeat, he thought of the watchtower's silence—the way people called him reckless, the way no one ever believed in the boy who kept chasing storms. And now, at last, the storm itself seemed to see him.

Every drop of rain struck with weight, hissing on rusted steel and fractured glass. Leo felt—not for the first time—that the world was watching him, waiting for him, judging him.

He tightened his jaw. No one waited for Leo Alekos. Not his father. Not the kids at school. Not anyone. The storm was the first thing in months that seemed to care whether he lived or drowned.

Bolts of white-blue energy branched down like roots across the skyline, not striking but erasing. Transformers blew, rails froze, skyscrapers winked out floor by floor. This wasn't lightning—it was something older, something hungrier, draining the city as though the storm itself had teeth.

Through the blur of rain, a figure stood across the tracks—too far to name, too close to ignore. When Leo blinked, it was gone, leaving only the echo of eyes in the storm.

A storm thousands of years in the making had been waiting. Silent. Patient.

Coiled above the world like a living thing, unseen by all but the gods who had chained it.

It was not born of clouds or wind or water.
It was born of prophecy.

The October air had that restless, brittle edge—cold enough to hint at winter, but still carrying the faint smoke of autumn bonfires.

And on October 31st, 2025, everything aligned.

The chains broke. And the storm split the sky.

Not just to drench the city below. Not just to howl its fury into the void.

But to change everything.
Forever.

◆ ◆ ◆

The first crack of lightning hit so close it felt like it split the bones of the earth.

A bank of dead fluorescents flickered in the gutted security shack, buzzing like angry wasps. The storm felt close enough to press a hand against his ribs from the inside.

The air itself waited for him to move.

Leo Alekos flinched as the ground beneath his boots shuddered, loose gravel skittering across the skeletal remains of the Chicago trainyard. Rusted tracks jutted from the dirt like broken ribs, twisted from decades of neglect. Abandoned cars loomed in the darkness like ghosts of a city that used to matter.

And across the world, millions stared into sudden darkness. In Athens, the Acropolis fell black for the first time in centuries. In Cairo, the Nile vanished into shadow. In Tokyo, neon bled away until the skyline looked like a grave. Everywhere, silence spread. The storm hadn't passed. It had only begun.

The air smelled like wet metal and ozone, sharp enough to sting the back of his throat.

The sky boiled.

It wasn't just a storm.

It was alive.

Leo pulled his hood tighter around his face, his breath fogging in the unseasonable chill. It was late October, but this didn't feel like any Midwestern weather he'd ever known.

This felt like the end of the world.

He checked his phone for the tenth time, though the screen had been dead since the first lightning strike. Figures.

He wasn't even sure why he'd come out here tonight.

No—that was a lie.

He knew exactly why.

Because when the city felt too big, too loud, too suffocating, this place was the only one that felt like it belonged to him.

The trainyard ruins didn't care who he was.

Didn't care that his dad had walked out when he was eight, leaving him and his mom to scrape by. Didn't care that his mom worked two jobs and still barely had time to look him in the eye. Didn't care that Leo Alekos—dropout, nobody, ghost of a kid—was one bad day from disappearing entirely and no one would notice.

Here, among the rust and the rot, he could breathe.

Or at least, he used to.

Tonight, the air was too heavy to breathe.

The wind picked up, howling between the train cars.

Leo cursed under his breath, shoving his hands into his pockets.

He needed to get back before this storm got worse—if that was even possible. But something kept him rooted in place.

Some instinct he couldn't explain.

Like the storm wasn't just above him.

It was watching him.

The second lightning strike came without warning.

It didn't just split the sky.

It ripped it open.

A blinding spear of white-blue fire slammed into one of the derailed train cars twenty feet away. The sound was so loud it felt like the world itself screamed.

Leo staggered back, throwing up his arms as a shockwave of heat and static rolled over him.

The car hissed where it had been struck, metal glowing faintly like it had been pulled from a forge.

And then he heard it.

A low, bone-deep hum threaded through the storm—not from the trainyard. From inside him.

"What the hell…"

Leo clutched at his chest, but there was nothing there—no injury, no wound. Just that impossible hum, vibrating through his ribs like a plucked string.

The storm roared again, the sky flashing with jagged veins of lightning.

He stumbled, boots skidding on the wet gravel, heart hammering.

For an instant, the boy inside him surfaced—the one who had prayed his father would come home, who had learned too early that some storms never pass. He shoved the ache down, but the memory lingered like salt in his throat.

That's when the voice came.

"Child of the Sea."

Leo froze.

The words weren't shouted.

They weren't whispered.

They just were—as present and undeniable as the storm.

"Who's there?!" His voice cracked, swallowed instantly by the howling wind.

No answer.

Just the storm.

And the hum, growing louder.

The ground trembled beneath him.

Puddles scattered across the trainyard rippled, pulling toward him like magnets.

Leo staggered back again, his chest tight.

This wasn't real.

Couldn't be real.

And yet—

"You were not made for silence," the voice said. "You were made to rise."

Lightning struck again.

This time, it didn't hit the trainyard.

It hit him.

The world went white.

Heat exploded through his veins, searing and cold all at once.

He should've died.

He should've been ash on the wind.

Instead, he was still standing.

The water at his feet surged upward, wrapping around his legs like it had been waiting for him.

Leo gasped, staggering as tendrils of water coiled up his arms, slick and heavy, yet impossibly light.

The hum in his chest became a roar.

Not pain.

Not exactly.

It was something deeper.

Like the part of him that had always been empty—the part his father left hollow—was being filled for the first time.

With power.

With fury.

With the sea itself.

"Stop!" he shouted, though he wasn't sure who he was talking to—the storm? The voice? Himself?

"Stop?" The voice chuckled. "You've been waiting for this longer than you know."

Leo fell to his knees, gripping his head.

"I don't want this!"

"Liar."

The word hit harder than the lightning.

The water surged higher, rising around him like a living tide.

Leo's panic curdled into something else.

Something hot and dangerous.

He wasn't just in the storm.

He was the storm.

The storm wasn't just around him.

It was in him.

The rain lashed sideways in sheets so thick it felt like the sky itself was falling, but Leo didn't feel cold anymore.

The water wrapped around him like armor, moving with him, through him, alive.

His knees hit the gravel, but it wasn't weakness—it was gravity. Some greater force pressing down on him, commanding him to bow.

"No," he hissed between clenched teeth.

The word was almost drowned out by the storm.

Almost.

"Defiance," the voice said, approvingly.

Lightning carved a jagged burn across the sky, its afterimage burned into his eyes.

And then the storm moved.

Not the wind.

Not the rain.

The whole storm.

And it was looking at him.

The world tilted.

The ground beneath him vanished.

Leo's stomach lurched as gravity became meaningless, the trainyard dissolving into black, endless water.

♦ ♦ ♦

He was falling.

No—sinking.

The storm above was just a distant smear of light, muted and far away.

The water was everywhere.

And it wanted him.

Leo thrashed, fighting for air.

But there was no air here.

Only the crushing silence of the deep.

His lungs screamed, and his chest convulsed, but he couldn't stop sinking.

Down, down, down.

Until the last glimmer of light vanished.

Until there was nothing but darkness.

And then the darkness spoke.

"Breathe."

Leo's chest seized.

"No," he choked out, though there was no air for the word to carry.

"I'll drown."

"You'll rise."

He couldn't.

Every instinct screamed at him not to.

But his body was done fighting.

The moment his mouth opened, the water surged in.

And it didn't choke him.

It filled him.

Warmed him.

He could breathe.

♦ ♦ ♦

Leo gasped and opened his eyes.

He wasn't in the deep anymore.

He was standing.

On marble.

The hall was impossibly massive, carved from stone the color of the sea in winter—blue-green streaked with veins of silver. The air smelled of salt and storms, brine stinging his nostrils as if he were standing on the deck of a ship in the middle of a hurricane.

Somewhere deep within the shadows above, something groaned—the slow, leviathan-deep sound of something massive shifting just out of sight.

The hall wasn't empty.

It was watching him.

Colossal pillars rose into an endless vault of darkness above, their surfaces etched with sigils that glowed faintly like bioluminescent creatures in the abyss.

The floor was a mosaic: a trident splitting the waves, surrounded by twelve symbols he didn't recognize.

At the far end of the hall, a throne waited.

It wasn't ornate.

It didn't need to be.

It was carved from a single slab of dark stone, simple and brutal, like it had been pulled from the bones of the ocean itself.

And on it sat a man.

No—not a man.

A god.

His skin was sun-browned and burned like weathered stone, his beard shot through with silver. His eyes—impossibly blue, impossibly deep—looked like they could swallow oceans whole.

He didn't wear a crown.

He didn't need one.

The sea itself bent toward him, waves of invisible power pulling at the edges of the hall.

"You've kept me waiting," the god said.

His voice was the tide—endless, patient, inevitable.

Leo's mouth went dry. "Who… who are you?"

The god leaned forward, elbows on his knees, eyes narrowing. "You know."

And Leo did.

Somewhere deep in his blood, in a part of him he'd never understood, he knew.

"Poseidon," he whispered.

The name tasted like salt and lightning.

The god smiled, sharp and dangerous.

"Child of the sea," Poseidon said. "You are mine."

Leo staggered back. "No. I'm not—I can't—"

"Can't what?" Poseidon's voice rolled through the hall, shaking the marble. "Can't carry what you already are? Can't face what you've always been?"

"I'm no one," Leo said, his voice breaking.

"You are my blood."

Leo's throat closed.

"I don't want this."

"Liar."

The word was soft.

Cruel.

True.

Poseidon stood.

The hall groaned as if the ocean itself strained to hold his weight.

"You think I care what you want?" His voice rose, a storm in human shape. "You were born for this. Shaped by it. Every moment you've cursed your life, every day you've wanted to disappear, every time you've wished for something bigger than the scraps you were given—it led you here."

The god raised his hand.

The mosaic at Leo's feet shifted, water spilling from the trident in its center. It coiled up his legs like serpents, cold and alive, winding tighter the more he struggled.

"You are mine," Poseidon said.

"No—"

The water surged higher, wrapping his chest, his throat.

Leo's knees buckled.

"Please," he gasped.

The god crouched, leveling his gaze with Leo's.

"You've begged enough," Poseidon said, his voice soft again. "Now rise."

The water pulled him under.

He didn't fight it this time.

He let it fill him.

Drown him.

Remake him.

The threads roared to life.

Leo doubled over, clutching his head as they slammed into his mind—a dozen connections sparking at once.

Some burned hot, fierce as wildfire.

Some were steady, slow, immovable.

Some flickered faintly, keeping their distance.

And one…

One was wrong.

Like a corrupted note in a perfect chord, scraping through his veins.

He sucked in a breath, shaking.

"What is that?" he rasped.

Poseidon tilted his head.

"The chain," he said simply.

"Something's off—"

"And you will learn why. In time."

The threads pulsed again, grounding him.

Twelve symbols in the mosaic glowed faintly at his feet, one brighter than the others.

A trident.

His.

"Do you feel it now?" Poseidon asked.

Leo swallowed hard. "Yes."

"Good."

The god's eyes softened, though they didn't lose their weight. "Then stand, child of the storm."

Leo did.

The water obeyed him now, coiling around his arms like living armor.

The hum in his chest had become a roar.

The god smiled.

And for a moment, Leo swore the sea itself smiled with him.

◆ ◆ ◆

The hall dissolved.

The throne.

The god.

The trident-etched floor.

All of it shattered like glass, replaced by screaming wind and torrential rain.

Leo gasped, lungs burning as he slammed back into his body, kneeling in the flooded ruins of the trainyard.

The storm hadn't ended.

If anything, it was worse.

Lightning split the sky in jagged veins of white-blue. Wind whipped so hard it felt like it was trying to tear the world apart. The derailed cars around him groaned, metal screeching as they were pushed against the tracks like toys in the hands of a furious child.

And the water—

The water wasn't still anymore.

It surged at his feet, swirling in unnatural patterns, coiling around his legs like it remembered him.

Claimed him.

Leo staggered to his feet, every muscle aching like he'd been hit by a freight train.

No.

Not hit.

Struck.

By lightning.

He looked down at his hands, expecting burns, broken bones, something.

Instead, golden light shimmered faintly beneath his skin, fading in and out with the rhythm of his pulse.

"What the hell…"

The word barely made it out of his mouth before the wind carried it away.

The threads hummed.

He could still feel them—those other presences tethered to him. Some pulsed steady and strong.

Some were faint and distant.

And one still scraped at him, sharp and wrong.

He shook his head, trying to shove the sensations aside, but the more he fought them, the stronger they became.

A low hiss cut through the storm.

Not wind.

Not water.

Something else.

Leo spun, heart hammering, and saw them.

Two figures at the edge of the trainyard.

Tall.

Slender.

Cloaked in black that the rain didn't seem to touch.

Porcelain-white masks stared at him with hollow, unblinking eyes.

They didn't move.

They didn't need to.

Leo knew they were here for him.

The threads convulsed, thrumming violently in his veins.

His instincts screamed at him to run.

But his feet stayed planted.

It wasn't courage.

It was something deeper.

Some unspoken understanding that running wouldn't matter.

Because these things would follow.

The first one tilted its head at him, jerky and inhuman.

"The storm awakens," it hissed. "And the chains weaken."

The second cocked its head the opposite way.

"The sea claims its child."

Its voice was metallic, scraping, like a rusted blade dragged across stone.

Leo's chest tightened.

"What are you?"

They didn't answer.

They glided closer.

The first raised a hand, and the air grew heavier.

Leo staggered as the storm itself seemed to pause—wind, rain, even the lightning holding its breath.

The Watcher's clawed fingers curled.

"You should not exist," it said.

"I get that a lot," Leo muttered, though his voice cracked.

The second hissed.

"Unmade."

It lunged.

Leo barely moved in time.

The thing was fast—impossibly fast—its claw slicing through the air where his throat had been a second earlier.

Instinct took over.

He threw his hands out, and the water obeyed.

A wall of liquid rose from the flooded ground, slamming into the Watcher like a battering ram.

The impact sent it sprawling back into the side of a derailed car, the metal crunching on impact.

Leo stumbled, breathless, staring at his hands.

He'd done that.

The second hissed and lunged.

Leo turned sharply, dragging water up from the puddles like a living whip.

He swung.

The strike caught the Watcher mid-charge, sending it skidding across the gravel.

His heart pounded, his blood roaring in his ears.

He was alive.

He was fighting.

And the water was his.

The first Watcher stood, head snapping unnaturally as its mask cracked where Leo's water had hit.

It hissed, tilting its broken face.

"The chain will break."

Leo clenched his fists, water swirling at his sides.

"Not tonight."

The second Watcher hissed again, its voice layered and inhuman.

"We'll see."

Then—as suddenly as they'd appeared—they vanished, swallowed by the rain.

The storm raged on.

Leo staggered, every muscle trembling, chest heaving like he'd run miles.

The threads thrummed one last time before quieting.

But not gone.

Never gone.

♦ ♦ ♦

Far below Olympus, in halls of obsidian veined with molten gold, Maelis traced her fingers across the living map.

The storm's pulse flickered through it like veins of lightning.

She smiled, though it did not touch her eyes.

"The first has awakened," she whispered.

The map glowed faintly, threads of white-blue energy spreading outward from the heart of the storm.

Her hand lingered over one link in the chain—bright, unsteady, fragile.

Her lips curled.

"It begins."

The storm howled above the world, and in its shadow, a whisper curled through the silence.

"But it will."

**Hellenic Institute of Mythology**

Athens, Greece                                Venice, Italy

**To Whom It May Concern,**

Following a thorough review of the recovered Codex fragments, we provide the following clarification for cataloging and interpretive purposes:

These fragments have been provisionally identified and numbered in the order in which they were uncovered during excavation and subsequent archival transfer. This numbering system is intended solely for reference and continuity within our working archive. It does **not** represent, nor can it guarantee, the original sequence in which these writings were composed or compiled.

The physical and linguistic evidence strongly indicates that a significant portion of the Codex material remains missing or unrecovered. As such, any reconstruction of their intended progression remains speculative, and *all numbering should be regarded as practical convenience rather than definitive order*.

It is our position that while these fragments provide valuable insight into Olympian-era transmission and pre-Olympian script traditions, the absence of the presumed "larger corpus" prevents absolute certainty in their original arrangement.

We recommend all readers and researchers approach the numbering with caution, recognizing it as a tool of modern cataloging rather than a reflection of authentic ancient structure.

Respectfully submitted,

**Dr. Eleni Makris**
Director, Hellenic Institute of Mythology
(on behalf of the Institute's Codex Review Committee

# *CODEX FRAGMENT*
# *THE FORGOTTEN NAME*

A VOICE BENEATH UNWATERS THE EARTH.
IT SPEAKS WITHOUT SPEAKING, WEARING
BORROWED FACES.
MIRRORS LIE; MASKS TELL THE TRUTH.
BEWARE THE NUMBER THAT IS NEVER
WRITTEN —
THE MARK THAT ANSWERS WHEN YOU DO
NOT CALL IT.
FOLLOW THE CURRENT UNDER CITIES OF
SALT AND SONG;
THERE THE OLD BARGAIN RUSTS, WAITING
TO BE TOUCHED.

# CHAPTER 11
# THE GIRL WHO SAW
# THE PATTERN

November 10, 2025

Cambridge carried the brittle silence of late autumn, weeks before Thanksgiving.

Wind rattled the empty streets of Cambridge, carrying with it the last breath of October. The storm of Halloween lingered in memory…

By the 10th of November, Cambridge lay in that in-between hush—students suspended between midterms and the promise of holidays ahead. Zara's world bent, constellations pulling into impossible alignment. Threads of light and shadow twisted together—not just prophecy, but a chain she could almost feel binding her to something larger, unseen.

Her hand burned as the glyph cut itself across her palm. The smell of singed skin clung to the air. Tiny embers hissed against her palm before fading into the shape of feathers. The pain wasn't fleeting—it branded.

Athena's wisdom etched in flame. The lines did not just burn; they solved themselves like a puzzle in fire. An owl's wings spread across her skin, feathers traced in molten clarity. The storm that split the sky had passed, but its echo pulsed in her veins, as if the glyph remembered what the city could not.

27

She gasped, not at the pain, but at the weight of knowing too much at once.

The voices of reason, strategy, prophecy layered over one another in her mind until she wanted to scream. It was too much, too soon, and yet a part of her whispered: finally.

The mural above her shifted, its glyphs glimmering like liars, as though some ancient hand had rewritten the truth. Something in them did not match the truth that pressed against her skull. She knew it. She just could not prove it. And yet, she could not shake the prickle that she was being studied, silently, by something that moved unseen.

♦ ♦ ♦

Zara Kane didn't remember the last time she slept through the night.

It wasn't insomnia.

It was the patterns.

They never left her alone.

Even now, under the soft yellow glow of the antique lamps in the Cambridge Observatory, her pen hovered over a sheet of graph paper as her mind swam with connections.

Numbers, star charts, battle formations, fractals—all twisting together into one endless tapestry.

She blinked hard, trying to force the thoughts into order, but they rearranged themselves the moment she made sense of them.

They always did.

It was exhausting.

And yet, she couldn't stop.

The observatory had been abandoned for nearly a decade, but Zara liked it that way. Still, the silence tonight wasn't the kind that comforted. It was the kind that waited.

The university students who came here in daylight hours only saw a ruin—flaking plaster, cracked lenses, dust-coated domes that didn't rotate anymore.

Zara saw a sanctuary.

Here, surrounded by forgotten star maps and obsolete equipment, she could think.

The outside world was too loud.

Her mother with her constant social climbing critiques.

Her father with his cold, distant praise for "results."

Her classmates with their hollow laughter and casual cruelty.

"Here, the only sound was the scratch of her pen and the faint creak of settling beams. Here, she wasn't Zara the overachiever. Not the 'ice queen.' Not the girl who corrected professors mid-lecture. Here she was simply the girl who saw too much."

Here, she could breathe.

Or she used to.

Tonight, the air felt heavy.

Like the room itself was holding its breath.

She glanced up from her notes.

The night sky through the cracked observatory dome glittered with November constellations—Cassiopeia, Perseus, Andromeda.

Except…

Her pen stilled.

That wasn't right.

Zara frowned and reached for the faded star chart tacked to the wall beside her.

She'd memorized it years ago.

The constellations had shifted, sure—Earth's slow wobble always did that—but these were wrong.

Not just rotated.

Rewritten.

She glanced back at the dome, then at her chart.

The stars weren't where they were supposed to be.

And it wasn't the sky that was wrong.

It was her.

Her pulse quickened.

She set the chart down and rubbed her temples, whispering to herself.

"Patterns don't rewrite themselves. You're just tired. You've been staring too long."

Except she hadn't.

She could stare at the same numbers for days without breaking.

This was different.

This was… deliberate.

She glanced back at her paper.

Her pen had moved on its own. Three symbols bled across the page in dark ink…

A circle split by a vertical line.

A spiral of triangles.

An eye with twelve spokes radiating from the pupil.

Zara's breath caught.

She didn't know what they meant.

But she knew they weren't random.

The sound wasn't just wood settling. It carried weight, like a footstep where none should be. A prickle ran along her spine, the same sensation she'd had in dreams where unseen eyes lingered just beyond the door.

The creak of old wood broke the silence.

Her head snapped toward the sound.

The door was still closed.

The hall beyond it was still empty.

But the shadows in the observatory seemed to shift.

Like someone else was here.

Watching.

♦ ♦ ♦

She grabbed her bag, shoving the paper inside, and rose to her feet.

The floorboards groaned beneath her, louder than they should have, like the building was protesting.

She told herself to leave.

Walk out, go home, forget about the stars and the symbols and the way the room felt like a trap.

Her body didn't listen.

She walked to the center of the observatory and tilted her head back, staring up at the sky.

The constellations were still wrong.

And yet…

They made sense.

Her mind raced, pulling the stars into new patterns—paths and arcs and angles she'd never considered before.

A new map.

A new order.

She could almost see it, glowing faintly between the stars:

A web.

Threads stretching between each point of light.

Pulling.

Connecting.

♦ ♦ ♦

Zara staggered, gripping the edge of the telescope for balance as the web burned brighter.

It wasn't just in the sky anymore.

It was in her.

Threads humming beneath her skin, each one singing a different note.

Some steady as drums.

Some sharp as knives.

Some faint and distant, hiding at the edges of her awareness.

And one…

One was broken.

Its note grated against the others, discordant and jagged, like a shattered piece jammed into a perfect puzzle.

Her chest tightened.

She didn't understand what she was feeling, but she couldn't shut it out.

It felt like drowning in starlight—a beauty so vast it pressed against her ribs until she thought they might crack. She had begged her mind to be quiet so many nights, but this wasn't noise. This was invasion, a chorus she couldn't silence.

She pressed her palms to her temples, squeezing her eyes shut.

The desert whispered against the stone, dunes shifting like oceans just beyond the walls. Even the jackals had fallen silent, as if the ruins themselves demanded to be heard. She thought, fleetingly, that the land was older than gods—older than the myths written to explain it.

"Make it stop," she whispered.

But the threads only pulled tighter.

Her pen clattered to the floor.

The lights above flickered, then steadied, glowing brighter than they had in years.

The air smelled of dust and ozone.

Zara forced her eyes open.

The observatory wasn't empty anymore.

At the far end of the room, half-hidden in the shadows between the bookcases, stood a figure cloaked in pale gold.

And though it didn't speak, Zara felt the weight of its gaze.

Assessing.

Measuring.

Like a player considering their next move.

The hum of the threads roared in her veins.

And Zara understood, in some small, terrible way, that she wasn't just looking at someone.

She was standing on the edge of a game she'd never agreed to play.

And the gods had just made their first move.

The figure stepped into the light.

Not a man.

Not a woman.

Something older than both, draped in a robe of pale gold stitched with constellations that shifted with every breath. The hem glimmered with script Zara couldn't read, yet somehow understood: not words, but strategies.

The room seemed to bend around them, the observatory stretching taller, wider.

"You're not real," Zara whispered. But the words felt hollow, like a pawn denying the board it stood on.

The figure tilted their head, like a teacher indulging a wrong answer.

"Reality is an overrated construct."

The voice wasn't loud, but it filled the room like a chorus of a thousand generals.

The stars above pulsed, constellations breaking apart and rearranging into new shapes—birds of prey, drawn bows, war banners.

◆ ◆ ◆

Zara's heart pounded as the dome dissolved.

The observatory was gone.

She stood at the center of an endless war room.

Marble floors inlaid with glowing constellations stretched in every direction.

Bookshelves rose like towers, their spines etched with battle maps and histories of wars she'd never read about.

Above, the ceiling itself wheeled like a living sky, constellations tearing apart and reforming with each heartbeat, as though the universe itself was being drafted into strategy.

Giant tables overflowed with maps that moved on their own, armies of tiny glowing figures clashing silently as new strategies scrawled themselves across the parchment.

The air smelled of ink, old leather, and something sharper: the metallic tang of blood.

Zara turned slowly, her breath quickening.

This wasn't just a library.

It was a place where knowledge became war.

The figure circled her, each step deliberate.

"You've felt it," they said.

Zara swallowed hard. "Felt what?"

"The chain."

Her pulse quickened.

"You saw its threads. You heard their song."

She opened her mouth, but no words came out.

She had felt them—the luminous web connecting her to people she didn't know.

She just hadn't understood it.

The figure stopped in front of her, golden eyes glimmering like twin suns.

They didn't smile.

They didn't need to.

"I am Athena," they said. The name rang like bronze, striking through Zara's chest like the toll of a war-drum. Not introduction, but declaration.

And Zara felt it sink into her skin, carving her open, reshaping her.

"No," Zara whispered, taking a step back. "This isn't—I'm not—"

Athena raised a hand, silencing her with a gesture.

"Do not deny what you are. I chose you long before you had words for your curse."

"My curse?"

Athena's gaze sharpened.

"The mind that cannot rest. The one that sees what others cannot. The sleepless girl who rearranges the world in her head a thousand times before dawn. You think it's madness. Weakness. But it is my blood in you. My gift."

She thought of nights curled under her blanket, whispering to herself, begging her mind to stop racing. Of the way silence never came, no matter how tightly she shut her eyes.

Zara's throat tightened.

She hated how much of it sounded true.

Athena stepped closer, close enough that Zara could see the constellations in her robe rearranging again, forming the shape of an owl midflight.

"You are my mind," Athena said, voice cold and precise.

"My blood.

My war."

Zara's knees nearly gave out under the weight of those words.

"No," she managed, her voice breaking. "I didn't ask for this. I don't want this."

"You were never asked," Athena said simply.

Her tone wasn't cruel.

It was factual.

"History is written by those who act, not those who want."

The floor beneath Zara glowed.

The constellations at her feet shifted, forming a web of twelve points—eleven steady, one flickering erratically at the edge of the pattern.

Threads connected them all, their light humming in her veins.

She knew what they were without being told.

The others.

The connections sang to her.

Some blazed bright, fierce as wildfires.

Some pulsed steady as war drums.

Some hid in shadow, faint and evasive.

And one—

One was broken.

Its light scraped against hers, jarring and offkey.

Like a corrupted star trying to force itself into a perfect constellation.

Zara flinched, clutching her head as the discordant thread pressed against her.

"What is that?" she asked through gritted teeth.

Athena's expression didn't change.

"A piece out of place."

"Then cut it out."

"No."

"Why?"

"Because every piece matters. Even the broken ones." "And every piece has its place," Athena continued. "Even those meant to be sacrificed. Victory is not won by sentiment, but by seeing the board as it is."

Zara's breath came shallow, her mind fracturing under the onslaught of new information, new visions.

She saw flashes—

Battles fought under different suns.

Faces she didn't know but somehow recognized.

A boy standing in a storm.

A girl surrounded by fire.

A hunter with blood on her hands.

The chain pulled her toward them, tightening like a noose.

Athena reached out and placed her hand on Zara's forehead.

Zara gasped as searing light burned through her skull, down her spine, flooding her veins with molten clarity.

The war room sharpened.

The noise in her head stilled.

For the first time in her life, the patterns made sense.

She saw the world as it was—a living game board.

Every piece in motion.

Every strategy visible.

Every path forward.

Her curse of overthinking wasn't a curse at all.

It was a weapon.

"You see it now," Athena said.

Zara's voice was barely a whisper. "Yes."

Athena nodded once.

"Good. Then play well."

The constellations on the floor surged upward, wrapping around Zara like living armor.

An owl—glowing white and gold—spread its wings across her chest.

The threads hummed in harmony.

For the first time in her life, Zara didn't feel cursed.

She felt chosen.

♦ ♦ ♦

The war room trembled.

The constellations on the marble floor flickered, their perfect geometry fracturing.

Athena's golden gaze cut toward the darkness at the far end of the hall.

"They come," she said, voice like a blade leaving its sheath.

Zara's chest tightened. "Who—?"

She didn't finish.

The shadows moved.

Two figures stepped into the light.

Cloaked.

Porcelain masked.

The Watchers.

The same shape she'd seen in her nightmares without knowing their names.

Their masks caught the light in a way that erased faces—a blank cruelty, like something that had never needed eyes to see.

They moved like liquid shadow, gliding between the bookshelves as if the space belonged to them.

The hum of the threads in Zara's veins roared like a warning.

Her whole body screamed at her to run.

She couldn't.

Her feet rooted to the marble, even as her pulse thundered.

Athena didn't move.

She stood, statuesque and silent, as the Watchers approached.

"They're here for you," she said at last, as if commenting on the weather.

"Me?" Zara's voice cracked.

"Your awakening cannot go unanswered. They are the answer."

The Watchers tilted their heads in unison, their hollow eye slits fixing on her.

"The mind awakens," one hissed.

"The game changes," the other replied.

Zara's hands trembled. "What do I—"

"Think," Athena cut in.

♦ ♦ ♦

The room warped.

The endless marble, the constellations, the bookshelves—they dissolved.

And in a blink, Zara was back in the crumbling Cambridge Observatory.

But it wasn't as she'd left it.

The air pulsed with otherworldly energy, the stars above the cracked dome burning brighter than they ever should.

The war room strategies, the constellations—they lingered in her mind, overlaid on this ruined place like two worlds colliding.

And she wasn't alone.

The Watchers had followed her back.

They split apart, moving to flank her.

Zara's breath came quick and shallow.

She had nothing.

No weapons.

No training.

No way out.

Think.

The voice wasn't Athena's this time.

It was hers.

Her curse.

Her gift.

She darted to the nearest table, sweeping up a rusted metal rod that had once been part of the telescope.

The Watcher to her left lunged, faster than anything human.

But she saw it before it moved.

Her mind had already mapped the room, plotted the angles, traced the trajectory of its leap.

She sidestepped, pivoting her whole body, and swung.

The rod connected with its mask, sending it crashing into a shelf of star charts.

Stone splintered, the shock of impact vibrating up her arms until her teeth hurt. Dust rained from the rafters, the observatory groaning as if it might collapse around her.

The other one came for her.

She dropped low, ducking its claws by inches, and scrambled toward the spiral staircase leading up to the viewing deck.

She didn't run blindly.

Every step was measured.

Every movement calculated.

Her mind spun with probabilities, escape routes, contingencies.

It wasn't panic.

It was clarity.

She reached the deck and grabbed a loose railing, wrenching it free with both hands.

The Watcher hissed below, its head jerking unnaturally as it tracked her movements.

It climbed the stairs, slow and deliberate, savoring the moment.

Zara didn't wait.

She hurled the railing down the steps, catching it square in the chest.

It stumbled.

She took the opening, sprinting across the deck to the opposite stairs, circling back down as both creatures adjusted their paths.

She couldn't overpower them. But war wasn't about strength. It was about the next move.

Her eyes darted to the central telescope, its base cracked and leaning from years of neglect.

The chains holding it in place were rusted, corroded.

Weak.

She ran to the far side of the room, baiting the Watchers toward her, then spun at the last second and sprinted for the telescope.

The first one lunged.

She ducked, shoving the rusted chains with all her weight.

They snapped.

The telescope groaned, then crashed like thunder.

The impact crushed the first Watcher beneath it, its mask shattering.

It dissolved into black smoke.

The second froze for just a moment.

A moment was all she needed.

She grabbed the metal rod again and swung hard.

The air in the observatory seemed to twist, pulling her focus through a gap she couldn't see. For a heartbeat, she was aware of every flicker of light on the glass, every shadow sliding across the floor—and then the cold was inside her bones.

The mask cracked. The creature shrieked—nails on glass—then tilted its head, as if memorizing her face. Frost spider-webbed across the floorboards. Her breath fogged as though winter had entered her bones.

Zara collapsed against the fallen telescope, her chest heaving.

Her hands were raw and bleeding from gripping the metal.

Her whole body trembled, but her mind—

Her mind was still.

♦ ♦ ♦

Athena's voice cut through the silence.

"Better."

Zara looked up.

The goddess stood where the Watchers had fallen, her robe unmarked by the chaos of the fight.

"You see now why you were chosen."

Zara swallowed. "Because I can think."

"Because you can win."

Zara closed her eyes.

The threads hummed in her veins again—bright, taut, undeniable.

She could feel them clearer than before, each one a point of light on her cosmic board.

The boy in the storm.

The girl in the fire.

Others she didn't yet know.

And one broken star at the edge of the constellation, grating against them all.

She opened her eyes.

"I see it," she whispered.

Athena's gaze lingered one heartbeat longer, as if already calculating her next move. Then the goddess unraveled into starlight, leaving only the scent of iron and ink behind.

The silence after the fight was deafening.

Zara stood in the ruined observatory, every muscle trembling, the rusted metal rod still clenched in her bleeding hands.

The rain outside had slowed to a mist, faint droplets tapping against the cracked glass dome.

The constellations above were wrong again—or maybe they were finally right.

She couldn't tell anymore.

Her knees buckled, and she sank to the floor, leaning against the broken telescope.

The threads pulsed inside her.

Not as a hum.

As a living map.

She closed her eyes, and the room fell away.

She stood on a web of starlight, each glowing point humming with its own rhythm.

Some burned fierce and bright—wildfires barely contained.

Some flickered faintly, elusive, keeping their distance.

And one…

One scraped like glass against metal.

A broken star, jagged and wrong, forcing itself into the constellation.

She shuddered at its touch, but she couldn't cut it out.

Athena's words echoed in her mind: Every piece matters. Even the broken ones.

Her awareness stretched further, following the threads outward.

She saw glimpses.

A boy standing in a storm, water bending to his will.

A girl surrounded by firelight, her hands unburned.

A shadow moving like a predator at the edge of a forest.

More faces.

More pieces.

Some familiar, some strangers.

All tethered to her by something older than memory.

Her breaths came steadier now.

The rusted rod slipped from her fingers, clattering against the marble floor.

The weight in her chest—the curse of seeing too much—felt lighter. It wasn't madness. It was truth: Athena's heir. Her blood. Her mind. Her war.

The observatory creaked, as if acknowledging the change. Zara caught her reflection in the cracked glass above. For once, she didn't look like the girl lost in her head. She looked like someone who could see the board. And win.

Yet even in that reflection, she swore she saw a shadow move just behind her—not Athena, not her own—but something patient, waiting. The victory in her eyes flickered, tempered by the knowledge that every board had a player she could not yet see.

But clarity had its own cost. The board didn't just show paths forward—it showed endings, sacrifices, moves she wished she couldn't see. And for a fleeting moment, the knowledge felt heavier than the gift.

◆ ◆ ◆

Far below Olympus, in the obsidian halls lit by veins of golden fire, Maelis stood over the living map of the world.

She traced a finger over the Northeast, stopping at Cambridge.

A new symbol pulsed there:

An owl, white gold light radiating outward in geometric rings.

Maelis' lips curved into a faint smile. "The mind wakes," they murmured, tracing the glowing owl. Golden fire gripped the map. And already, the first piece tilts the whole board toward ruin.

CHAPTER III

# THE GIRL WHO WALKS WITH SHADOWS

November 19, 2025

In the narrow lanes of Spaccanapoli, November shadows stretched thin…The catacombs breathed around Selene, shadows curling like living smoke—like Watchers hidden in the dark, patient and waiting.

Whispers threaded through the dark—names she should not know, chains rattling where no chains existed. Selene let the shadows curl closer, but this time she noticed they seemed to respond to her breath. It was not just darkness—it was presence, as if something old had chosen to stand at her side.

Her whole life, she had felt like an intruder in her own skin. But here, with the cold stone and whispering dark, she felt… seen.

Her glyph ignited, searing itself into her palm. The smell of scorched stone and cold iron filled the air as chains of black-silver etched across her skin. Shadows spilled like ink into her veins, branding her as Hades' heir.

She shivered as if someone watched from behind the walls. Eyes she could not see, patient and waiting. She fled the catacombs with the certainty she had not been alone.

Naples was too alive for Selene Marino.

Too loud, too bright, too full of people laughing in the streets like the world hadn't ended a hundred times already.

From her apartment window above the crowded Via Toledo, she could watch the city pulse—scooters weaving between cars, tourists crowding piazzas, lovers lingering at café tables long after the wine had gone warm.

It made her skin itch.

♦ ♦ ♦

Everyone down there belonged to life, to a rhythm she'd never been able to hear.

She turned away from the window.

The city above had nothing for her.

The city below did.

Her boots echoed down the worn stone steps of Castel dell'Ovo, the oldest fortress in Naples.

It clung to the edge of the sea like it had grown there, its yellowed walls weathered by centuries of storms and sieges.

But Selene wasn't here for its history.

She was here for what was beneath it.

The catacombs.

No one came here at night.

Not the tourists.

Not the guards.

Just Selene.

She knew every twist of the crumbling staircases, every cold breath of air that rose from the crypt below.

Down here, the noise of the city couldn't reach her.

Down here, surrounded by stone and shadow, she could breathe.

The smell of salt and dust grew stronger as she reached the lowest level.

The catacombs opened like a wound—a maze of tunnels and ossuaries lined with bones that had been nameless for centuries.

The air pressed against her chest like damp stone. Each step echoed too loud, too alive, and the silence that followed made her feel less like a trespasser than a trespassed-upon.

♦ ♦ ♦

A hush pressed tighter than stone. For a breath, Selene thought she saw a lacquer-white mask, pale and unblinking, staring from between the ribs of the wall. She spun—only shadows remained. But the certainty of being watched clung to her like frost.

It should have been terrifying.

It wasn't.

Selene felt more at home here than she ever had above ground.

She reached into her jacket and pulled out a candle stub, lighting it with a cheap plastic lighter.

The flame flickered, casting long, restless shadows against the walls—shadows that seemed to wait for a command she hadn't yet spoken.

She'd been coming here for months now, sneaking away when the weight of Naples became too much.

At first, it was just to escape.

Then it became something else.

She didn't just come here to be alone.

She came because the dead listened better than the living.

Selene stopped in front of a crumbling fresco.

It had once been a saint, or maybe an angel, its face long since eroded into blankness.

She traced her fingers over the faded paint, her skin prickling at the chill seeping through the stone.

Her father used to tell her that ghosts didn't haunt places like this.

She disagreed.

She thought the dead liked company.

Her throat tightened as she sank to the floor, pulling her knees to her chest.

The quiet here didn't erase the grief.

It just made it manageable.

Some nights, she still dreamed of the accident... the sound of sirens smothered by the silence that followed, a silence that never left her."

Her mother had been the only one who understood her silences.

Now Selene carried them alone.

The candle flickered.

The air shifted.

Colder.

Deeper.

She froze, lifting her head.

No wind reached this far down.

No windows opened to the night.

And yet, the shadows on the walls moved as if something had passed through them.

"Hello?" Her voice echoed weakly down the corridor.

No answer.

But the silence wasn't empty anymore.

It was heavy.

Waiting.

She stood, grabbing the candle as she followed the corridor deeper.

She shouldn't have gone further—she knew that.

There were tunnels even the guides refused to map.

But something pulled her on, past the frescoes, past the stacked skulls grinning in the dark.

The walls narrowed, forcing her to turn sideways to fit.

Her candle guttered, nearly going out, but she shielded it with her hand, heart hammering in her chest.

The air smelled different here—like earth that hadn't been touched in centuries.

She'd never been this deep before.

◆ ◆ ◆

At last, the tunnel opened into a crypt.

The ceiling arched low, its stone etched with strange sigils that seemed to writhe in the flickering candlelight.

A cracked marble sarcophagus sat at the center, ringed by unlit torches.

Selene's breath caught.

She'd found something older than the catacombs themselves.

Something meant to be hidden.

The candle trembled in her grip.

She took a step toward the sarcophagus.

The chill deepened.

The shadows thickened, bleeding across the floor like ink.

And then she felt it.

A pull in her chest.

Like invisible strings tightening around her ribs.

Threads.

Her knees went weak as the sensation spread—a dozen faint heartbeats thrumming beneath her skin.

Some pulsed steady, like ancient drums.

Some burned like open flames.

Some flickered faintly, keeping their distance.

And one—

One seared cold.

Wrong.

Like fire that didn't burn, but froze.

She gasped, clutching her chest.

"What—what is this?"

The shadows answered.

They shifted toward her, reaching like hands from the corners of the crypt.

She stumbled back, pressing herself against the wall.

Her candle went out, plunging her into darkness.

But the dark wasn't empty.

It was alive.

And it knew her name.

◆ ◆ ◆

The darkness swallowed Selene whole.

Not like stepping into a shadow.

Like falling into one.

The crypt walls dissolved into black mist, the stone floor giving way beneath her feet.

She didn't scream.

The silence here was too complete for that.

The weight of the world above fell away, leaving her suspended in something deeper than air, deeper than water.

Deeper than death.

Her boots touched solid ground again.

Selene blinked.

She wasn't in the crypt anymore.

She stood at the edge of a river that wasn't a river—black glass, perfectly still, reflecting a sky she couldn't see.

The air tasted like iron and smoke.

An ashen wind carried whispers, voices that weren't words, but grief distilled into sound.

Some of the whispers seemed to know her, curling around her name, fragments of voices she thought she'd buried with the dead. They didn't speak like strangers. They welcomed her like someone coming home.

It wasn't frightening.

It felt… familiar.

Like coming home.

She followed the bank, her own reflection pacing her in the black glass.

Fields of pale flowers stretched beyond the river—asphodel, their ghost white petals glowing faintly in the eternal twilight.

In the distance, a throne rose from the earth itself, carved from a single block of obsidian.

It wasn't adorned with gold or jewels.

It didn't need to be.

It was authority made stone.

Someone sat on it.

A figure draped in shadow, still as death.

Selene stopped breathing.

She didn't need to ask who it was.

Every instinct in her blood knew.

Hades.

The name wasn't spoken, yet it thundered through her veins like earth collapsing into a grave.

He was not the monster she'd been told to fear as a child.

He didn't wear a crown.

He didn't need one.

The weight of his presence was crown enough.

His skin was pale as marble, his hair black as a raven's wing. His robes moved like smoke, threaded with faint silver symbols that burned and faded as she tried to read them.

His eyes—gods, his eyes—were pools of endless night.

Not empty.

Full.

With every soul, every secret, every silence ever spoken.

Selene's lungs seized, her body forgetting the rhythm of breath. She felt not stared at but swallowed, as though her secrets had already been claimed before she could speak them.

Selene fell to her knees.

Not because he commanded it.

Because anything else would have been a lie.

"You've been walking toward me for a long time," Hades said.

His voice wasn't loud.

It slid into her bones like a memory.

Selene's lips trembled. "What… what is this place?"

"The threshold," he said. "Where the living brush against the dead."

She swallowed hard. "Why me?"

Hades leaned forward, resting his hands on the arms of his throne.

"Because you've lived with one foot in the grave since the day you were born."

She flinched.

"You don't know me."

"I know you better than you know yourself."

He rose, and the ground shivered.

Every shadow in the field bent toward him.

"You carry grief like a lantern, Selene Marino. You hide in it. Breathe it. Survive by it. But grief is not just suffering. It is power. And it has brought you to me."

He stopped in front of her.

She didn't move.

Couldn't.

"Stand."

It wasn't a request.

She stood.

Hades reached out and brushed his fingers against her temple.

The cold was instant, blooming through her skull, down her spine, until even her bones felt like ice.

But it wasn't a lifeless cold.
It was the cold of stillness.
Of quiet.
Of finally being seen.
"You are my shadow," Hades said, his voice low and absolute.
"My silence."
He pressed his palm against her chest.
Selene gasped as black silver light seared through her veins,
spreading like shadowveins beneath her skin.
"My key."
Her knees buckled, but she didn't fall.
The black glass river surged, reflecting images that weren't
hers—
A boy wielding a storm like a weapon.
A girl surrounded by constellations in an endless library.
Others she didn't know.
Others she would.
Threads tethered them all to her, faint but unbreakable.
The chain.
She felt it now, clearer than in the crypt.
Each connection a heartbeat, a distant candle in the dark.
Some steady.
Some burning.
Some hiding.
And one—
One seared like cold fire.
A wrongness that didn't belong and yet couldn't be cut away.
Her breath hitched.
"What is that?"
Hades didn't answer.
He didn't need to.
The chain didn't care if it hurt.
It only cared that it bound.
The visions dimmed.
Her pulse slowed, syncing with the river, the field, the god.
The shadows didn't just surround her anymore.
They moved with her.

Became her.

Hades withdrew his hand and stepped back.

"Do you understand now?"

Selene nodded, her voice barely a whisper. "Yes."

"Good."

The corners of his mouth lifted, but it wasn't a smile.

"Then walk with me."

♦ ♦ ♦

The throne room dissolved.

The river.

The fields.

The throne.

All gone.

Selene stood once more in the crypt beneath Castel dell'Ovo.

But it wasn't the same.

She wasn't the same.

The crypt hadn't changed.

The cracked marble sarcophagus still sat at its center. The torches were still unlit.

But Selene felt everything differently.

The shadows weren't just shadows anymore.

They shifted when she moved.

Bent toward her like living things.

Waiting.

A hiss cut through the silence.

Not the whispering of the dead.

Something else.

Selene turned sharply, her pulse spiking.

At the mouth of the corridor stood two Watchers.

Not like the ones Leo or Zara had faced.

These were worse.

Their lacquer-white masks were fractured, sharp edges curling like teeth.

Their cloaks clung to their spindly frames like wet burial shrouds, dripping with a black ichor that ate through the stone where it fell.

They moved like corpses jolted awake.

51

Stiff.

Wrong.

The hum of the chain roared in Selene's veins, the threads pulling taut.

She staggered back as they glided forward, claws dragging against the walls.

"The shadow awakens," one hissed, voice like the grinding of a tomb being sealed.

"The key turns," the other rasped.

Selene backed against the sarcophagus, her chest heaving.

Her mind screamed to run, but her feet stayed rooted.

She couldn't outrun them. Not like this.

A cold voice cut through her panic.

"You are the boundary."

Selene gasped. "Hades—?"

Her glyph flared white-hot beneath her ribs, and the shadows answered.

"You are the place where the living end and the dead begin. You are the door. And the door does not flee from what it was made to hold back."

The Watchers lunged.

Selene threw up her hands on instinct.

The shadows obeyed.

They surged upward like a wave, forming a wall of black between her and the creatures.

The first Watcher slammed into it, screeching as the barrier burned its flesh.

It clawed and thrashed, but the darkness clung like tar, pulling it in.

The second Watcher darted low, skittering along the floor like a spider.

Selene spun, sweeping her arm.

The shadows lashed out like whips, wrapping around its limbs and yanking it back.

It writhed, shrieking, but couldn't break free.

Selene's breath came fast and shallow.

She didn't know how she was doing this.

She just knew it worked.

The barrier quivered, threads of shadow unraveling into claw-shaped tendrils that dragged the first Watcher deeper into the dark.

Its scream cut short as the shadows swallowed it whole.

Gone.

The second screeched, thrashing against its bindings.

Selene clenched her fists.

The darkness tightened, crushing its brittle frame until the mask cracked.

It dissolved into black smoke, fading like it had never been there.

Silence.

The shadows rippled once, then stilled.

♦ ♦ ♦

Selene lowered her hands, her entire body trembling.

Her knees nearly buckled, but she forced herself to stay upright.

She'd done that.

Not Hades.

Not anyone else.

Her.

"Good."

The god's voice slid through the crypt like a whispering wind.

"The dead obey you. And the living will learn to fear you."

Selene swallowed hard, staring at her hands.

They still trembled, but not from fear.

From power.

The darkness shifted again, returning to the corners of the crypt like obedient hounds.

Selene wiped her palms on her jeans, smearing them with cold sweat and dust.

The Watchers were gone.

But the hum of the chain remained.

She felt them more clearly now.

The boy who carried a storm in his veins.

The girl who saw constellations in everything.

Others—distant but undeniable.

And one.

That same cold fire, scraping against her like a blade drawn too slow.

She didn't want to touch it.

But she couldn't ignore it.

She exhaled, letting her shoulders relax.

The fear hadn't left her.

But it no longer ruled her.

The crypt was quiet again.

Selene stood in the center, every nerve buzzing like a plucked string.

The fight hadn't been long, but it had changed everything.

She stared at the sarcophagus, its cracked marble lid still sealed.

She wondered what—or who—had been buried there.

And if they knew she'd just claimed this place as hers.

Her hands shook.

Not from fear.

From the fading rush of what she'd done.

The shadows still hummed in her veins, sluggish now, like they were waiting for her next command.

It should have burned her.

It didn't quiet her.

Selene sat on the cold floor, leaning back against the sarcophagus.

Her breathing slowed, her body sinking into the stillness of the crypt.

For once, she didn't feel like a trespasser in this city.

She didn't feel like an intruder in her own skin.

She felt… home.

Her mother's face came to her unbidden—the warmth of her hand, the sound of her laughter.

Selene had thought she'd been coming here to grieve.

To stay close to the dead.

But now she understood.

She hadn't been running from life.

She'd been walking toward this.

Toward him.

Toward herself.

The hum of the chain drew her deeper inward.

She closed her eyes, and the darkness opened like a door.

She stood on a shadowweb stretching into infinity.

Each thread pulsed like a heartbeat.

Some steady.

Some burning.

Some faint, half-hidden.

She saw them—the others.

The stormbringer.

The stargazer.

The girl of fire.

The hunter who bled twilight.

Faces she knew but didn't know.

All tethered to her.

All bound by something older than any of them.

And there it was again.

That cold fire.

The wrong thread.

It burned differently, a frozen brand against her skin.

Her stomach twisted at the touch of it, but she couldn't pull away.

Athena had called it a broken piece.

Hades hadn't named it at all.

But Selene knew one thing:

Whatever it was, it didn't belong.

And it couldn't be ignored.

The crypt felt smaller now—not because it had changed, but because she had.

The boundaries of this place no longer defined her.

She was the boundary.

The door between worlds.

The place where endings and beginnings touched.

For the first time, that didn't sound like exile.

It sounded like purpose—but purpose had its price. If she was the door between worlds, she belonged to neither side. The thought clung to her like the crypt's cold air—she was not just Selene anymore. She was the threshold.

Selene rose to her feet, brushing the dust from her jeans.

The candle she'd carried here was still on the ground, long burned out.

She didn't need it anymore.

She could see in this darkness just fine.

But even with sight restored, she couldn't shake the certainty that something still watched from deeper within the dark—not Hades, not the dead, but something that lingered just beyond the chain.

♦ ♦ ♦

Their pale fingers drifted across Italy, stopping at Naples.

A key, black silver light radiating outward like veins of frost.

Maelis' lips curved into a faint smile. "The door opens," they murmured, their smile thin as ash. "And already, the game changes."

CHAPTER IV

# THE BOY BENEATH THE WAVES

November29, 2025

Kai paused at the base of the hill, listening. The city below murmured with ordinary life—bicycles clattering over stone streets, the faint hum of televisions spilling from paper-thin walls, the laughter of schoolmates released from cram sessions. All of it felt distant, like a world he stood outside of.

Kai's heartbeat echoed like temple bells underwater. In that ringing he thought he heard a koto string plucked pure and sharp. The sound carried sunlight with it, and the water no longer felt cold but alive.

Exams would begin soon, and every friend he had left seemed to Orbit that fact like moons around a crushing planet. His grandfather expected excellence, the same way he expected dawn to rise—without excuse. Yet Kai felt none of it fit. He drifted through classrooms like a shadow, more familiar with the silence of libraries than the chatter of his peers.

When he turned from the city toward the mountain, that silence deepened. The path rose into cedar groves where wind whispered in low, constant tones. Prayer ribbons still clung to some trees, their kanji washed pale by years of rain. Once, entire festivals had wound through this slope, lanterns blazing, drums echoing across the valley. Now only his steps disturbed it.

He remembered climbing this same path as a boy, his small hand wrapped in his grandfather's, dragged too quickly to keep pace. Lanterns had burned bright then, the air alive with the scent of grilled chestnuts and the thunder of taiko drums. For a moment he had lingered at the edge of the procession, watching fireflies lift from the grass. His grandfather's sharp tug had snapped him forward, his voice cutting sharper than the drums: "Stay focused, boy."

♦ ♦ ♦

The memory clung now like smoke, a reminder of how easily wonder had been pressed from his hands. The empty slope seemed to echo with those lost drums, and the silence weighed heavier because of it.

The air cooled the higher he climbed, carrying scents of earth and pine resin. Kai's fingers brushed a broken offering box as he passed. Coins, long tarnished, rattled faintly inside. The shrine might have been abandoned by the living, but he could not shake the sense it had never been abandoned by something greater.

Kai Watanabe pulled his coat tighter as he crossed the worn path that wound through the trees. His breath came in small clouds, mist rising and fading with each step. The path had been abandoned for years. Fewer locals spoke of the shrine at its end, and fewer still dared climb to it after nightfall. The place was haunted, they said, cursed by storms that never touched the rest of the valley. But Kai had learned that sometimes rumors clung to truth, the way mist clings to mountains.

His hands tightened on the strap of his satchel. Inside, wrapped in cloth, rested the cracked remnant of a mirror he had found two nights before. The fragment pulsed faintly even now, as though it contained light trapped beneath its surface. He hadn't told anyone about it—not his teachers, not his classmates, not even his grandfather, who had raised him with quiet discipline since childhood. Something in his bones whispered the discovery was meant only for him.

The wind pressed through the trees, carrying with it the faint scent of cedar resin and the brittle rustle of leaves. Kai's stomach tightened. He had been uneasy for weeks, plagued by half-dreams that slipped away when he woke: a storm splitting the heavens, a bow drawn of fire, a voice calling his name from across an endless sea of light.

One dream had lingered longer than the others. In it, Kai stood at the shore of an ocean that stretched forever, waves rimmed in gold. A figure waited beyond the water's edge, face hidden by light. When the figure spoke, the words carried both comfort and command: Rise, heir. But before Kai could answer, another sound split through—whispers that did not belong to the sea or the light.

◆ ◆ ◆

They slithered across the dream like oil across water. Light cannot rise without shadow. Give me your hand, boy, and I will lift the burden from you. The voice was female, velvet and venom entwined. Each time he woke from it, his chest ached as though a hand had truly pressed there, steady and unyielding.

◆ ◆ ◆

Even during the day, fragments clung to him. The crack of chalk on a blackboard became the snap of a bowstring. The gleam of sunlight on glass caught his eyes like a glyph half-formed. Once, as he crossed the river near Gion, he thought he saw a woman reflected in the water though no one stood beside him—hair like black silk, eyes that burned even in ripples.

◆ ◆ ◆

He had told himself these were nerves, tricks of exhaustion. But part of him knew the truth: dreams like that did not come from inside alone. They came from somewhere else, somewhere waiting. He told himself it was exhaustion from exams, from the weight of expectations, from the sense that his life was poised on the edge of something vast and nameless. But he knew better.

He slowed on the path, boots scuffing against damp stone. His mind returned, as it always did, to his grandfather. The old man had been a stern figure, razor-straight posture even in his eighties, with a voice that could silence a room by lowering to a whisper. To Kai, he was less guardian than judge, a constant reminder that excellence was not a goal but a demand.

Discipline is the bow, restraint is the string, truth is the arrow. Never forget, boy.

59

The words looped in Kai's mind like a mantra carved into the walls of his skull. He had lived by them. Tried to. But lately he had begun to wonder whether they were meant to shape him—or cage him.

The path curved, opening into a clearing. The ruined temple loomed before him. Its once-grand torii gate leaned at an angle, one pillar cracked and moss-covered. The shrine itself crouched in shadow, roof tiles missing, cedar beams blackened with age. Yet threads of golden light traced the air, as though the stones themselves remembered something the world had forgotten.

Kai swallowed hard. The satchel tugged heavier on his shoulder, as though the shard within longed to return to this place. His pulse quickened. He should turn back. He knew it. He had exams next week, assignments due, and the relentless rhythm of life that allowed no room for haunted shrines or cursed relics.

But his feet carried him forward anyway.

♦ ♦ ♦

As he stepped beneath the torii, the air shifted—colder, sharper. His breath misted thicker, curling before him like incense smoke. The mirror shard pulsed brighter, answering some unseen call.

He froze. For a moment he wanted to drop the satchel, to flee back down the mountain. But a current seemed to draw him onward, as though he had already stepped into a stream that would not release him until it carried him to its end.

Inside the shrine, silence reigned. The floor creaked faintly beneath his weight, but even that sound seemed swallowed by the cold. His gaze fell to the center of the ruin, where a cracked stone basin sat. Once, it had been used for purification rituals. Now, water no longer flowed into it, yet mist curled above its surface, lit faintly from below—as though some hidden fire still breathed there.

Kai approached slowly, heart hammering in his chest. The satchel throbbed against his side, heat seeping through the cloth. His fingers shook as he set it down, loosening the wrap around the mirror fragment.

The shard pulsed harder, faster, as though it would split if he didn't act. Each beat scorched hotter against his ribs, a countdown written in fire. He knew—without knowing how—that if he hesitated, the shrine itself would bury him.

For an instant, he simply stared at it. The shard looked ordinary in the dim light—jagged, weathered, its silver backing mottled with age. But then it flickered, faint gold chasing across its fractured surface.

The world tilted.

Mist thickened, spilling across the cracked stones. The air hummed, low and resonant, like the first note of a song played by an instrument too vast to see. The hairs on Kai's arms lifted. He stumbled back, but the shard rose from the satchel on its own, drawn upward as though by invisible threads.

Golden light burst from it, filling the chamber. Threads spun outward, weaving across beams, tracing patterns too complex for his mind to follow. They crawled across the stones, igniting ancient glyphs that flared to life: prophecy, light, healing, plague, archery, sun. Symbols he did not recognize yet somehow understood, their meanings unfolding in his mind like forgotten memories.

Kai staggered, breath caught in his throat. His legs buckled. He dropped to one knee, clutching at his arm as heat lanced through it. With a strangled gasp, he tore back his sleeve.

A glyph burned itself into his skin. Lines of fire etched outward like rays of a rising sun, spreading across his forearm. The stone basin cracked under the force, a jagged line racing across its surface. Dust and shards scattered as if the glyph were carving its mark not only into him, but into the shrine itself. The pain was unbearable, searing into bone. Yet beneath it was something worse— something that stole his breath with its clarity.

Recognition.

This was not discovery. This was not new.

It was awakening.

Kai staggered back against the stone basin, clutching his arm as the glyph seared deeper into his flesh. The lines glowed like molten gold, branching in rays across his skin until his entire forearm blazed. His vision blurred, tears springing to his eyes—not from weakness, but from the impossible heat of divinity etched into mortal flesh.

The shrine groaned around him, timbers creaking, dust cascading from broken beams. Golden fire licked across the wood, weaving in patterns like constellations born from flame. Mist thickened around him, and in the fire that seared his arm, Kai glimpsed flashes not his own. A boy stood at the edge of a storm-lashed sea, lightning crowning his hands, waves rising in answer to his breath. A girl knelt in shadows, eyes like obsidian, skeletal hands reaching yet recoiling from her command. Another hammered in a cavern, fire leaping with each strike, sparks spinning like stars around her. A huntress drew her bow in the glow of a fjord, her arrows silver as the moon. A trickster laughed from a mountain peak, shadows and wind bending at his feet. Twelve figures, scattered across the world—twelve glyphs igniting like stars in a night sky he had never seen.

For an instant, he felt them. Their breath, their fear, their awakening. He was not alone.

But the vision twisted. The stars were smothered by black coils. The twelve were hunted, their light drowned beneath shadow. A thirteenth mark flared—darker, sharper, a void where fire should be. It pulsed, and the others faltered.

Kai gasped, clawing at his arm as though he could rip the visions free. His knees buckled against the cracked basin, breath ragged. He didn't understand what he had seen—but he knew it was no dream.

♦ ♦ ♦

The ruined torii at the shrine's entrance blazed suddenly as though newly built, every crack sealed by light. The dead shrine lived again, burning with borrowed divinity.

Mist at the basin's surface thickened, churning, splitting into shapes. First only coils of gold and white. Then arms. Then a torso. Then the radiant outline of a man.

A figure stepped forth—impossible, terrible, crowned in light. His presence pressed on Kai's chest until it ached to breathe. The air stank of cedar smoke and lightning, sharp and ancient. The man's eyes shone like the sun cresting the mountains.

"Heir of my blood," the figure intoned. His voice carried as though spoken by a thousand dawns, each word resonant with history. "You bear the mark of Apollo. The bow is yours, the light is yours. Do not falter. The storm comes."

Kai's knees hit stone. He braced on trembling hands, sucking in ragged breath, arm still burning with celestial fire. His world had split open. Every lesson, every expectation, every half-dream—suddenly revealed not as burden but as prophecy.

He forced his gaze upward. The god's brilliance was unbearable, yet beautiful. Tears cut clean lines down his cheeks. He wanted to speak, to ask what storm, what mark, what he was meant to do—but his voice was a rasp swallowed by light.

The figure—Apollo—lowered his hand, reaching as though to steady Kai. Yet before the god's touch could fall, something in the light fractured.

The brilliance cracked. Lines split across the vision, like a mirror breaking in silence. Through those cracks, darkness seeped. Shadows pooled along the shrine's edges, thick as ink spilled across stone. They crawled between fallen beams, slithering closer.

Kai's skin prickled. He felt them before he saw them—cold wrongness, heavy as pressure in his lungs. Shadows darker than night itself, moving as though cast by nothing.

A whisper rose from them—low, silken, coiling around his ear. "Light cannot rise without casting shadow, boy." The words brushed against him like breath, close and taunting.

Kai froze. That was no dream, no hallucination. Someone else was here.

Apollo's figure blazed brighter, voice ringing. "They come for you, heir. The Watchers will not let the blood of Olympus rise unchallenged."

The word struck Kai's chest with weight. Watchers. It tasted of iron on his tongue.

The first shadow surged forward. Its form was vaguely human, yet faceless, its body flickering between smoke and flesh. It crossed the broken floor with inhuman speed.

Kai stumbled back, heart hammering. His glyph still glowed furiously, heat crawling through his veins. He wanted to run. But instinct rooted him. His arm lifted.

Light answered.

A bow unfurled from his glyph, woven of pure radiance. The string shimmered, humming like struck glass. His other hand drew back on nothing—yet an arrow of flame leapt into being, golden shaft blazing brighter the further he pulled.

Kai loosed it.

The arrow tore across the shrine, slamming into the faceless shadow. It shrieked—not a sound but a vibration, like stone grinding against stone, like ice splitting on a frozen river. The creature collapsed into smoke, scattering on an unseen wind.

Kai gasped. The bow remained, glowing fiercely, its weight both foreign and familiar—like remembering a song he had never learned but had always known. His hands shook.

Another shadow lunged. He loosed a second arrow, then a third. Each struck true, ripping the things apart. They dissolved, leaving only mist.

◆ ◆ ◆

But one shadow did not dissolve. It lingered at the far wall, taller than the others, its chest marred by faint burns that glowed like a half-burned glyph. When it moved, it did not screech like the others—it whispered.

"Kai…"

His blood turned to ice. The sound was his mother's voice, soft as memory, though he had not heard it since childhood. The figure stretched an arm toward him, smoke rippling like silk. For an instant he faltered, bow lowering, breath shaking.

Then the glyph on his arm blazed in answer, rejecting the false call. He loosed, and the shadow shattered into nothing—but the echo of his mother's voice clung like frost inside his chest.

But more came. Dozens. They spilled from every crack, crawling from between broken tiles, sliding from the rafters. The shrine filled with them, a tide of darkness pressing against golden fire.

Kai's bow sang, arrow after arrow leaping from it, his body moving faster than thought. He turned, loosed, turned again. The arrows burned through shadows, scattering them into ash. Yet with each shot, his chest heaved harder, sweat stung his eyes, his limbs grew heavier.

The timbers groaned. Dust rained. The ruin quaked beneath the clash of light and shadow.

Then the shadows parted.

A figure walked among them.

A woman, tall and poised, her presence commanding as though even darkness bowed to her. Her hair rippled like black water, her eyes sharp as cut obsidian. She moved without hurry, her steps soft yet final, the ruin itself seeming to lean toward her.

Kai froze. This was no faceless shadow. She was more.

"You are late," she said. Her voice was smooth, measured, threaded with a resonance that echoed beyond mortal sound. "But you awakened nonetheless."

Her gaze fell to his arm. The glyph flared brighter, answering her attention like prey twitching beneath a predator's eyes.

"Apollo's heir," she murmured, the corner of her mouth curving. "How fitting. You will be useful… once you learn obedience."

Kai's bow trembled. He forced his stance to steady, raising it higher. His throat was dry, but the words scraped out: "Who are you?"

The woman tilted her head, amusement glinting in her gaze. "Names are for those who still serve Olympus. You may call me what your kind always has—Maelis."

The name slammed into him with inexplicable force. His chest tightened. He didn't know why, but history recoiled from it, his bones remembering something his mind could not.

The shadows stirred restlessly behind her.

Maelis extended one pale hand. "Come to me, boy. Cast aside their chains." "Olympus abandoned you long ago, "Maelis said, her voice weaving through the ruin like silk and smoke." They chained the world in lies, then turned their thrones to stone when it no longer suited them. Do you know what Olympus was, boy? Not a myth. Not a dream. A world—shattered and buried so mortals would never remember. They broke it to keep their power, and they will break you the same."

Her gaze sharpened, obsidian bright. "And still you kneel for them. Still you burn when they tell you burn. You carry their mark as if it were honor. But what is it truly?" She stepped closer, shadows curling at her feet. "A leash. A brand. A promise that you will bleed, fight, and die for gods who will not rise to bleed for you."

The words sank deep, heavy as iron. For an instant, Kai's bow wavered.

Her voice wound around him, thick with temptation. For an instant, his knees weakened. He saw himself stepping forward, bow dissolving, surrender offered freely. The vision was intoxicating— his classmates bowing before him, his grandfather's stern face finally softened with pride. No more exams, no more discipline, no more failure. Only freedom, sweet and absolute.

Freedom without weight.

The vision pulled him forward. He almost obeyed.

♦ ♦ ♦

His breath caught—between the weightless freedom she offered and the fire still burning in his arm.

Then a memory cut sharp. His grandfather's words: Discipline is the bow. Restraint is the string. Truth is the arrow.

Kai's breath steadied. His grip tightened. He raised the bow fully. Light gathered, the glyph burning hotter, brighter.

Maelis' smile thinned. "So. You choose defiance."

He loosed.

The arrow screamed through the shrine, tearing into the shadows at her feet. They unraveled, smoke hissing into nothing. But Maelis did not move. The light passed through her untouched, as though her body were smoke itself.

Still, her eyes narrowed. "Interesting."

Shadows surged at her command, flooding the shrine. The ruin shook, wood splintering as the horde pressed in.

Kai fought—arrow after arrow, his breath ragged, his limbs leaden. Yet the bow sang louder with each release. The glyph on his arm pulsed in rhythm with his heartbeat, hotter, sharper, until it felt as though the sun itself had been carved into his skin.

The shrine shook as if the ruin itself recognized the duel between light and shadow. Splinters fell from the rafters, broken tiles clattered to the floor, dust clouding the air. The glyph on Kai's arm burned white-hot, searing every nerve. He gritted his teeth, refusing to cry out.

Shadows clawed closer, too many for him to hold back. His lungs burned, his arms trembled, each arrow heavier than the last.

Maelis only watched. Calm, assured, her eyes gleamed with something sharper than amusement. "Your power is new. Unshaped. Every arrow costs you. The Watchers do not tire. How long before you collapse beneath the weight of your god?"

Kai's knees buckled. She was right—he could feel himself breaking.

But then the light surged again.

Apollo stepped forward, radiant, raising one blazing hand. A wave of brilliance exploded outward, slamming into the shadows. They shrieked as they were hurled back, bodies unraveling into ash. The god's presence filled the shrine like the dawn itself had broken through its shattered roof.

"Stand." Apollo's voice thundered, sharp as a command, steady as sunrise. "You are my heir, Kai Watanabe. Remember: the sun rises because it must, not because it is asked to. Your strength is inevitability." The words burned through Kai's chest, deeper than any lesson carved into him by his grandfather.

Apollo's gaze blazed with both pride and warning. "Do not mistake light for mercy," Apollo intoned. "Light is not forgiveness. It is choice—choice to reveal, to burn, to heal. The Watchers will twist that truth until freedom tastes of ash. Remember: light endures not because it never breaks, but because it rises. Guard your choice, heir. In choice lies all power.

"The words rooted in Kai's chest, heavier than any lesson his grandfather had ever drilled into him. His breath steadied. His arms straightened. The bow of light re-formed, stronger, its golden curve blazing against the dark.

He drew.

This time the arrow split into three. Then seven. Then more—each line of fire humming like a chord in some divine song. When he released, the arrows cascaded outward in a storm of brilliance, flooding the shrine with sunrise.

The horde dissolved in waves, ripped apart by light. The shadows shrieked, burned, then vanished, leaving nothing but curling smoke.

Silence fell.

The ruined temple smoldered, every stone glowing faintly as though remembering the touch of dawn.

Kai sagged, chest heaving, sweat running down his temples. His arms trembled, but he had not broken. The bow of radiance faded, yet the glyph across his forearm continued to blaze—etched now into his flesh, permanent.

Maelis remained.

Her form flickered at the edges, her body wavering like a reflection in disturbed water. Yet her gaze cut sharp and steady. She studied Kai, her lips curving into something between admiration and warning.

"You learn quickly," she murmured. "Too quickly. Apollo chose well. But choice—" she lingered on the word, her tone twisting around it, "—choice is fragile."

The glyph pulsed angrily in answer.

Maelis tilted her head, obsidian eyes narrowing. Her form unraveled, edges blurring like ink in water, but her voice lingered, carved into the ruin itself.

"You will kneel, boy. Not today. Not tomorrow. But the storm always breaks its heirs."

Her words clung like frostbite long after her form unraveled. Even when the mist dispersed, Kai swore he felt her presence linger—a cold weight pressed against his chest, promising to return.

He staggered, bow fading from his grasp, and nearly fell against the cracked basin. His arms ached from loosing arrows that no quiver had ever held. Sweat slicked his temples though the night air was freezing. He could not tell whether his trembling came from exertion or from the echo of Maelis' voice curling in his thoughts.

For the first time, he realized how close he had come to yielding. A single step forward, and her hand would have closed around his. A single word, and he might have abandoned everything—his grandfather's lessons, the discipline etched into his bones, the self he had tried to build. The possibility shook him more than the battle itself.

Apollo's fading light stirred once more, less a figure now than a glow that hovered near. "You resisted because you chose," the voice whispered. "Choice is the core of all light. Guard it well."

Kai lowered his eyes to the glyph burning across his arm. The lines seemed carved into his very veins, pulsing in rhythm with his heartbeat. Pain had given way to something heavier: responsibility. He could never undo what had happened tonight.

The weight of that distance pressed on him harder than the battle had. For them, tomorrow would bring exams, crowded trains, late-night ramen shops. For him, there would be no return to that rhythm.

He gripped the satchel strap, though the shard inside was gone, consumed into him. The boy who once walked unnoticed through classrooms was ash now. Something new stood in his place— burned, marked, burning.

Lights blurred as his vision stung, not with weakness but with the knowledge of what he had lost: the illusion of being ordinary.

The shrine sagged around him, timbers split by fire and shadow. Smoke drifted through broken beams, carrying the faint tang of ozone. He imagined the villagers far below whispering of storms that struck only this hill, never knowing what had stirred above them.

Slowly, he rose to his feet. His body ached, but his resolve held. Maelis had promised to return. The Watchers had seen him. Apollo had named him heir. There would be no returning to the quiet boy who slipped unnoticed through classrooms.

Kai clenched his fist over the glyph and whispered into the ruin, voice hoarse but certain.

The silence after the storm pressed thick, every beam groaning like a warning. Smoke drifted upward in slow spirals, the ruin holding its breath to hear his words.

"Then let them come."

The storm had come for him. And it would not let him go.

Nor, he realized, would he ever let it go again.

# CODEX FRAGMENT

## THE MIRROR AND THE MASK

REFLECTIONS DEVOUR THE FACE THAT
LINGERS.
THE MASK REMEMBERS WHAT THE MIRROR
CONSUMES.
FALSE SELVES BIND THE TRUEST CHAINS,
YET ONLY IN THE BREAKING OF GLASS
CAN THE HIDDEN OATH BE SEEN.
BEWARE THE EYES THAT LOOK BACK TWICE,
FOR THEY ARE NOT YOURS — NOR THEIRS.

# THE EYES THAT WATCH

As November's chill deepened across the northern cities, the Watchers moved through streets already forgetting the warmth of autumn. They gathered where the world had no name.

They did not speak in words, but in fragments of the First Tongue—marks carried across centuries, waiting for the heirs to awaken.

"The Mother stirs," one hissed, their voice carrying like a knife through silence.

On the table lay a map of the world, twelve glyphs smoldering faintly. A thirteenth glimmered beneath the parchment, brighter, hungrier, until a hand pressed flat and smothered it.

"Not yet," the Watcher whispered.

"The storm has only begun."

It was not a room. Not a temple. Not a place that mortals could walk. It was the hollow between—where light had no courage to exist, where the walls were nothing but shifting silhouettes, and the ground pulsed like the hide of some buried, sleeping beast.

The Watchers did not belong to the world of gods or men. They belonged here. And from here, they saw everything.

One of them broke the silence.

"Four." Its voice was a hiss that scraped like glass on stone.

Another answered, higher-pitched and layered like two voices speaking at once.

"Four awaken."

"Four disturb the chain."

The words overlapped, tangled, echoed like a chorus in a cavern.

"Storm."

"Mind."

"Door."

Each title dripped from different masks, their heads tilting in jerks that didn't follow the logic of human anatomy.

"The chain grows louder."

"The pieces move."

They turned toward the living wall at the center of their gathering place. It wasn't stone or flesh, but something between—a smooth, veined surface covered in shifting glyphs that blinked like eyes.

Each Watcher placed a clawed hand against it. The wall shuddered, and images bloomed across its surface: a boy kneeling in a drowned trainyard, lightning in his veins. A girl standing in an endless library of stars, constellations burning in her eyes. Another girl in a crypt, her hands dripping with shadows that moved like living things.

"Storm."

"Mind."

"Door."

Their whispers layered together again, their masks reflecting distorted pieces of the images.

"Four chosen."

"Four claimed."

"Four added to the game."

The wall darkened, the images splintering into a web of threads—some glowing steady, others flickering. One pulsed erratically, its light broken and wrong, shivering like a star on the edge of collapse.

The Watchers hissed.

"The broken one."

"The thirteenth."

"The unmade."

Their voices grew louder, overlapping into a discordant hum.

One mask tilted lower than the rest, its voice a broken rasp. "I do not trust it."

Another snapped its head toward it, voice sharp as flint. "Doubt is weakness."

The hum faltered, jagged edges of discord revealing cracks in the chorus.

"It does not belong."

"It does."

"It breaks the chain."

"It completes it."

They did not agree. They never did.

The air shifted. Cold. Heavy. Predatory. The Watchers froze.

From the far end of the hollow, a figure emerged. Tall. Clad in robes of black so deep they seemed to swallow the light. Where the Watchers were twisted fragments of something inhuman, this figure was terrifying because it looked almost human—too symmetrical, too deliberate, too still.

Their hair was white as bone, falling in precise, unbroken strands. Their skin glowed faintly, like a candle shielded in glass. And their eyes—Gods, their eyes. Pale and burning, like coals left in a dead fire.

The Watchers bowed their heads.

"Maelis," one hissed.

"Maelis," another echoed.

"Maelis," the rest chorused, voices falling into imperfect unison.

Maelis did not acknowledge them at first. They walked to the living wall and placed a hand against its surface. The glyphs writhed, shifting into a map of the world—oceans pulsing faint blue, continents carved in glowing gold.

Maelis traced the map slowly, their long fingers brushing over Chicago, Cambridge, Naples. Each touch left behind a smoldering mark. The surface rippled at each touch, the glow spreading outward in trembling rings, as though the map itself resisted being claimed.

For an instant, the trident mark flared too bright—then dimmed, as if something unseen had pressed back.

A trident.

An owl.

A key.

"Four," Maelis said at last, their voice soft but carrying more weight than all the Watchers' chattering combined.

The Watchers shifted, claws clinking against the floor.

"Four awaken," they murmured.

"Four disturb the chain."

"Four do as they are meant to," Maelis corrected, and the whispers fell silent.

They studied the four marks glowing on the map. The trident over the drowned ruins of Chicago. The owl burning above Cambridge. The key buried in Naples.

"The storm."

"The mind."

"The door."

They said the words like pieces of a puzzle, considering how they fit.

"How far they've come."

"How far they'll fall."

The Watchers tilted their heads in unison.

"Do we unmake them?"

Maelis did not answer. Instead, they turned to face them, their pale eyes glowing faintly in the hollow.

"The unmade one," Maelis said.

The Watchers hissed, masks jerking violently.

"The thirteenth."

"The broken."

"The one that should not be."

"The one that completes."

The discordant hum rose again, louder this time, as they circled Maelis like carrion birds.

Maelis raised a hand. The hum stopped.

They did not raise their voice. They didn't need to.

"It is not yet time to decide what should not be," Maelis said. Their tone was patient. Measured. Like a player explaining rules to children who could not hope to understand the game.
"The thirteenth will play its part. As will the twelve. As will you."
The Watchers tilted their heads, quiet now.
Maelis returned their gaze to the map.
"The chains are loosening," they murmured, as though to themselves.
"The pieces are moving."
They pressed their hands harder against the map, and the surface rippled like water disturbed by a stone.
"Let them."

The Watchers bowed again, their masks nearly touching the ground.
Maelis turned away from the map, their robes trailing like smoke.
"The game has begun," they said.
"And the eyes that watch will not close until it ends."
The Watchers slithered back into the shadows, masks glinting faintly in the hollow's dim glow. But they did not leave. They never left until dismissed.
Maelis let them linger. Fear made them useful.
The map still pulsed under their hand, glowing faintly—four marks shining brighter than the rest.
Trident.
Owl.
Key.
Pieces of the game, finally waking up.
"You are troubled," Maelis said without turning.
The Watchers froze, their discordant chorus silenced. Then, one spoke:
"The thirteenth."
Another layered over it:
"The broken piece."
"The chain does not hold."
"The chain fractures."

Maelis closed their eyes for a moment, listening. Not to their words.

To their fear.

"The chain," Maelis said, almost gently, "has always been imperfect. You mistake its flaws for new breaks because you have forgotten what it was built to carry."

The Watchers tilted their heads, masks creaking.

"Chaos."

"Order."

"The prophecy," one hissed.

"The prophecy," another echoed.

Maelis withdrew their hand from the map. The surface rippled once, then stilled.

They walked to the far end of the hollow, where a great iron frame jutted from the wall—a cage forged of chains that glowed faint red. Inside hung strips of parchment, countless and overlapping, floating as though underwater.

Each strip bore fragments of script, carved in languages the Watchers had forgotten how to read. Some glowed faintly. Others burned like live coals. A few were blackened, their words too dangerous to be touched.

One of the blackened strips twitched as Maelis passed, exhaling a faint, wordless scream that echoed like a trapped memory. Even the Watchers shifted back from it, claws scraping nervously against the floor.

Maelis stopped in front of the cage, their pale hand wrapping around one of the chains.

"The prophecy does not change," they said softly.

"We do."

The Watchers pressed closer, masks reflecting the flickering fragments.

"The thirteenth unravels it."

"The thirteenth rewrites."

"The thirteenth corrupts."

Maelis smiled faintly, though there was no warmth in it.

"Or perhaps the thirteenth clarifies."

They tugged one of the burning strips free. The chain holding it hissed, slackening under their touch. The parchment floated to them like it knew its master.

Maelis held it up, reading the words aloud:

"When the thirteenth breaks the silence, the gods will hear what they buried."

The Watchers hissed as one, their voices echoing like a storm of knives.

"Betrayal."

"Blasphemy."

"Unmaking."

Maelis ignored them. They read another fragment, this one faint, barely glowing:

"When the chains tremble, the board will shift, and those who watch will be seen."

They folded the parchment between their fingers.

"Would you like to be seen?" they asked.


The Watchers recoiled, their chorus stuttering.

"No." "No." "No."

Maelis returned the fragment to its place in the cage. The hollow groaned softly, as though relieved.

"The game cannot be stopped," Maelis said, turning back to them. "It can only be played well."

One of the Watchers stepped forward, its mask twitching in sharp, unnatural angles.

"And if you are wrong?" it hissed.

Maelis did not look at it.

"Then you will learn what becomes of pieces who forget their place."

The Watcher recoiled, the hum of the others softening into uneasy silence.

The Watchers hesitated. One stepped forward, clawed fingers curling.

"And if we lose?"

Maelis tilted their head, studying them like an entomologist regarding an insect that didn't know it had already been pinned.

"Then you'll understand why I do not tolerate failure."

They walked back to the map. Four glowing marks pulsed like heartbeats.
Chicago.
Cambridge.
Naples.

The first wave. The beginning of something larger than the heirs could comprehend. Larger than the Watchers, too.

Maelis traced the edge of the map, their hand lingering over the darkened parts of the world where no marks glowed yet.
"Eight more to wake," they said.
The Watchers shifted.
"Eight.", "Eight pieces.", "Eight fractures."
Maelis' smile returned.
"Eight inevitabilities."

They pressed both hands against the map, the surface shuddering beneath them. The chains across the world tightened, faintly glowing, trembling under pressure unseen.
"When eight stand," Maelis whispered, "the chains will tremble."

Their voice softened, almost reverent.
"When twelve rise, the sky will bleed."
The Watchers hissed, recoiling from the words like they burned.
But Maelis didn't flinch.
They leaned closer to the map, their reflection warping in the rippling surface.
"And when thirteen speaks," they said, voice a thread of silk and venom, "we'll all finally hear what we've been waiting for."

But in the hollow's silence, one mask trembled. Its claw tapped against the stone, once, twice, a rhythm out of sync with the others—like a heartbeat it could not silence.
For all their devotion, even Watchers could feel fear.
And the Watchers moved unseen again.

# *CODEX FRAGMENT*

## *THE LAST THRONE*

TWELVE THRONES REMEMBER THE HANDS

THAT FORGED THEM.

ONE THRONE REMEMBERS THE HAND THAT

REFUSED IT.

LOVE IS AN EMPIRE AND A WOUND.

WHEN THE CROWNS ARE CIRCLED AND THE

CHAINS COMPLETE,

A HEART MUST CHOOSE BETWEEN THE

LIGHT IT CARRIES

AND THE SHADOW THAT PROMISES IT

FREEDOM.

THE PATH OPENS ONLY BY A GIFT THAT

CANNOT BE TAKEN.

COUNT NOT THE

THRONES—COUNT

THE COST.

# CHAPTER V
# THE CROWN THAT WAITED

December 2, 2025

Naia Morrigan hated mirrors.

They lied.

They showed her smiling when she wasn't.

They made her look effortless when every inch of her body ached from the corsets, the heels, the hours of pretending to be what her mother demanded.

They told the world she was perfect when she felt like glass—brittle, breakable, one careless touch from shattering.

She smoothed the sequined emerald fabric of her gown as she glided through the ballroom, keeping her posture flawless, her face serene.

Her mother's voice was always in her head at moments like this:

"Poise, Naia. Shoulders back. Don't just walk—arrive. You are a Morrigan. They should feel it when you enter the room."

Naia could perform that role perfectly.

And she did.

Even when it hollowed her out.

When she was alone, Naia let the smile slide from her face. It was only then she felt the crown again—not a symbol of strength, but a chain no one else could see.

♦ ♦ ♦

Outside, Dublin's December air bit with winter's first true chill. It was three weeks until Christmas and the lights flickered over Grafton Street, fresh and fragile as if the city was still learning how to shine against the long nights. The season of celebration had begun, even as Naia felt herself unraveling.

Gold-leafed walls stretched high above her, chandeliers spilling artificial stars across polished marble floors. Every guest wore the same mask: smiling too wide, drinking too much, laughing at jokes they didn't find funny.

Naia knew how to play her part in this masquerade.

Her job was to be dazzling—the beautiful daughter of Evangeline Morrigan, the "promising young socialite" the magazines fawned over.

She held herself like a statue carved for worship.

Inside, she wanted to scream.

She caught her reflection in the mirrored columns that lined the ballroom.

At first glance, it was perfect.

Emerald gown draped elegantly.

Raven hair cascading in sleek waves to her shoulders. Golden-flecked hazel eyes framed by flawless makeup.

A queen, or at least the idea of one.

But when she looked closer, her reflection didn't quite move the way she did.

It tilted its head a second too late.

Smiled a fraction too wide.

And the eyes—

The eyes weren't hers.

They were older. Colder. A version of her that had seen every mask for what it was and learned to wield them like weapons.

Her stomach twisted.

She blinked hard and looked away.

She'd been seeing things like that for weeks now.

Shadows where there shouldn't be shadows. Faces in mirrors that didn't belong to her.

Her mother called it stress.

Naia called it losing her mind.

The string quartet in the corner shifted to a waltz, the music lilting and shallow.

Her hand trembled around her champagne glass.

The room felt too warm, the perfume and cologne mixing into a nauseating haze.

She needed air.

Naia slipped away from the bar, ignoring the disappointed glance from her mother across the room.

The ballroom doors opened onto an empty corridor lined with more mirrors, each one framed in ornate gold.

She walked quickly, heels clicking against the marble, her reflection following in the glass.

At least, it should have.

Halfway down the hall, she stopped.

Her reflection didn't.

It kept walking.

Naia's breath caught in her throat.

She turned sharply, heart pounding, but the glass showed only her.

Perfect. Poised. Smiling.

"Who are you?" she whispered.

Her reflection blinked.

But she hadn't.

The glass rippled like water.

Naia stumbled back, the champagne glass slipping from her hand and shattering against the floor.

The ripples spread until the mirror wasn't a mirror anymore.

It was a pool of shifting gold.

From its depths, a voice emerged.

"Child of the Crown."

Naia froze.

The voice wasn't a sound.

It was inside her.

Soft as velvet.

Sharp as a blade.

"You've been wearing their masks so long, you've forgotten what your face looks like."

Naia's knees went weak. "Wh… what are you?"

The golden surface of the mirror swirled, forming the vague outline of a woman's face.

"I am the one who gave you the spine to stand. The beauty they covet. The voice they ignore. You are mine."

The corridor pulsed with heat.

Every mirror shuddered, their glass surfaces warping until they became endless golden pools reflecting versions of Naia she didn't recognize—some younger, some older, some crowned in gold, some cloaked in shadow.

Each one smiled at her.

Each one waited.

Naia couldn't breathe.

"What do you want from me?"

"Not from you."

The voice softened, almost amused.

"For you."

The mirrored Naia closest to her stepped out of the frame.

She wore a laurel crown of gold, her eyes glowing like candlelight through whiskey.

She radiated authority.

Power.

The kind of presence that didn't ask for attention—it demanded it.

"Take it," the crowned reflection said.

Naia's voice cracked. "Take what?"

"What was always yours."

Her chest ached.

Her whole life had been a performance for someone else—her mother, the tabloids, the men who looked at her like she was a prize instead of a person.

Was this her?

The woman in the crown?

Could she be?

Naia reached out.

The glass was warm under her fingertips, pulsing like a living thing.

The warmth grew hotter, pulsing faster, until it burned like a heartbeat that wasn't hers. Each beat quickened, the heat building toward a shattering point. If she didn't take it now, she knew the mirror would burst—and take her with it.

The crown-bearing reflection smiled.

"Good."

The corridor melted into light.

Naia gasped, shielding her eyes as the world burned gold.

◆ ◆ ◆

When she blinked again, she wasn't in the corridor anymore.

She was in a throne room.

It was endless and opulent, lined with towering columns of white marble veined with gold.

Thrones sat in a ring, empty but for one.

At its center lounged a woman draped in emerald silk, her black hair coiled into a crown of braids.

A golden laurel rested on her brow.

Her eyes—

Naia's eyes—

Met hers.

"Hera," Naia whispered.

The goddess of queens smiled.

"Child," she said.

"Are you ready to stop playing at royalty?"

Naia's heart hammered as the woman on the throne rose.

Every movement was deliberate, every gesture so graceful it felt rehearsed, like Hera had been perfecting this role for eternity.

Maybe she had.

The goddess descended the steps, the train of her emerald gown whispering against the marble.

Her presence was suffocating, not because it pressed on Naia like a weight, but because it demanded space—a presence that couldn't be ignored or diminished.

She wasn't beautiful the way the magazines defined it. She was beautiful the way storms are: inevitable, dangerous, impossible to ignore.

"You've been wearing masks," Hera said, circling Naia as one might examine a painting.

Her voice was soft velvet over sharpened steel.

"The dutiful daughter. The dazzling socialite. The prize worth winning. Masks they gave you. Masks they praised you for."

She stopped in front of Naia, tilting her head.

"Do you even remember what your face looks like beneath them?"

Naia swallowed hard.

"No."

Hera's expression softened, almost pitying.

"Then it's time you remembered."

The goddess gestured, and the mirrored walls of the throne room shuddered.

They rippled like water, reshaping into hundreds of versions of Naia.

Some wore crowns, some chains.

Some dripped with blood, some knelt, some stood tall and unbroken.

All of them stared back at her.

Naia's stomach twisted.

"What is this?"

"A court of your own reflections," Hera said.

"The versions of you the world has tried to make. The ones you've tried to be. The one you are meant to become."

Naia's eyes locked on one reflection—the crowned woman she'd seen before, standing straighter than Naia ever had, her gaze calm and commanding.

For a moment the air thickened, sharp with the scent of ozone, and the walls pulsed as though every version of her was breathing in unison. The weight of a hundred gazes pressed on her chest, daring her to look away.

"Is that really me?"

"It will be, if you claim it."

Naia shook her head.

"I don't know how."

Hera stepped closer, lifting Naia's chin with one cold, perfect finger.

"You don't need to know. You only need to want."

The goddess snapped her fingers.

Chains of molten gold erupted from the floor, coiling around Naia's wrists, her ankles, her throat.

The marble floor cracked under the force, a golden fissure splitting outward from her feet. Dust rained from the vaulted ceiling as if the entire corridor shuddered to witness the bond.

Naia gasped, but the chains didn't hurt.

They pulsed like heartbeats, warm and alive, as if they recognized her.

"The chain," Hera said.

"The legacy that binds you to the others. Twelve links of gold, unbroken."

Naia's mind reeled.

"Others?"

"Children of Olympus," Hera said simply. "Heirs, like you. Some blaze bright. Some lurk in shadow. All are bound. All are mine as much as they are theirs."

Naia's gaze dropped to the chains at her feet.

They stretched out across the floor, connecting her to unseen points in the golden marble.

As she watched, faint silhouettes flickered at the ends of the links—strangers she didn't recognize but somehow felt.

She reached toward one.

It burned with steady warmth, regal as sunlight.

Another flickered like candlelight in the wind—fragile, unsteady.

Another pulsed like a drumbeat, sharp and violent.

And one—

One corroded link.

Rust-eaten, jagged, wrong.

It scraped against the others like a discordant note in a symphony.

Naia winced.

"What is that?"

Hera's expression darkened.

"A broken link."

"Why is it here?"

"Because it refuses to be anywhere else."

Naia clenched her fists.

"Then cut it out."

Hera's gaze sharpened.

"Would you cut off a finger for being ugly? A limb for being burned? Even the flawed are part of the whole."

Naia stared at the rusted link.

The discordant scrape clawed against her soul, sharp as broken glass.

She wanted to recoil, to reject it—but Hera's gaze pinned her.

Even the fractured are part of the whole. Without them, the chain breaks.

She didn't want it there.

Hera reached behind her and lifted something from the throne—a golden laurel crown, simple yet divine.

"You were not made to kneel."

Her words dripped with authority, not suggestion but law.

"You were crafted to bind and command. To stand in the halls where others falter. To be seen—and to make them tremble when they do. You were made to rule."

Naia's breath caught as Hera placed the crown gently on her head.

It seared against her scalp, but the pain was cleansing, stripping away the performance, the hollow smiles, the years of being her mother's perfect doll.

For the first time, she felt like herself.

The warmth in her chest didn't fade when the light dimmed.

It felt like standing beneath a summer sky, even in the December cold.

And somewhere deep inside, a voice she didn't recognize whispered that the crown hadn't just been waiting—it had chosen.

The chains pulsed, brighter now, linking her not just to the others but to herself.

She stood taller.

Straighter.

The crowned reflection in the mirror smiled.

Hera stepped back.

"You are my heir, Naia Morrigan. My voice. My vengeance."

Naia inhaled deeply, feeling the words sink into her bones.

"Then I'll never kneel again."

Hera's smile turned razor sharp.

"Good."

◆ ◆ ◆

The throne room trembled, the mirrored walls shattering into a thousand pieces.

Naia didn't flinch.

She was ready.

The golden marble, the endless mirrors, the divine glow of Hera's presence—gone.

Naia stood once again in the hallway outside the ballroom.

The champagne glass lay in glittering shards at her feet, and the waltz still played faintly in the distance.

But everything felt different.

She felt different.

The chains were still there.

Not physical.

Not visible.

But she could feel them, coiled around her wrists and ankles, pulsing faintly beneath her skin.

They hummed with power, ready to be used.

"Pretty little doll."

Naia stiffened.

The voice wasn't Hera's.

It came from behind her.

She turned slowly.

Two figures stood at the end of the hall.

Tall.

Cloaked in black that seemed to bleed into the air around them.

Porcelain masks hid their faces, but Naia felt their eyes on her.

"The doll thinks she's a queen," one hissed, its voice like splintering glass.

The other tilted its head.

"The doll should stay on her shelf."

Naia's pulse spiked, but she didn't back away.

They weren't human.

She didn't know what they were.

But she knew what they wanted.

To make her small again.

Breakable.

Silent.

She straightened her spine, lifting her chin the way Hera had taught her in the throne room.

"I'm no one's doll," she said, her voice steady.

The Watchers didn't rush her.

Instead, they moved in slow arcs, circling as if measuring the space between every breath she took.

Their gaze pressed on the crown still gleaming at her brow, a silent test of its weight.

Naia's pulse quickened, but she held their stare.

Only when she lifted her chin higher did the nearer shadow recoil, mask twitching in a jagged snap of motion.

The silence thickened, a breath held too long.

Then the other lunged, claws slashing toward her throat.

A chain burst from the marble, snapping around the first Watcher's torso and pinning it to the wall.

The second Watcher darted to her side, claws extended.

For a heartbeat she froze.

The doll in her wanted to scream, to run, to shatter.

But the crown pressed heavier on her brow, Hera's voice whispering like thunder through her bones: You were not made to kneel.

Fire surged where fear had been.

Her arm shot out on instinct.

Another chain exploded from the wall, wrapping around its neck and yanking it backward.

The creature slammed into the mirror, the glass spiderwebbing in golden cracks that pulsed like veins of fire.

Naia stepped forward.

Her heels clicked against the marble like the toll of a bell.

The Watchers strained against their bindings, but the chains held fast, glowing brighter with every attempt to escape.

"You don't touch a queen," Naia said.

Not a warning.

A verdict.

The first Watcher hissed, jerking against the chains.

"The doll plays dress up."

Naia tilted her head, studying it.

"No," she said.

"The doll grew teeth."

She tightened her fists.

The chains constricted.

Golden fire raced through the porcelain, splitting it apart; the mask screamed as it cracked, then dissolved into ash.

The second one thrashed, clawing at its bonds.

Naia glanced at it, the crown burning like sunlight in her eyes.

"Kneel."

The word wasn't spoken—it was unleashed.

The chain snapped down, and the Watcher crumpled, forced to the marble floor.

The creature hissed, but it couldn't rise.

Naia felt a flicker of fear beneath the power, but it was distant. Muted.

Hera had been right.

This wasn't a mask.

This was her face.

She walked between the two Watchers, her gown brushing the marble like the train of a queen's robe.

"You came here thinking I was weak," she said.

The chains tightened.

"You came here thinking I was yours."

She looked between them, meeting the hollow slits where their eyes should've been.

"Now kneel."

Both creatures hit the floor.

The power thrummed through her veins, intoxicating and terrifying all at once.

She could feel their resistance—their hatred—but they couldn't disobey.

They couldn't not kneel.

Naia raised her hand.

The chains pulsed once, then ignited.

Both Watchers screamed as they dissolved into black smoke, leaving only the faint smell of burnt ash in the air.

The chains retracted, slipping back beneath her skin like obedient servants.

Naia exhaled, steadying herself.

Her heart still pounded, but she didn't feel afraid anymore.

She felt alive.

For the first time, she didn't feel like her mother's doll.

She felt like the woman in the mirror.

She felt like a queen.

And she knew, with a clarity sharper than any blade, that she would never wear their masks again—not her mother's, not society's, not the ones they built to keep her small.

She had shed them in the fire of Hera's gaze, and there would be no putting them back on.

◆ ◆ ◆

Naia stood in the quiet corridor, the faint smell of burnt ash lingering in the air.

The ballroom doors loomed at the end of the hall, the muffled sound of waltz music and meaningless laughter bleeding through.

A few minutes ago, that room had felt like a cage.

Now, it felt like a court.

Her court.

She caught sight of herself in one of the fractured mirrors.

Her hair was a little wild, the crown of golden laurel gleaming faintly at her brow like a brand of light only she could see.

Her eyes—

They weren't the hollow, glassy ones she'd seen earlier tonight.

They burned.

Steady.

Unflinching.

The chains hummed under her skin, warm and waiting.

She didn't need to see them to know they were there, coiled around her wrists and ankles like adornments made for royalty.

They weren't shackles.

They were power.

Her pulse steadied.

Every step toward the ballroom doors felt heavier and lighter at once—like walking into judgment and coronation in the same breath.

It wasn't her mother's voice guiding her spine, demanding perfection.

It was her own.

Naia walked back into the ballroom.

Every step clicked like a gavel striking marble, the sound cutting through the waltz, through the idle chatter, through the meaningless performance.

Heads turned.

They couldn't help it.

She wasn't just dressed like a queen anymore.

She was one.

And they felt it.

Her mother's gaze found her from across the room—Evangeline Morrigan, the architect of Naia's every mask.

The woman blinked, her poised expression faltering for just a second as she took in her daughter.

Naia didn't break stride.

She didn't bow her head.

She didn't smile.

She didn't need to.

When she reached the center of the room, she paused, letting the eyes linger.

The string quartet faltered for a moment, as if sensing the shift in the air.

Naia smoothed her gown with steady hands, adjusted the invisible crown on her head, and let the silence press down like judgment.

Let them feel the weight of her.

The chains whispered.

She could sense the others again.

Distant, flickering silhouettes at the ends of her links.

Some steady and bright.

Some unstable and dim.

Some burning hot as fire.

And one—

That corroded, rust-eaten link.

It scraped against her again, a discordant weight in an otherwise perfect chain.

She hated it.

But she couldn't deny it belonged.

Naia's chest swelled with the strange, awful knowledge that she wasn't alone.

That she wasn't just part of this chain.

She was holding it together.

Yet even as she steadied the chain, the rusted link scraped louder, a discordant sound no crown could silence. It was waiting. Watching. And Naia felt, with a chill, that it wasn't broken at all—it was awake.

♦ ♦ ♦

Far below Olympus, in halls of obsidian veined with molten gold, Maelis traced their fingers across the living map.

They stopped over Ireland.

A new symbol glowed over Dublin:

A golden laurel, crowned and gleaming.

"The queen rises," Maelis whispered, lips curling into the faintest smile.

"The chain tightens."

The Watchers knelt behind them, silent, their masks bowed low to the floor.

Maelis didn't look at them.

They only pressed their palm against the map, and the chains across the world thrummed in response, singing a tune that only they could hear.

"When the queen rises," Maelis said, their voice a silken thread of prophecy, "the court will kneel… or burn."

# CODEX FRAGMENT
## THE FIRST CHAINS

CHAINS SING WHERE THUNDER SLEEPS.
THE LINKS ARE NOT IRON BUT OATH —
BLOOD RECOGNIZES BLOOD AND
REMEMBERS ITS SHAPE.
COUNT THEM, AND YOU REACH ONLY
TWELVE;
DO NOT COUNT, AND YOU WILL FEEL
ANOTHER.
SEEK THE WATCHTOWER SHATTERED BY
LIGHT;
GATHER THE MARKED BEFORE THE SKY
SPLITS TWICE.

# CHAPTER VI
# THE FORGE THAT WOULDN'T DIE

December 14, 2025

Above, winter storms pressed against the coast. December gales swept across the caldera, the sea's roar faint beneath the heartbeat of the forge."

If Santorini had a heartbeat, Isla Damaris knew where to find it. The island lay quiet in the off-season, ferries running on winter schedules and most tourist shops shuttered against the Aegean wind.

It wasn't in the whitewashed villas stacked like sugar cubes on the cliffs, or in the tourist-clogged markets selling overpriced olives and cheap leather sandals. It wasn't in the postcard sunsets tourists screamed about on Instagram, all fiery skies and champagne toasts.

Santorini's heart wasn't up there.

It was below.

Isla tightened the straps on her work boots, ignoring the way the sharp volcanic gravel bit into her ankles.

Her uncle had forbidden her from coming down here again— said it wasn't safe, said the tunnels were unstable, said she had no business wandering volcanic veins in the middle of the night.

But staying still was worse than danger.

Her mind didn't know how to stop.

It hummed constantly, a swarm of thoughts and ideas and blueprints that never quieted unless her hands were moving.

When she wasn't building, she was unraveling.

The cave's entrance yawned ahead, a jagged tear in the black rock.

Even from here she could feel its breath—hot, mineral-laden air rising from deep within, tinged with sulfur and ash.

She ducked inside, her flashlight beam cutting across rough walls streaked with veins of glimmering ore.

The deeper she went, the more the island changed.

The air grew thicker, humid with the memory of ancient fire.

The sound of the sea above vanished, replaced by the slow, rhythmic hiss of steam escaping unseen vents.

She'd been coming here for months, scavenging metal scraps and dragging tools to the small cavern she'd claimed as her sanctuary.

It wasn't much—a soot-stained worktable, some salvaged gears and broken mechanisms, a box of rust-spotted tools her uncle would have thrown away.

But it was hers.

She set the flashlight on the table and touched the tools like a priest handling relics.

The cave smelled like scorched stone and old smoke, the air buzzing faintly with heat.

It felt alive.

And she felt alive when she was inside it.

Her uncle had called her obsession "too much like your father."

He'd meant it as an insult.

Isla wore it like armor.

♦ ♦ ♦

She pulled out her notebook and sketched in the dim light, quick strokes bringing gears and levers and intricate locking mechanisms to life on the page.

She didn't even know what she was designing yet.

She never did.

The ideas came first.

The purpose followed.

She grabbed a half-finished contraption from the table—a gear-driven tool she'd been tinkering with for days.

She adjusted its alignment with a rusted screwdriver, tightening the screws until it clicked into place.

Better.

But not done.

Never done.

The ground vibrated.

Just slightly, like a cat purring beneath her feet.

Isla froze.

The tunnels didn't usually tremble like that.

She set the tool down and listened.

The hiss of steam grew louder.

The air shimmered, waves of heat distorting the edges of the cavern.

Golden veins in the rock began to glow, faint at first, then brighter, until they pulsed like molten arteries.

Isla stepped back, heart hammering.

This wasn't a normal tremor.

This was… something else.

The worktable rattled, spilling screws and bolts onto the floor. Her flashlight flickered, then died.

Darkness swallowed the cavern—but not for long.

The golden veins flared, filling the room with a warm, unnatural light.

The glow traced patterns across the walls, spiraling and interlocking like the insides of some colossal machine.

Gears.

That's what they looked like.

Gears turning beneath the skin of the island.

Isla's mouth went dry.

She'd studied enough machines to know this wasn't random.

The patterns had purpose.

They fit together like teeth on a cog, like a lock slowly opening.

The forge wasn't just alive.

It was waking up.

Isla's pulse roared in her ears.

She should've run.

Instead, she moved closer.

The golden patterns on the walls shifted, forming a doorway she'd never seen before.

The rock groaned as it split open, revealing a passage lined with veins of fire and metal.

It beckoned her, glowing brighter the longer she stared.

Every instinct screamed to stay back.

She stepped inside.

The heat enveloped her, oppressive but not unbearable, like standing too close to a forge fire.

The air smelled like molten iron and oil.

Her boots crunched over black stone until the tunnel opened into a massive chamber.

She gasped.

It was a forge.

Not the kind she'd cobbled together above.

This one was divine.

Anvils the size of cars lined the walls, glowing with faint embers.

Massive bellows pumped on their own, driven by unseen mechanisms.

Chains dangled from the ceiling like metallic vines, each one humming with barely restrained power.

At the center of it all sat a single pedestal.

On it rested a hammer.

The forge quaked, gears grinding louder, sparks spitting from chains above as though straining to hold. Cracks spidered across the pedestal, heat pulsing in waves so fierce she thought the chamber might collapse before she reached it.

It was no ordinary hammer.

Its head shimmered like heated steel, carved with glowing runes that shifted and rearranged themselves.

Its handle was obsidian, wrapped in leather that hadn't aged a day.

It radiated strength.

Purpose.

Like it had been waiting for her.

Isla approached slowly, her breath shallow.

Every step felt like walking deeper into someone else's dream.

When she reached the pedestal, she hesitated only a moment before wrapping her fingers around the hammer.

The world exploded in light.

The cavern dissolved.

The heat, the stone, the scent of sulfur—gone.

Isla floated in a void of glowing embers, each one pulsing like the slow beat of a heart.

Then the embers burst, and the void became a workshop.

It was unlike anything she'd ever seen.

An endless space where the walls were alive with mechanisms—colossal gears turning in perfect rhythm, chains snaking across molten beams, constructs assembling themselves from fragments of metal.

The heat here did not burn—it baptized. The air tasted of iron and smoke, heavy with the ghosts of a thousand creations, as if every invention Hephaestus had ever forged still whispered in this place. The weight of it stole her breath. For a heartbeat she thought her ribs might crack beneath the pressure, as if the forge itself tested whether she could withstand its rhythm. The clanging of unseen machines was not noise. It was music, raw and unyielding, a symphony of labor and persistence.

Workbenches floated in midair, cluttered with tools that hummed with divine energy.

The floor beneath her feet shifted like a living machine, reconfiguring itself with every step.

At the far end of the workshop, a man stood at a forge.

He was massive, broad-shouldered, his arms corded with muscle and marred by deep, jagged burns.

His beard was ashy gray, his hair wild and blackened by soot.

He wore a leather apron, scorched and battered, as if he hadn't taken it off in centuries.

And in his burned hands, he held a hammer the size of her torso, bringing it down on an anvil that glowed like molten gold.

Every strike shook the workshop, sending ripples through the air.

Each blow birthed sparks that floated upward like captured stars.

He didn't look at her.

But she knew who he was.

Hephaestus.

Isla's throat tightened.

She'd never believed in gods—not really.

But she'd always believed in work.

In building.

In taking broken things and making them whole.

And here was the god who had been doing it for eternity.

He set the hammer aside and turned.

His face was weathered, burned, his left eye a pale, milky white. But the other…

The other burned like the forge.

"Damaris."

His voice was rough, like gravel dragged across metal. But it wasn't cruel.

It was the voice of someone who'd worked too long and suffered too much to waste words.

Isla swallowed.

"You know my name."

Hephaestus grunted.

"I know my blood when I see it."

Her pulse spiked.

"Blood?"

"You build like me," he said simply.

"Restless. Obsessive. You make tools because stillness would kill you. You fix what others throw away. That isn't learned. It's inherited."

Isla felt the truth of it settle in her chest like molten iron.

He gestured to the workshop around them.

"This is the forge of gods. Every chain, every cog, every weapon in Olympus' arsenal was born here. You are not the first to stand where you are. But you may be the last."

Her gaze flicked to the walls—to the massive gears and pulsing chains that crisscrossed the workshop.

They weren't just mechanisms.

They were alive.

The longer she stared, the more she saw them differently.

They weren't just pieces of a machine.

They were connections.

Threads.

She blinked, and the workshop shifted.

The chains and gears stretched out into a web of interlocking links, each one glowing faintly.

Some turned smoothly, strong and steady.

Some clicked unevenly, as if straining to keep up.

And one—

One was corroded, jagged, grinding against the others with every rotation.

The sound of it scraped against her skull.

Isla winced.

"What is that?"

Hephaestus followed her gaze.

His burned mouth pulled into something like a grimace.

"A broken cog. It wasn't made for this machine, but here it is. Grinding. Refusing to break."

"Can't you fix it?"

Hephaestus huffed a laugh—bitter, heavy.

"Not everything can be fixed. Some things just have to be endured."

The words cut deeper than she expected.

She'd spent her whole life fixing things.

She hated the thought of leaving something broken.

Hephaestus stepped closer, the floor adjusting itself to bear his weight.

"You think building is about perfection."

Isla's breath caught.

"Isn't it?"

"No."

He leaned down until his burned face was level with hers.
"It's about survival." It's about making something strong enough to
bear the weight of its flaws."

Her chest ached.
She didn't know if he was talking about the machine.
Or her.

◆ ◆ ◆

He gestured to her hands.
"Pick up the hammer."

Isla's fingers tightened around the one she'd taken from the
pedestal.
It felt heavier now.
Not just a tool.
A burden.
A promise.

Hephaestus rested his massive hand on her shoulder.
It was warm.
Steady.

"You are my heir. My forge. My hands in the world. Build well,
Isla Damaris."

The workshop flared with light, so bright she had to shield her
eyes.
The heat roared, not painful, but purifying, burning away everything that didn't matter.

When she lowered her arm, Hephaestus was gone.

But the forge still hummed inside her.
The forge's glow didn't just light the cavern—it lit her from the inside. Every strike of the hammer still echoed in her ribs, steady and
certain, as if the heartbeat of the island had aligned with her own.
She didn't have to be told it would answer her again.

And the hammer still burned in her grip.

The hammer's runes blazed hotter, searing against her skin. Isla
gasped as fire threaded through her veins, burning a mark deep
into her palm. She nearly dropped it, but the pain steadied into
something stranger—alive, deliberate.

When she pulled her hand back, the skin was unbroken, yet the glyph glowed there: a golden flame etched in shifting lines of metal and fire. Her forge. Her inheritance.

The forge quieted.

The hammer in Isla's hand still glowed faintly, its runes shifting like molten script.

She could feel its hum in her bones—steady, alive.

She thought the vision was over.

She thought she was alone.

Then the temperature dropped.

Not by much.

Just enough to make her skin prickle.

The forge lights flickered.

The massive bellows groaned.

The gears and chains that had turned with divine precision began to stutter, grinding like they were being forced against their will.

Isla's stomach sank.

She wasn't alone.

"Little smith. The Marionette that bends iron."

"The child of chains that dreams of fire. The chains will claim you."

"The forge roars… but even flame breaks in shadow."

She spun, gripping the hammer with both hands.

Two Watchers emerged from the glowing walls.

Their bone-white masks glossy as shell were cracked, their cloaks trailing black smoke that hissed when it touched the floor.

They moved like broken marionettes, jerking unnaturally as they stepped toward her.

Her grip tightened.

"I'm no one's Marionette," she said.

The words came out steadier than she felt.

The first Watcher didn't strike for her directly. Instead, it turned toward the forge's heart, a clawed hand rising as the glow dimmed where its shadow fell.

The hiss of cooling metal cut through the chamber, sharp and wrong.

Heat surged under Isla's skin in response, and she stepped between the creature and the forge.

The shadow hesitated, its cracked mask tilting as though measuring her—then it lunged.

She swung the hammer with a burst of molten light, the impact flinging the Watcher into the wall.

The hiss died, and the glow steadied.

The second one skittered low, claws scraping sparks against the metal floor.

Its weight struck so hard the floor dented, molten cracks radiating outward with each lunge. Every impact shook her bones, the cavern threatening to tear itself apart under their clash.

Isla pivoted, swinging again, but it was faster.

It slammed into her side, knocking her into one of the floating workbenches.

The impact stole her breath.

She scrambled up, chest heaving.
The hammer felt heavier now.

The Watcher stalked toward her, its limbs too long, its mask splitting wider as it hissed.

"You don't belong here," it rasped.

"Neither do you," Isla spat.

She reached for the bench.
Her hands found scraps—gears, a twisted length of pipe, a jagged sheet of metal.

Her brain didn't think.
It just built.

♦ ♦ ♦

She jammed the gear onto the pipe, wrapping the connection with the glowing chains that dangled from the ceiling.

The metal responded, shifting, welding itself under her grip.

In seconds, she'd made something new: a spiked, gear-driven mace.
Crude.
Ugly.
Hers.

The Watcher lunged again.

Isla met it head on.

The mace connected with its head, the gears grinding as the spikes bit deep.

It shrieked, black smoke pouring from the cracks in its mask.

She didn't stop.

She swung again and again until the creature dissolved into smoke.

The first Watcher screeched, rising from the floor.

Its mask was shattered, exposing something underneath—a writhing void that made Isla's skin crawl.

It rushed her, claws outstretched.

She dropped the mace and raised the hammer.

This time, she didn't just swing.

She brought it down like she was forging a blade.

The runes flared, molten and blinding, and the hammerhead struck the Watcher with a deafening impact.

The creature convulsed, then burst into a cloud of black ash.

The forge fell silent.

Only her ragged breathing filled the air.

♦ ♦ ♦

Isla dropped the hammer, her hands trembling.

Her arms ached from the weight of the fight, but she couldn't let go of the adrenaline humming through her.

She'd built her first weapon.

Not to make something beautiful.

Not to fix what was broken.

To survive.

She stared at the hammer.

It wasn't just a tool anymore.

It was an extension of her.

And she understood what Hephaestus meant.

Building wasn't about perfection.

It was about making something strong enough to bear its flaws.

Even herself. The forge quieted again, but not to silence.

It hummed, steady and low, like the deep breath of something alive and patient.

Isla leaned against the workbench, her hands still trembling from the fight.

The mace she'd built sat disbanded at her feet, crude but effective.

The hammer still burned in her grip, its runes glowing faintly, as though pleased.

Her uncle had called her obsession a problem.

Her teachers had called it wasted potential.

Her friends had called it strange.

She'd always built because she couldn't stop.

Now she understood why.

It wasn't compulsion.

It was purpose.

The forge wasn't just a place.

It was part of her.

Every chain, every gear, every hiss of steam sang to her now. She could feel their rhythm, their interlocking motion.

The chains were no longer just tools—they were threads, connecting her to something bigger than herself. She followed them with her mind.

Some links turned smooth and steady, humming with strength. Others rattled, grinding under unseen pressure.

And one—

That corroded cog, jagged and wrong, grinding against the machine with every painful rotation.

It screamed in defiance of the harmony, a fragment that refused to fit yet refused to break.

Its presence infected the rhythm, a reminder that even divine machinery carried flaws too stubborn to erase.

It scraped against her skull, a discordant note she couldn't unhear. She clenched the hammer tighter.

"Can't fix you," she muttered under her breath.

"Not yet."

Her gaze shifted to the forge itself.

It wasn't just a divine workshop.

It was a crucible.

And she'd been inside it. Isla lifted the hammer and brought it down against the anvil, not to build, but to claim.

The glyph on her palm seared bright as the hammer struck, molten fire answering molten fire.

The sound rang through the workshop like a bell, deep and final.

The chains above her pulsed in response, glowing brighter, as though acknowledging her. She was no longer just Isla Damaris, the restless girl who fixed scraps to quiet her mind.

She understood now: she wasn't meant to tinker in the margins of other people's designs.

She was meant to build her own—to craft herself, flawed and unbreakable, in the fires that would try to consume her.

She was the forge.

A creator.

A weapon. But even as the forge dimmed, the discordant cog screamed louder in her skull, rattling the perfect rhythm with its refusal to break. For the first time, she wondered if it was watching her back. The forge light dimmed, softening until the chamber felt almost restful.

When she looked around again, the workshop had begun to dissolve.

The anvils faded first, then the bellows, then the endless walls of gears and chains. When the light fully died, she was back in the cavern beneath Santorini.

The golden veins in the stone still glowed faintly, but the rest was still.

Silent and Waiting.

Isla exhaled, her breath shaky but steadying.

She wasn't afraid anymore.

"Far above, the caldera quaked. On the cliffs of Oia, shutters rattled and lamps swayed. Her uncle would wake. The island had felt her forging."

She felt anchored, like she'd finally found the blueprint for herself.

She turned toward the tunnel, hammer slung across her shoulder.

It didn't feel heavy anymore.

It felt right.

Far below Olympus, in the obsidian halls lit by veins of golden fire, Maelis stood over the living map.

Their pale fingers traced across the Aegean Sea, stopping at Santorini.

A new symbol glowed there:

A hammer wreathed in flame.

"The forge roars," they murmured.

"The chain tightens."

The Watchers knelt behind them, their cracked masks lowered to the ground.

Maelis didn't look at them.

They only pressed their hand against the map, and the chains stretched across the glowing continents shuddered like a machine straining against its own weight. "When the forge roars," Maelis said softly,

"even the unbreakable will bend.

**Institute Archive Reference – Document 447-B**

Fragment recovered from a collapsed archive vault in Delphi.

Initial translation is unstable; the language shows irregularities not seen in other Olympian codices.

Further verification required before authentication.

— *Filed by Dr. Eleni Makris, Senior Archivist*

FOR HIDDEN CODEX FRAGMENTS AND LOST GLYPHS, ENTER THE VAULT:

WWW.JOINTHEAWAKENED.COM

# CHAPTER VII

# THE BATTLEFIELD OF ASHES

December 24, 2025


Damien Holt hated memorials.

They always felt like lies.

Stone statues, engraved names, polite plaques telling the world to "never forget."

But they always forgot.

People forgot.

They forgot the bodies, the blood, the screaming. They forgot what it meant to be left behind while everyone else moved on.

Antarctica's old battlefield memorial wasn't different. The sea air carried a brittle winter chill, sharp with salt and the scent of distant rain.

It was beautiful, sure—rows of weathered headstones lined up like teeth, marble statues watching over the dead like stone-faced gods, flowers left by families who could afford to remember.

But beneath all of it, Damien smelled the rot of hypocrisy.

This wasn't a graveyard for people like him.

It was a gallery for ghosts that mattered.

Even the statues seemed to sneer—not guardians of the fallen, but stone jurors staring down from their pedestals. Their silence wasn't reverent. It was a verdict.

He walked past the names carved into the ossuary wall without reading them. He didn't want to see who was worth remembering.

The night air was cool, heavy with salt from the nearby sea. The kind of night that should've calmed him.

It didn't.

Not anymore.

Not since his mom left.

Not since his dad drank himself into a grave instead of trying.

Not since the foster homes. The streets. The fights.

Being forgotten wasn't new.

It was the only thing in his life that stayed the same.

He sat on the memorial steps, his hood pulled low, staring at the flickering candles someone had left at the base of the marble statue.

The statue was of a soldier—faceless, rifle in hand, cloak billowing in a wind that wasn't there.

"Hero," the plaque called him.

Damien spat on the ground.

"Heroes," he muttered. "Just another word people use to forget the ones who didn't come back."

He rubbed at the burn on his knuckles, the one from last week's fight outside the bar where he wasn't old enough to be drinking but did anyway.

It had been stupid—two guys twice his size, one bad joke about his mom, and he'd seen red.

It always went that way.

Red.

No thoughts, no fear, no pain.

Just red.

That was the only time he ever felt… alive.

Not good.

Not safe.

Just alive.

A sound broke the silence.

A hum.

Low, steady.

At first, Damien thought it was the wind.

But the air was still.

And the sound wasn't coming from outside.

It was coming from below.

He stood slowly, scanning the dark cemetery.

"Hello?"

His voice echoed off the stones.

Nothing answered.

The hum grew louder, pulsing in his bones.

His stomach tightened.

Something was pulling him toward the memorial's ossuary—the underground chamber where the bones of long-dead soldiers were kept.

He didn't know why.

He just knew he had to go.

He pushed open the heavy iron gate, its rusted hinges screaming in protest.

The stone steps leading down were slick with moisture, the air growing colder with each step.

The hum in his bones turned into a rhythm.

A heartbeat.

Not his.

The ossuary was massive—rows of skulls and bones stacked in geometric patterns along the walls, forming grim mosaics of death.

It smelled of stone and dust and something older.

Something that had been waiting.

At the far end of the chamber, a single torch burned, though he hadn't seen anyone light it.

Its orange glow illuminated an altar—cracked, bloodstained, and older than the memorial above.

The hum intensified.

It was coming from there.

The air shivered as if the chamber itself had lungs, every torch guttering against a draft that came from nowhere. The hum wasn't just sound now—it was a pressure, a weight sliding beneath his skin.

His boots crunched over scattered bones as the hum pulled him deeper.

The closer he got, the heavier the air became.

It pressed on him, like the weight of every soul buried here had their eyes on him.

He set his hands on the altar.

It was warm.

Too warm.

"Do you feel it?"

The voice wasn't his own.

It wasn't in his ears.

It was in his blood.

Damien jerked back, his chest heaving.

"Who's there?"

"You bleed for them," the voice said, layered with centuries of war and rage. "You fight because they left you nothing. You are mine."

The heat from the altar surged up his arms, searing but not burning.

Damien stumbled back. "Mine? What the hell are you talking about?"

"You are the abandoned. The ones left behind," the voice thundered. "And war does not wait for the willing. It takes the broken and makes them into weapons."

◆ ◆ ◆

The hum became a roar, drowning out his thoughts.

Damien clutched his head, falling to his knees.

Images flooded his mind—battlefields soaked in blood, soldiers screaming, swords clashing against shields, the air thick with smoke and death.

He saw himself standing among them, his hands dripping red, his heartbeat matching the rhythm of the war drums.

"You are my heir," the voice said, fierce and proud. "You are the weapon. You are the war."

The ossuary shook.

Dust rained from the ceiling as the walls groaned like they were alive.

Bones tumbled from their careful patterns, spilling across the floor in a clattering wave.

The altar cracked open, glowing veins of molten red racing through the stone like blood through veins.

Damien screamed.

Not from fear.

From the fire tearing through his veins.

His skin burned, his muscles spasmed, his teeth clenched until his jaw ached.

And beneath the pain, he felt it:

Power.

Raw.

Untamed.

Alive.

"Rise, Damien Holt," the voice commanded. "Rise, my heir. Take your place among the Twelve."

When the pain finally subsided, Damien was on his feet, panting, drenched in sweat.

The altar's glow dimmed, settling into a dull, steady thrum.

His hands were shaking, but not from weakness.

From adrenaline.

From rage.

"What the hell did you do to me?" he asked the empty chamber.

"I gave you what was already yours," the voice said. "You were born of war. You were forged in blood. Now claim it."

The hum hadn't stopped.

Even with the altar quieted, the rhythm was still in his bones, still pounding in his chest like a second heartbeat.

Damien flexed his fingers. They felt strange—stronger, heavier. His whole body did.

It was like his skin didn't quite fit anymore.

He stepped back from the altar, his boots crunching over the scattered bones.

The skulls along the walls stared at him, hollow eye-slits glowing faintly in the torchlight.

They'd been silent for centuries.

Now they felt like an audience.

"Do you feel them?" the voice rumbled, less of a question than a command.

Damien didn't answer.

"These dead. These warriors. They do not sleep. They do not forget. They watch, as you watched. They waited, as you waited. Forgotten. Left behind. You are theirs now. And they are yours."

Damien shook his head, trying to clear the voice from his skull. "This isn't real," he muttered.

"Real?" the voice scoffed. "Was it real when they abandoned you? Was it real when you bled on their streets and they stepped over your body? This is the only thing that has ever been real, Damien Holt. The only thing that matters."

Damien clenched his fists.

He wanted to deny it.

But the words landed like they'd been pulled straight from the marrow of his bones.

A sound broke his thoughts.

Not the hum.

Not the voice.

Something else.

Footsteps.

Slow.

Deliberate.

Damien spun toward the ossuary's entrance.

The torchlight flickered, shadows stretching unnaturally across the walls.

"Who's there?"

No answer.

Just another step.

And another.

He reached for anything that could be used as a weapon.

A rusted sword rested against the wall—probably ceremonial, but it would do.

He gripped it tight, the leather-wrapped handle flaking under his fingers.

The weight felt good.

Familiar.

Like he'd held one before.

"Steel remembers the hand that wields it," the voice said. "And it remembers you."

"Shut up," Damien growled.

A shape appeared in the doorway.

Cloaked.

Tall.

Its face was smooth porcelain, featureless except for two narrow slits where eyes should have been.

A Watcher.

Damien didn't know what it was.

But every instinct screamed danger.

The same part of him that saw red in every fight told him this wasn't a man.

This was something worse.

The Watcher tilted its head, the movement jerky, insect-like.

Its neck snapped sideways with a brittle crack, glazed ceramic mask fracturing further, as though its body had forgotten how to be human.

When it spoke, its voice was a metallic whisper. "Blood of the war-god. Curse and gift, bound in one."

The cracked mask didn't move when it spoke—the words slithered straight into Damien's skull, as if his ears had been bypassed.

Damien raised the sword. "Back off."

The Watcher dragged one claw slowly across the damp stone floor, frost blooming in its wake and creeping toward Damien's boots. The gesture wasn't an attack—it was a claim.

His jaw tightened, the war-god's fire pushing back the cold, and he stepped forward, forcing the shadow to give ground.

Only then did it lash out, claws slicing for his chest.

Damien crashed forward, driving it back into the wall—bone racks rattled—and a length of chain slithered from the stacked ossuary ribs, snarling around its torso.

He met it with steel, the rusted blade striking the mask hard enough to send spiderweb cracks across the porcelain.

The creature reeled, and when it shrieked, the sound rattled the bones along the walls.

The cry was so sharp his vision blurred; for a heartbeat he thought the ossuary itself screamed with it. Skulls cracked against the floor as if the dead themselves were fracturing under the sound.

The ossuary trembled.

Dust rained from the ceiling.

The altar pulsed, its cracks glowing like molten veins.

"Yes," Ares said, his voice rumbling with approval. "Feel it. This is not rage. This is war."

The mask split further, hairline cracks glowing faintly as shadow leaked through.

The fight wasn't graceful.

It was brutal.

Damien ducked and swung, letting instinct guide him.

Every strike, every block felt familiar, like his body had done this a thousand times.

Like the blood in his veins remembered war even if his mind didn't.

The Watcher lashed out, claws raking across his arm.

Pain flashed hot and bright.

He didn't stop.

He drove the sword into its chest, pushing until the cracked mask was inches from his face.

"You are the weapon," Ares roared. "Now act like it."

With a guttural scream, Damien ripped the blade upward, splitting the Watcher's mask. Shards scattered across the ossuary floor like glowing teeth, flickering before they dissolved into smoke.

It howled, collapsing back in a plume of black smoke before vanishing completely.

He didn't know what it had been.

But he'd killed it.

And it felt good.

Damien stood in the center of the ossuary, chest heaving, knuckles white around the rusted sword.

His whole body shook, but not from fear.

From something else.

Something hotter.

Alive.

He glanced at the altar.

The cracks in its surface still glowed faintly, like veins of cooling magma.

It hummed again, matching the rhythm of his heart.

Not a hum.

A drum.

"You understand now," Ares said.

Damien didn't answer. He wasn't sure he could.

"They left you to rot," Ares continued, his voice rumbling through Damien's bones. "But war does not waste what is useful. It takes the forgotten. The broken. The abandoned. It makes them into weapons."

Damien dropped the sword with a clatter.

His hands were still trembling, but the adrenaline dulled every-thing—the cuts, the pain, even the fear.

He wasn't just Damien Holt anymore.

He wasn't just some angry kid from Antarctica.

He was something else.

He ran a hand over his face, smearing sweat and blood across his skin.

"This is insane," he muttered.

"No," Ares said. "This is truth. You are my heir. You are the weapon. You are the war."

Damien squeezed his eyes shut, but the images from earlier came rushing back.

Battlefields. Blood. The rhythm of marching feet.

And at the center of it all, a towering figure in bronze, crowned in fire.

He didn't have to ask who it was.

He knew.

"You're really in my head," Damien said, voice hoarse.

"I am in your blood," Ares corrected. "In your marrow. You carry me as you carry every fight you've ever survived."

Damien laughed bitterly. "Great. So I'm some god's pet project."

"You are my heir," Ares growled. "Not a pet. Not a project. My legacy. My war given flesh."

Damien opened his mouth to respond—but then he felt it. A tug deep in his chest.

Not the hum of the altar.
Not the voice of the god.
Something else.

Threads.

He staggered back, clutching his chest as the sensation spread. It wasn't just in his body.
It was everywhere.

One thread pulsed gold and steady—calm, like sunlight through storm clouds.
Kai.

Another hummed sharp and electric, buzzing with restless ambition.
Naia.

A third burned hot and steady, like living steel.
Isla.

And faintly, at the edges, threads not yet burning—sleeping, inevitable, waiting for their turn.

Each thread vibrated with its own rhythm, its own life, but together they felt like a single chain pulling him forward.

The sensation sharpened, and suddenly he wasn't just feeling them.
He was in their heads.

A boy on a mountain, clutching a violin, his breath shallow with fear.
Kai.

A girl in a torn green gown, her crown-mark glowing as she clenched her fists, her mind sharp and calculating.
Naia.

A girl in a forge lit by molten veins, hammer in hand, her heart thrumming with purpose.
Isla.

They all turned toward him.

Not physically. Not really.

But they felt him.

And he felt them.

Damien flinched.

He hadn't felt this exposed since the first time someone pinned him in a fight.

The threads weren't just connecting them.

They were bleeding into each other.

Kai's fear.

Naia's hunger.

Isla's steady resolve.

They were in his veins like they were his own.

And they felt his rage.

Kai's breath hitched in his distant mountain refuge.

Naia's hand trembled as she gripped her crown-marked arm.

Isla blinked, her hammer faltering mid-swing before she steadied it.

They didn't know his name.

But they knew him.

"They feel you as you feel them," Ares said, thick with satisfaction. "This is the chain. The binding of the Twelve. You will not fight alone. You will not bleed alone."

Damien sucked in a shaky breath.

He'd spent his whole life being left behind.

Now he was chained to people he'd never met.

And for the first time, it didn't feel like a prison.

It felt like power. All his life he'd been left behind. Now, even if he wanted to, he couldn't be.

"Who are they?" he asked.

"Your kin," Ares said. "Children of gods. Heirs of Olympus. The last war-forged souls who will decide what is broken and what endures."

Damien stared at the altar, jaw clenched.

He didn't know them.

Didn't know what they wanted.

But he knew one thing:

If they were going to war, he'd be ready.

"Good," Ares said, reading his thoughts. "War waits for no one. It takes what it needs. And now, Damien Holt, it takes you."

Damien flexed his bloodied hands, the fire in his veins burning hotter than ever.

"Then let it."

The threads quieted, but they didn't disappear.

They stayed coiled in his chest like living chains, their faint hum matching the war drum in his veins.

Damien stood there for a long time, staring at the cracked altar, his fingers still trembling from the fight.

The silence pressed in around him, but it wasn't the same silence he'd known his whole life.

It wasn't empty.

It was waiting.

"You feel it now," Ares said, voice like distant thunder. "The chain that binds you to the others. The blood that binds you to me."

Damien exhaled through his nose. "I feel... something."

"It is not something," Ares growled. "It is everything. It is purpose. It is survival. It is war."

Damien dragged a hand down his face. He'd spent years blaming himself for being left behind—by his mom, by his dad, by every adult who promised him help and gave him scraps instead.

But now?

Now he had a god's voice in his head telling him that being abandoned wasn't his curse.

It was his origin.

"The world does not save boys like you," Ares said, low and sharp. "It consumes them. Breaks them. Leaves them to rot."

"Yeah," Damien muttered, staring at the bone-lined walls. "I know."

"But you are not broken," Ares said. "You are forged."

Damien flexed his hands. His skin still felt hot, like his blood had been replaced with molten iron.

Forged.

That sounded better than abandoned.

He thought about the others—the ones he'd felt through the threads.

Kai, Naia, Isla.

He didn't know them, but he'd felt them.

Their fear.

Their hunger.

Their purpose.

And they'd felt him.

The raw, ugly rage that had carried him through every fight, every night alone, every moment of being someone nobody wanted.

"You are not alone anymore," Ares said. "The chain binds you. But it does not bind you to kneel. It binds you to rise."

Damien barked a laugh. It sounded harsh, bitter.

"Rise?" I've been trying to rise my whole life. All it's ever gotten me is knocked back down."

"Then rise higher," Ares snapped. "Until nothing can reach you."

The words burned like truth.

For as long as he could remember, Damien had been swinging blind—at people, at the world, at himself.

Now he wasn't blind.

He saw the chain.

He saw the war coming.

And he wasn't going to be anyone's victim.

"You are my heir," Ares said. "You are not prey. You are the predator. You are the weapon. You are the war."

Damien clenched his fists.

For the first time in his life, he believed it.

He looked at the rusted sword lying near the altar.

It wasn't good steel.

It wasn't even sharp anymore.

But it had felt right in his hand.

Familiar.

Like the altar. Like the voice. Like the fire in his blood.

He picked it up, felt its weight steady him — then set it back against the altar. A weapon for the dead, not for him. His war would be fought with something older, now burning in his veins.

"This place remembers you," Ares said. "As do all places where blood has been spilled. The world has forgotten your name. But war does not forget its own."

Damien smirked faintly. "Guess I should say thanks."

"Don't thank me," Ares said. "Use me. And make them all remember your name."

The god's voice faded, leaving Damien alone with the drumbeat in his chest.

He took one last look around the ossuary—at the torch still burning, at the skulls lining the walls, at the altar that had cracked open and remade him.

Then he climbed the steps back to the memorial above.

◆ ◆ ◆

The night air was cool against his sweat-slicked skin.

The marble statue of the faceless soldier still loomed over the rows of headstones, candles flickering at its base.

Once, it would've filled him with bitterness.

Now?

It was a challenge.

He stood there for a long moment, staring up at the statue. "Guess I'm one of you now," he muttered.

The faceless soldier's stone eyes seemed to watch him still. Damien smirked faintly. "Stone doesn't forget. And neither will I."

No one answered.

But the hum in his bones did.

The threads pulled faintly at his chest, tugging toward the others.

Kai.

Naia.

Isla.

The chain wanted him to find them.

And for once, Damien didn't mind following where something led.

Yet even in that moment, the rusted link scraped louder through the chain in his chest, discordant against the war drum. It didn't feel like an ally. It felt like a shadow marching in step.

The street beyond the memorial blurred in the damp winter air.

For years, he'd told himself it didn't matter that no one had come back for him.

But now, with the chain humming in his chest, he realized he'd never been waiting for rescue.

He'd been waiting for a reason—and now he had one.

Across the square, the memorial wall seemed to hold its breath, shadow pooling against the stone as if something unseen were watching the empty street, waiting for it to move.

The air snapped faintly, a pressure shifting in his ears. "Exactly," a thought hissed—not his, not fully.

Damien froze. The mist seemed to lift its head, listening. For a heartbeat, the static that had haunted the edges of his mind was gone. In its place, the chain thrummed louder, answering some signal he couldn't name.

He turned, half-expecting someone to be there. But the square was empty. Only fog moved, curling back into itself as if a figure had dissolved into its folds.

Damien started walking, his heart still beating to the rhythm of a war that hadn't started yet
But when it did, he knew where he'd be.
At the front.

◆ ◆ ◆

Far away, beneath Olympus, the obsidian map pulsed like a living thing.

A new name burned across its surface in molten red:
DAMIEN HOLT.

Veins of light spiderwebbed outward, connecting him to Kai, Naia, Isla—and to countless other faint names waiting to awaken.

The chain grew stronger.
The drumbeat of war echoed louder.

In the shadows of the chamber, Maelis stepped closer, their pale fingers hovering just above Damien's glowing name.

"The warrior awakens," they whispered.

Their ember-red eyes burned with quiet delight as they traced the web of light.

"And the drums of war begin to sound."

CHAPTER VIII

# THE HUNTRESS AT DUSK

January 1, 2026

Dusk in Bergen always came quietly. The sun barely skimmed the horizon before dusk returned, a January sky painted in bruised purples and cold golds.

Ayla's arrow quivered in the dusk, the wind carrying a sound too steady to be mere weather. Somewhere beyond the fjord she thought she saw the outline of chains, or a wolf waiting, though when she blinked the mist was empty again.

The world didn't burn into sunset here. It dimmed. Softly. Slowly. Like the light itself didn't want to disturb the fjords. Somewhere far beyond the fjord, she could feel faint tugs on the chain—others had awakened, their presence threading through her own.

The wind off the fjord tasted of iron, sharp as blood on her tongue. The cliffs loomed like beasts holding their breath, their shadows stretched long across the water as if they too feared to break the silence.

Ayla Solberg liked it that way.

Quiet was safer.

Quiet didn't ask questions.

♦ ♦ ♦

She crouched low in the pine needles, her breath steady as she watched the elk in the clearing.

It was young—too young to be out here alone.

She studied the way it moved, favoring one leg. Wounded. Probably from a fall or a predator that hadn't finished the job.

Her fingers tightened on the bow.

Not yet.

Her eyes flicked to the horizon. The ruins of an old watchtower jutted from the rocky shoreline like broken teeth, silhouetted against the fading light.

That place had been her refuge for weeks.

When her aunt's house felt too small.

When the people in town whispered too loudly.

When the memories pressed too hard.

She exhaled, long and even, the way her mother had taught her before she was gone.

Aim. Wait.

The elk lifted its head, ears twitching, sniffing the air.

Ayla didn't move.

Then she felt it.

Not the wind. Not instinct.

Something deeper.

Threads.

♦ ♦ ♦

She froze, bow still drawn.

She'd felt this before—faintly, like a dream she couldn't remember upon waking.

But now it was stronger.

Alive.

One thread glowed gold and warm, like sunlight breaking through clouds.

Kai.

Another was sharp, buzzing with purpose and ambition.

Naia.

A third burned hot and steady, like a forge at full heat.

Isla.

And the last throbbed like a drumbeat, raw and unrelenting.

Damien.

Her pulse quickened.

They weren't just threads.

They were people.

And somehow, she knew they could feel her too.

The elk bolted.

Ayla blinked, lowering her bow as it vanished into the trees.

She didn't care.

Not anymore.

Whatever this was, it was bigger than dinner.

♦ ♦ ♦

She stood, brushing pine needles from her knees, and turned toward the watchtower ruins.

If she was going to lose her mind, she might as well do it somewhere familiar.

The path to the ruins wound through a dense grove of pines, the air growing cooler with each step.

Twilight crept between the trees, painting the world in shades of silver and gray.

She didn't use a flashlight.

Her feet knew the way.

The watchtower was older than anyone alive.

A relic from a time when men still thought they could tame the fjords with stone and iron.

Now it was nothing but crumbling walls and moss-covered steps leading down into a hollowed chamber.

Ayla had made it hers—or as much as you could claim a ruin.

She ducked under a fallen arch, landing lightly on the damp stone floor.

Her bow stayed in hand.

The threads were stronger here.

Tugging.

Calling.

She reached the center of the chamber.

The last of the daylight filtered through the cracks in the stone, illuminating a half-collapsed altar.

It had always been there.

She'd always ignored it.

Tonight, the silence around it felt crueler than usual. The altar waited, patient as the townspeople's stares, as her aunt's pity, as every reminder that she was not built to belong.

Until now.

The air grew heavy.

The forest outside went silent.

Even the threads seemed to hold their breath.

"You walk alone," a voice said.

Ayla jerked back, arrow nocked, scanning the chamber.

No one was there.

"You choose solitude because you fear the pack. But even the lone wolf has a purpose."

Her throat tightened. "Who are you?"

"The moon," the voice said. "The wild. The hunt. You are mine, Ayla Solberg."

Her grip on the bow faltered.

The words weren't just in her ears.

They were in her blood.

"You feel their pull," the voice continued. "The chain that binds the Twelve. But you are not bound to kneel. You are bound to rise. To judge. To endure." "Once, the moon was chained to the sky, worshipped but never free. I broke that chain. And so will you."

The altar glowed, faint at first, then brighter, veins of silver light racing across its cracked surface.

Ayla stepped closer, drawn despite herself.

◆ ◆ ◆

"You are my heir," the voice said. "The huntress. The Moon's fang. You will stalk the shadows and strike with my judgment."

She swallowed hard, staring at the altar.

"Only what you already are," the voice replied. "You are the predator. You are the shield. You are the hunt."

The glow intensified, flooding the chamber with silver light.

Ayla raised a hand to shield her eyes, but it didn't help.

The light wasn't blinding.

It was consuming.

She gasped as the forest flooded into her senses—not the forest outside, but something older, wilder.

Every tree had a heartbeat.

Every stone had memory.

Every shadow had teeth.

And they all belonged to her.

She dropped to her knees, bow clattering against the stone.

The voice was everywhere now—in the cracks of the ruins, in the rustle of unseen leaves, in her chest.

"Rise, Ayla Solberg," Artemis commanded. "Rise, my huntress."

When the light faded, she was still kneeling, trembling, her palms pressed flat against the damp stone.

Her bow was in her hand again.

Different now.

Its wood gleamed like polished ivory, its string glowing faintly with silver light.

A gift.

A weapon.

A promise.

The bow felt alive in her hands.

Not warm—not exactly.

But awake.

Like it recognized her.

Like it had been waiting.

The dusk air felt sharper now, every sound along the fjord cutting clean against her ears. Somewhere beneath her skin, the huntress's presence stretched, testing her limbs like a bowstring drawn for the first time. She could almost hear the forest breathe with her.

Ayla rose slowly, testing the weight of it.

It wasn't heavier than her old bow, but it was different—perfectly balanced, as if it had been carved for her and no one else.

When she drew the string, it hummed faintly.

The sound sent a chill up her spine.

"Do you feel it?" Artemis asked.

Ayla swallowed hard. "What… what is this?"

"It is judgment," the goddess said. "Your judgment. My judgment. The wild has teeth, Ayla Solberg. And now, so do you."

♦ ♦ ♦

Ayla's fingers tightened on the bow.
The threads in her chest pulsed, sharp and alive.
Kai. Naia. Isla. Damien.
And more, faint in the distance.
The others.
The Twelve.

♦ ♦ ♦

She let the sensation settle, closing her eyes.
They weren't faces or voices.
They were instincts.
Flickers of fear.
Surges of anger.
A steady thrum of resolve.
They didn't know her name.
But they knew she was there.
And she knew them.
"You have felt their pull," Artemis said. "Now feel their weight. The chain binds you to them—not as prey. As the huntress. The Moon's fang."
Ayla opened her eyes.
The silver glow from the altar was fading, settling into the runes carved along its base.
The ruins felt different now.
Not abandoned.
Not dead.
Alive.
Waiting.
That's when she heard it.
A faint crunch of stone behind her.
Too heavy for an animal.
Too deliberate to be the wind.
Ayla spun, bow drawn, arrow nocked.
"Who's there?"
Her voice echoed through the chamber, sharp and steady.

134

Silence.

Then another step.

The air grew colder.

Her skin prickled.

She stepped back, keeping the bow raised, her eyes sweeping the ruins.

The threads in her chest pulled tighter—not toward the others.

Toward something else.

Something wrong.

"They come for you," Artemis said, her voice low. "They come for all of you. But you are not prey. Do not run."

"I wasn't planning to," Ayla muttered.

The shadows near the entrance shifted.

Something stepped inside.

It was tall. Cloaked.

Its face was smooth porcelain, featureless except for two narrow black slits where eyes should have been.

A Watcher.

Ayla had heard the stories from her grandmother—of shadowed figures that haunted the edges of the wild, taking the unworthy.

She'd thought they were just stories.

But this wasn't a story.

This was real.

And it was here for her.

The Watcher tilted its head, the movement unnervingly slow.

"The Moon's fang," it hissed, voice like grinding metal. "The wild awakens."

Ayla tightened her grip. "You picked the wrong prey."

"Prey?" the Watcher asked. "You misunderstand. The chain does not bind hunters or hunted. It binds all. And you will kneel, as they all will."

Ayla's heart pounded, but her breathing stayed even.

She couldn't afford to panic.

The Watcher stepped forward, its movements jerky, unnatural.

"The ones who forged the first chains fear you most," it said. "The fangs that turn against their masters."

Her pulse quickened.

"The first chains… what are you talking about?"

The Watcher's mask tilted. "You think the gods forged your bond? No. They stole it. They twisted it. You wear a leash and call it a gift."

It didn't answer. "Every time it flickered, her ears filled with a sound that didn't belong—like bones grinding underwater, like the forest itself was choking."

"Do not falter," Artemis commanded, her voice like steel. "You are the predator. This thing is nothing."

♦ ♦ ♦

Ayla's breathing slowed.

Her hands steadied.

She'd hunted wolves bigger than this thing.

She'd tracked bears through the snow for days without faltering.

This was no different.

This wasn't fear.

This was the hunt.

She bolted for the stairs, taking them two at a time.

The Watcher followed, gliding more than running, its cloak dragging against the stone like a living shadow.

She reached the treeline as twilight bled into night.

The mist off the fjord clung to her skin.

The pines loomed like silent sentinels.

Perfect.

Her terrain.

She darted into the woods, moving fast and silent, weaving between the trees.

Her every step was measured.

Every breath controlled.

She could feel the Watcher behind her, closing in—but she knew these woods better than it ever could.

She skidded to a stop at a fallen tree, grabbing the rope she'd left tied there days ago.

One swift pull.

The snare sprang to life.

The Watcher lunged—and a crude but strong net snapped up from the ground, tangling its legs and yanking it skyward.

It shrieked, thrashing, clawing at the ropes.

Ayla didn't waste the opening.

She drew another arrow, this one glowing faintly with the same silver light as her bow.

She fired.

The shot hit its chest, embedding deep.

The Watcher howled, the sound rattling through the forest.

The ropes strained.

Then snapped.

The Watcher crashed to the ground, its lacquer-white porcelain mask, hairline-cracked and leaking black smoke.

It turned its head toward her, those empty eye slits locking on her.

"You cannot change what you are," it hissed. "Chains do not break. They only tighten."

Ayla nocked another arrow.

"Then I'll strangle you with them."

She loosed.

"The arrow hit its mark. Silver light split the lacquer-white mask down the middle, shards falling like broken moonlight before dissolving into smoke. The Watcher convulsed, shrieked one final time, and dissolved into the mist."

Ayla lowered her bow, her breath coming fast and shallow.

The forest was silent again.

No wind.

No Watcher.

Just her.

"Good," Artemis said. "You did not run. You did not beg. You hunted. You endured."

Ayla exhaled, long and steady.

This wasn't survival.

This was judgment.

And for the first time in a long time, she felt alive.

Ayla stayed crouched in the clearing, the bow still raised though there was nothing left to shoot.

Her breath came fast, but steady. Controlled.

The Watcher's smoke lingered like a stain in the air, curling and twisting before dissolving into the mist.

She slowly lowered her weapon.

Her fingers tingled. Her chest felt tight, not from fear but from…something else.

The fight had awakened something in her.

No—not the fight.

The hunt.

"Do you understand now?" Artemis asked, her voice quieter now, but no less commanding.

Ayla swallowed hard. "Understand what?"

"*Why I chose you,*" Artemis said. "*Why you walk alone. Why you are the fang in the dark? You are not prey. You are judgment. The moon does not beg to be seen. It hunts. It endures.*"

♦ ♦ ♦

"All her life, she'd thought solitude was punishment. But now it was purpose. Isolation hadn't broken her—it had forged her teeth.

She looked at the ground where the Watcher had fallen, at the ropes that had failed to hold it.

Even dead—or whatever counted as dead for things like that—it made her skin crawl.

It hadn't come for her because of who she was.

It had come because of what she was.

And that terrified her more than the fight.

She rose, brushing the dirt from her knees.

Too quiet.

That's when she felt them.

The threads.

They didn't just tug this time.

They burned.

She gasped, clutching her chest as they pulled tighter, sinking into her bones.

She staggered back, nearly tripping over a tree root as the world tilted around her.

And then—

They were there.

Not in front of her.

Not in the forest.

In her.

♦ ♦ ♦

A boy on a mountain, clutching a violin like it was the only thing keeping him standing.

Kai.

A girl in a ruined courtyard, her gown torn, her crown-mark glowing as she stared defiantly into the dark.

Naia.

A girl in a forge that breathed and roared, hammer in hand, her pulse as steady as the molten channels around her.

Isla.

A boy in a catacomb of bones, blood on his hands, his eyes burning with a rage so deep it felt endless.

Damien.

And she knew them.

Her breath caught.

She didn't just see them.

She felt them.

Kai's uncertainty, trembling like a burned animal in the dark.

Naia's ambition, sharp and electric, like a blade on her tongue.

Isla's steady purpose, a forge-fire that never went out.

Damien's raw, unyielding rage, hot enough to burn anyone who got too close.

She hissed through her teeth, staggering back again.

It was too much.

Too loud.

Too alive.

"You feel them as they feel you," Artemis said.

"What…what are they to me?" Ayla whispered.

"The chain binds you. They are your Twelve. Prey. Hunters. Pack. All."

The words cut deep.

Prey. Hunters. Pack.

Which were they?

Which was she?

Ayla pressed a hand to her chest, breathing through the flood of sensations.

Her body wanted to categorize them, the way she would any living thing.

Kai—Prey, Fragile. Hesitant.

Naia—Predator. Calculating. Dangerous.

Isla—pack. Steady. Reliable.

Damien—a threat. Wounded, but lethal if cornered.

The threads didn't feel like chains.

They felt like belonging.

She hadn't felt that in a long time.

Maybe ever.

"You are no longer alone," Artemis said. "But solitude will always be your nature. You are the huntress. The Moon's fang. You judge. You protect. You endure."

Ayla closed her eyes.

She didn't want to belong.

She didn't want to be bound to strangers.

♦ ♦ ♦

Part of her did.

She thought of her mother—of the stories she used to tell her about Artemis, about the Huntress who walked alone but guarded the lost.

She thought of the whispers in town, the pitying stares, the way people looked at her like she'd broken too young.

She thought of every night she'd slept under the pines, pretending the woods could fill the hole in her chest.

And for the first time, she wondered if maybe she hadn't been hiding.

Maybe she'd been waiting.

"You are my heir," Artemis said. "The huntress. The judgment. The shield. The fang. Take this gift, Ayla Solberg. Wield it. Use it. Decide who lives and who falls."

Ayla exhaled slowly.

Her hand tightened on the bow.

It wasn't just the hunt.

It was purpose.

She turned her eyes skyward.

The moon had risen, pale and sharp against the blackened sky.

It felt like it was watching her.

Judging her.

And, for the first time, she felt like she could meet its gaze without flinching.

Ayla stayed in the clearing long after the threads dulled to a steady hum.

She could still feel them—Kai's quiet fear, Naia's sharp ambition, Isla's steady purpose, Damien's molten rage—but the flood had receded.

Now they pulsed like a distant heartbeat.

Not overwhelming.

But constant.

She sat with her back against a pine, her bow across her lap, and breathed.

The mist curled low, silvered by moonlight.

The forest smelled of sap and soil, alive and awake.

She had walked these woods for years, but tonight they felt different.

Not just a home.

An extension of herself.

"You see now," Artemis said.

Ayla nodded slightly. "I do."

"You are the huntress. Not prey. Not victim. Not child. You are the fang in the dark. My judgment."

The words settled in her bones.

For so long she'd believed her isolation made her hollow.

Now she saw it for what it was:

Preparation.

She tilted her head back, watching the moon through the break in the trees.

It felt close enough to touch.

♦ ♦ ♦

"The chain will pull you toward them," Artemis said. "The other heirs. Some will be wolves. Some will be deer. All will be judged."

"By me," Ayla said.

"By us," Artemis corrected. "You are my fang. My voice in the wild. The predator that shields the pack and strikes the unworthy. You will decide who walks with the Twelve—and who falls beneath their weight."

A shiver crawled down her spine.

This wasn't even about the Watcher.

This was about the Twelve.

The chain had shown her their faces.

She'd felt their hearts.

And Artemis had given her a role to play in their story.

She exhaled slowly, letting the truth of it settle.

Her grief, her loneliness, the years of walking as a shadow in the world—none of it had been wasted.

It had forged her.

"Go now," Artemis said. "The forest knows your step. The hunt will always welcome you. But you are no longer walking alone."

Ayla rose, sliding her glowing bow across her back.

Her movements were lighter than they'd been when she entered the ruins.

More certain.

She wasn't just Ayla Solberg anymore.

She was the Huntress.

The threads tugged faintly at her chest.

They weren't as sharp as they'd been in the ruins, but they were there.

Alive.

Kai.

Naia.

Isla.

Damien.

And others, faint as whispers at the edges of her mind.

She couldn't name them yet.

But she would.

They weren't just strangers anymore.

They were hers.

Her prey.

Her pack.

Her judgment.

The pines seemed to part for her as she left the clearing.

The night didn't feel cold anymore.

The silence wasn't empty.

For the first time in years, she felt like she belonged. "Not to the town that whispered. Not to the family that pitied. But to the hunt. To the moon. To the Twelve."

And yet, even in belonging, solitude clung to her ribs like marrow. The chain didn't erase the silence she'd lived with—it weaponized it.

Far away, beneath Olympus, the obsidian map thrummed like a living heart.

A new name burned across its surface in silver light:

AYLA SOLBERG.

The veins of light webbed outward, pulling her toward the others—binding her into their chain.

Maelis stood over the map, fingers poised above her name without touching.

Their pale face was unreadable in the dim glow.

"The huntress awakens," they said softly.

They traced the lines of light with careful precision, mapping the web in their mind.

"And the moon sharpens its teeth."

They paused, tilting their head as though listening to something only they could hear.

"Eight of twelve," they murmured. "The chain grows. The game begins."

**Hellenic Institute of Mythology**
Athens, Greece                                        Venice, Italy

To Whom It May Concern,

In compliance with the request of Mr. Ginn for authentic
reproductions of the recovered Codex material, the accom-
panying images have been rendered with minimal interfer-
ence.
 Readers are advised that certain plates may appear blurred,
faint, or otherwise imperfect. These conditions reflect limi-
tations inherent to the conservation process.
The fragments were photographed under low-intensity
lighting and without the use of restorative enhancement in
order to reduce strain upon the original substrates. As a
consequence, the resulting facsimiles preserve not only the
content but also the irregularities of the source material.
Such irregularities—whether in clarity, line, or surface deg-
radation—should be regarded as features of the record rather than flaws of reproduction.
It remains the position of this Institute that presenting the
Codices in this manner, even at the expense of modern clarity, provides the most faithful means of transmitting their
condition to contemporary readers while safeguarding the
integrity of the originals.

Respectfully submitted,

**Prof. Alexandros Stavros**
Archivist and Conservation Lead
Hellenic Institute of Mythology

# CHAPTER IX
# THE TRICKSTER'S MARK

January 9,2026

January heat shimmered over the streets, but banners for Carnival still hung from balconies like faded laughter.

It clung to Eryx Draven like a challenge, daring him to run, to sweat, to give up the chase. But he didn't. Not because he liked the heat. But he'd learned something in the last few weeks: you don't outrun the gods—you steal from them when they're not looking.

And right now, he was alone.

Not abandoned—by choice. No Zara watching his every smirk. No chains tugging at him like he wasn't alone. No awkward silences between heirs who didn't know if they were a team or a ticking time bomb.

He moved quickly through the winding trail that snaked up the Tijuca mountainside. Jungle mist curled at the edges of the path, thick and warm, alive with birdsong and the occasional rustle that suggested something watching—monkey, jaguar, or something older. He didn't care.

He was after something real. Something hidden.

He'd found the first clue in the corner of an old temple mural in downtown Rio—Hermes' winged sandals half-sketched beneath a layer of vines and soot. Then, a half-whispered riddle scratched into a subway pillar in Copacabana:

"Where silence breaks and stars rewind, The thief of gods leaves marks behind."

The echo of another voice told him not to go alone. Zara had raised a brow and muttered something about impulsiveness and poor judgment.

Thane had just laughed and handed him a bag of dried mango slices.

"If you die, I call dibs on your boots."

Eryx had replied with a grin. "You can't afford them."

"Roots tangled across the path like snares. The jungle fell quiet too fast, and Eryx knew what that meant: something was waiting."

Not the peaceful kind. The kind that falls too fast. That chokes the air.

Eryx stopped.

He knew this feeling. He'd felt it in Cairo, just before the fire. In Prague, just before the Watcher passed him on the train and vanished into smoke.

Something was close.

His grin faltered. He hated admitting it—even to himself—but Part of him wished Zara—or anyone—were here. Someone to prove he wasn't the only one who felt the air turn heavy.

A shape loomed ahead.

The trail ended in a clearing where the mountain dropped off into sky. Beyond the ledge stood a stone archway carved into the cliffside—half-swallowed by moss, but unmistakably divine.

Symbols spiraled across the frame in old Greek, but even without reading them, he knew. The shape of the staff. The looped sandals. The two snakes winding around a central flame.

Hermes.

His heart kicked harder.

"I found it," he muttered.

And the arch opened.

Not like a door swinging. Not like anything real.

The air shimmered—a mirage folding inward, peeling back like a curtain—and behind it, a hallway appeared. Cool. Dark. Waiting.

Eryx glanced behind him.

No one.

He rolled his shoulders, flicked the sweat from his brow, and stepped through.

♦ ♦ ♦

The transition was instant.

From sweltering jungle to shadowed marble corridor in half a heartbeat.

Torches lit on their own, lining the passage with flickering green-blue flame. The walls curved in smooth arcs, carved with shifting inscriptions that refused to stay still when he looked directly at them.

"Classic," he muttered. "Trickster god's house. Nothing makes sense. Cool cool."

His voice echoed more than it should've.

He walked slowly. Not because he was afraid, but because—well, okay, he was afraid, but in a healthy way. He called it strategic caution.


Never rush into a trap when you can saunter in looking unbothered.

The corridor opened into a circular chamber.

A shrine.

At the center stood a pedestal—simple stone, no ornamentation—supporting a mask.

Half-gold, half-smoke. No eye holes. No straps. Just… there. Balanced like it belonged to someone clever enough to leave it behind without losing it.

On the floor beneath the pedestal was an engraving:

The words crawled into his head and wouldn't leave. No truth. No path. No self. He almost laughed—almost. But part of him wondered if the shrine wasn't mocking him, if it already knew how many lies he'd told just to survive.

Eryx raised an eyebrow.

"Liar's mark, huh? Now you're speaking my language."

He stepped closer.

The air shifted.

The torches dimmed.

And then the mask moved. Not with sound, but with reflection. His face splintered into a dozen grins, each wider, crueler, hungrier than the last. One eye glowed, another wept black smoke, a third vanished entirely, leaving only a hollow socket staring back.

"Are you a trickster, or just a boy who runs?"

The voice didn't come from the shrine. It came from everywhere—from the walls, the mask, from him.

He didn't answer. Not out loud.

But he felt it. The question wasn't new.

Eryx had always run. From foster homes, from dead ends, from truth.

But lately… running hadn't worked.

The mask trembled.

And then a gust of wind burst from the pedestal—not warm, not cold—just sharp. It spun around him, lifting the dust, pulling at his jacket.

"His glyph burned—collarbone, sudden and clean."

He gasped, dropping to one knee as the mark seared across his collarbone.

For a heartbeat, the flame wasn't gold but black—shadow-light crawling under his skin like ink. Then it was gone, leaving him shaking, unsure if it had been real.

He staggered back toward the shrine—and froze.

Two Eryxes stared at him from the mask's reflection. One smirked with the same crooked charm he knew too well.

The other bled shadow from its eyes, its grin stretching wider, sharper, until it looked hungry.

◆ ◆ ◆

Only one reflection faded. The other lingered in the glass. Watching.

Not a mirror. A window.

◆ ◆ ◆

A laugh rippled through the chamber.

Not his own. Not Hermes's.

Something older, sly and cruel.

"The laugh thinned. 'The labyrinth remembers more than Daedalus.' Then silence.".

And then it was gone.

"Messenger, thief, deceiver, guide…"

"Do you wear the mask, or has it already worn you?"

He gritted his teeth.

"I'm not a liar," he growled. "I just know how to survive."

Silence.

Then laughter.

Not cruel.

Worse.

Knowing.

The glyph blazed.

Symbols appeared across the walls—riddles in motion, clues in looping script. Doors formed where none had been. Paths appeared, then vanished.

And Eryx knew: This was the trial. This was the shrine of the god who never gave straight answers.

And to leave… he'd have to outwit the god who made the maze.

He cracked his knuckles.

"Alright, Hermes," he said. "Let's play."

♦ ♦ ♦

The moment Eryx stepped away from the mask, the shrine shifted.

The circular chamber twisted, stretching outward in impossible directions like it had inhaled space itself. The floor rippled underfoot, stone folding like cloth. Arched doorways emerged where flat walls had been, each marked with a symbol.

One glowed with a feather. Another, a coin. A third, a snake curled into an infinity loop.

"Choose wrong, and be trapped forever."

The words echoed from nowhere and everywhere—Hermes' voice, maybe. Or just the part of Eryx's mind that had always feared being tricked and never knowing it.

149

He stood at the center of the new crossroads. The glyph burning under his collarbone pulsed faintly in time with the torches now flickering along the walls—green, gold, violet. Trickster colors.

"Okay," he muttered. "Riddle me this."

He turned slowly, reading the inscriptions above each door.

Feather Door:

"Light as truth, heavy with consequence."

Coin Door:

"Value lies not in face, but in choice."

Snake Door:

"What sheds skin may lie beneath it."

Eryx smirked. "Gods and their poetic nonsense."

But his heart was pounding. Because something in the room had changed again.

There was a fourth door now—no symbol, no inscription, just shadow. And from it, a voice called softly.

"Eryx… come home."

His eyes narrowed.

That voice—

He turned sharply, breath catching in his throat.

It sounded like his brother.

He hadn't heard that voice in three years—not since the fire that tore apart the last foster home they'd shared. Not since they were separated and sent to opposite ends of the country. Not since Eryx had stopped believing anyone would come back for him.

He stepped toward the shadow door.

A foot closer.

Then he stopped.

"No," he whispered. "You're not real."

"We waited," the voice said, calm and aching. "You left us. You always leave."

Eryx closed his eyes. The old guilt rose again like smoke from an extinguished fire—charred but never gone. He felt the heat. The screaming. The hands pulling him away from the building while the others—

"Stop," he said, fists clenched. "Not real."

The glyph under his collarbone flared, searing now. A warning. Maybe even a shield.

He turned back to the three marked doors.

Hermes wouldn't test him with guilt. That wasn't the trick. That was the distraction.

Eryx breathed through his nose, grounding himself.

He scanned again.

Feather: Light as truth… but weighed down. Deception through honesty?

Coin: Not the face, but the flip. A choice. Risk.

Snake: Skin-shedding. Illusion. Transformation.

All three could be traps. All three could be answers.

He bit his lip, then made a decision.

"Not the one that speaks loudest. The one that waits."

He walked to the snake door.

◆ ◆ ◆

The second he crossed the threshold, the world fractured.

The floor vanished. He fell—not down, but sideways—through threads of golden rope and glimmering words suspended in the dark.

Then—impact.

He landed on smooth marble, rolling to a stop. When he stood, he found himself in a vast hall of shifting mirrors—not unlike what Zara had described days ago, but this was… off.

These mirrors didn't reflect him.

They showed other people.

People he'd stolen from.

People he'd lied to.

People he'd pretended to care about so he could slip out of their lives with what he needed and without their questions.

A woman crying by a broken register in a corner bodega. A teacher calling his name in a crowded hallway. A foster parent flipping through an empty photo album.

Each reflection held a piece of him—or what he'd left behind.

And in the center of the room: a boy.

Small. Curly hair. Barefoot. Just like Eryx had been at eight.

The boy was watching him. Silent.

Eryx approached slowly. "I know what this is."

"Then what will you do about it?" the boy asked.

He stared. "You're me. From then."

The boy nodded. "You were supposed to protect us. But you ran."

Eryx swallowed. "I didn't have a choice."

The boy frowned. "You had many. But you always took the one that made you disappear."

The floor beneath them lit up—symbols spreading in circles. Runes. Glyphs. Directional markings like those on ancient maps.

And at the center: a coin.

One side bore Hermes' face, smiling. The other—Eryx's own.

The coin spun slowly in the air.

"Choose," the boy said. "Your past, or your path."

Eryx's hands curled into fists.

He didn't want to choose. He wanted to keep dancing through life, slipping between responsibilities like a shadow.

But he knew, deep down—

That wouldn't work anymore.

Not with the glyph growing under his skin. Not with Olympus waking.

He reached out.

And grabbed the coin.

Instantly, fire raced across the marble.

The mirrors exploded—not violently, but shimmering into dust, like lies being erased.

The boy disappeared.

And the room folded in on itself.

Eryx stood alone once more—back in the shrine.

The pedestal was gone.

The mask was gone.

But a new door stood open, and beyond it, a bridge of golden light stretching across a chasm of pure shadow.

No illusions now.

No riddles.

Just one final test.

He touched the glyph at his collarbone. It glowed steady now—etched with wings, flame, and two interlocking rings.

A messenger's mark.

A trickster's legacy.

And maybe, just maybe—a leader's beginning.

The golden bridge shimmered beneath Eryx's feet like spun thread from a god's loom—narrow, silent, suspended over nothing. Not night. Not sky. Not space.

Just absence.

The kind of nothing that whispered things to you. That made you doubt whether you'd ever been real in the first place.

Eryx stepped forward.

The moment he did, the bridge rippled—like water catching light—but held.

One step.

Two.

The echo of his boots didn't sound like footsteps. It sounded like questions.

"Why do you hide?" "What do you fear?" "Who will you become?"

He didn't answer. Not aloud. But the questions didn't stop.

And neither did he.

Midway across the bridge, the air changed.

He could feel it—the stillness behind him, the tension ahead.

And then he wasn't alone.

A man stepped from the edge of the path—not walking from the far side, but stepping into existence itself, as though peeled from the world like a sticker from glass.

He wore a cloak made of shadow and smoke, and a crooked smile that didn't reach his eyes. One eye was gold. The other, silver. He looked too old and too young all at once.

Eryx froze.

"Are you—?"

"No," the man said. "I'm not your god. Just a messenger. Like you."

His voice was velvet laced with razors.

"Then what are you doing here?" Eryx asked.

The man shrugged. "Delivering options. That's what messengers do."

He reached into his robe and pulled out a coin. Not like the one in the trial—this one was flat black on one side, and blank white on the other.

He flipped it once.

Caught it.

Then extended it toward Eryx.

"No inscription. No meaning. No prophecy. Just a coin. Just a choice."

Eryx didn't move. "What happens if I take it?"

"That's the trick, boy." The man leaned closer, his voice silk-soft now. "Nothing happens when you take it. Everything happens when you choose how to use it."

The coin shimmered. Almost too perfect. Unknowable.

Eryx's mind raced.

It had to be a trap. Right?

But then again—wasn't that the point of being the heir of Hermes?

The trap is the lesson. The trick is the truth.

"He could live with that.

He took the coin.

The moment his fingers touched it, the bridge shattered.

Not with a bang.

With a laugh.

The man was gone.

And Eryx was falling—not down, but through.

Through moments.

Through memories.

Through pieces of himself.

◆ ◆ ◆

He landed in a familiar hallway.

Fluorescent lights buzzed overhead. Locker doors slammed shut. The smell of pencil shavings, cheap cologne, and unwashed gym towels filled the air.

A school.

His school.

Fifth foster home. Ninth school. Tenth name.

People passed him without seeing him.

Then one did.

A girl—fifteen, maybe—stood in front of him. She was crying.

He remembered this.

He'd taken the answers to her test. Tricked the teacher into giving him a copy. Swapped her paper when she wasn't looking. She got expelled. He didn't.

She was real.

So was the hurt.

So was the betrayal.

"You never came back," she said. "You just moved on."

"I had to," Eryx whispered.

"No," she replied. "You chose to."

She vanished.

Another memory unfolded.

He was in a corner store. Pocketing medicine. The clerk distracted. The alarm silent. He walked out.

Behind him, a voice begged. "Please… that was for my daughter."

He hadn't turned back.

Not then.

Not now.

The room dissolved into a thousand fragments—each a trick, a lie, a half-truth that helped him survive.

They spun around him like shards of broken glass.

And in the center of it all—

a new version of himself.

Older.

Sharper.

Colder.

Wearing the same smirk, but no humor behind it.

"Don't lie to yourself," this version said. "You don't want to be a hero. You want to be the one who lives. The last one standing."

Eryx stared.

And then smiled—soft. Small. But real.

"Maybe," he said. "But I'm tired of doing it alone."

The fragments stilled.

The coin in his hand cracked.

And his glyph exploded with light.

◆ ◆ ◆

Wings of gold unfurled across his back—illusory, not physical—flashing with a thousand interwoven messages. Symbols danced across his collarbone and down his arms, like ink catching fire.

The trickster's mark.

But also—the guide's.

He wasn't just the messenger now.

He was the one who understood the path because he'd walked every wrong one.

The illusions vanished.

And he stood again at the shrine.

This time, not alone.

A woman stood in the doorway now. Bronze-skinned. Sharp-featured. Her robes fluttered with threads of wind that weren't blowing. On her wrist coiled a silver snake with eyes like galaxies.

She did not smile.

But her gaze was steady. Knowing.

"Hermes," Eryx said.

She tilted her head. "His echo. His legacy. You passed the trial."

"Did I win?" he asked.

"Winning is for games," she replied. "This was an invitation."

"Invitation to what?"

"To be more than clever. To be true."

◆ ◆ ◆

The coin he still held pulsed with light.

The woman stepped forward and pressed her fingers to his chest—directly over the glyph.

And whispered:

"All roads cross. All doors open. But only one will know them all."

Then she vanished into wind and ash.

Eryx staggered forward, breath ragged.

He looked down at the glyph. It had settled—etched in glowing silver and gold, wings stretching behind a key.

And in that moment, he understood:

He wasn't just meant to deliver messages. He was meant to unlock them.

◆ ◆ ◆

And the next door had already begun to open.

Eryx stepped out of the shrine into light that didn't look real.

The sky had turned the color of melting copper, and the sun—what little of it pierced the mountain mist—looked cracked at the edges, like it had watched too much and forgotten how to burn.

He rubbed the back of his neck.

The glyph still glowed faintly on his skin, the heat ebbing now, settling into something steady. Fused. It wasn't just a mark anymore.

It was a compass. And it pointed inward.

◆ ◆ ◆

The world felt… quieter.

Not empty, Just like it was listening now.

He knew what that meant.

Hermes wasn't a god of noise. He was a god of signals. Subtle. Disguised. Hidden in plain sight. Eryx had always thought his tricks were games.

But the shrine had made something clear:

Hermes' greatest trick wasn't in what he showed. It was in what he never said.

And now… Eryx was part of that silence.

He found the dirt path again and followed it down the slope, boots crunching dry underbrush, the jungle stretching its limbs in the dying light.

The city flickered far below—Rio's heartbeat dimmed under the storm clouds that still lingered at the edge of the horizon.

Something had changed here, too.

Not visibly. Not to tourists or locals.

But Eryx could feel it. A current in the air. A new thread pulling.

His glyph pulsed once.

A message, One that wasn't meant for words.

The jungle held its breath. He stood alone at the tree line, sweat drying on his neck, the glyph under his collarbone a steady ember. The coin warmed in his palm—one face black, one white—refusing to tell him anything he could spend.

He slid down onto a sun-bleached root and let the hush settle. For once, quiet didn't feel like a test. It felt like a reply.

The chain stirred.

Not a voice—pressure. Threads tugging at him from very far away, like someone plucked a harp in another city and the echo reached his ribs. Heat—someone forging fire under the earth. Cold—stone that remembered names. A breath like drawn bowstring. The salt-thick weight of a tide deciding whether to rise.

They weren't here. Not really. But the pulls were real enough to tilt him.

"Some messages," he murmured, "aren't meant to be delivered."

He balanced the coin on a knuckle and flicked it, catching it without looking. Head, tail—wasn't the point. The point was whether he'd run, and he didn't feel like running anymore.

A leaf shivered. He glanced up—nothing on the trail but mist. Still, something watched. Not a person. The world, maybe, deciding whether to let him pass.

He stood and started down, boots whispering over powder-dry soil, then grit, then old asphalt the jungle had started to eat. Rio's lights pulsed far below like a heartbeat under gauze. He used to love that—so many exits, so many pockets to disappear into. Tonight, the map in his head re-drew itself. Not alleys and doors. Lines. Routes only he could feel.

The chain tugged again—faint pulses in sequence. He paused, touching the new mark beneath his collarbone. Wings. A key. Rings interlocked.

A whisper of rain came and went without falling. He moved on.

Halfway down he found an overlook—the city spread like spilled coins. He took the coin out again and turned it over in the dim. Blank black. Blank white. Unwritten.

"Fine," he said. "Be that way."

A shape at the edge of sight shifted—just mist slipping between trunks. He didn't pretend it wasn't there. He lifted two fingers in a half-salute and kept walking.

When the trail broke into a service lane, he stopped beside a rusted fence strangled in vines. The air was different here—quieter than quiet, the kind that waits for your answer. He palmed the coin, then crouched and pried up a loose shard of concrete. A nest of roots coiled beneath, damp and patient.

"Hide-and-seek," he said softly. "Your game."

He didn't bury it. Not yet. He pressed the coin to the concrete instead, left a print of heat, felt the echo travel. A signal laid down where only someone like him would feel it later.

"Not delivered," he told the dark. "Marked."

The chain thrummed once in approval—or warning. Hard to tell with gods.

He leaned back against the fence, watching the city flicker and slow. Messages everywhere, most of them lies, some of them good enough to live by. He'd spent years learning which was which. The shrine had taught him something uglier and truer: the best trick wasn't the one that fooled someone else. It was the one that stopped fooling him.

Belonging wasn't an exit. It was a *lock you chose to fit*.

He closed his eyes and let the threads pass through him: a cadence like marching breath; a hush like a door closing gently but firmly; a bright flare of thought that bent the sky into patterns. The wrong note was there too, thin and cold, scraping where it shouldn't. He didn't look away from it this time. He filed it where good thieves keep their best alarms: in the part of the mind that never sleeps.

The mark under his skin cooled from ember to compass.

"Alright," he said into the waiting night. "I'm listening."

He pushed off the fence and headed for the switchback, trail dust ghosting around his ankles like smoke that had forgotten how to burn. Somewhere above, a bird called once—three notes, then silence. Somewhere below, a siren hiccuped and thought better of it.

He smiled—small, real. The kind you can't forge.

He didn't speed up. He didn't slow down. He walked like a messenger who finally knew which door he was meant to knock on, even if he wasn't going to knock yet.

And the jungle, satisfied, let him pass.

Far above him, clouds shifted.

And in a pocket of clear sky, a spiral of stars formed—tight and turning, like the center of a coin caught in mid-flip.

He stared up at them.

Then whispered, "Alright. Let's see where you land."

# INTERLUDE 11
## THE WATCHERS MOVE

The chain wakes. Something has already chosen.

In January's silence, when the solstice shadow held longest, the Watchers moved.

The Watchers Move

Beneath the bones of Olympus, the chain hummed.

It pulsed faintly in the obsidian map carved into the floor—nine points of divine light scattered across the world, each burning with its own rhythm. No longer just echoes. No longer myth.

Nine heirs. Nine awakenings.

The time for prophecy had passed.

The time for movement had begun.

Maelis stood at the edge of the chamber, cloaked in stillness. They watched the light flicker across the stone like stars in slow motion, not with awe but calculation.

The heirs had risen faster than anticipated. The chain should've taken months. Years, even. But now…

Now it surged.

Something ancient was stirring beneath the world, and not all of Olympus was ready to face it.

Maelis walked the perimeter of the obsidian map, hands clasped behind their back. Their robes whispered over the stone, silent as snowfall. With each step, they passed a name now glowing bright in Olympian glyphs—divine resonance etched in molten precision.

LEO ALEKOS—The tidebreaker. Wild and unyielding. He had not yet learned that storms don't only destroy—they reshape. The obsidian pulsed hotter at his name, the map's surface fracturing like ice under pressure. For a breath, Maelis thought the stone itself might splinter if Leo's power surged unchecked.

ZARA KANE—The mind. Sharp as a blade's edge. She questioned too much already. She would be the first to see what lay beyond Olympus' mask.

SELENE MARINO—The shadowwalker. Her grief was her armor, but also her cage. She would walk closest to the veil.

KAI WATANABE—The lightkeeper. Beautiful in his hesitance. There was something inside him struggling to be heard.

NAIA MORRIGAN—The queen without a crown. Cold, calculating, and ambitious. She would either rule the chain or break it.

ISLA DAMARIS—The flame that builds. The heart of creation in mortal hands. And hearts, Maelis knew, could burn just as easily as they could forge.

DAMIEN HOLT—The war reborn. Maelis could still feel the echo of his awakening—fire and blood. If he turned, he would not hesitate.

AYLA SOLBERG—The fang in the dark. Judgement cloaked in silence. Her solitude made her the most dangerous. She would not need convincing.

ERYX DRAVEN—The thief of paths. Quick as breath, restless as wind. He would carry more than messages; he would carry secrets too heavy for any chain to hold.

Maelis paused. Nine of Twelve. The chain was more than half complete.

They exhaled slowly. "Faster than last time," they whispered.

A flicker passed through the air—not wind, but memory.

They looked down at the center of the map. It still held no name. No glow. No glyph. Just a faint ring, darker than the stone around it.

The convergence point.

Maelis touched it gently, as if checking the pulse of a sleeping beast.

It stirred beneath their hand.

Not in body.

In intent.

Not yet.

But soon.

They withdrew their hand and turned toward the inner wall. With a single step, they crossed from the chamber of light into the hall of silence—a vault of uncut stone carved before language had names.

The walls here whispered. Not in sound, but sensation.

And something else whispered with them.

The Watchers.

They were already here—in the walls, in the air, in the spaces between heartbeats. The Watchers did not arrive so much as reveal themselves, stepping into form from where their gaze had already lingered.

They stepped from cracks in the walls. From beneath the stone. From corners where there had been no corners before.

Thirteen forms cloaked in liquid shadow, each face concealed behind glazed ceramic masks. Smooth. Cold. Silent.

Not one mask was identical.

Some were split by jagged lines. Others bore faint sigils etched like burns. One had no eye slits at all.

Maelis did not speak at first.

They simply watched the Watchers as the Watchers watched them.

Thirteen seconds passed.

Then Maelis raised one hand.

"The chain is growing unstable."

The Watchers did not move.

"You were tasked with observing," Maelis continued. "With measuring the weight of power as it returned to mortal veins. That balance has tipped."

They walked among the Watchers like a general before a silent army.

One bone-white mask glossy as shell tilted just slightly, its mouth fissured into the suggestion of a grin. "And if the heirs break themselves?" it rasped, voice like rust over glass. Maelis didn't look at it, but the pause in their step was enough to silence the rest.

"Nine heirs now carry the gods' legacy. And while Olympus rejoices, the silence beneath grows louder."

A flicker of tension passed through the chamber—not emotion, but atmosphere.

"Soon, the heirs will find one another." Maelis stopped before a Watcher whose mask was cracked clean across the center. "And when they do, they will begin to remember."

Still no sound.

But Maelis felt the anticipation gather like static in the stone.

"Some will resist their roles. Others will embrace them. But at least one will stray from the path entirely."

They turned toward the wall, where a shadowed glyph pulsed faintly.

Not yet ignited.

But nearing the spark.

Thane Virelli.

Venice.

The boy with too much charm and not enough clarity. A mask behind a mask.

"He is the next to awaken," Maelis said. "But his path is blurred. He is watched—by others, not just us. There is something in him... unfinished."

They gestured toward the cracked-mask Watcher. "Mark him. But do not act. Let him choose his path. Let him believe it is his own."

The Watcher bowed once, then stepped backward into the wall and vanished.

To the rest, Maelis said, "Deploy new veils," Maelis commanded, her voice a blade through the silence

Santorini. Dublin. Alexandria. Chicago. Naples. Bergen. Antarctica. Watch the places where power has bloomed."

They turned slowly in place. "And prepare the unknowns."

Another Watcher stepped forward—mask pristine, but humming faintly.

Maelis handed it a scroll sealed with a glyph none of the heirs would yet recognize.

"Deliver this to the silent shrine."

The Watcher accepted the scroll and dissolved into mist.

Maelis stood alone once more.

The map chamber behind them now pulsed more rapidly— nine glyphs glowing brighter, faster, as if aware of each other.

The chain wasn't just forming.

It was binding.

That was more dangerous than Olympus would ever admit.

There had been chains before.

And there had been breaking.

Maelis looked up at the ceiling, where nothing was carved— where the stone remained untouched, unmarred, waiting.

Some truths were not recorded.

Some names were never written.

But even those forgotten by history could still be remembered by the earth.

And the earth was stirring.

They returned to the map. Watched the lights flicker.

And whispered the names of those still to awaken.

Thane Virelli.

Lysandra Korr

Cassian Wolfe.

Twelve heirs.

But Olympus had never understood that twelve was never the end.

Only the edge.

And edges cut both ways.

Somewhere deep in the stone, a faint sound answered—not echo, not tremor, but a rhythm. A heartbeat where no heart should be.

# PART III – THE THREADS OF FATE

# CHAPTER X
# THE MIRROR AND THE MASK

January 15, 2026

The wind off Siberia had teeth. It chewed through fur, leather, and flesh, gnawing at bone until even thought felt brittle.

Thane Virelli trudged across the frozen shore with his collar pulled high, though no amount of fabric could soften a cold like this. This wasn't weather. It was something older. A patience that had outlived empires. A silence that swallowed the world whole.

For days the chain had pulled him here. He hadn't chosen Baikal—he'd barely known its name before—but the pulse inside his veins had given him no rest. On trains rattling eastward, in towns that spoke languages he didn't understand, across plains where the sky pressed down like a lid, the pull had never weakened. Each night he told himself he could stop. Each dawn his feet betrayed him. Now, at last, the lake stretched before him—an ocean imprisoned in ice, vast and gleaming, so flawless it hurt to look at.

They called it the Blue Eye of the World. He understood why. The surface was so clear it reflected sky and star alike, a mirror that made him dizzy if he stared too long. It felt less like a lake and more like a wound in the earth, open and watching, unblinking.

Somewhere beneath that perfect glass lay depths older than Olympus, so deep the world could drown in them.

He thought of the villagers at the last station who had crossed themselves when he asked about the lake.

They had muttered old words, too fast for him to catch, but one phrase returned again and again: "The eye remembers."

One man had touched Thane's wrist, right where the glyph burn burned faintly under his sleeve, and whispered that Baikal swallowed what it loved.

The stories clung to him now.

Fishermen lost without a trace, whole sleigh teams vanishing on clear nights, hunters who walked out on the ice and never came back.

It was said that in winter the lake dreamed, and in its dreams it borrowed faces.

He could almost hear them—voices moving just beneath the wind, slipping between reeds and frost.

The chain's pulse urged him forward, but his chest rebelled.

The others had awakened in storms and shadows, in temples and ruins that rang with triumph.

Leo in thunder. Selene in silence. Damien beneath ice that bled red.

Each story had weight, had grandeur.

His? A frozen lake in the middle of nowhere.

It felt wrong. Or maybe he was the wrong one.

♦ ♦ ♦

Thane's throat tightened as the horizon shimmered.

A faint green glow danced across the sky—the aurora—and for a heartbeat it looked like chains of light, spanning across the heavens, drawing him closer.

He clenched his fists and stepped toward the mirror that waited.

He tightened his grip on the strap of his satchel, though it carried nothing but the coin he had picked up days earlier, slipped into his pocket almost without thought. He hated the way it burned cold against his thigh, as if it too had followed the pulse of the chain.

Carnevale came back to him unbidden. Venice in winter, lanterns shining on black water, laughter echoing across narrow bridges. Masks everywhere—painted faces that smiled when the mouths beneath did not. He had been good at wearing them. The charming one. The smiling one. The one people liked to look at but never looked into. For a moment, he almost wished he were back there, under silk and candlelight, instead of here in the raw silence of Siberia where nothing could be hidden.

Snow scoured the shoreline, rattling through dry reeds. He stopped at the edge of the lake.

The surface was so smooth it looked like polished marble, stretching to the horizon in a single, unbroken sheet. Beneath it shimmered faint light, deep as buried fire.

His heart beat faster.

The chain whispered faintly in his ears, not words but threads tugging taut. He felt the others in it—distant flares in the dark. Storms breaking. Shadows stirring. Arrows loosed. Drums of war. Their awakenings had come in thunder. His came in silence.

He shivered. It wasn't awe he felt. It wasn't even fear. It was dread, sharp and certain, the kind that grows in the gut and refuses to leave.

The pulse inside him demanded more. Demanded he step forward.

Thane's breath fogged the air as he whispered to no one but himself:

"It's just a lake."

But even as he said it, the Blue Eye of the World looked back at him, unblinking, and he knew that was a lie.

Thane stepped onto the ice.

The sound rang sharp, brittle, echoing across the endless flat. A crack darted outward like lightning, spiderwebbing beneath his boots before vanishing into the dark. His reflection wavered in a dozen shards: pale eyes, too-wide smile, skin leeched of color. The pieces stared back at him like strangers.

He froze, afraid the lake would shatter beneath him. But the ice held. It did more than hold—it hummed faintly, as though the weight of his body had woken something vast and patient below.

He forced himself forward, step after step. Each time his boot struck, more fractures leapt outward, splitting his reflection into further fragments. Dozens of Thanes stared back: some smirking, some grim, some hollow-eyed. He could not tell which was real.

The shards shifted as he moved, each reflection peeling away into something stranger.

One smirked back at him, cruel and sharp. Another wept openly, eyes hollow.

One leaned forward with hunger, lips whispering words he couldn't hear.

It was like walking past windows into futures he might have lived, fragments of himself carved by choices he had never made.

He pressed a hand to the glass.

For an instant, one shard smiled back with warmth—genuine, unmasked.

He staggered, breath caught, almost desperate to reach through and take that boy's hand.

But the ice buckled, cracks racing outward, and the vision was gone.

◆ ◆ ◆

A laugh echoed beneath the surface.

Not his. Never his.

The sound slid along the fractures until it dissolved into silence again.

The silence pressed harder. There were no birds, no water beneath the ice, no sound but the faint crack and shift of frozen glass. His own breath rasped too loudly, fogging the air. The mist drifted down, clinging to the surface like frost, and where it touched, the ice glowed faintly.

He knelt, squinting. Light pulsed beneath him—gold and rose, dim at first, then brighter. It beat in time with his heart. He tugged back his sleeve, revealing the faint glyph burn on his wrist. The mark was shining through his skin, its glow echoing beneath the ice as if the lake had claimed it before he had.

A chill not born of weather ran up his spine.

He bent closer, peering into the depths.

Movement.

At first he thought it was his own shadow—stretched and distorted by the glow. But no. Too tall. Too bent. Masked faces moved under the surface, pale and luminous, their edges blurred by water and distance. They did not drift. They paced, deliberate and slow, as though waiting.

The Watchers.

He knew them without knowing how. His pulse thudded in his throat. He should have recoiled, should have fled, but his body refused. His feet felt locked to the ice, his chest tight as though invisible hands held him in place.

One of the figures paused. Its mask tilted, a hollow gaze fixing on him through the fractured surface. Then, impossibly, it inclined its head. A bow. Not mockery. Not threat. Recognition.

Thane's knees nearly buckled. The Watchers should not bow. Not to him. Not to anyone.

The cracks spread further, lacing outward in thin white threads. The ice groaned beneath him, alive with strain. He staggered forward, driven by the pulse in his blood even as his instincts screamed to retreat. Each step was agony, waiting for the moment he plunged through into the frozen depths.

He whispered between clenched teeth, "It's just a lake."

But the words rang hollow, muffled against the vast silence. The Blue Eye of the World gazed back at him, reflections multiplying, shadows pacing below. He could not pretend anymore.

This was no lake.

It was a mirror.

And he was already trapped inside it.

The ice beneath him shifted again—not cracking this time, but rippling. As if the frozen surface were not solid at all, but water given the shape of glass. Shadows welled upward, and then faces pressed against the surface, blurred and shimmering.

At first, he thought they were drowned souls clawing for escape. Then the shapes sharpened. He knew them. Or he thought he did.

A girl whose laughter he had once chased across a Venetian bridge. A boy who had clasped his shoulder with too much devotion. Strangers from crowded rooms who had met his gaze with worship in their eyes. Lovers he had never kissed, friends he had never held, admirers he had never spoken to—all staring up at him through the glass.

They smiled. They reached. They adored. Their mouths moved in silent promises. You are enough. You are beautiful. You are loved.

One vision stepped closer than the rest.

It was Zara, her eyes bright with trust. "You'll never be alone," her lips shaped, though no sound passed through the glass.

Another flared beside her—Leo, hand outstretched, storms at his back but steady as stone.

Selene followed, her shadow curling protectively around him.

Kai, Ayla, Damien, Isla, Naia—each appeared, each smiling as though he were theirs, as though he belonged.

His chest ached.

It was everything he wanted and everything he feared.

They would never look at him like this in truth.

They didn't know him. Not really.

Behind them rose still more: strangers from Venice, faces from parties, lovers' eyes he'd never earned.

All promising. All reaching.

Their hands pressed against the ice as though they could draw him in, baptize him in their adoration.

Then came his own reflection again—brighter, sharper, impossible.

That boy smiled like a king, radiant and adored.

He hated him. He needed him.

The surface trembled. Frost lifted, curving upward, sculpting itself into ivory.

The mask emerged slowly, lips first, then cheekbones, then hollow eyes.

It was not carved. It was grown from desire, shaped from every look he had ever longed for.

The voice that followed was inevitable.

"Wear it. They will love you. They will follow you."

The words slid into his chest like a blade of silk.

His hand rose before he could stop it.

The mask waited, patient and perfect, promising he would never be unseen again.

Behind every painted smile he had ever worn, people had believed. They had seen charm, not hollowness. They had loved the mask, not him.

This mask was more. This mask was everything.

His throat ached. For all his bravado, for every grin he'd ever wielded like a shield, he had never truly been seen. Never truly been enough.

Here was the chance to change that. Here was the face that could make the world see what it always refused to.

He lifted the mask.

The ivory shimmered as he raised it, edges blurring as if it were made of both glass and smoke. His reflection smiled wider, waiting. His admirers beneath the ice pressed closer, eyes shining.

Thane pressed the mask against his skin.

It fused instantly, seamless, cold as stone.

His reflection smiled back at him. Too wide. Too perfect. Not his. Never his.

And yet, as the lake reflected him in endless shards, he felt their eyes. He felt their devotion. For the first time in his life, the world adored him.

Hollow adoration. Worship for a mask.

It was everything he wanted. And nothing at all.

The moment the mask sealed to his skin, fire tore through his veins.

It wasn't warmth. It was a searing blaze that licked bone, rushing through him with the violence of a storm uncaged. He gasped and staggered, falling to his knees, palms splayed against the ice. The lake hissed under his touch, steam curling where his skin met glass.

His glyph exploded into light.

For a heartbeat, it was brilliant—rose-gold, luminous, radiant with all the promise of Aphrodite's lineage. The beauty of allure, the command of desire itself. His reflection blazed, and for an instant he believed. Believed he was whole.

Then the light split.

A jagged crack ran through the glow, splitting it down the center. One flame stayed gold, dazzling, but the other bled black, shadows unfurling like ink in water. They twined together, gold and void, warring across his veins.

Thane screamed. The sound echoed across the empty expanse, carried on winds that swallowed it whole.

The chain roared to life.

Voices surged in his mind—twelve threads woven together, twelve presences burning like stars in the dark. He felt them all: storms thundering, shadows rising, arrows loosed to pierce the night, war drums pounding under ice. Each heir's glyph sang, their power straining to hold, to bind.

And his thread.

His was discord. A rasping screech against the harmony, like glass dragged across iron. No matter how tightly the chain bound, his link scraped wrong, sparks leaping from every connection.

The fire in him flared again, doubling. He saw their faces flicker—Leo, Zara, Selene, Damien, Ayla, Isla, Naia, Eryx, Kai—all illuminated in a storm of visions.

A whisper slithered through the thunder of the chain: "Twelve will complete." But not unbroken."

The words tore through him, and with them came visions not of strangers but of the others—each thread flashing in the storm.

Leo's tide surged, powerful and steady. Zara's mind blazed like silver fire. Selene's shadows coiled, patient and cold.

Kai burned with sunlight, Damien thundered with rage, Ayla's arrow split the dark.

Naia's crown weighed heavy with judgment, Isla's forge rang with fire, Eryx slipped between paths like smoke.

Each one flared brilliant, whole, certain.

His thread scraped against them, jagged and raw. Sparks leapt every time he brushed another, until the chain rattled with unease.

It was not harmony. It was fracture.

◆ ◆ ◆

The Watcher beneath the ice moved closer. Its mask caught the glow, pale and expressionless, but the tilt of its head was unmistakable.

It bent low, then sank to one knee.

A gesture of allegiance.

A gesture that made the ice sing like broken glass.

Thane's heart stuttered. He wanted to recoil. He wanted to deny. But the mask on his face grinned wider, until his jaw ached, and in that moment he felt it—recognition.

For the first time, someone, something, saw him.

And bowed.

Thane clutched his head, choking on the sound, desperate to deny it.

With a cry torn raw from his throat, Thane clawed at the mask.

The ivory sealed cold as bone. For one blinding heartbeat his glyph burned rose-gold—then split: gold on one side, ink-black on the other, twining like barbed wire through his veins.

"Get off—!" His voice cracked, swallowed by the emptiness.

The glyph surged, pain searing down his arm. He gripped the edges of the mask, pulled with every ounce of strength. For an instant it held, as though fused to his very soul. Then a jagged crack split down the center.

The mask shattered.

Shards scattered across the ice, vanishing into the fractures below like teeth falling into an endless maw. His palm blazed with fire where the glyph had burned wrong, a burn etched across his skin like a fracture that would never heal. He curled his fist around it, hiding it from the frozen world.

The lake fell still. The visions faded. The admirers, the worship, even the perfect reflection—gone. All that remained was the silence of Siberia and the reflection of a boy on his knees.

He forced himself upright, body trembling, lungs heaving. The cold gnawed at him, but the greater chill was inside, carved into him by the mask's absence.

Behind him, the chain still whispered, unstable, uncertain. He could feel the others faintly—threads burning with strength—but every time his own strand brushed theirs, sparks leapt and hissed. Wrong. Misfit. Flawed.

He dragged air into his lungs, shaping it into something steady. His lips pulled into a smile, practiced and hollow. It was the smile he had given strangers in crowded rooms, the one that kept people close without letting them close enough to see the emptiness.

"When they see me," he whispered, the words shivering in the air, "they'll see only this."

He looked down at the lake. The surface gleamed back at him, fractured by thin white cracks. His reflection stared upward. Two Thanes.

One whole. One broken.

Both waiting.

The whole Thane leaned forward in the glass, lips moving in silent encouragement.

The fractured one said nothing, only watched with eyes that bled shadow.

For a heartbeat, Thane thought he saw chains trailing from its wrists, sinking into the depths below.

◆ ◆ ◆

He forced his smile wider, rehearsing it until his jaw ached, until it felt like part of him again.

That was who he would be. The charming one. The mask others loved.

He would bury the fracture so deep no one could see it.

◆ ◆ ◆

The Watchers shifted beneath the ice, their silhouettes dissolving into the depths.

The ripples they left behind looked like links of a chain, sinking, sinking, until they vanished.

◆ ◆ ◆

Thane straightened, breath unsteady, and whispered: "It's enough."

But the lake's reflection disagreed.

It showed him whole and broken both, and the cracks in the ice gleamed faintly, as though the world itself had already judged him.

The wind screamed across the ice, carrying his words away. The glyph in his palm pulsed faintly, light spilling between his clenched fingers. He forced the smile to remain even as his jaw ached from it.

It was enough. It had to be.

The Blue Eye stared back, cracks gleaming like runes.

**The chain was whole-just not unbroken**

*I was right. My intuition was not madness, not nostalgia. I felt it in the marrow of the storm — the air itself cracked open. This was no ordinary weather. These were chains breaking.*

*Whispers reach me already. Twelve heirs, they say. Twelve... and yet I know the stories always hid a shadow beyond the number. The Institute must be ready. You must be ready. If Olympus stirs again, it will not be in silence. I will see to that.*

*—M.M.*

CHAPTER XI

# THE VERDANT PATH

January 22, 2026

Lysandra Korr hated the way Alexandria whispered.

It wasn't the wind. Or the sea. Or even the call to prayer that echoed from the distant mosques above.

It was the ground itself—ancient, heavy with secrets, pressing in on her with every step. The desert night carried a chill that didn't belong to spring, the kind that slid into her lungs and stayed.

The Nile's flood season was still weeks away, but the air already smelled faintly of wet earth, as if the river knew what was coming before anyone else.

She stood at the edge of a collapsed alleyway behind a forgotten spice shop, staring at a rusted iron grate sunk into cracked limestone. Sand clung to her boots, sweat beading beneath the burn wrapped around her curls.

The air was dry, brittle as old parchment.

No one stood behind her.

The chain hummed faintly—distant heartbeats braided through the night: a crown's cool pressure, a forge's breath, a bowstring

179

drawn and held, a tide deciding whether to rise, a coin refusing to speak. Not here. Not with her. Just resonance.

♦ ♦ ♦

She didn't call them. You crossed thresholds alone.

She set her boot on the grate. Metal sang underfoot—a high, deliberate note that didn't belong to rust. The air cinched tight, as if the city itself braced.

"It groaned—not with rust or age, but recognition."

There was no warning when the grate gave way. No dramatic cracking sound. Just a soft sigh—like the earth exhaling—and then Lysandra dropped.

The city seemed to gasp.

Too late.

She landed hard, coughing in a plume of dust and shattered stone. Stone grit clicked between her teeth; a green flash pulsed under the floor like something ancient had opened one eye. Something sliced her arm. Blood bloomed beneath her sleeve, warm and immediate.

Her hand shook as she pressed it to the wound. Not from the pain—but from the thought that this place demanded blood before it would open to her.

It didn't matter.

Because when she looked up, she saw it:

A staircase descending into shadows carved in patterns of vines, grain, and coiled serpents. Symbols of harvest and rot. Of growth and grief.

It wasn't just old.

It was buried on purpose.

She took a shaky breath and pressed her hand to the glyph on her forearm. It sparked gold beneath her skin—Demeter's mark. Not just alive now, but awake.

Then a voice—distant, rusted, older than language—brushed her mind:

*"To grow, you must first let go—again and again"*

She stood slowly.

And walked down the steps.

Alone.

"The descent was short, yet every step pressed centuries onto her shoulders. Roots pierced the walls, veins of earth clutching at her ankles as if the city itself wanted her to turn back.".

At the bottom of the staircase, a massive stone door waited. No hinges. No handle. Just an emblem carved deep into the center.

A single stalk of wheat, bound in chains.

This was it.

This was Demeter's gate.

The air shifted.

Not colder. Not warmer.

Just… expectant.

She pressed her palm to the carving. The glyph ignited, gold spilling through her veins until it felt like her skin would tear. The chains across the wheat screamed, splintering into sparks of light that rained down as the stone shuddered open.

Inside was a temple, long forgotten and carved directly into the bedrock.

The ceiling was domed and cracked, spilling narrow shafts of light from the world above like celestial vines. Reliefs of Demeter covered the walls—arms outstretched, grain rising from her palms, eyes mournful.

Not divine.

Human.

She walked slowly, the sand muffling her steps, eyes tracing the murals. In each, Demeter offered life—but shadow stole it away. A child dragged beneath the earth. Fields devoured by flame. A throne left empty, its crown burning with dark fire. The losses were not accidents. They were warnings.

In each, Demeter was offering life—but surrounded by loss.

A child swallowed by shadow.

Fields set ablaze.

A throne left empty.

"Loss feeds the soil. Only what is buried may bloom", the voice whispered again, its echo threading through stone and bone alike.

The floor drank her blood. Vines writhed up from the cracks, coiling around her wrist and arm.

She tore free with a cry, but when the ivy retreated, its mark remained—dark, jagged burns twining her skin like a chain.

The altar pulsed once, green fire spilling into the reliefs.

Hairline fractures spidered from the stone into the floor, tracing the same pattern as the burns winding her forearm.

"The harvest must always cost," the voice whispered, softer now, as if satisfied.

Her glyph flared bright emerald, then dimmed faster than she had seen in the others.

As though even her awakening had come hungry.

Lysandra flinched.

She wasn't ready for this.

Not yet.

A breeze stirred the dust.

It didn't feel natural.

At the far end of the temple stood an altar choked in vines. Flowers—some dead, some impossibly fresh—grew in scattered bursts around it. In the center, a figure knelt.

Not a statue.

Not a shadow.

A girl.

Thin. Small. Curled in on herself like a forgotten blossom.

Lysandra's knees buckled.

No.

She ran to her.

The girl didn't move.

Didn't speak.

But Lysandra knew her.

Even after all this time.

Even after the fire.

"Callia", she whispered.

Her sister.

◆ ◆ ◆

She reached for her.

And the vines snapped upward, wrapping around Lysandra's wrist.

Thorns dug in.

She gasped in pain—but not fear.

Because the vines weren't attacking.

They were remembering.

The air around her shimmered.

The temple blurred.

And then she wasn't standing in the present anymore.

She was back in Cairo. Thirteen years old. Smoke in the sky. Callia screaming. Their mother gone. Her hands full of dirt. A garden she'd tried to grow burned to ash.

Lysandra fell to her knees, clutching her head.

"Stop", she said." This isn't real. She's gone. I couldn't save her."

The vines around her arm pulsed.

And the voice said:

"But you still carry her."

Tears blurred her vision.

"You don't understand. I wanted to grow something. I tried. But everything dies."

"Then plant again."

◆ ◆ ◆

The temple snapped back into focus.

The altar cracked down the center.

And the girl vanished in a shower of petals.

Lysandra screamed.

Then—silence.

Real silence.

And in it… a heartbeat.

Not her own.

Not human.

The pulse of the earth.

It rose from below. From the roots. From the bones of the city. It rose through her skin and into her soul.

And her glyph exploded with green light—spiraling leaves and gold—veined petals unfurling across her arm and shoulder, wrapping like armor grown from grief.

The vines fell away.

But she didn't move.

She just sat there, alone in the dark temple, breathing.

Because something had been buried.

And now it was growing again.

Lysandra didn't remember standing.

One moment she was on her knees in the dust of a long—dead goddess, breath caught between grief and awakening.

The next, she was walking—guided by the pulse of her glyph, drawn deeper into the temple's roots.

The vines had parted for her.

Not just around her body—but through the air itself. They slithered back into cracks in the stone, revealing a staircase behind the altar that hadn't been there before. Hidden not by illusion.

By grief.

"To heal, you must bury the lie."

The words weren't spoken. They bloomed in her thoughts like seeds split open by the rain.

She descended.

The staircase grew colder with every step.

The stone here was damp, blackened by centuries of silent weeping. Roots protruded from the walls like skeletal fingers reaching for something that never came.

At the bottom was a doorway of moss—stained marble carved with a familiar image:

A girl cradling a cracked urn, from which a single vine grew.

Lysandra pressed her hand to it.

The glyph on her arm pulsed.

The door opened—not with force, but invitation.

The room beyond was not what she expected.

It wasn't a crypt.

It wasn't a treasure chamber.

It was a garden.

Underground.

Impossible.

And alive.

Light streamed from an unseen source above, casting golden patterns across a lush floor of soft moss, spiraling ferns, and blossoms she didn't recognize—red—gold petals shaped like open mouths, purple vines that curled around one another in slow—motion embrace.

It smelled of rot and bloom.

Death and life.

And in the center of the garden stood a stone pedestal with something resting atop it.

A seed.

But not a small one.

It was the size of her fist. Cracked. Pulsing faintly with internal light—like a heartbeat made of starlight and soil.

Lysandra stepped toward it.

The air shifted.

Suddenly, she wasn't alone.

A figure stepped from behind a curtain of ivy.

A woman.

Not young. Not old. Her skin dark like her own, but tinged with the green sheen of chlorophyll. Her hair was a crown of braids entwined with dried wheat, vines, and bone.

Her eyes—those eyes—were what made Lysandra freeze.

Because they looked like the fields of her childhood.

Vast. Quiet. Watching.

"Demeter", she whispered.

The woman smiled softly.

"No", she said." I am what remains."

The voice wasn't unkind.

But it was heavy.

It was not the voice of Olympus triumphant.

It was the voice of a mother in mourning.

"You were called here", the woman said." Because you have already tasted what most heirs fear."

Lysandra swallowed." Loss."

"Worse". The woman moved closer." Rootlessness."

She turned and gestured to the seed.

"This is yours. A relic. A promise. And a burden. Within it sleeps all that once grew where gods walked. But it cannot awaken unless you understand the truth."

Lysandra hesitated." What truth?"

The garden changed.

Suddenly, Lysandra stood not in the temple—but in her own memory, distorted and flooded with green light.

Cairo.

Nine years old.

She sat in the back of a refugee tent, surrounded by strangers, clutching a small clay pot with a sprouting flower that had no name.

Her sister's flower.

The one she'd coaxed to life with warmth and patience.

A soldier stormed in, barking orders. Someone screamed. In the chaos, the pot was kicked, shattered, and lost in the trample of boots.

Callia wept.

Lysandra said nothing.

She hadn't cried.

Not once.

The vision rippled again.

Now older.

Fourteen.

Placed in a new home with a family that didn't believe in emotional indulgence". She remembered the garden behind the house—a perfect patch of soil, untouched.

She never planted anything.

Not even once.

"I didn't want to lose it", she said aloud.

Demeter's remnant stood behind her now.

"You didn't want to watch it die."

Lysandra clenched her fists." Isn't that the same thing?"

The woman tilted her head." No. One is fear. The other is love."

The garden returned.

The pedestal pulsed brighter.

The woman stepped closer, and this time, her presence was divine. Heavy. Mythic.

"You are the heir of cycles", she said.""" The living emblem of rebirth. And rebirth requires death. Grief is not failure. It is a season."

The vines stirred with her words.

"Do you understand what must come next?"

Lysandra looked at the seed.

"I have to bury it", she said." Don't I?"

The woman nodded.

"But first—" She reached forward and pressed her fingers to Lysandra's temple.

"—you must grieve everything you buried in yourself."

The seed pulsed once beneath the earth.

Then again—brighter.

And then the floor beneath Lysandra split open.

Not violently.

But with a sound like roots cracking through stone.

She lurched back as vines exploded from the soil—thick, luminous, alive. They spiraled into the air, wrapping the chamber in a helix of glowing flora that didn't belong to any world she knew.

Golden pollen glittered in the air like suspended fireflies. Ferns uncurled in time—lapse motion. A tree sprouted from the center of the garden—wide—trunked, flowered, crowned with emerald leaves that hummed with unseen power.

Lysandra gasped.

And then the chamber above began to collapse.

It started with a tremor.

Then stone fell in sheets from the cracked ceiling above the temple, smashing into the garden with thunderous weight. The trunk of the great tree bent beneath it but did not break.

She scrambled to her feet, vines brushing her skin like frantic warnings.

There was no exit.

The staircase behind her was gone—swallowed in earth and rock.

"No", she breathed." Not now—"

The glyph on her arm pulsed wildly.

Then she heard it.

Not a voice.

Not prophecy.

A heartbeat.

The tree before her shimmered.

And a face appeared in its bark—feminine, ancient, carved of bark and breath and something older than gods.

The Spirit of the Seed.

Lysandra didn't know how she knew. She just knew.

"All things born of the earth must return to it", the spirit said, voice deep and green.

"But I just found it!" she cried." I just woke it up!"

"And now it must choose."

The ceiling above groaned again. Stones split. Roots twisted.

"You were the key", the spirit continued. "But keys do not walk through the doors they open."

Lysandra shook her head. "What are you saying?"

"The seed must take root in the world. Not beneath it."

"You must carry it—or it dies here with you."

A blinding flash seared across her glyph.

And then the tree began to fold.

Not withering.

Transforming.

Its trunk split into a thousand threads of golden light, each coiling around the roots, the vines, the walls—until the entire chamber pulsed like a living lung, drawing air and memory into itself.

The seed rose from the earth, hovering now, burning like a second sun.

And her glyph flared in response.

"Bind it to your blood", the spirit whispered." Or it will be lost."

Lysandra stepped forward.

Tears streaming down her face.

Not from fear.

From knowing.

She opened her arms.

The seed touched her chest.

And sank into her.

A surge of green flame blasted from her spine. Her hair lifted, braided by wind she couldn't feel. Glyph—lines shot down her arms, across her collarbones, twisting into symbols that weren't just Demeter's—but hers.

New.

Floral. Fierce. Rooted in loss, but reaching toward light.

She screamed—not in pain, but in awe—as the garden collapsed.

Not into rubble.

Into her.

The spirit bowed its head.

"Let it bloom through you now."

And vanished.

♦ ♦ ♦

The ceiling finally gave way.

Stone roared downward—

—only to be caught.

By roots.

By vines.

By her.

Lysandra raised her arms and the entire temple surged upward—not through strength, but growth.

Pillars of flowering root snapped into place beneath the collapsing roof, holding the weight of centuries on fresh life.

Cracks filled with moss and golden ivy. Dust blew backward. The tree did not regrow.

She had become the tree.

A girl of flesh.

And earth.

And grief.

And rebirth.

The temple stopped shaking.

Silence returned.

But it was a different silence.

Not absence.

Balance.

Lysandra exhaled hard, dropping to one knee.

And the vines bowed with her.

A whisper rose from her skin.

"What dies returns. What returns must bloom."

She clutched her chest, breath ragged. The glyph still glowed—no longer flaring, but warm. Constant. Like a compass rooted in her heart.

She wasn't just carrying Demeter's legacy.

She was it now.

But not the old goddess.

Something new.

The path ahead unfolded—vines receding to reveal a narrow tunnel slick with old roots and moonlit dew.

She staggered to her feet and walked through it.

The tunnel was tight at first.

But with every step, it widened—brighter, lusher, alive with echoes of flora and memory. As if the temple was reshaping itself for her.

A final root curled aside.

And she emerged—

—not into the alley she'd fallen through.

But into a hidden garden beneath Alexandria's foundations. A place that had not seen sun in two thousand years.

Now lit by her arrival.

Naia stood there.

Waiting.

"I felt it", "she said." The others did too."

Lysandra gave a weak smile." Good. I was worried I'd have to grow a ladder."

Naia looked her over—eyes catching on the vines still clinging to her boots, the soft glow of her glyph, the new pattern on her neck that looked suspiciously like a wreath made of bone and blossom.

"You okay?"

"No", Lysandra said." But I think that's the point."

Naia didn't ask questions.

She just helped her up the path, back toward the surface.

Behind them, the garden closed again.

Hidden.

But not lost.

Not anymore.

The night air above Alexandria had shifted.

Not just in temperature.

In tone.

It felt heavier—thicker with expectation, as if the city had exhaled something it hadn't known it was holding for centuries.

Lysandra stood alone on the hostel roof, palms braced on the warm parapet. Markets murmured below.

A neon sign crackled, failed, then tried again, stubborn as a sprout pushing through stone

She should have felt relief.

Instead she felt pressure. Not a hand. A root.

Her glyph had settled into a radiant wreath of grain rimmed in living script—seed—veins and spirals that glimmered when she breathed. Demeter's mark, yes. But also hers. Not 'growth' alone. Grief endured. Growth chosen.

The chain throbbed once, soft as a pulse taken at the wrist. Threads brushed her ribs—cool crown; forge—heat; drawn bow; storm—salt; a coin refusing to speak. No faces. No bodies. Only presence. She didn't reach back. She didn't need to. They would feel that she had changed.

♦ ♦ ♦

Clouds loosened. Between them the stars opened like seed—heads. The pattern formed slowly, insistently—a tightening spiral she had seen in the garden and, now that she knew how to look, in the whorls of her own glyph.

♦ ♦ ♦

Not symbol. Mechanism.

A wrong note scraped faintly through the chain, cold and thin, like wire dragged over bone. She didn't flinch from it this time. She logged it the way a gardener notes blight: watch, isolate, learn what feeds it.

Wind skimmed the roof. Somewhere a fox barked twice and went silent.

"Let it bloom," she said to the city, to the seed in her chest, to the season that wouldn't be hurried and wouldn't be denied.

Far below, roots she had never planted found room in cracks no architect had drawn.

♦ ♦ ♦

Far beneath Olympus, the obsidian map woke.

A new name flared there in living green:

LYSANDRA KORR.

Veins of light webbed outward, touching other points, testing their strength, tightening the chain. In the dark beyond the map's rim, something old shifted its weight, listening for failure.

Maelis stood at the edge of the chamber, gaze unreadable. Their gloved hand hovered over the Alexandrian glimmer but did not touch.

"The Verdant Path opens," they murmured. "And famine remembers it is only a season."

The Watchers bowed as one, porcelain faces to the stone.

"Mark her garden," Maelis added softly. "And mind the spiral. It is a lock before it is a sign."

In the ceiling's black glass, a thirteenth pulse beat once—dark, patient, unspent—then went still.

# CHAPTER XII
# THE LIGHTNING THAT REMEMBERS

January 27, 2026


It was late January when winter storms clawed the Atlantic raw. Change always came with thunder—but this storm carried memory, and it had waited for him."

Other pulses woke in him, flickers he knew but did not know: Leo—water beating iron in a Chicago yard; Selene—a cold key turning under Naples; Damien—a burn drum under polar glass; Ayla—silver breath drawn in a Norwegian dusk. He wasn't alone; the chain remembered twelve.

Cassian Wolfe didn't remember falling asleep.

He only remembered waking—heart pounding, hands clenched, the sound of thunder rolling behind his eyes like a memory that hadn't happened yet.

The motel room was dark. Cold. A faint arc of static leapt now and then from the lamp to the metal base of the nightstand, as if the storm outside had reached in to mark this place as its own.


He didn't touch it.

He just stared.

And when the first flash of lightning lit up the sky outside the window, he knew.

It was calling.

An hour later, Cassian stood alone at the edge of the world.

For a moment he looked like a boy again, frightened of storms—not the heir who carried one inside him.

The old watchtower jutted from the Maine cliffs like a broken tooth, stone scorched black by a thousand storms. The Atlantic crashed far below, waves roaring against the rocks, angry and relentless.

The place reeked of ozone, rust, and something older—like time had curled around this place and forgotten how to pass.

The others had offered to come.

He told them no.

This was his storm.

And it had waited long enough.

♦ ♦ ♦

Once used to track hurricanes and signal ships during World War II, it had been abandoned for decades. Nature had taken its tribute—walls collapsed, stairs broken, metal supports warped by wind and salt.

But the top still stood.

Barely.

He climbed.

Boots scraping against cracked stone. The wind screamed. Thunder cracked again—closer now.

He reached the summit and stopped.

The floor was gone. Only the skeletal frame remained, exposed to the sky.

And in the center of it, like a burn etched into the stone, was a single symbol:

A spiral of broken lines ending in a jagged bolt.

It wasn't there last time.

He was sure of it.

But it was here now.

Waiting.

He stepped toward it, heart hammering.

And then the storm spoke.

Not aloud.

Not in words.

In memory.

The wind snapped sideways, carrying images with it.

He staggered.

The watchtower blurred

—and suddenly he wasn't standing there anymore.

He was watching.

A different time.

A different sky.

The same storm.

He saw Zeus—a storm made flesh, a crown of lightning splitting the sky. Golden armor shattered and reformed with every flash, his hand gripping a bolt that throbbed like a heart torn from the sky itself. The storm bent around him, not against him.

Cassian felt it in his chest.

A pull.

A weight.

Cassian's throat tightened. He wasn't just seeing Zeus's memory—he was being measured against it. And he wasn't sure he wanted to know which way he would fall.

This was no weapon.

It was a key.

The memory shifted.

Zeus thrust the bolt downward into a vault of storm—forged metal, and Cassian saw chains made of clouds, locks built from thunder, and something inside—

—something screaming in silence, chains of cloud straining as shadow—light bled through, a presence that should never wake."

♦ ♦ ♦

The thunder wasn't empty.

It roared with voices—dozens, maybe hundreds—shouting, pleading, dying.

We failed. Don't forget us.

They weren't strangers. They were storm—bearers before him, each bolt carrying their last breath. Their deaths branded into the storm itself.

Now they lived inside him, echoing through his veins like static.

Cassian dropped to one knee, clutching his skull as lightning threaded through his blood.

When the storm finally dimmed, his glyph still blazed. His hand trembled violently, refusing to steady.

The storm had remembered him.

And it would never let him forget.

Then the mountain split.

The memory broke.

Cassian gasped.

The wind around the tower intensified, lifting his jacket, crackling against the metal.

The glyph on his forearm began to burn.

Not from heat.

From recognition.

He dropped to one knee, breathing hard.

"What was that?" he whispered. "What was he locking away?"

A voice—soft, familiar—brushed his thoughts.

"Not what. Who."

He spun.

But no one was there.

Only the wind.

Only the storm.

Another flash.

And suddenly—

He was a child again.

Age ten.

Standing in the rain outside a foster home.

Alone.

Unwanted.

Thunder rolled overhead, and for a moment, he swore the sky whispered his name.

No one else heard it.

They just called him a freak.

Fifteen now.

In the hospital.

They told him his last remaining relative was dead.

He didn't cry.

He just walked outside into the downpour and looked up.

And the lightning curved around him.

Didn't strike.

Didn't retreat.

It watched him.

Back to the present.

The storm howled now.

Not with rage.

With reminder.

Cassian stood.

His glyph now flared in time with the thunder—each pulse brighter than the last.

The storm wasn't reacting to him.

It was remembering through him.

And then it struck.

A bolt of lightning ripped down from the sky—straight toward the center of the tower.

Cassian didn't move.

Didn't flinch.

He let it hit.

But instead of burning—

—it froze.

Midair.

The bolt stopped inches from his chest, humming, vibrating, alive.

Cassian reached out.

And touched it.

Pain.

Memory.

Power.

He saw it all:

Zeus, casting the vault downward into the sea… and something unseen-vast and watching-cloaked behind the storm.

The gods arguing, not over how to save the world—but how to contain one of their own.

A choice made in secret

A betrayal hidden in thunder

And a vault that never closed

Cassian screamed.

And the lightning finally struck.

The blast shattered the top of the tower.

Stone exploded outward.

But Cassian stood at the center, arms wide, eyes glowing with electric fire, glyph flaring now into a full storm sigil—a swirling cyclone of bolts and broken rings, circling his forearm like a storm with no eye.

He wasn't just being chosen.

He was being charged.

And the storm had finally remembered its heir.

The storm was gone.

Not passed.

Not faded.

Cassian stood in stillness—alone at the top of the crumbled watchtower—but the world around him had shifted.

No rain. No thunder. Just sky.

Silver and unmoving.

Like the storm had paused time itself.

He looked down at his hands, still sparking with threads of gold and white lightning. His veins glowed faintly, his glyph now fully unfurled along his arm and into his chest like a constellation wrapped in storm rings.

He wasn't just lit from within.

He was being watched from within.

"You carry more than power", said a voice, close and ancient. "You carry the lock."

Cassian turned.

No one stood there.

Only sky.

And then the ground vanished.

♦ ♦ ♦

Not shattered.

Not dropped.

Just… removed.

One moment he stood atop the ruins of a forgotten tower—

The next, he stood in a void of clouds and stormlight, surrounded by slowly circling bolts suspended in air like threads of light woven into the atmosphere.

A sky that had no ground. No sun.

Only memory.

A temple of storm made of thunder, mist, and time.

And in the center—

A vault.

It wasn't large.

Only the size of a sarcophagus, hovering in the air, sealed with twelve interlocking glyphs.

As he drew closer, a twelfth sigil—his—kindled from dark to blinding, locking into the ring like a final tooth in a gear.

Lightning arced across its surface in rhythm, not chaos. It breathed.

And beneath it…

Cassian staggered back.

There were chains.

Not wrapped around the vault.

Hanging beneath it, falling endlessly downward into nothing, like anchors sunk into the fabric of the world.

And something at the bottom of those chains was pulling.

Trying to rise.

◆ ◆ ◆

"This is what Zeus feared", said the voice again.

Cassian spun around.

This time, the figure stood clear before him.

Not a god.

Not a man.

A memory of one.

Zeus.

Or a shadow of him.

A mirrored echo standing tall, crowned in stormlight, eyes glowing gold, face not angry but tired.

Like the sky when it's too heavy to hold the rain.

"You are my heir", the echo said." But not my legacy."

Cassian's jaw clenched. "That's not what the world sees."

"Then show them otherwise."

The echo gestured toward the vault.

"This was not built to cage a monster," the echo said

"It was built to seal a truth."

Cassian stared. "What truth?"

The echo's eyes burned brighter.

"That Olympus was never unified. That the gods did not agree. That there was once a thirteenth."

Cassian froze.

He felt the chains shift beneath the vault again—groaning, strained.

"The others denied him. Feared him. Feared his gift."

"They sealed him away. But they didn't destroy him."

"Because they couldn't."

Cassian took a slow step toward the vault.

The closer he came, the more he felt it—not just its presence, but its remembrance.

Like it had been waiting for him.

And when he reached out his hand—

The glyphs on the vault flared.

One of them matched his own.

"You are one of twelve keys", the echo said. "Even twelve together cannot open it fully."

It flared in answer, and the other eleven answered back— twelve points locking into a single, terrible geometry.

"The final lock was made not of lightning or blood…"

"But of choice—the lock no glyph can turn."

Cassian's fingers trembled. "Choice?"

"One of you must choose to bear the burden the others deny."

"To remember what should have been forgotten."

"To become more than heir."

"To become… storm."

Cassian stepped back.

"No. That's not me."

"It could be", the echo said.

"It will be. Or it will be her."

Cassian's breath caught.

"Who?"

The sky pulsed.

The chains groaned.

And an image shimmered in the mist beside the vault.

Zara.

Eyes glowing. Hair wind—blown. Standing before a burning city. Her hands raised—not in defense, but command.

People kneeling.

Others running.

The sky behind her cracked with thunder.

Her face unreadable.

Cassian looked away.

"I don't want that. I don't want any of this."

The echo stepped closer.

"Then you are not ready."

Cassian's fists clenched.

"I didn't ask to be ready. I didn't ask to be chosen."

The echo's gaze hardened.

"Neither did I."

"And because of that, the world burned."

The vault pulsed again—louder now.

Each chain trembling.

The glyphs shimmered brighter.

And the storm began to move.

♦ ♦ ♦

Wind returned. Slowly at first.

Then in a spiral.

The bolts above shifted direction, circling now—around Cassian.

Not the vault.

Not the echo.

Him.

The storm had stopped watching.

It had begun to obey.

The echo raised a hand.

"You don't have to accept it yet. But you do have to see it."

He pressed a finger to Cassian's chest—where the center of the glyph spiraled.

A sound like thunder cracking inside a cathedral echoed through the void.

Cassian screamed.

Suddenly, visions crashed into him—

Twelve heirs, standing at a chasm of fire, unsure who will cross

A throne of cloud and chain, unclaimed

The vault, shattered—its chains snapped—and something rising

Himself, alone, lightning spiraling around him, eyes glowing like stars

Zara, whispering a name that had no sound

And a final flash—

A bolt that strikes the world itself.

◆ ◆ ◆

Cassian collapsed.

Darkness flooded in.

And the storm fell silent again.

He blinked.

And opened his eyes to find himself back atop the tower.

The sky overhead churned with clouds.

But the lightning?

The vault?

Only the glyph remained—alive on his skin, glowing in a slow rhythm like the calm eye of a storm.

He didn't feel chosen.

He felt…

charged.

Like a blade that had just been pulled from fire.

He turned and walked back down the crumbled staircase, each step slow and deliberate.

The storm would return.

But next time?

It would answer to him.

The air in the motel was tense when Cassian returned.

The storm hadn't followed him.

But something else had.

He stepped into the room, soaked to the bone but calm in a way that felt unnatural—like the storm had taken everything it needed from him, and now he was only what remained.

Thane was the first to notice.

"You're glowing", he said flatly.

Cassian didn't reply. He wasn't sure how to.

Zara stood. "Are you okay?"

Cassian looked at her—really looked—and saw the edges of the same exhaustion he felt. The pull of prophecy. The weight of inheritance. The fractures that didn't show on skin, but behind the eyes.

"We're not okay", he said softly. "None of us are."

He walked to the sink, turned the faucet, and let the water run over his hands.

No lightning sparked.

No glyph activated.

He exhaled.

Kai leaned against the wall, arms folded. "Did it happen?"

Cassian didn't look up. "Yeah."

Naia spoke next. "The glyph?"

Cassian lifted his shirt slightly, revealing the full mark spiraling across his ribs and shoulder like storm—braided thread.

Thane whistled. "Zeus, huh? Guess that explains the thunder."

"It doesn't explain anything", Cassian muttered.

Zara watched him carefully. "But you saw something."

Cassian met her eyes.

"I saw everything."

◆ ◆ ◆

They were quiet for a beat.

Then Eryx walked in holding a bag of vending machine snacks. "So… are we all casually unlocking ancient storm powers now, or should I just keep trying to make shadow jokes?"

Isla smacked him lightly on the back of the head.

Cassian gave a small smile. "It's fine. Let him cope."

He didn't elaborate on what he'd seen.

Didn't describe the vault, or the chains, or the moment the lightning stopped being wild and started waiting.

He just sat.

And let the silence fold around him.

Later, while the others slept, he stood alone outside the motel.

The sky was clear now, moonlight brushing the pavement like a blessing.

He looked up—not out of superstition, but longing.

"You were supposed to be the protector", he whispered.

"And you left it all behind."

He didn't know who the words were for.

Zeus?

His father?

Himself?

Maybe all three.

The wind shifted.

Not hard.

Just enough to rustle the trees.

Enough to make the hairs on his arms rise.

He wasn't alone.

Not completely.

The glyph pulsed gently beneath his skin.

No longer violent.

Just… present.

Like the storm didn't need to rage anymore because it had found its anchor.

He held out a hand.

A soft crackle of energy danced along his palm—like a spark waiting to become something greater, but choosing not to.

For the first time, he didn't feel like he was controlling the lightning.

He felt like it was listening.

And that terrified him more than power ever had.

"I'm not him", he told the quiet sky.

"And I won't become him."

No one answered.

But a small arc of lightning curled up from the asphalt, coiled around his wrist, and faded like a nod.

♦ ♦ ♦

Cassian looked to the sky one last time that night.

And for the first time in his life…

… the sky did not thunder back.

It simply waited.

♦ ♦ ♦

The motel coffee tasted like burnt clouds.

Cassian didn't mind.

He sat alone in the corner booth of the roadside diner next to the motel, the neon light outside flickering a soft OPEN in red and blue over the fogged windows. Dawn hadn't broken yet, but something in the air felt new. Stilled. Coiled.

He spun the mug in slow circles on the table, watching his glyph fade and flare in rhythmic pulses.

Each beat was faster now.

Like it wasn't just reacting to him.

Like it was keeping time with something else.

Zara slid into the booth across from him, wordless.

She didn't need to ask.

She just nodded toward the window.

Cassian followed her gaze.

Out in the darkness, the clouds weren't moving randomly anymore.

They were swirling.

A spiral.

Not large enough to be a storm system yet—just mist threading itself into a shape that matched the one etched into their memories, their glyphs, their futures.

"You think it's coincidence?" Zara asked.

Cassian shook his head. "No. And I don't think it's weather either."

She sighed. "You said you saw the vault."

"Felt it," Cassian said. "Chains like anchors. Pulling. But not on the vault. On us."

205

Zara looked away, expression tight. "We're unlocking something."

"No", Cassian said, eyes darkening." We're unsealing it."

Then Zara reached into her jacket and pulled out the coin.

Still cracked.

Still etched with both sides: the owl and the spiral.

She set it gently on the table.

"I keep thinking I should throw it away."

"But it keeps showing up."

Cassian stared at the spiral side.

"It's not a symbol", he said. "It's instructions."

Zara didn't flinch. "It's a map."

The bell above the diner door jingled.

Naia, Kai, and Isla entered, bleary-eyed but alert.

Thane was already sitting by the counter, unreadable as always.

Eryx leaned in from the jukebox. "Storm's building again. All the way down the coast. Weird spiral pattern. Weather service says it's a freak occurrence."

Kai muttered, "We're way past freak."

Naia pointed toward Cassian. "And it started when he lit up."

Cassian didn't deny it.

Thane finally stood and walked toward them, hands in pockets.

"Question is", he said, "is the storm building because of your awakening—"

"—or because we're all waking up in the wrong order?"

Zara looked at him. "What do you mean?"

Thane's eyes glittered. "What if this was all supposed to stay buried? What if we were never meant to awaken at all?"

Silence.

Then Isla said softly, "Then why were we chosen?"

Thane didn't answer.

But he looked at Cassian.

Then at Zara.

Then at the coin.

Cassian stood, suddenly needing air.

The sky outside was beginning to glow faintly—purple bleeding into orange along the horizon. But the clouds above were thickening, not breaking.

A single roll of thunder echoed through the stillness, distant but deliberate.

He walked to the edge of the lot and stared upward.

And he felt it again.

That hum.

That awareness.

Like someone was watching.

Not from the clouds.

From behind them.

A whisper tickled the edge of his mind:

"Twelve are threads…"

"…but storms do not follow thread."

"Storms cut."

He blinked.

The glyph on his chest flared, then settled again.

No pain.

No prophecy.

Just… warning.

Zara joined him.

She didn't ask what he'd heard.

She just said, "The coin flipped."

Cassian nodded.

"And I think we're all standing on its edge."

Back inside, the others had gathered around the table.

Naia rolled out a map they'd been marking with locations—their awakenings, their encounters, and now… spirals.

Lysandra had left vines burned into parchment that mirrored the underground temple's shape. Eryx had added symbols from the shrine in Rio. Kai was still sketching fragments of the glyph he couldn't decipher.

And in the center of them all—they began to see it.

A convergence.

Not just of geography.

Of intention.

Zara traced it with her finger. "It's not a trail. It's a pattern."

"A lock", Naia murmured.

"A trap", Thane said flatly.

Cassian looked up. "Then what's in the center?"

They all turned.

But no one had an answer.

Later that night, as they packed up to leave Maine, Cassian lingered behind.

He walked once more to the ruins of the watchtower.

The lightning—burned floor was still cracked, still scorched, but his boot prints were gone.

Wiped clean.

As if the storm had taken them.

Or someone else had.

A low rumble sounded far out over the water.

Cassian squinted toward the sea.

For a heartbeat he saw it beneath the waves.

A pulse, then the suggestion of links turning in the dark.

Not current.

Chains—deep, silent, old.

And in a place far from the reach of heirs or gods, a presence stirred.

Not seen.

Not named.

Not free.

Yet.

"The storm remembers", it whispered, voice like wind dragged across bone.

"And soon… the sky will forget its masters."

"The lock is cracking."

"And I am listening."

CHAPTER XIII

# THE FIRST LINKS

Global—February 4, 2026

The storm had ended, but its echo still prowled inside Cassian Wolfe like a beast that refused its cage.

Snow fell steadily across the ruins of the watchtower, burying blackened beams and stone that had been scorched when lightning split the sky. He had slept little since that night. Every time his eyes closed, the same images repeated: the sky tearing open, chains of light clashing across the heavens, thunder cracking as though Olympus itself had exhaled.

Even now, eight days later, he swore he could hear it under his skin. His pulse did not sound like a heartbeat. It rumbled. Every breath sparked faint static in his chest, like a stormcloud he carried within. Sparks feathered between his fingertips if he clenched his fists too tightly. He was afraid to touch anything—afraid of what he might set alight.

Cassian had grown up on the Maine coast, where storms came sudden and violent off the sea. He'd learned to love them, to stand at his window and count the beats between flash and thunder. But this… this was not weather. This was possession.

He wrapped his coat tighter, though the cold wasn't the problem. The silence was. The storm should have passed, but the world around him felt heavier, as though snow and sky conspired to press him down. Too still. Too empty.

And then it wasn't.

Who are you?

The voice rang through him like a struck bell, so sharp and unexpected he staggered back against a crumbled wall. He twisted toward the empty doorway, breath fogging the air. "Who's there?" His voice cracked, hoarse from shouting into wind and rain.

No answer. The watchtower was empty but for snow and ruin.

He pressed a hand to his chest. The tug came again—sharp, unnatural. Not pain. A pull. Something hooked deep inside his sternum, drawing taut like a chain being reeled in.

He dropped to his knees in the snow, gasping. The ruined stones around him blurred. He clutched at them like they might anchor him, but the world tilted, folded, as if gravity had found a second direction.

Who are you? The voice again. Not his own. Not a memory. Too precise, too alien.

Cassian's teeth ground together. He shouted, though it felt like shouting inside his skull more than into the world. "I said—who's there?"

Only the hiss of snow answered him. Yet beneath it came another sensation: not a sound, but a presence brushing his thoughts. Faint, feminine, sharp. A thread brushing against another thread.

The storm inside him surged at the contact. His veins glowed faintly blue-white in the dusk light, lightning answering lightning. He dragged in a breath that felt like swallowing fire.

"I can feel you," he whispered. His voice shook with both awe and terror. "I don't know how—but I can."

The air itself seemed to respond, as though unseen chords vibrated around him. His hair lifted in static. Sparks crawled over the stones at his feet. The storm had found others to echo against.

And Cassian, though he had spent his life preparing for solitude, knew with a dread certainty: he was not alone anymore.

◆ ◆ ◆

Zara The observatory hadn't been used in decades, not since the university abandoned it for a shinier dome across town. Now its cracked lens and weather-beaten walls belonged to dust, frost, and Zara Kane.

Snow had blown in through broken panes, feathering across the marble floor like forgotten chalk marks. She sat cross-legged in the center of the chamber, notebooks scattered around her, each crammed with half-finished diagrams, scrawled numbers, and lines of text she had stopped pretending were homework.

They were fragments. Fractals. Patterns that came whether she wanted them or not.

Since the storm, the world had not been silent for Zara. Where others saw randomness, she saw arrangement. Rain dripping from a gutter struck in threes, then sevens, then threes again. Streetlights that still worked blinked in rhythms she could almost read. Even the stars had rearranged, tugging themselves into constellations that whispered of chains and crowns.

She hated how much sense it made.

She tugged her glove higher, trying to ignore the faint heat beneath her skin. The glyph burn had been quiet for days, a dull throb she could keep hidden. Tonight, it flared.

Her whole arm jerked as pain seared upward from her palm. Zara hissed and pressed her hand to the floor, as though the cold marble could bleed the fire out. The heat didn't fade. It spread, crawling into her chest, rushing behind her eyes.

The chamber warped. The snow-dust patterns stretched into shapes she didn't understand, equations written by no human hand. For a heartbeat, she thought she saw a web of lines stretching across the floor—threads linking her to points she couldn't name.

Then came the voice.

Her breath caught. It wasn't her thought. It was rougher, storm-cracked, filled with static like radio left on in a thunderstorm.

Zara froze. Her instincts screamed for silence, for control. But the patterns pulsed, pressing her to answer. "I should be asking you," she whispered.

The words didn't echo in the observatory. They reverberated in her head, carried into somewhere else—someone else. She reeled back, knocking over a notebook. Her eyes darted across the frost-dust floor. Empty. Yet she could feel it. Another mind brushing against hers.

♦ ♦ ♦

Her glyph burned again, searing so bright beneath her glove that she ripped it off. The burn glowed faint gold, its lines feathering like cracks of lightning through stone. She clutched her palm, breath stuttering.

Then she felt it again—another weight pressing into the resonance. This one heavier, steadier. Regal, like iron forged into a crown. A second thread braided itself into the chain.

"Who's there?" she demanded, though the words left no sound in the room.

A voice answered her. Calm, deliberate. *The chains are forming.*

Zara staggered back, heart pounding. Someone else was here—not in Cambridge, not in the observatory, but in her mind. Across an ocean, through stone and storm, she could feel them.

And worst of all—part of her knew this was exactly what the patterns had been leading her toward.

♦ ♦ ♦

Naia

The monastery had no roof anymore. Its ribs of stone arched against the winter sky, open to snowfall and silence. Naia Morrigan walked slowly through the cloisters, boots crunching on frost that webbed the flagstones.

She had come here every day since the crown awoke on her brow. It was invisible, intangible, and yet it pressed against her skull with a weight that no mortal metal could match. Even now, she could feel it shaping the way she carried herself—chin higher, shoulders squared, each step deliberate. She hated it almost as much as she feared it.

She paused at the center of the courtyard. Broken pillars stood like teeth around her, their capitals buried in snow. Wind slipped through the gaps and tugged at her hood.

Naia closed her eyes.

The chains were always there, somewhere deep in her bones. Twelve links, faint and half-formed. She had felt them flicker in

212

and out since the night of the storm—phantom sensations like voices just beyond hearing. Tonight one pulled sharper, brighter. The twelfth link had joined.

Cassian.

His presence was raw storm and confusion. The resonance carried his ragged breath, the way thunder carried across valleys. Naia gasped as she felt him—not as a voice in her ear, but as a tug inside her chest.

Another thread joined. Sharper, keener. A girl's voice, steady despite fear. Zara.

Naia swallowed against the weight pressing at her ribs. The crown seemed to tighten as if in recognition.

The chains are forming.

She had not meant to think it aloud, but the words traveled. Her declaration rang through the tether, steadier than Cassian's storm, surer than Zara's tremble.

Zara flinched at it; Naia felt her recoil. Cassian muttered something half-strangled.

Still, the links held.

"Naia pressed her palm against the ruined column, the chain thrumming through her ribs as if the stone itself carried its weight."

She had been raised to stand straight, to command. But she had not been prepared for this—for the sensation of others in her mind, for the threads binding her fate to theirs.

She looked up at the sky through the broken ribs of the monastery. Snow whirled through the arches, vanishing into the dark. "We are bound whether we wish it or not," she whispered.

The words did not vanish into the night. They joined the chain. And for the first time since her awakening, Naia did not feel entirely alone.

◆ ◆ ◆

The Resonance

The chain tightened.

Cassian knelt in the snow of the watchtower ruin, lightning still crawling faintly under his skin. Zara clutched her burning palm in Cambridge, eyes locked on the glowing glyph burn. Naia stood in the monastery courtyard, her invisible crown anchoring her even as her breath quickened.

They were three strangers separated by an ocean. Yet each felt the others as if standing a breath away. Thoughts bled across threads, broken and stuttering.

Cassian: "What is happening to me?"

Zara: "This isn't possible."

Naia: "It has begun."

The resonance was jagged, a half-tuned frequency. Images flickered unbidden: Cassian glimpsed the shape of an observatory dome beneath snowfall. Zara saw ruins roofless against the night sky. Naia tasted salt air and ozone, lightning flashing behind her eyes.

It was too much. Too fast.

Cassian dug his fingers into the snow. "Make it stop—"

The resonance quivered. And then—another presence pressed in.

Silken. Intentional. Wrong.

Beautiful, isn't it?

The voice slid through the bond like velvet over glass. It came not from Maine, or Cambridge, or Dublin, but from further still—Antarctica's frozen silence.

Thane Virelli had awakened days earlier, but his presence in the chain was different. Not raw like Cassian, not honed like Zara, not weighted like Naia. He slipped between them as though the links were threads he could braid to his liking.

Zara recoiled instantly. Her glyph burn seared, burning hot enough that she nearly screamed. "Who are you?"

Thane's laugh curled through the resonance. Light, careless, practiced. A friend. For now.

Naia's voice sharpened with warning. "This link is not yours to twist."

Cassian trembled. He didn't understand what was happening, only that the storm inside him raged louder in response.

The resonance flared. Threads pulled taut until they screamed with pressure. Zara's glyph blazed, flooding her vision with broken equations, chains corroded, an Orb flickering cold in shadow. She staggered back, clutching her palm. "Something's wrong—there's something else in this weave."

Naia braced herself, eyes fierce in the snow. "Then we will hold it together."

The chain recoiled. For a moment, the link threatened to snap. But it held. Flickering. Unstable. Alive.

♦ ♦ ♦

Far below the earth, in halls carved of obsidian and veined with molten gold, the Watchers gathered around their living map. Threads of light stretched across it now, weaving between points scattered across the world.

"Twelve," one whispered, voice sharp as breaking glass.

"Not twelve." Another shadow touched the center, where the Orb pulsed faintly—not Olympian gold but cold, pale, alien, like fire drowned beneath water."

The Orb flickered once—blue fire like a star smothered under water. The shadows bowed their heads. Not in reverence. In agreement.

"They gather too fast," the tallest intoned. "The chains close sooner than foreseen."

"Then we will break them before they are whole."

The Orb pulsed again, as though it had heard.

♦ ♦ ♦

Cassian collapsed in the snow, sparks dimming against the blackened stone. His chest heaved, every breath tasting of lightning. He was not alone anymore. He wished he was. He had felt them: a girl sharp as a blade, a queen weighted with chains, a boy smiling in shadows. And beneath them, something else—something wrong. He pressed his forehead to the frozen ground and whispered: "What have I been pulled into?"

♦ ♦ ♦

In Cambridge, Zara tore her glove away. The glyph burn glowed faint as an ember, stubborn and alive. She traced it with shaking fingers, remembering Cassian's storm voice, Naia's steady command, and that other one—that silken laugh she did not trust. Her heart pounded, mind racing. "There aren't just twelve," she murmured into the empty dome. "Something else is in the weave."

215

◆ ◆ ◆

Naia knelt in the cloister courtyard, snow catching in her hair. She felt every link in the chain, some bright, some unstable, one corroded. The invisible crown pressed heavy on her brow, binding her to the weight of responsibility she had never asked for. She closed her eyes, whispered a vow into the winter air: "I will not let it break."

◆ ◆ ◆

In the Antarctic silence, Thane opened his eyes. The resonance hummed in his veins, threads alive under his skin. The others had flinched. Pulled back. But not him. He had seen enough. They were bound—and he could tug those threads whichever way he pleased. He smiled into the endless night, the frozen wind scattering across ice. His reflection gleamed faintly in the blade of ice before him, eyes glinting with secrets.

Across continents, heirs lay restless and haunted by voices not their own. And in the obsidian halls of the Watchers, the Orb flickered once more—an echo of the Fourteenth waiting to be claimed.

The First Links had formed. And nothing would ever be the same.

◆ ◆ ◆

Cassian lingered longer among the ruins, every breath laced with the phantom thunder. He thought he saw sparks dancing along the walls, illusions or truths he could not tell. Memories of storms from childhood crashed into the present, but none had ever carried voices. His fear tangled with awe as the resonance clawed deeper.

◆ ◆ ◆

Zara could not release the glyph burn. Patterns reshaped themselves faster than she could write them. She hallucinated numbers in the frost, golden veins in the marble, whispers echoing in constellations above. Her logic began to unravel, leaving behind raw instinct and terror. Yet she knew she was needed, her wisdom the only shield against madness.

◆ ◆ ◆

Naia stood taller though the chains tore at her ribs. She thought of Hera, of crowns undesired. She whispered confessions to the snow: that she resented the burden, that she feared failing them all. But she refused to let the chain break. She remembered her mother's voice, Dublin's old myths, and steeled herself with the knowledge that without her, their unity would fracture.

♦ ♦ ♦

The resonance expanded, no longer a whisper but a storm of voices. Cassian shouted over thunder, Zara calculated patterns that shredded into nonsense, Naia commanded the chain to hold. Their visions bled into one another: seas boiling, skies splitting, labyrinths carved beneath cities. And through it all, a new presence coiled— Thane, smooth and deliberate. He delighted in their recoil, testing words like blades. His laugh lingered, and for a moment they thought they heard other whispers behind him, darker still.

♦ ♦ ♦

The Watchers bent closer over their map. Ritual chants thickened the air. The Orb glowed defiant, rejecting Olympian etchings as cracks in the stone bled light. The shadows murmured of the silence that watches, of prisons beneath, of thrones lost to time. They did not speak reverently but hungrily, calculating the moment when the heirs would break themselves. The Fourteenth glyph pulsed again, like a heart not yet claimed.

Cassian's closing breath carried both terror and surrender. Zara's whisper trembled but carried prophecy. Naia swore to carry the weight no matter the cost. Thane smiled into the frozen silence, savoring the discord. And the Orb, far below, flickered as though laughing with him.

The resonance swelled beyond a whisper, becoming a storm that clawed at their minds. Cassian shouted against thunder, Zara's thoughts fractured into broken equations, Naia pressed commands into the chain, each struggling to assert order.

Their visions spilled: fire racing across seas, towers collapsing into waves, voices whispering names they did not yet know. The tether screamed with pressure, threads glowing then dimming as if alive.

Fragments of words from other heirs flickered, half-heard, pieces of laughter, screams, and whispers of prophecy. It was not just connection. It was invasion. Each carried glimpses of the others' fears, secret thoughts they had never spoken.

217

Cassian saw Zara's notebooks tearing themselves apart in fire. Zara glimpsed Naia bowed under her crown, sobbing where no one could see. Naia felt Cassian's storm ripping him open. Their breaths tangled into one desperate rhythm, then unraveled again, leaving only chaos.

Naia braced herself, but inside, fury brewed. She had not chosen this crown. She had not wanted to feel chains forged of bloodlines she never asked for.

She thought of her mother's voice warning her about legacy, about burdens that outlive choice. She thought of Dublin's myths—queens who carried kingdoms only to be forgotten in stone.

The resentment burned, but alongside it burned resolve. If she let go, the chain would break. She straightened her spine and whispered, not just to the others but to herself, "I will not falter."

Her vow was not only for them. It was for herself. To prove she could carry weight without being crushed. To prove that Hera's bloodline was not doomed to silence.

◆ ◆ ◆

The Watchers leaned closer to their map, the air trembling with ritual cadence. Glyphs carved into obsidian walls writhed, their lines shifting like serpents.

The Orb pulsed defiance, each flicker cracking Olympian inscriptions etched as prison around it. One shadow drew a spiral in the air, a mark not Olympian but older, curling back into itself like a serpent eating its tail.

Whispers carried across the chamber—The Forgotten Chain, the drowned throne, chains hammered beneath waves.

"The fourteenth is restless," the tallest shadow said. "It stirs at their link, as though mocking them. It waits to be claimed." The others bowed, not in reverence, but in hunger.

Cassian lay back in the snow, exhausted, staring at the night sky. Lightning no longer flashed above, but he saw it still behind his eyes.

He thought of isolation, of years spent silent, and how now silence was impossible. He whispered to the ruins: "I never wanted this. But I cannot undo it." The storm hummed in answer.

Zara sat amid her scattered notebooks, fingers trembling as she tried to write what she had seen. The numbers slipped, ink blotted.

One corner of the Codex caught her eye. A name in the margin, scrawled in a different hand, half-faded: Eleni Makris—Ca' Foburni. She had skimmed it before, dismissed it as another scholar's note. Now, it pulsed in her mind like it belonged to the pattern.

For the first time, the patterns did not feel like knowledge but like prophecy written against her will. She whispered, "Wisdom was supposed to guide me. Now it may be the chain that binds me."

Naia bowed her head, snow freezing against her lashes. She whispered promises she would never admit aloud—that she hated the chain, that she needed it, that she feared it was already corroded. Still, she swore to bear it until it shattered her.

And Thane—Thane smiled into the void. The others recoiled in fear, but fear was fuel. He leaned into the chain, savoring every shiver of their unease.

He whispered to the endless ice around him, "If chains exist to bind, then I will use them to rule." The wind carried his words into silence, but the Orb, far below, flickered in time, as though answering his ambition.

# PHONETIC LEGEND

Leo Alekos – LEE-oh AH-leh-kohs

Zara Kane – ZAH-rah KAYN

Selene Marino – Seh-LEEN-eh Mah-REE-noh

Cassian Wolfe – KASH-eean WULF

Naia Morrigan – NAY-ah MOR-ih-gan

Kai Watanabe – KAI Wah-tah-NAH-beh

Ayla Solberg – EYE-lah SOL-berg

Damien Holt – DAY-mee-ahn HOHLT

Isla Damaris – EYE-lah DAH-mah-riss

Thane Virelli – THAYN vee-REL-lee

Eryx Draven – EH-riks DRAY-ven

Lysandra Korr – Lee-SAN-drah KOR

# CHAPTER XIV
# THE CHAIN ASSEMBLES

En Route to Venice—February 15, 2026

Winter had not loosened its grip on Cambridge.

Snow lay heavy on rooftops, softening angles into white silence. The Charles River ran dark beneath ice, sluggish and reluctant, while lanterns in student windows glowed through the long February nights. By now, most of the city had grown used to outages. The storm that split the sky had stripped half the grid bare, and each neighborhood took turns between flickering light and darkness.

Zara Kane had stopped marking the blackouts on her wall calendar. They had ceased being anomalies. They were part of the season now, like frost or exams.

It was deep in the night when she dreamed of the labyrinth.

♦ ♦ ♦

The labyrinth gave way. Walls folded into bridges; corridors melted into canals. The marble beneath Zara's feet softened into slick stone, black water lapping at its edges. Lanterns drifted on the surface, each a tiny flame sealed inside glass, floating aimlessly until currents gathered them into constellations that shimmered like stolen stars.

The masks were everywhere now. From balconies, from shadows, from reflections in the canal—ivory faces streaked with crimson tears, gilded smiles too wide, feathered plumes that trembled without wind. When she counted, they multiplied. When she looked away, she felt them staring. Eryx's voice slipped out sideways, half a joke, half a dare. "Storms don't herd us for nothing. Word is, Venice has a director—Dr. Makris—reads storms like scripture. If she's real, maybe she's the one pulling us through the fog." His grin faltered when no one laughed. Music knifed through the fog: violins sawing, a tune that broke on every note yet continued, part dirge, part celebration.

Zara turned a corner and saw the lion of stone, wings half-spread, perched above an arch like a sentinel. Its eyes gleamed not with light, but with patience, as though it had been waiting centuries for her to look up. Her glyph flared so violently she almost dropped her notebook. She glanced down and froze—page after page bore the same word, written in a hand more frantic than hers: Venice. Venice. Ink tore the parchment.

A bell tolled, deep and wrong, not bound to any hour she knew. Its echo rolled along the canal, through fog that smelled of salt and smoke, until it reached her chest and rattled her ribs. The flame-lanterns on the water flickered in time with it, and for one sickening instant, Zara thought they were breathing.

She walked, notebook clutched to her chest, until the corridors bent and mirrored back on themselves. Each turn revealed masks hanging from the walls—porcelain faces painted with gold, feathers, jewels. Venetian, though she had never been there. Their vacant eye-wells followed her, mouths frozen in eternal half-smiles.

She pressed her hand against one, and the glyph burn beneath her skin seared awake. The burn shot up her arm and into her ribs, stealing her breath.

◆ ◆ ◆

Zara jerked awake with a gasp.

The observatory dome loomed above her, cracked lens letting in a shaft of moonlight. Frost had crept along the walls during the night, sketching veins across stone. Her notebooks lay open around her in a chaotic sprawl, their ink blurred from the damp.

Her hand still burned. She tore the glove away, hissing through clenched teeth. The glyph burn glowed faint gold, ember lines etched into her palm. She curled her fingers into a fist, as if she could hide it from the world—and herself.

It was not silent.

Her breath frosted in the air, but beneath it she heard another cadence: the faint hum of resonance, like distant voices bleeding through a faulty radio.

Not again. Her pulse hammered. The chain had pulled taut once before, days ago, after Cassian's storm. She had told herself it had been shock, or madness, or the storm clinging to her. But the pattern had not been random.

Tonight, the threads tugged sharper.

Zara rose shakily to her feet. The dome felt different, as though the frost itself strained toward her. She pressed her palm to the marble; glyph burn searing against the cold. For a heartbeat, she swore she felt the floor breathe beneath her.

A voice brushed her thoughts. Familiar this time. Heavy with storm.

I don't want this.

Cassian.

Her chest tightened. The resonance returned with more force now, no longer jagged chaos but a fractured signal aligning. She closed her eyes, and the labyrinth swam behind her eyelids again. Corridors lined with books. Venetian masks staring.

Another presence joined, steady as iron.

Hold the chain.

Naia.

The links braided tighter, drawing Zara into their current. She staggered, clutching her notebook, breath ragged. She didn't choose this. None of them did. Yet as the season deepened, as the last hours of January collapsed into February's long frost, she knew the resonance was not going away.

It was only growing stronger.

♦ ♦ ♦

The storm had not left him.

Cassian Wolfe leaned against the shattered stones of the watchtower ruin, breath steaming in the cold. January had yielded to February, though winter showed no mercy. Snow still came in waves off the Atlantic, burying the coast until fences disappeared and rooftops sagged. He had tried to measure time by the wind, the rise and fall of drifts, but everything blurred since lightning carved itself into his veins.

Sleep was no refuge. Every time his eyes shut, he saw the sky split open. The thunder still rumbled in his bones. Sparks snapped along his knuckles even when he sat still. He was afraid to touch the wood beams or the frozen stones, afraid of what might burn.

And now there were voices.

He pressed his palms against his temples. It wasn't silence he feared anymore—it was the resonance humming under his skin, a thread pulling taut. It was Zara's sharp intake of breath, not carried by air but straight into his skull. It was Naia's steadiness, pressing iron into the chain.

Cassian gritted his teeth. "Get out of my head."

"You think I want this?" Zara's thought-voice crackled with panic, words half-formed and jagged.

"Neither do I," Naia answered, her tone controlled, regal, though Cassian felt the weight in it. But wishing won't undo it. The chain exists whether we wish it or not.

Cassian snarled into the cold air. He hated being tethered, hated the thought of strangers inside him. He had been alone for so long that even comfort felt like intrusion.

Lightning sparked across his fingertips. He saw Zara flinch through the tether, heard her muffled cry in Cambridge. Naia gritted against it, forcing calm into the resonance.

"You'll tear it apart," she warned.

"Maybe that's better." Cassian's voice carried aloud this time, echoing across empty snow. His chest heaved, every breath sharp as ice. He wanted freedom, even if it meant breaking the link.

But the chain did not snap.

It shuddered, bending under storm and fear, yet Naia's steadiness braced it. She stood in the monastery courtyard, snow swirling around her, head lifted as though her invisible crown alone could keep the chain whole.

Inside, her resentment burned. She had not chosen this crown, this duty carved in bone. She had not asked to be the one who carried balance. But the chain pressed against her ribs, and she refused to let it collapse.

You speak of breaking as if it would free you, she said, her thought steady though her heart pounded. It would only destroy us all.

Cassian's storm surged in defiance. He saw her—saw her standing in broken arches, snow threading through her dark hair. It wasn't a true vision, more like a mirror shard thrown into his mind. But it was enough to make him falter.

Naia felt his hesitation. She pressed harder, chains tightening. "I will not let it break."

♦ ♦ ♦

The words were not whispered aloud, yet they resounded in the resonance like an oath. For the first time since his awakening, Cassian did not push back. The storm subsided to a growl, uneasy but restrained.

Zara's breath shuddered across the tether. "Then you'll hold it together for all of us?"

Naia closed her eyes. She wanted to scream that she was tired, that the crown burned, that she resented every link dragging at her soul. Instead, she lifted her chin.

"Yes," she said. Even if it breaks me.

♦ ♦ ♦

The thread steadied—not smooth, not safe, but steadier than the first night. It felt like the world catching its breath after a February squall: wind fading, snow hushing into the hollows, the air holding tight and cold.

Zara pressed her bare palm to the marble and let the glyph's heat seep into the stone. Somewhere far north, Cassian's storm growled at the edge of control. Across the ocean, Naia held the chain as if it were the last rope on a cliff. Zara didn't know if any of them were breathing in the same rhythm, only that she could hear each inhale as if it were her own.

Count it, she told herself. Order it. Bring it into numbers and it will stop being a monster.

"Three counts in, five counts out," she whispered, and the words went nowhere and everywhere at once.

The tether brightened. And then a new shadow pressed gently into the space between thoughts—a cool dark that wasn't absence but presence, like standing at the lip of a cavern and feeling air move past you from a world below.

♦ ♦ ♦

Selene flickered.

It wasn't a voice at first. It was temperature. The way night falls fastest in winter when the sun gives up all at once; the way a room grows quiet when someone mentions a name that belongs to the dead. Then, softly—I see you. Her words touched them without pushing. No storm, no iron, no blaze—only the velvet hush of the underworld breathing.

Zara went still. Cassian flinched, lightning jittering along his knuckles. Naia's crown pressed heavier, yet her shoulders eased by a fraction, as if some invisible weight had shifted from bone to air.

I'm not here long, Selene said—or perhaps thought—and threadlike images spilled: a ferry dock at night, a candle guttering behind frosted glass, coins laid on a windowsill "in case." A black river ran under stars that weren't entirely the sky's.

Zara's notebooks rustled in an absent wind. "You're... different," she said before she could stop herself.

We all are, Selene answered, and the hush of her receded to the edges, like a tide that promised to return.

Before the quiet could settle, a bright thread snapped through the tangle, quick and clever, the thought-equivalent of a grin.

Finally found the party.

♦ ♦ ♦

"Who—" Cassian began.

Eryx, the thread announced, not waiting for invitation. A flash of mirrored sunglasses in a winter night, the click of a lighter, the squeak of a sneaker on tile. Hermes' heir came in like a courier slipping past a door just before it shut, hands full of messages that may or may not belong to you. Signal here was a mess. You all were shouting over the frequency like gulls over a dock fight.

"Keep your distance," Naia said, the warning as much instinct as command.

"Nah," Eryx replied, and Zara could feel the smile in the syllable. We're all distances right now. You should thank me-I can thread this better than any of you. I live in static. It's sort of my art.

Zara's glyph pricked in protest. "If you're threading it, then fix the feedback. You're making it worse."

Am not. Well… A pause, like a shrug. Not on purpose.

For a breath, the link clarified. The white hiss softened; the edges of each presence brightened. Cassian's storm retreated a step, caged but pacing. Naia's iron held. Zara's patterning sharpened enough to make sense—and hurt.

◆ ◆ ◆

At the edge of the network, a silk thread brushed the weave.

It was so light it could have been the memory of touch, a draftsman's line rather than a hand. But silk is strong. The line curled once around the others, testing tension.

You're improving, came the velvet voice.

Zara's palm burned. Cassian's storm snarled from somewhere cold. Naia's jaw set until it might have cracked.

"Leave," Naia said.

I'm not in your way, Thane replied, and the Antarctic dark that rode his words leaked into the link: a horizon with no features, a quiet too vast to be silence, the taste of air too clean to belong to cities or people. I'm admiring the architecture.

"You don't get to touch it," Zara said, surprised by the steadiness in her own voice.

Of course he smiled. The chain felt the curve of it. Touch is such a strong word for winter.

Lightning skittered from Cassian's fingers, a sound like ice fracturing on a river. The chain thrummed in warning—too many threads, too many currents in the same narrow channel.

"Back off," Cassian said. He meant it to be a growl; it came out a plea.

Thane's silk loosened—not gone, never gone—but slack enough not to cut.

The resonance held.

Zara dragged air into her lungs. She forced herself not to look at her palm. The labyrinth from her dream rose up behind her eyes without her permission—corridors of books, walls like clockwork, and the masks. Porcelain, feathered, gilded; eyes that weren't eyes staring without blinking. Her mind snagged on a carving above an arched doorway: a winged lion worn smooth by time.

"Do you see that?" she asked before anyone could tell her not to.

"See what?" Cassian demanded.

"The lion," Selene murmured, a shadow-soft echo. With wings.

"Oh ho," Eryx said. Feathers and gold? Must be terribly subtle. Does it come with confetti?

Zara chased the image, refusing to lose it to the static. In the labyrinth, a corridor opened onto water. Not the black river in Selene's breath, but water with a skin of lights floating on it—candles in windows, reflections bending. Wooden rails. The creak of an oar in an oarlock. A bell striking somewhere at an odd hour: not midnight, not dawn. An hour that belonged to masks.

"It's a city," she said. "A city of bridges. No roads."

"Boats," Eryx put in, satisfied. Gondolas, if we're being romantic. Or… if we're being accurate.

"Venice," Naia said, almost before the word reached them, as if the crown had whispered it into her bones. Snow gusted in her cloister, and she felt the damp of a place she was not standing in. She tasted salt that wasn't the Atlantic.

Thane's thread hummed. Not agreement, exactly. Appreciation. A fine stage.

"Stay out of it," Cassian snapped, and the storm pressed hard enough that the chain sang.

Zara closed her eyes and let the image assemble the way a proof assembles when the last needed number is found. Winter anchored it: February's breath in her lungs, frost on the observatory windows, the knowledge—because her brain wouldn't stop knowing—that Carnival fell midmonth. That what she saw belonged to a city readying itself for masks even as the blackout kept whole neighborhoods dark. Even as travel stretched time thin.

"Something is pulling us there," she said. Her voice shook only a little. "Not now. Not yet. But… it's the vector. This is where the chain wants to close distance."

You don't close distance with water between, Cassian said, angry because fear had nowhere else to live.

"You do," Eryx countered gently—more gently than Zara expected. You cross it. Might take days now with the grid playing dead. Might take more than days. But there are ferries. Trains. Roads that remember how to carry feet.

Naia's breath steadied the link. "Then we prepare. We do not run blind into a masquerade." The word landed heavy, born of the crown and of some old story she refused to name.

Images bled together—the watchtower and the observatory and the monastery overlaying a city none of them were standing in: low fog curling under bridges, windows like eyes along a canal, a lion with wings staring down from a salt-stained facade. A child's paper mask blowing along a flooded alley, caught against a step where someone had nailed boards for high water. Candlelight pooled like gold in a world that had largely gone dark.

Selene's cool touched them again. There are banquets for the living and other banquets for the dead, she said, not quite prophetic, not quite anything else. Be careful which one you sit for.

"Enough," Naia said—but there was no anger in it, only care. She gathered frayed edges, as if she were braiding hair she didn't have the hands to touch. "We hold until we're ready. We do not let this tear us."

Zara opened her eyes to the observatory dome. Frost had traced new filigree on the glass, and in it, for one heartbeat, she saw the blank oval of a mask where the moon should have been. She flinched, blinked, and it was just winter again.

"Can you keep the storm from chewing through the walls?" she asked softly into the link.

Cassian stared at his hands. Tiny sparks leaped and died like fireflies in a jar. "I'll try."

"And you," Naia said, and though she didn't say a name, the silk thread at the edge of the bond loosened further. "You will not pull at us while we learn."

Thane's answer was a smile no one could see. Learn fast. Winter is short when someone is hunting you.

The thread cooled. Eryx whistled a tune that sounded like a train slice through snow. Selene's hush faded with the care of a night nurse leaving a room without waking the patient.

The link held its shape. Frail. Real. The last hours of Feb 15 gave way to Feb 16, and somewhere seas shifted and somewhere grids ached and somewhere a city full of masks waited under blackout candles for strangers who did not yet know how to arrive.

Zara drew a line in her notebook with a shaking hand: a lion's wing. Under it she wrote pathway, then crossed it out and wrote invitation, then crossed that out and wrote nothing. Her palm throbbed. In the frost along the marble's edge, a flake melted and refroze, leaving the faint impression of an oval as bland and eerie as a face without eyes.

"Hold," she said, to the chain, to herself, to winter.

And for this breath—this night—the chain obeyed.

◆ ◆ ◆

Far beneath the world of snow and blackouts, the Watchers gathered.

The chamber had no torches. It needed none. Light crawled up the walls on its own, twisting into glyphs that shifted when you weren't looking. The map stretched before them was alive: continents traced in molten gold, oceans heaving like a breathing beast. Threads of light arced across its surface, fragile lines that did not belong to Olympian craft.

"Twelve," murmured one shadow, its voice like iron dragged across stone.

"Not twelve." The tallest leaned forward, a hand almost—but not quite—touching the map. "Do you not feel the fault line?"

At the center of the glowing web, an Orb pulsed faintly. Not warm Olympian gold, but pale blue fire. It beat like a heart smothered under water. Each flicker cracked against the Olympian inscriptions carved around the map, as if rejecting their cage.

The Watchers did not merely observe; they began to chant. The cadence was low, harsh, as if dragged from a language the earth itself had tried to forget. Each syllable rippled through the chamber, making the molten lines of the living map convulse. Glyphs slithered across obsidian, rearranging into symbols no Olympian archive would acknowledge: a spiral within a spiral, burning bright before dissolving to smoke; an eye nested inside a crown, flaring and then vanishing as if it despised being seen.

The air thickened until it tasted of salt and iron. Though they stood deep beneath the world, Zara would have sworn later that she felt the bite of sea-spray, the cold slap of waves against stone. The shadows raised their hands as one, and the cavern ceiling shifted as if something enormous turned in its sleep overhead.

The Orb pulsed again—harder, louder—splintering another inlay of Olympian gold. Cracks raced outward like veins of lightning, spilling pale blue fire into the grooves. The chamber quaked. For a heartbeat the map itself threatened to unravel, oceans sliding away from continents, the threads snapping apart. Then it steadied, trembling but unbroken.

One Watcher's voice scraped through the dark: The One Beneath remembers. The words were echoed, taken up by the circle, whispered again and again until they became tide. The tallest shadow lowered his head, not in reverence but in conspiracy. "The Fourteenth waits," he said. "Their dreams already carry them here. When they arrive, they will already be undone."

♦ ♦ ♦

Another shadow spoke, voice reedy with hunger. "The Fourteenth stirs. Their link woke it. It is mocking them already."

A ripple moved through the circle of Watchers, robes whispering against stone. Some bowed their heads, not reverently but calculating. Others whispered names older than Olympus, names buried in drowned thrones and sunken walls. The glyphs on the chamber's walls writhed, shifting into spirals, serpent coils, and the mark of the eye that never closed.

"They should not have reached this harmony so soon," the tallest said. His voice was low, but it filled the cavern until the molten lines themselves quivered. "It was meant to be scattered, chaotic. The Olympians ensured distance, ensured delay. And yet…" He gestured to the glowing threads that had already found each other. "Already they braid."

"Then the harvest begins early," another whispered. Its voice cracked like frozen branches snapping. "Better. The chain will strangle them before it steadies."

The Orb pulsed again, harder this time, flaring like drowned lightning. The Olympian glyphs etched around the map blackened, as though the very metal resented its prisoner. A crack ran through one golden inlay, glowing blue for the briefest moment before it faded.

The shadows stilled. Some hissed. Some smiled.

"The Fourteenth waits," the tallest intoned. "But the Thirteenth has already marked itself."

A long silence followed, broken only by the slow groan of the chamber walls. The map dimmed, but the threads remained. They had not broken. Not yet.

"We will strike," the tallest said, "before they can gather in flesh. Masks will be their undoing."

And the chamber darkened, leaving only the Orb's heartbeat echoing in the stone.

♦ ♦ ♦

Zara woke with a gasp, cheek pressed to a page. Ink had smeared across her skin where she'd fallen asleep writing, but the words bled nonsense. Equations repeating in circles. Chains crossing chains. A lion with wings scrawled three times in increasingly shaky hand.

Her palm burned. She flexed her fingers, but the glyph refused to dim. It throbbed like a second pulse, answering something she couldn't see.

She closed her eyes, and the labyrinth returned—not in fragments now, but whole. The corridors bent toward a single image: a canal, black water slick with candlelight. Bridges arched low overhead. Masks bobbed in the reflection, feathered and gilded, faceless and watching. A bell tolled midnight, but the sound was wrong—it stretched, echoing like water dripping in a cavern.

Zara staggered back from the vision, but there was nowhere to retreat. Every corridor led to water. Every archway held masks. A lion of stone crouched above it all, wings folded like judgment.

She heard the voices again: Cassian's storm muttering in fury, Naia's crown pressing steadiness, Selene's hush, Eryx's laugh sharp in the static. Even Thane's silken amusement lingered at the edge, curling where she could not cut him out.

The resonance dragged at her, not violent this time, but insistent. Pulling. A vector with only one solution.

Venice.

Her eyes snapped open. Frost glazed the observatory walls, and for an instant, she swore she saw a mask etched into the ice: blank, pale, staring. She rubbed at it, but the mark remained until the ice melted under her hand.

The chain had chosen its next step. Whether she wanted it or not.

Zara pulled her glove back on, breath shaking. "Then we follow," she whispered.

And outside, as February began in earnest, the wind carried her words into the night.

◆ ◆ ◆

The resonance did not simply hum now—it surged, overflowing their boundaries. Cassian's storm roared, straining its cage, sparking against Zara's patterns until her equations shattered into fragments of fire and ice.

Naia's crown pressed hard, chains stretching into sparks of molten light. Voices overlapped: Selene's hush, Eryx's laugh, Cassian's thunder, Zara's frantic logic—all colliding until the link was a storm inside a storm.

Each heir caught glimpses not meant for them: Naia saw the observatory dome bending under weight of storms, Zara glimpsed cloisters bleeding snow into fire, Cassian glimpsed masks staring from every arch. Their breaths tangled, becoming one rhythm then breaking again.

Lightning split across their minds, and for a heartbeat Zara thought she heard someone else—not heir, not Watcher, something older—murmur beneath the chaos. It vanished as quickly as

233

it came, leaving only the resonance screaming with too many voices at once.

Naia stood straighter in the ruined cloister, though inside her bones burned with defiance. She had not wanted the crown. She had not asked for chains that bound her to strangers she did not know.

She thought of Hera, her bloodline heavy with thrones and betrayals. She thought of Ireland's forgotten queens who carried kingdoms only to be carved into statues, their voices stolen by time.

The resentment scorched her even as she anchored the chain. "Why must it always be me? "she thought, not sending it across the link. She swallowed the words, pressing them into silence. And in that silence of self, Naia made a vow: she would carry it anyway, even if it crushed her.

Not because she loved the crown, but because she would not let the chain break, not when the others faltered.

◆ ◆ ◆

The Watchers' chamber seethed. Obsidian walls rippled with glyphs that shifted when no eyes were on them, curling into shapes that belonged to a language forbidden since the First Age.

The Orb flared, cracks spiderwebbing through Olympian inlays. One shadow raised a hand and the glyphs writhed into spiral after spiral, serpent jaws closing around circles, eyes blooming open in the stone.

They spoke in names that had not been uttered in centuries: thrones drowned beneath waves, palaces torn from the earth, prisons sealed under oceans. Each syllable carried dread that eroded the chamber like tide grinding stone.

The Orb answered them with a pulse that shook the cavern like a heartbeat under the sea. Blue fire seeped through cracks, and the shadows bowed their heads in hunger. "The Fourteenth wakes," the tallest said. "And it listens."

◆ ◆ ◆

Zara's dream deepened. The labyrinth bent again, corridors widening into bridges, walls turning into canals. Water lapped at stone, carrying the flicker of candlelight like veins of gold.

She saw masks more clearly now—ivory streaked with crimson tears, feathers black as midnight, grins carved too wide. None were worn, yet all watched her. Each mask turned toward her though no hand wore them.

She walked through fog that smelled of salt and smoke. Bells rang, not hours but warnings. A lion of stone crouched above it all, wings folded, watching as though it had always waited for her.

Her glyph burned until she thought it might sear through bone. She woke gasping, whispering, "Venice," though she had never been there. Her notebook lay open, ink blotting a page where she had scrawled the word over and over without memory of writing it.

♦ ♦ ♦

# *Codex Fragment*

## *The Verdant Lie*

Green growth conceals the bones of
famine.
Fields rejoice, yet roots drink sorrow.
The harvest is taken twice —
once by the hand, once by the oath.
Beware the gift that binds the earth,
for it withers even as it blooms.
What feeds the chain will one day
starve it.

INTERLUDE III

# THE GATHERING STORM

The chain wakes. Something has already chosen.

Archivist's note: The tally that reads 'thirteen' may be a scribal error—the original mark is scratched away, and two counts overlap. We proceed under caution.

Far beneath the world that mortals knew—beneath its cities, its ruins, its faith—there stood a chamber no map had ever dared mark.

Above, February storms clawed at the Atlantic, but here beneath, the air was still. Too still—as if the earth itself was holding its breath.

A sanctum carved from stone not found in this age. Not built, but remembered into place.

It did not exist.

It simply endured.

◆ ◆ ◆

Twelve mirrors lined the circular chamber, their frames etched with languages too old for myth and too cursed for god. Between them, threads of silver light hummed in geometric rhythm—forming the spiral that had no beginning and would have no end.

The spiral was moving now.

Not just spinning.

Tightening.

♦ ♦ ♦

At the chamber's center stood a figure in a robe woven from darkness and dust. No face could be seen beneath the hood. Only eyes—mirrored like the walls, reflecting things not present.

A Watcher.

Not the first.

Not the last.

One who remembered Olympus not as a beacon, "…but as a wound still bleeding shadowlight through history."

The wound pulsed again in the glass, and for an instant the mirrors fractured into rival words—one language etched by gods, another older, cut by chains.

Half the glyphs reversed themselves, as if refusing the Olympians' story.

The Watcher saw both.

And neither was whole.

"The spiral shifts," the Watcher whispered. Their voice echoed unnaturally—soft but stretching, as if time bent to hear it.

"Faster than we projected."

Another mirror rippled.

From it stepped a second figure—taller, robed in midnight blue, glyphs stitched into their sleeves with thread that moved like smoke.

This one did not bow.

"Two more glyphs have awakened. The storm child. And the Verdant heir."

The first Watcher turned.

"And still no sign of the Chainbreaker?"

"None. But… her presence stirs. The earth recoils again."

♦ ♦ ♦

The mirrors pulsed in sync.

One showed a burning observatory. Another, a collapsing forge cavern. Another, a blade suspended in violet starlight.

"They move faster than expected," the first Watcher murmured.

"Or perhaps," the second offered, "fate is correcting itself."

♦ ♦ ♦

The spiral in the center brightened.

A thirteenth ring shimmered—faint, like a ghost behind glass.

The Watchers both fell silent.

Then the first one spoke, quietly:

"He stirs."

"The One Beneath?"

"He does not sleep as they hoped. He remembers. And so do we."

Another mirror lit—this one showing Cassian Wolfe standing alone atop the ruined tower in Maine, his hand outstretched, lightning spiraling around him.

For a moment, the mirror slipped. Not gods, not heirs—mortals.

Fishermen along the Maine coast clutching their chests as thunder rippled through their bones.

A child waking screaming in Dublin as vines coiled outside her window.

Pilots above the Atlantic radios crackling with words no one spoke.

The storm was no longer theirs alone.

It was spilling.

"He touched the Vault," the second Watcher said. "And lived."

"He was meant to."

"But not yet."

♦ ♦ ♦

Silence again.

Then a third voice spoke from the shadows beyond the mirrors.

Female.

Resonant.

Old as the lock itself.

"Perhaps that is the point."

The other Watchers stilled.

None turned.

They knew that voice.

Not divine.

But close.

Maelis.

◆ ◆ ◆

She stepped into view slowly—face still cloaked, but the air bent differently around her. Softer. Heavier. Like gravity remembered her weight and dared not forget it.

Even the mirrors faltered, their reflections stuttering as if time itself struggled to remember her place in it.

"The spiral is not a warning," she said. "It is an invitation."

"We are not ready," one Watcher whispered.

"Neither are they," Maelis replied.

"But readiness is irrelevant. The Gathering begins now."

The prisms around the chamber pulsed in unison, each showing an heir's face.

But one shimmered strangely.

Thane Virelli's reflection rippled twice, as though two glyphs warred beneath his skin.

Neither fully Aphrodite's. Neither fully known.

The spiral shuddered in response, tightening with hunger.

She turned to the thirteenth ring—the one barely glowing, barely present—and reached toward it.

It flared.

Not fully.

Just enough to be seen.

Enough to be known.

"He calls for his heir," she said. "And soon, they will answer."

◆ ◆ ◆

The other Watchers shifted.

One stepped forward and asked what none dared:

"Is it true? That one of the Twelve already questions their allegiance?"

Maelis did not answer.

She didn't need to.

The spiral pulsed again—twice.

A warning.

Or a heartbeat.


240

"Let them awaken," Maelis said. "Let them chase purpose and prophecy. Let them believe they choose."

"The spiral will turn. The locks will break. And when the storm gathers—"

"He will rise."

♦ ♦ ♦

And somewhere—far beneath the vault, far beneath even memory—something smiled without a face.

The chamber dimmed.

Not by shadow, but by will.

As if the spiral had blinked.

As if something behind the mirrors had leaned closer.

The Watchers stepped back as one, forming a ring around the central dais. Above them, the ceiling split into panels—revealing a vault of stars etched in metal, each constellation tied not to the heavens but to names long erased.

At the center of the room, the First Watcher extended a hand.

A black scroll unraveled into the air.

Not parchment.

Not digital.

Not any material of the mortal world.

It shimmered as if made from pressed smoke and lightning.

♦ ♦ ♦

Codex Fragment XI.

Lost to all but the Watchers.

Forbidden even among their own.

♦ ♦ ♦

The First Watcher began to read:

"When storm forgets its master, the lock will tremble. When twelve threads burn through mortal skin, the spiral shall tighten. But the thirteenth was never thread—the thirteenth was chain, forged to bind gods themselves."

Silence followed the reading.

The scroll folded into itself and vanished.

No one spoke.

No one moved.

The spiral hovered at the center of the room, spinning more rapidly now. The thirteenth ring pulsed again—no longer faint.

Present.

♦ ♦ ♦

And then came the whisper.

Not from any voice in the room.

Not from Maelis.

Not from the mirrors.

"The chain remembers…"

The sound slithered from beneath the floor.

The stone itself darkened.

The glyphs on the walls flickered—not in fear, but in recognition.

"Let the threads dance. Let the gods forget. Let their heirs awaken to fire and ruin."

"But when the final lock shatters…"

"…they will see who held the key."

♦ ♦ ♦

The Watchers remained still.

Even Maelis did not speak.

The voice did not continue.

It didn't need to.

Its echo lingered not in the air—

—but in them.

In their minds.

Their glyphs.

Their bones.

♦ ♦ ♦

The First Watcher finally said, voice brittle:

"He has not spoken since the Sundering."

Maelis turned toward the mirror showing the heir glyphs, now fully arranged in a circular pattern—eleven shining.

The twelfth flickered.

The thirteenth?

Shadow.

"He was waiting," she said.

"Now, he watches."

♦ ♦ ♦

The spiral glowed once more—brighter than before.

Then dimmed to nothing.

As if it had blinked again.

Watcher Virel had not spoken since Delphi fell.

Not aloud.

Not to the others.

He preferred silence now.

Silence held truth better than prophecy.

♦ ♦ ♦

While the rest of the circle remained in the sanctum, parsing glyphs and whispers, Virel walked the inner corridors—vaults of moving shadow, relics etched into glass, memories suspended in oil like insects in amber.

This level wasn't seen by most.

Even among the Watchers, he was old.

Old enough to remember the day the thirteenth was chained.

Old enough to know the gods were not omnipotent—

Just afraid.

♦ ♦ ♦

He stopped before a suspended scroll labeled only with a sigil: a cracked heart surrounded by seven downward arrows.

The Fragment That Never Was.

He'd helped scribe it.

Then helped bury it.

Now, it pulsed again, like a wound reopening.

♦ ♦ ♦

"It's happening too fast," he whispered.

"The threads are not aligning… they're fraying."

♦ ♦ ♦

He moved toward a series of crystal prisms hovering in the air—each one reflecting the face of an heir in real-time.

Twelve.

Then—

He paused.

One prism shimmered differently.

Its reflections fragmented—not broken, but out of sync.

As if the face within was changing.

Shifting.

◆ ◆ ◆

Beautiful.

Charming.

And dangerous in a way even the Watchers had not foreseen.

◆ ◆ ◆

Virel pressed a finger to the prism's surface.

It resisted.

Then rippled.

"You're not lost," he whispered. "You're not confused."

"You're already choosing."

◆ ◆ ◆

He turned to the wall behind him—covered in overlapping maps drawn from codices, time-looped prophecy spirals, and threads mapped to bloodlines long forgotten.

Most pointed to one convergence point—an alignment the Watchers had counted on for centuries.

But now…

He blinked.

"No."

The convergence had split.

Two new endpoints glowed on the timeline—neither marked in the original prophecy.

One burned gold.

The other pulsed with shadow.

◆ ◆ ◆

Virel stepped back.

"One will break the chain."

"The other… will become it."

◆ ◆ ◆

The chamber around him dimmed.

Footsteps echoed behind him—quiet, deliberate.

He didn't turn.

He knew who approached.

◆ ◆ ◆

"You shouldn't be here," said the voice. Calm. Female. Controlled like the coil of a serpent.

Maelis.

244

$$\blacklozenge\ \blacklozenge\ \blacklozenge$$

"Neither should the thirteenth thread," Virel replied.

"Yet here we are."

She stopped beside him, hands clasped before her like a priestess before judgment.

"You doubt the spiral," she said.

"I doubt our control over it," Virel answered.

"It's not meant to be controlled."

He looked at her for the first time.

"Is he guiding it?"

Maelis tilted her head.

"Would it matter if he was?"

"It would if he's choosing an heir."

$$\blacklozenge\ \blacklozenge\ \blacklozenge$$

Silence.

Then Maelis smiled—not with cruelty, but with something older.

Sadness.

Maybe pride.

"The gods chose by blood."

"But blood lies."

"He will choose by will."

$$\blacklozenge\ \blacklozenge\ \blacklozenge$$

Virel looked again at the prism showing Thane.

The reflection was clearer now.

But the glyph on his arm… had begun to twist.

A ripple.

A change.

"Not Aphrodite. Not any glyph the Olympians dared record.".

$$\blacklozenge\ \blacklozenge\ \blacklozenge$$

"If he does choose," Virel said, "what happens to the rest?"

Maelis turned to leave.

Her answer was simple.

"Then the storm won't gather."

"It will be born."

$$\blacklozenge\ \blacklozenge\ \blacklozenge$$

And she vanished.

Leaving Virel alone with twelve prisms.

And a thirteenth reflection that had no face yet.
Only potential.
Only danger.
Across the world, the spiral moved.
Not as symbol.
Not as storm.
As presence.

♦ ♦ ♦

In the sands beneath Alexandria, forgotten vines withered overnight, curling into spiral shapes before blackening into ash. In Rio, mountain birds fell silent at once—one thousand heartbeats halted in unison, as if cued by a song only they could hear. In the fjords of Norway, the northern lights bent southward, carving the spiral into the night sky for an instant too long.

Then vanished.

♦ ♦ ♦

Humans called it anomaly.
The Watchers called it alignment.
But nature?
Nature remembered.

♦ ♦ ♦

In Santorini, the forge's flames sputtered and turned silver.

In Kyoto, ink bled from ancient scrolls unbidden, sketching unformed eyes.

In Dublin, a field of white flowers bloomed overnight, only to twist into spiral patterns by morning—petals open like mouths.

"In Bergen, hunters whispered of a silver stag crossing the fjord at dusk, though no antlers cast its shadow."

In Naples, a cemetery door blew open where no wind reached. In Cambridge, an owl was born with two heads and no eyes. In Marseille, lightning struck the same hill twice—twelve minutes apart.

"In Chicago, waves rose against the lake wall though no wind touched the water."

Somewhere in the Atlantic, deep beneath the sea where no heir had yet stood, something shifted.

A chain moved.

246

A vault groaned.

♦ ♦ ♦

The world was remembering the storm before the storm.
The one that split Olympus itself.

♦ ♦ ♦

And in a cave unseen by mortals, carved into the root of an island long wiped from maps, a circle of runes began to glow.
Not gold.
Not white.
Not even red.
But black.
Inkblack.
Like the void behind stars.

♦ ♦ ♦

A single stone pillar stood in its center, surrounded by chains embedded in the rock.
The pillar bore no name.
Only a symbol:
A spiral inside a shattered circle.
Around it, thirteen smaller sigils—twelve glowing faintly.
The thirteenth?
Dim.
But waking.

♦ ♦ ♦

Above the pillar, suspended in nothing, an eye pulsed.
Not open.
Not closed.
Not yet.
Just aware.
Like it had spent centuries dreaming of the sky, and now remembered it existed.

♦ ♦ ♦

Wind screamed across a mountain range.
Lightning rippled across oceans.
Birds took flight.
Glyphs across the world flared in sync, some unnoticed, some felt like a chill crawling across skin.

247

The chain remembers. The vault trembles. The lock is almost ready.

♦ ♦ ♦

And in the Watchers' sanctum, the spiral shimmered.
All thirteen rings present now.
One still dark.
But no longer absent.

♦ ♦ ♦

Watcher Virel stared at it, fingers pressed together, eyes wide.
Maelis stood beside him, face unreadable.
Zara Kane had awakened the mirror. Cassian Wolfe had remembered the sky. Others would follow.
Too fast. Too soon. Too aligned.

♦ ♦ ♦

"It won't hold," he said.
"No," Maelis answered.
"It's not meant to."

♦ ♦ ♦

A final beat of silence. Then thunder cracked across the world—not from above.
From below.
And far beneath it all, a whisper not in words, not in language, but in intention—It crawled into glyphs etched on mortal skin. It curled into bones not yet broken. It trembled through the spiral. One word. Not command. Not plea. A memory demanding to be lived again. Awaken.

# *Blood of the Immortals:*

# *The Last Prophecy*

# Book Release Dates

1. **Book I – The Storm That Split the Sky**
   Release: **October 31, 2025** (Halloween)
2. **Book II – The Rising Shadows**
   Release: **March 20, 2026** (Spring Equinox)
3. **Book III – The Shattered Crown**
   Release: **June 21, 2026** (Summer Solstice)
4. **Book IV – The Fallen Legacy**
   Release: **December 21, 2026** (Winter Solstice)
5. **Book V – The War of Gods**
   Release: **May 1, 2027** (Beltane / May Day)
6. **Book VI – The Final Awakening**
   Release: **August 1, 2027** (Lughnasadh / Lammas)

# PART IV – THE CITY OF GODS

CHAPTER *XV*

# THE CITY OF MASKS

Venice—February 21, 2026

It had taken eleven days to cross what should have been a single night's journey.

She paused, letting silence gather at the edges of her thoughts. The city did not hurry; neither would she. She breathed and let the stillness settle.

Zara's mistrust deepened with every step across the square. She studied Cassian's clenched fists and the sparks he tried to hide, and she watched Naia's poise, the way she carried her unseen crown like an executioner's blade. The chain tugged them closer, but chains could bind enemies as easily as allies. Her mind flickered back to nights on the road—stations without light, trains that never came, and the haunting thought that she might be the only one moving toward this fate. Now, two strangers stood tethered to her, and Zara wondered if destiny's design was a salvation or a trap.

Naia slowed on the stones and simply breathed, a measured stillness. She let the moment linger, refusing to be rushed by masks or crowns.

Zara's eyes kept darting between the storm crackling under Cassian's skin and the weight of judgment in Naia's stare. Logic told her to trust no one, yet instinct pulled her toward them. She thought of the eleven days crossing blackout Europe, faces glimpsed and lost, nights of silence pressing down. Now, here

251

stood two heirs bound to her by chains she had never chosen. Her hand tightened around her notebook. Could she trust them? Or was survival the only bond that mattered?

♦ ♦ ♦

Cassian eased the storm down until it whispered. He waited, head tipped back, choosing the slow breath over the sudden spark.

Cassian's storm crackled restlessly at his edges. Every corner of Venice pressed against him, smothering his control. He hated the silence of the canals, hated the masks that stared without blinking. The Rialto bridge felt like a cage, every step reminding him of Maine and the storm he could not master. He clenched his jaw until sparks bled from his teeth, resenting the tether that bound him closer to heirs he did not trust. The city mirrored his fury back at him, until he wondered if Venice itself wanted to see him burn.

Cassian's storm never rested. He loathed the city, its silence, its masks that stared too long. Every step along the Rialto bridge felt like walking inside a storm cage. He could feel his control fraying, sparks crackling at his sleeves, the tether binding him tighter to the others. He hated being dragged like this, hated the memory of Maine gnawing at him, hated that the chain knew him better than he knew himself.

Under ordinary skies, Venice lay only hours away by train and ferry. But nothing had been ordinary since the storm that split the sky. The blackout had gutted every timetable, severed every line of certainty. Power grids lurched on and off like wounded things. Trains stopped mid-journey without warning, stations went dark, ferries sat moored until fuel could be scavenged. What maps promised in neat lines unraveled into detours and waiting, days swallowed in a silence that hummed with unease.

♦ ♦ ♦

Zara Kane had marked the dates, because she always marked them.

The resonance had seized them on the last night of January, its threads pulling taut until her glyph burned hot under her skin. That had been February second. She had counted the days since: ten of them spent moving, eleven now, each one heavier than the last.

252

A voice threaded through the resonance, silken and cruel. '*The Thirteenth waits*, 'it whispered, a sound that might have been the sea itself. Zara's glyph flared, the golden lines twisting into a symbol she did not recognize—one that shifted as though it resisted translation. Naia hissed as her crown pressed sharper, Cassian scowled at the phantom voice. None of them spoke, yet all heard it. A secret seeded in silence, older than Olympus, waiting to bloom.

A journey that once took eleven hours had stretched to almost two weeks.

She remembered overhearing a traveler in Milan muttering the same thing while waiting for a train that never came: "Eleven hours, they said. Eleven days now." The words had clung to her, a bitter refrain. She carried them across every delay, across the silent nights when generators failed and she wrote equations by candlelight in her notebook just to steady her thoughts.

Now it was mid-February, and Carnival had come—but Carnival in blackout was no celebration.

The city greeted her with silence first. Then with masks.

From the ferry deck, Zara saw them clustered on the docks: rows of painted porcelain faces, pale and unblinking. Some smiled with gilded lips. Others wept crimson tears. Their feathers stirred in the wind though no one touched them. She pressed her gloved hand to her chest, feeling the sear of the glyph under the leather, as if her dreams had leaked into the waking world.

The vaporetto shuddered against the dock. Zara shouldered her pack and stepped down, boots striking the stone. The resonance throbbed faintly in her ribs, sharper here, closer. She tried to tell herself it was only nerves. But the burn in her palm said otherwise.

Somewhere in the fog, the bells of San Marco tolled, their sound muffled and warped. The city exhaled a sigh older than its stones, a welcome that felt more like a warning. Venice was not greeting them—it was watching

The city held its breath with them. Blackout lanterns flickered, casting ripples of gold across the water. For the first time, the twelve saw each other whole—not as shadows in dreams, but as living proof of everything their chains had whispered. Wonder warred with suspicion in their eyes, and no one dared speak first.

Venice did not welcome her. It watched her.

Every bridge was a question. Every alley bent the wrong way. Candlelight bled through fog, but whole districts slept dark, their windows black holes in the night. Carnival had come anyway. Costumed revelers drifted across squares in silence, their laughter too thin, their masks too heavy.

Zara pulled her hood lower and tightened her glove over her hand. Eleven days late. Eleven days heavier. And the city was waiting.

Winter clung to Venice like a shroud.

The canals were rimmed with ice at their edges, black water swallowing moonlight whole. Lanterns hung from balconies, their flames guttering against the February wind, but the city's bones were still in blackout. Generators thrummed faintly in some districts, a few floodlights sputtered to life above piazzas, but most of Venice remained half-lit, half-dead, moving through Carnival like a dream that could not decide if it was alive.

Venice itself seemed to decay as they moved. Banquet tables sagged with plates of ash, masks wept seawater that pattered onto stones, and bridges curved too steeply as though the city had been bent in agony. One canal ran with ink instead of water, reflections rippling in distorted shapes. The masquerade was not a festival—it was a funeral written into stone, a city that had chosen to wear its death as costume.

Zara Kane stepped off the vaporetto with her hood low and notebook clutched close. The ferry had taken twice as long as usual; power outages had cut half the routes, and rail lines leading north were still broken. What should have been an eleven-hour journey from Cambridge had stretched into days of limping progress: missed connections, dark stations, and long nights staring at the labyrinth carved across her palm.

Venice did not welcome her with warmth. It stared back at her through masks.

On the dock, vendors had set up tables of Carnival masks despite the blackout, rows of painted porcelain faces staring at her with wide, lightless sockets. Others wept crimson tears. Their feathers quivered in the wind, though none of the sellers touched them. Zara's chest tightened. They were identical to the masks from her dreams—the ones that had haunted her since the resonance pulled taut.

Her glyph burn seared. Beneath her glove, the burn lit faintly, like a coal hidden in fabric. She curled her fingers into a fist, forcing her hand into her pocket. No one could see. No one could know.

The city pressed close around her. Venice was not built for order. Bridges tilted at odd angles. Alleyways broke into courtyards that fed back into alleys. Water replaced streets. Everything doubled itself in reflections, so that Zara felt she was being followed by copies of herself moving under the waterline. She tried to map it as she walked—counting bridges, marking turns—but the patterns dissolved. Numbers she could normally control slipped like water through her grasp.

She hated it. And she loved it.

Because for the first time, the labyrinth was not inside her alone. It was around her, alive, drawing her deeper.

She passed a group of masked figures clustered near the Rialto. Their costumes were faded, patched with scraps; blackout had made Carnival hollow. Yet their laughter echoed anyway, loud and sharp, though no mouths moved behind their masks. Zara's steps faltered. The glyph under her glove burned hotter.

Venice was not a city. It was a masquerade.

Zara stepped off the dock into streets that were not streets at all but stone ribs stretched across black water. Bridges leaned like bones, alleys twisted into loops, and every reflection doubled itself until she no longer trusted what she saw. Lanterns burned in a scattering of windows, but the city's arteries pulsed mostly with shadow.

Carnival had arrived anyway.

Figures drifted through the fog, their faces hidden behind fired-clay masks with hairline cracks. Once, Carnival meant music—crowds laughing, violins sawing, drums echoing across canals. But blackout had muted everything. Generators coughed in some piazzas, sputtering out fragments of song from old speakers, but the silence between notes swallowed more than it gave.

The revelers did not dance. They wandered.

She passed a procession near San Polo: masked women in gowns patched together from curtains and sheets, men in velvet jackets faded from decades of use. Their masks gleamed, some painted with gold tears, others with crescent moons. They should have been singing. Instead they walked as if in a funeral line, their steps measured, their hands holding candles whose flames bent against the wind.

A boy darted across the crowd wearing a fox mask. His laughter rang sharp against stone, and for a moment Zara almost smiled. Then he vanished down a side alley, and she realized no footsteps followed him.

Her glyph burned hotter.

The city did not yield to logic. Zara had tried—counting bridges, timing her pace, sketching crude maps in her notebook—but the alleys looped back on themselves like mirrored equations. She turned left three times and found herself at the same canal. She marked a square and returned to it from the wrong side. Numbers blurred. Angles bent. Patterns betrayed her.

She hated it. She loved it.

Because the labyrinth wasn't hers alone anymore. It was everywhere, outside her skull, drawn across the city like a riddle written in stone and water.

On the steps of a church, a man in a plague doctor mask leaned against a column. His beaked face glistened with rain, lenses blank. Zara hurried past, only to glance back and find the steps empty.

On a bridge near the Rialto, a line of children in skeletal masks stood shoulder to shoulder, staring into the canal. None moved as she crossed. None blinked.

Her throat tightened. She pressed her gloved hand deeper into her pocket, holding the burn.

The resonance pressed harder here. Cassian's storm muttered at the edge of her thoughts. Naia's crown weighed against her ribs.

And always, faint and silken, Thane's voice curved through the tether, amused, waiting.

♦ ♦ ♦

Naia's walk through Venice was a pilgrimage through silence. Carnival's revelers turned their masks as she passed, but their movements were too exact, too rehearsed. Children in skeletal costumes bowed, their porcelain faces blank of joy. Naia felt the weight of expectation pressing on her shoulders like the crown itself, each step forward a judgment she did not want to pass. She had been raised for command, but not for trust, and the chain that hummed inside her ribs felt less like unity and more like a sentence.

Naia drifted through Venice's fog-draped streets as if moving through a dream of ruin. The silence was heavy, broken only by distant laughter that ended too sharply. Her cloak gathered the damp air, her every step ringing with the crown's invisible weight. The Carnival's masks turned toward her as if awaiting judgment, and she hated them for it. She had been trained for command, not for trust, and she feared the chain might demand both.

Venice was a city alive with masks, and every mask stared at her.

She stopped in a narrow alley where laundry hung frozen stiff across windows. A mask dangled among the clotheslines, feathers tattered by wind, its painted mouth grinning wide. No one reached for it. No one claimed it.

The city wore too many faces. And not all of them belonged to the living.

♦ ♦ ♦

Cassian Wolfe hated the city before he even stepped into it.

The moment his boots struck the dock, the storm surged under his skin. The air was damp, charged, alive with salt, and it found every fracture in him. Sparks feathered across his fingertips. He shoved them into his coat pockets, trying to look like just another traveler. But no traveler carried thunder in his chest.

The blackout had stripped Venice of its noise. The revelers were fewer, their costumes half-complete, their music muted by silence between notes. The city smelled of wax and wet stone. Candlelight shimmered in windows, but entire streets slept in shadow.

257

He walked them anyway, because the resonance tugged at him like a leash.

The chain had grown heavier since Maine. Stronger. He could feel it each night when he closed his eyes, Zara's logic brushing against him, Naia's crown pressing iron into the tether. Here in Venice, the pull sharpened until it throbbed against his ribs. It was dragging him toward something he wasn't ready for.

Cassian ducked into a narrow alley, then froze. Ahead of him, a figure stood motionless under an arch: a mask of gold with black plumes rising, cloak heavy around its frame. The eyes behind the mask caught light—but too much light, as if reflecting a storm not present. Cassian's hand twitched. Lightning licked his skin. The figure tilted its head, then stepped back into shadow, vanishing into the city's folds.

He clenched his jaw. Venice was a maze of masks, and he had no patience for games.

♦ ♦ ♦

Across the city, Naia Morrigan moved with quieter steps.

She carried herself as if the blackout did not exist, as if Carnival had been lit for her alone. Her cloak trailed like royal train, her head high though no crown was visible. The monastery had prepared her for solitude, but the chain denied it. Every step in Venice pressed more weight into her bones, dragging her toward others.

The Carnival unsettled her. She remembered pageants in Dublin, parades that blurred faith with revelry, but this was different. The blackout had starved the city. Its masks felt less like celebration and more like a funeral procession. Figures drifted across bridges, candlelight glinting off porcelain faces, but the air behind them was too silent. Their laughter did not warm the street.

Naia's hand brushed the wall of a canal-side building. The stone felt damp, alive. She closed her eyes, steadying herself against the crown's pressure. The chain tugged stronger here. Each link hummed, sharper, louder, insistent.

Venice itself was calling them.

♦ ♦ ♦

The chain thrummed so hard Zara thought it might drag her to her knees.

Cassian had stepped out of the shadows, sparks feathering under his coat, storm grinding against control. Naia stood on the opposite side of the square, cloak trailing like a coronation robe, her gaze iron-sharp. Between them, Zara held her ground near the lion pillar, notebook clutched to her chest.

Her hand betrayed her.

The glyph burned hot enough to blister. She felt the leather of her glove heating, the seams tightening. She pressed her hand hard into her side, trying to hide it in the folds of her coat. But the burn seared through, golden lines pushing against her skin like they wanted to be seen.

Cassian's eyes narrowed, his storm hissing louder. Naia's gaze cut across the square, too perceptive, too sharp.

Zara's pulse spiked. She flexed her fingers inside the glove, desperate to cool the fire, but it only burned brighter. The resonance fed it. Every heartbeat of the chain pressed more light into her palm.

Not now. Not here.

The air around her shimmered faintly. She yanked her notebook tighter to her chest, angling her body so the pillar's shadow masked her hand. If either of them saw—if they realized her glyph was different—everything could fracture before it even began.

Cassian shifted closer, storm crackling at the edge of sight. Zara's throat clenched. She imagined the burn flaring through her glove in the next instant, exposing her.

"Cold tonight," she forced out, voice flat, her other hand gesturing vaguely at the candles guttering on the basilica steps. It was nonsense, but it drew their eyes away for a breath.

Naia did not answer. Her crown pressed harder, suspicion threading her stillness.

Zara's glove slipped. For one terrifying heartbeat, the glyph's golden lines glowed through leather, faint but real.

Cassian's head snapped toward her.

Zara dropped her notebook. Papers scattered across the stones, skittering in the wind. She dove after them, heart hammering, glove hidden under her sleeve as she scrambled. She let the storm of paper distract them—Cassian crouching to pin one sheet with his boot, Naia's cloak fluttering as she bent to lift another.

By the time she gathered the last page, her hand was buried deep again, the glow smothered.

"Careless," Naia said, holding out the sheet she had caught. Her voice was neither kind nor cruel, only heavy with judgment.

Zara took it with shaking fingers. "I have too many patterns in my head."

Naia's eyes lingered on her a moment longer before she turned away. Cassian grunted, storm muttering under his skin, gaze already pulled toward the canal.

Zara exhaled slowly, clutching the notebook against her ribs. Her hand still burned, but at least the glove held. For now.

The chain thrummed again, harder, as if amused by her failure to control it.

They found each other in San Marco.

The square was half-dark, its lamps long dead. Candles guttered along the steps of the basilica, their flames bending in the February wind. A scattering of masked revelers moved like ghosts across the flagstones, their costumes tattered by blackout burn city.

Zara stood near the lion pillar, notebook clutched to her chest. The glyph under her glove seared, threatening to burn through the leather. She pulled the glove tighter, pressing her hand into her side so no one could see.

The resonance throbbed. Chains strung taut. She felt them before she saw them.

Cassian stepped out from an alley, shoulders tense, storm sparking under his coat. His eyes caught hers across the square, and the tether snapped hard enough she gasped. He flinched, sparks lighting his knuckles before he shoved his hands deeper into his pockets.

Naia appeared on the opposite side, cloak trailing, crown heavy though invisible. Her gaze swept the square like judgment. The chain hummed harder, dragging them together whether they wished it or not.

None of them spoke. None of them dared.

Zara forced her expression calm, hiding the panic clawing at her. If they saw the glyph burn—if they knew what was written into her skin—everything would fracture. She pulled her glove higher, turning slightly so the lion shadow masked her. The burn flared anyway, hot as betrayal.

Movement in the crowd caught her eye. A jester mask, feathers curling, slipped between revelers with a grin too sharp. Eryx. She knew it before he even laughed. The sound was quick, bright, mocking, darting through the tether like static.

"Nice of you to find the party," his voice brushed across them, though his body vanished into the crowd. A hand tipped his mask once before he melted back into the labyrinth of Venice. The square should have emptied after midnight, but the masks multiplied.

One moment there had been only a handful of revelers drifting past; the next, a dozen more stood in the shadows, their painted faces turned toward the heirs. Gilded grins. Crimson tears. Black plumes bending in the wind. Their bodies swayed to a music no instrument played, their hands clapped without sound.

Zara's chest tightened. The glyph under her glove seared hot enough to numb her fingers.

Cassian's storm snapped along his arms, sparks lighting the air. "They're not real."

"They are real enough to be watching," Naia answered, voice low but steady. Her crown pressed like a chain through her ribs, iron anchoring her against the rising dread.

The masks turned as one, empty panes gleaming in candlelight.

One fell from a balcony and struck stone with a brittle crack. It left no shards—only a smear of black ash that the wind lifted and erased.

Eryx's laugh crackled again, quick and mocking, darting through the resonance like a spark across static. *Not all masks hide the same thing*, his voice teased, and then it was gone, leaving only echoes.

Selene's shadow appeared in the canal, stretched by ripples. Her reflection moved when she did not, lips curved in a whisper that carried no sound. Zara felt a chill as if the chain itself had frozen. Cassian's storm dimmed, his sparks swallowed by a sudden hush. Naia's crown weighed heavier, dragging at her breath. Selene's presence was reminder enough: death walked with them, whether or not she stood among them in flesh. The reflection lingered until the water stilled, and then her eyes faded into blackness, leaving only silence.

Selene's presence rippled through the canal like frost on glass. Her reflection was a shadow layered on the water, eyes glinting with obsidian calm. She said nothing, yet her silence was heavier than words, a reminder that death lingered close, even here. Zara shivered under the weight of it, Cassian's storm faltered, and Naia's crown pressed heavier. Selene did not need to step ashore to remind them she was part of the chain.

The heirs stood together, though none of them had chosen it. The chain had dragged them into formation.

The laughter of the masked figures warped—longer, sharper, breaking into silence. One stepped forward, tilting its head. Another followed, then another. Their movement was too precise, too synchronized.

Watcher infiltrators.

Between the clapping and the hush, they lingered—one heartbeat, two—drawing a slow breath as the silence widened.

The Watchers made theatre of the heirs. A line of masked figures clapped in perfect unison without sound, their motions too precise to be human. One mask followed the trio through alleys, always ten paces behind. When Zara raised her hand, it raised its own. When Cassian's sparks flared, the mask tilted its head as if in admiration. Naia could not bear its mimicry; she quickened her pace, but still it followed, porcelain grin widening with each turn. When the chain dragged them further south, the mask finally stopped. Its smile cracked until shadow spilled through, a silent promise that the performance was not over.

The Watchers turned the city into theatre. One mask broke from the chorus and followed them, keeping ten paces behind. Its steps echoed theirs, its head tilted at the same angle as Naia's, its arm lifted when Zara's glove shifted. Cassian's storm flared and the mask froze, porcelain face gleaming with reflected sparks. Then, with deliberate slowness, it clapped once, the sound hollow as a coffin lid. The others copied, silent applause that chilled the air. They were not merely watched. They were performed.

Above the square, thunder rolled though no storm touched Venice. Zara felt the glyph burn until visions seared behind her eyes: chains stretching across the oceans, binding temples that cracked in far-off deserts, storms raging over mountains she had never seen. Naia staggered as her crown pulsed with echoes of Olympus itself, a memory of thrones trembling. Cassian's sparks flared skyward, and for an instant the heavens answered. The Hellenic Institute of Mythology was not only for them—it was for the world that shook beneath their steps.

Terror clawed through Zara's chest, raw and unreasoning. It was not the cold logic of dread, nor the sharp sting of panic—this was deeper, older, an instinct that told her to run though the chain held her fast. The silent applause of the masks became unbearable, a theatre of shadows that promised they were not just being watched, but condemned. Her mind screamed that this was no longer performance. It was judgment, and terror was its language.

The masks did not only watch; they imitated. One figure followed them ten paces back, copying every movement with eerie precision. When Cassian's storm flared, the mask tilted its head as though savoring the sparks. Naia felt her skin crawl when it clapped once—sharp, hollow—then froze in silence as the others mirrored it. The heirs moved faster, but the figure kept pace until the chain yanked them southward. Only then did its porcelain face crack into a grin too wide to be human.

Zara's pulse spiked. She pressed her notebook against her chest, glove clamped tight over her palm. The glyph inside her hand beat faster, as if answering theirs.

The masks closed in, surrounding the basilica steps. Candlelight bent against them, flames guttering low. The air thickened until every breath tasted of salt.

Naia raised her chin, eyes hard. "We do not run."

But the chain thrummed different now. Not chaotic, not random—it tugged. Southward. Away from the square.

Cassian stiffened, storm answering the pull. "Something wants us gone."

Zara felt it too. The resonance was not retreating. It was guiding.

The masks pressed closer. Fingers twitched beneath sleeves. Painted mouths cracked in smiles that weren't smiles.

And then the chain yanked.

Zara stumbled forward, nearly falling. Naia caught her elbow. Cassian cursed, sparks snapping from his boots against the flagstones. The resonance pulled all three of them toward the southern arcades, past the basilica, down an alley that wound between shuttered windows and fog.

The masks followed. Silent. Patient.

They ran. Not from fear, not entirely, but because the tether would not let them stand still. The chain burned in their chests, dragging them through alley after alley, across bridges slick with frost, until the square was far behind.

Lanterns thinned. Water lapped against stone. A bell tolled once, then again, echoing too long.

A pale mask drifted between pilings, facedown. Without wind, it rolled over, empty eyes catching the lanternglow—then slipped under, as if something beneath had turned it to look.

The heirs stopped only when the resonance slackened.

They stood before a gate.

It rose from the fog like a fortress carved into the city itself: ironwork latticed with symbols worn by centuries, its arch etched with words half-erased by time. Behind it, a courtyard stretched dark, the silhouette of towers rising faint against moonlight.

The Hellenic Institute of Mythology.

Zara's breath caught. She had seen sketches of it in old texts—fragments of floor plans, mentions in forgotten papers—but never whole, never here. The resonance vibrated harder than ever, pressing the glyph in her palm to the edge of pain.

Cassian's storm growled low, uneasy. Naia's crown pressed heavier, as if recognizing the threshold.

The masks had not followed this far.

For a moment, the only sound was water lapping against stone and their own ragged breathing.

Naia placed a hand against the gate, her voice solemn. "The chain has brought us here."

Cassian scowled, sparks dying reluctantly. "Then it's not finished with us."

Zara pulled her glove tighter, hiding the glow seeping through the seams. The glyph burned so hot it felt alive. She pressed it hard against her side and said nothing.

Above them, in the shadows of the courtyard beyond, a single lantern flickered to life.

The Hellenic Institute of Mythology was awake.

Cassian snarled low. Naia's lips pressed into a line. Zara said nothing.

Then the canal rippled.

Selene's reflection shimmered across the black water, shadows layering into her shape for only a moment. She did not speak. She only looked, eyes dark as obsidian, and the cold she carried with her slid into the tether. Zara's breath hitched. Cassian's storm faltered. Naia's crown pressed harder.

The square held its breath.

Venice closed around them.

The masks multiplied. Figures crowded the edges of the piazza, their eyes too still behind painted porcelain. Some laughed, but the laughter had no breath. Some clapped, but their hands made no sound. Zara's pulse raced. She knew—she knew—not all of them were human.

The Watchers were here.

Not directly, not unveiled. But in the silence between Carnival songs, in the way masks tilted their heads too precisely, in the flicker of wrong light across painted eyes, the Watchers had slipped into Venice. Hidden among masks, they needed no disguises.

Cassian's storm surged, his control fraying. Naia lifted her chin higher, crown anchoring the tether. Zara bit the inside of her cheek, forcing her face into calm as fire burned through her palm. She would not reveal it. She could not.

The chain thrummed, binding them in the square though none of them stepped closer. They did not trust each other. They did not even fully believe yet. But Venice was a stage, and it had drawn them into the same scene whether they wished it or not.

A bell tolled midnight. Its echo stretched too long, warped, as though the city itself rang hollow. Candles flickered in windows. Masks turned in unison.

Zara shivered. Venice was not merely a place. It was alive. Watching. Waiting.

And though the heirs did not yet move as one, the city had bound them together.

The City of Masks had chosen its audience.

♦ ♦ ♦

# CHAPTER XVI
# THE CHAINS COMPLETE

Venice—February 22, 2026

The storm had left Venice bruised.

Blackouts rolled through the lagoon city like a fever that wouldn't break. Lamps flickered and died. Shop shutters hung crooked, glass webbed from pressure waves that no one could fully explain. Gondolas moved without song—oars dipping in silence, the water black as lacquer. Whole neighborhoods breathed by generator light, then fell back into darkness, like a chest struggling for air.

It was here, in a city that knew a thousand versions of drowning, that twelve heirs of the old thrones stepped onto the same stone at the same time.

None of them were ready for the others to be real.

♦ ♦ ♦

Leo Alekos reached the fondamenta first, boots slick on the wet stone. The canal smelled like copper and rain and city rot; under it all, something wild, something like ocean. His glyph—Poseidon's mark—throbbed beneath his sleeve, a steady, tidal ache. He had felt the others for weeks, flickers at the edge of sleep, a tug at the base of the skull when lightning marched across the horizon. But a tug was one thing. A person standing ten paces away, watching back, was another.

He didn't have to turn to feel her. He did anyway.

Zara Kane stood between a pair of shuttered stalls. The abandoned observatory's dust hadn't washed completely from the seams of her coat, and she wore that fact like a choice. Her eyes were not hard, not kind—just awake. She saw everything. Leo lifted a hand. She didn't wave back; she tucked her right hand under her arm instead, hiding a palm that had not stopped stinging since the vault in the hills. The burn was small, almost invisible unless the light caught it, but it pulsed to the same rhythm as the world's new silence.

Across the canal, the bell of San Zaccaria tolled once and stopped, sound swallowed. Selene Marino appeared next, black hair damp with mist, Naples' catacombs still clinging to the angle of her shoulders. When she glanced at Leo and Zara, the air around the three of them felt colder by a single, deliberate degree.

Kai Watanabe slid from the gloom soon after, moving with the listening posture of someone who lived by pitch and resonance. A faint, impossible beam of daylight skimmed the underside of the clouds when he exhaled, and then was gone.

Naia Morrigan came in a velvet coat the color of old wine, chin high. Even when she stood alone, there was the sense of a procession about her. The weight of Hera's line was a set of invisible epaulettes; her gaze carried judgment like a burden she did not relish but would not put down.

Damien Holt walked as if an enemy might turn any corner. He kept his fists loose, his jaw tighter, his eyes never on one thing for long. Every step felt like it belonged to a field that had once had a name and a map and now only had ghosts.

Ayla Solberg had wind in her hair though the night was still. Her boots were laced as if for a climb, not a party. She looked at the water the way Northmen once looked at fjords—like a path that sometimes lied.

Isla Damaris smelled faintly of smoke and iron filings. There was a forge-callus on the thumb of her right hand that caught lamplight like a coin edge. Even the metal bollards along the dock seemed to angle themselves to listen.

Thane Virelli arrived with a lateness that felt like choreography. He came ribboned in shadow, a handsome boy cut too exactly to be comfortable to look at, and when his eyes drifted over the rest of them—curious, amused, almost tender—something else inside those eyes drifted, too, like silt in deep water.

Eryx Draven hopped a chain and landed lightly, hands in the pockets of a jacket that had too many zippers to be practical. He scanned sightlines, counted exits, smiled like he had decided to like everyone and no one at once.

Lysandra Korr stepped from behind a stack of crates with the patience of a field in winter. She was not dramatic. The stones underfoot felt steadier with her standing on them.

Cassian Wolfe came last, shoulders set against a sky that seemed to remember him. He paused at the edge of the fondamenta; a thin, foxbright fork of lightning walked the cloud rim and folded itself away as if it had been checking his pulse.

They formed a circle by not forming one. Their chains—those invisible lines of force that had been tugging them toward and away from one another for months—thrummed at the same frequency for the first time. That note was not pleasant. It was not meant to be.

No one spoke.

The city did it for them. A generator coughed and died. The dark pressed closer.

◆ ◆ ◆

A door rasped open.

Zara clocked the face from the university headshot she hadn't dared click open—spectacles catching lamplight like coins.

"You made it," Dr. Makris said, her voice steady as the storm outside. "Not all do." She stood in a low doorway, lamplight turning the lenses of her spectacles to gold coins. She wore a black wool coat and the posture of someone who had argued long and often with men who ran committees and won anyway. Her hair was pinned back as if it intended to escape and she had, repeatedly, told it not to.

Leo expected marble halls and columns. Instead, Eleni led them through a side entrance into a corseted corridor of the Hellenic Institute of Mythology that had been starved of budget and respect for decades. Shelves bowed under the weight of improperly cataloged scrolls. Marble torsos lay in straw like beached whales. A crate stenciled with "FRAG. 0—PROVEN. PENDING" had a coffee mug perched on it where a paperweight should have been.

"Director?" Naia said, the title half-question, half-glove thrown.

Eleni nodded once. "Director. Though for most of my career, 'woman who kept the lights on with duct tape and threats' would have been more accurate. After Halloween, the calls changed tone." She pushed her glasses up with a knuckle. "Now the world asks me what's happening. I have questions of my own. For once, I suspect we can help each other."

They reached a final door, the wood burned by the long fingernails of time and neglect. Eleni slipped a key from a chain around her neck. For a heartbeat she did not use it. Her mouth thinned.

"Please understand," she said without turning. "I do not bring people into this room. I do not bring anyone into this room. Until the storm, I would have denied this room existed. The storm rewrote more than weather maps."

She unlocked the door.

It was an old storage chamber, long sealed and forgotten.

Rusting shelves leaned under the weight of dust and disuse, stacked with spare bulbs, cracked crates, and toppled plinths no one had touched in decades. The stone walls carried a faint vibration, as if the storm had shaken something awake within them.

In one corner of the chamber stood a small vault, half-buried behind boxes draped in cloth that might once have been white and had since become a geography of stains. The air around it felt… pressurized. Not heavy. Just—aware.

This was the vault—the one in all the visions, the place that had been tugging and leading them the entire time.

Eleni stepped closer and laid her hand on the vault's frame.

"No one recognized the pattern until the storm. The ancients recorded an Orb not built but bound—a vessel meant to carry what should never have been loosed."

She pulled back the cloth to reveal what she now believed to be that Orb.

It was black in the way deep space is black—less a color than an invitation to fall. Not polished. Not faceted. Its surface drank light and returned it grudgingly through hairline veins that moved when you were not looking at them. The shape was almost a sphere and not interested in becoming more perfect than that. It pulsed.

Not like a machine. Like a heart that had learned patience.

Kai inhaled through his teeth. "There's a note," he whispered. "Under here."

Isla leaned closer, breath fogging. "It's pulling on the metals in the shelving," she said, surprised at the certainty of her own voice. "Like heat warps air."

"It was excavated near what we've called Fragment Zero," Eleni said, as if reading from an internal catalog card to keep from feeling too much of anything else. "A site in the Aegean with strata… that make no sense. It sat since then. Then Halloween. Then the hum started. Then the lights went out. I do not believe in coincidence." She folded the cloth neatly, an act of control. "I suspect you are why it woke. Or what it was waiting for."

Damien braced his hands on his hips to stop them from shaking. "What do you need us to do?"

"Understand it," Eleni said. "Then decide what to do with understanding."

"That isn't an instruction," Eryx said, but there was no mockery in it. Only fear masked as swagger.

"No," Eleni said. "It's a request. I am not a priest; I don't give absolution. I am a historian. I ask the dead to speak. I think this speaks. I would prefer it speak to you first."

Her gaze moved around the ring of them, weighing who would go first and seeing, to her credit, where that decision did not belong to her. She inclined her head, a director who knew when to cede the stage.

The twelve looked at each other.

Leo stepped forward.

◆ ◆ ◆

When his palm met the Orb, the world changed shape around the point of contact.

The air swelled; the floor heaved like deck planking under a surprise swell; a column of sea-green light climbed the dust into the rafters and burned a thread through the paint. Leo's glyph avalanched up his arm in bright tide-marks. Somewhere not-here but unmistakably present, waves hit stone with the ecstatic violence of a storm agreeing with itself.

Outside, every gondola line in sight snapped taut in unison and then went slack as if some great creature had passed under the canal and brushed them with its back.

Leo snatched his hand away, eyes wild, hair damp with sweat he had not earned. The Orb did not chase him. It settled, offended and delighted in equal measure.

Zara stepped into his place before anyone could ask her to.

She pressed her hand to the black and expected pain. She got something worse—clarity. Lines raced into being in her head: star paths that used to map gods, ley lines disguised as aqueducts, trade routes that were not commerce but choreography. The column that blasted from the Orb was not gold, not exactly; it was the color of problems revealing their shapes. Zara's glyph bit her palm and glowed across her wrist with Athena's cold grace.

On the other side of the world, in Cairo, scaffolding rattled at the same instant the muezzin's call paused and resumed, one breath late. In a lab with no windows, a seismograph ticked a signature that had no place in any table.

Zara pulled her hand away and hid it under her coat, fighting the urge to look. A dull heat crawled across the old burn in her palm. Something there was noticing the Orb, or the Orb was noticing it. She smoothed her sleeve and said nothing.

Selene touched the sphere as if it might bite her and stood while it decided not to. The lights in the vault guttered, not out, but inward, and shadows ran down the walls like water. The column that rose was night. In Naples, in passages mortals should have closed and never did, bones sighed against one another as if remembering a dance. Selene lifted her hand and the dark went back where it belonged, chastened but not sorry.

Kai laid two fingers on the Orb like a musician checking a tuning fork. The column that answered was a chord you might hear at dawn on the day a new instrument gets invented. A thousand grids half a world away found the same frequency for just a moment, Tokyo streetlamps blinking in time as if a conductor had raised a hand behind the sun.

Naia's palm was regal, measuring. Bells rang in Dublin with no rope pulled. The column was crown-light. Wherever she went, rooms had always wanted to arrange themselves around her; the Orb did not arrange—it acknowledged. She drew back with her chin higher and her doubts heavier.

Damien slapped his hand to the black like you slap a stallion you mean to ride or fight. The column that erupted was percussion—a heartbeat that had learned to be a war drum. In Marseille, a fissure traced itself across the face of a stone set up to remember men whose names Damien could list faster than laughter. The stone smoked and did not crack further.

Ayla went still, gathered herself, then reached. A skin of frost slicked the metal shelving; a draft thread its way along the floor though the door was shut tight. Somewhere in Norway, wind changed direction and old snow slid, choosing a new resting place.

Isla touched the Orb like an apprentice asked to hold a master's hammer for the first time. Sparks guttered along the edges of the shelving; every screw turned a fraction as if reconsidering its commitments. Forges that had been cold since Santorini's nights were not needed hummed with the memory of flame.

Eryx's fingers dragged. The column was quicksilver, a liar's mirror; the vault felt larger and shorter, closer and farther. In Rio, birds snapped from one flight pattern to three and back to one, as if receiving three conflicting orders and deciding to obey all of them.

Lysandra's hand brought the smell of rain into a room that had forgotten what green was. Hairline roots lifted at the baseboards where no soil lay. In Alexandria, a fig's subterranean fingers curled around the crack in a tomb and decided to keep it from widening for one more year.

Cassian touched, and the universe cleared its throat. Lightning stitched the seam of the clouds outside and didn't come down; thunder spoke its native language—old, amused, in no hurry. A tower in Maine that had sworn never to stand again felt a tremor that was not an insult but a memory.

Eleven hands. Eleven columns. Eleven answers from a thing that had not been asked a question in an age.

Thane looked at Eleni.

Eleni did not nod. She did not look away either.

Thane stepped forward as if onto a stage designed with his measurements in mind. He placed his hand on the Orb.

◆ ◆ ◆

Light came. The same as the others and not. His glyph woke with the bright, impossible generosity Aphrodite's line should have carried into a room—the ache of love that is a choice, not a compulsion. Everyone in the vault exhaled at once, relief and the first unguarded breath of the night.

Then the second thing arrived.

It came like an answer that had been waiting behind a door for years, barefoot, patient, unkind.

The column choked into shadow the way a sound catches and resolves into a second, lower note. The veins in the Orb squeezed and then inverted, a negative image revealed in a photographer's tray: black where light had been, a seam of darkness tracing itself from Thane's palm across the curve of the sphere.

The crack was not loud. Every chain in that room—seen and unseen—jerked.

Isla cried out as if she'd been stung. Selene stumbled and caught herself on a shelf that had the decency not to collapse. Zara's palm burned so suddenly she bit the inside of her cheek hard enough to taste iron rather than lift her sleeve. Damien shoved Eryx by reflex, and Eryx let himself be shoved, which was how you knew he was burned.

The column died. The room did not grow dark. It grew accurate.

Thane pulled his hand away as if from a stove he'd been certain wouldn't be hot. He looked at Eleni quickly, at Damien slower, at the floor last. For the first time that night, the beauty that had always been his perfect mask flickered.

"I didn't—" he began, and stopped because he did not know which word came next: mean to. Want to. Expect to. Fight to. His throat worked and found a version that would not betray him. "I touched it like you asked."

"No one asked you," Damien said, voice low enough that the words had edges. "We followed. You chose."

"We all chose," Naia said, not to defend him but to defend the room from shattering into too many arguments to mend. "Don't be a child."

"Don't be a queen," Damien snapped back, automatic, stupid, a shield. Regret tightened his mouth even before the last word evaporated. He didn't apologize. He didn't know how to in a way that mattered.

Eleni had gone bone pale. She collected herself one angle at a time: shoulders, jaw, eyes. "It cracked for none of you," she said. She was not asking a question. She knew the answer. She wanted to hear it rejected and understood it could not be. "Only you."

Thane couldn't look at anyone properly now, so he looked at the Orb, because a broken thing owed him less judgment than a person did. The crack did not ooze shadow. It sat like a closed eye in rest.

Something moved in the silence behind his heart.

*Child of choosing,* said a voice that was not a sound and not a thought and could be both forever. Not foe. Not heir. *Mine.*

Thane's knees almost failed him. Almost. He had learned, early, to give nothing to any audience he hadn't hired himself.

"Say something," Eryx said, too soft for mockery, too loud for prayer.

"It knew me," Thane said. He meant for it to sound like a joke, like an accusation, like a shrug. It sounded like a confession.

♦ ♦ ♦

Venice exhaled.

Lights that had been off surged, held, stuttered, and went down again. A woman pushing a grocery cart under a portico stopped and put her hand to her chest with no idea why. Somewhere on the far side of the lagoon, a dog howled, and another, and another until someone threw open a window and cursed them into silence. Water lapped with new insistence at the hulls of boats that had been empty and stayed empty, because there are nights when even thieves stay home.

The Institute trembled minutely, as if rediscovering how old its stones were.

"Again," Isla said, breathless, eyes bright not with delight but with the fierce, practical hunger of someone who had just seen how a mechanism wanted to move. "Not Thane. Not yet. The rest of us. Together."

Eleni shook her head once—No—and then, after counting something to herself, nodded. "Quickly," she said, horrified by her own permission and possessed by it. "Before the power fails again. Before I remember who I am supposed to be."

"Circles," Zara said. She did not reach for her palm. She did not look at it. "Order matters."

"Storm to sea to stone," Cassian said, understanding the old math of elements as if he had been born with it etched under his ribs. "Or sea to storm to stone."

"Or crown first," Naia said, defiant, because her line had been first too long to accept any other calculus without a fight.

"Not crown," Selene said, voice a twilight. "Grave. We start with what is honest."

"Honest is fire," Isla said.

"Honest is the way out," Eryx countered. "Trickster's prerogative."

"Honest is what grows back," Lysandra murmured.

Leo listened to them not as a parliament but as weather, and when the weather exhausted itself he said, "Honest is what keeps the city from flooding tonight. Storm to sea to stone."

Eleni watched them with a sensation she had never expected to feel again: the feeling of meaning assembling itself into a shape in front of her eyes. For all the years she had begged administrators to fund the work of naming what mattered, here were twelve arguments that mattered and needed no grant.

They reached, eleven hands and then twelve, not touching each other, touching what had dragged them into a vault and called it a chapel.

The Orb responded. Not in columns now, but in a halo that gathered itself from forked points: storm, sea, crown, harvest, forge, hunt, messenger, sun, grave, wisdom, love-that-was-and-wasn't, and something else—the thirteenth that refused a name. The light was not one color. It was one agreement.

The sound it made was the sound of chains drawing tight. Not shackles. Not prison. The sound a bridge cable makes when it accepts the weight it was built to carry.

Across the world, resonance answered like applause from balconies.

In Tokyo, the commuter line that had been delayed for hours rolled into a station with a sigh and a cheer and no one could tell you why precisely that moment felt like forgiveness.

In Cairo, a scaffolder set down his wrench and looked up because the metal under his hand had hummed like a throat clearing to speak. He laughed, though the joke was not one he understood.

In Rio, the birds returned to the line they'd abandoned and sat, suddenly content, like a choir finding its pitch.

In Dublin, bells rang, then stopped, then rang again, two tones arguing and reconciling.

In Santorini, a forge that had not been used since summer sent up a single curl of smoke that dissipated politely.

In Maine, the tower that should not stand not yet stood not yet, but it felt a hand on its bones and did not hate the hand.

"Enough," Eleni said, because directors exist to call a curtain, and if she did not claim the right to say when, something older would do it for her. "Enough."

They broke contact like swimmers surfacing. The light went out. The crack did not heal.

◆ ◆ ◆

No one spoke. Not because there was nothing to say, but because everything had become a thing you could be wrong about.

They trickled into the corridor like survivors of a birth. The Institute hummed underfoot. Somewhere, very far away and very near, a generator coughed and chose life again.

Eleni shut the vault door and leaned her forehead against the wood, just for a second, like a penitent. She turned back with her face composed and her eyes not.

"I will not pretend competence I do not possess," she said. "If any of you need ceremony, find a priest. If you want weapons, Damien will point you to someone who thinks steel still means what it used to. If you want answers, you will hate what I have to give. They are mostly better questions."

"That's… reassuring," Eryx said, because someone had to be the person who kept the room from freezing over entirely.

"It should be," Eleni said. "I am not here to rule you. I am here to witness. To warn. To measure. To remind you that the world has records, and it keeps them badly, and when you do a thing, it becomes harder to lie about it after. That is the function of an institute. We make lies more expensive."

"Then warn us," Naia said. "Properly."

Eleni glanced down the hall, as if checking whether the building itself would mind the next words. "Whatever that is," she said, nodding toward the closed door and the thing behind it, "it is not an artifact. It is not a battery. It is not a relic that will sit politely where we put it. It is a participant, and we keep pretending we are the subject of its study instead of the other way around."

"Plain speech," Damien said. "Please."

"It is alive," Eleni said. "And it remembers you."

"Remembers or recognizes?" Zara asked. She did not touch her palm. She did not acknowledge the way the burned glyph there had begun to prickle as if matching the rhythm of her heart to something more ancient than pulse.

"Yes," Eleni said. "Both."

"And Thane?" Leo asked. The question lifted all the other questions onto its back. He had not wanted to be the one to ask it. It had wanted him.

Eleni faced Thane, not unkind. "What did it do to you?" she asked. "Before you tell me what you did to it."

Thane swallowed. He had the look of someone walking along the edge of a roof and choosing, over and over, to pretend he was on a sidewalk. "It spoke," he said softly. "Or I heard something and my pride is big enough to call it speech."

"What did it say?" Selene asked, dusk and mercy.

Thane lifted his chin a fraction. He could lie without effort. He elected not to. "That I was not a foe. Not an heir. Its."

No one shouted. In the silence there were a dozen things: the scrape of a shoe on stone, the faint metal complaint of a shelf settling in the next room, the beat of Kai's pulse in his ears like a metronome that had not been turned off.

"Lovely," Eryx said after a moment. "A haunted bowling ball wants to adopt you."

"Eryx," Naia warned.

"What?" Eryx said, hands up. "It's either a joke or an argument; I only get paid to deliver one of those well."

"It cracked for him," Isla said, the engineer's mind leaving comfort to those who could make use of it. "Crack is how stress draws a map. If something recognizes him, it's because he carries a geometry the rest of us don't."

"Or because he is wrong," Damien said.

"Or because he is necessary," Zara said, and hated herself for saying it, and said it anyway because truth is not a democracy. "Those are not mutually exclusive."

"Enough," Cassian said, not loud but authoritative in the way thunder can be quiet and still promise you the rest of the sentence. "We will not solve this in a hallway with bad lighting and dust on the floor."

"The dust itself was historic—centuries layered, each mote a witness to forgotten truths," Eleni said, out of habit. Then she pinched the bridge of her nose and let the joke sit where it landed. "There are rooms upstairs. Not grand ones. I wasn't given many of those. But they lock and the windows open and my staff have gone home because I told them to well before any of you arrived. You can rest. Or not. No one will bother you."

"Your staff," Naia said, catching the plural like a rope. "Who knows we are here?"

"Fewer people than should," Eleni said. "More than I like." She hesitated, then added, "Professor Alexandros Stavros—field archaeology; good head, bad knees. Dr. Callista Theron—linguistics; the rare scholar who believes translation is betrayal and does it anyway. Dr. Nikolas Petrou—archives; he loves paper more than people and will therefore be useful. Dr. Helena Damaris—comparative mythology; she thinks all stories want to be neighbors. I sent them home with instructions to sleep and to ignore whatever their consciences tried to insist upon. They will not obey me. Good scholars don't. But they will be late to their disobedience."

"Can we trust them?" Leo asked.

"No," Eleni said with academic cheerfulness. "Of course not. That is not how trust works. But we can involve them carefully. And we can decide what to tell them and what to let them guess badly."

"Good," Eryx said. "I like a plan that includes lying."

"Lying is expensive," Eleni said. "Choose who pays."

♦ ♦ ♦

They climbed to a room that had once been a lecture hall and now looked like a library had spilled some of its more fragile feelings onto a table: atlases open to pages that had been annotated in pencil and fury, bundles of photographs clipped with paper that had rusted through the clips. Eleni lit two oil lamps on principle.

"Why lamps?" Ayla asked softly.

"Because the grid is a rumor tonight," Eleni said. "And because there is a certain kind of conversation one has more honestly by flame."

They took seats not by hierarchy but by accident. Leo at the corner of the table. Zara standing, because sitting would mean admitting the tremor in her right hand. Selene on a windowsill, looking at her reflection and seeing through it. Kai in a chair whose wobble he corrected by shifting his weight every few minutes, a small duet with furniture. Naia at the head of the table because furniture, like rooms, chose its own rulers whether we acknowledged the vote or not. Damien in a threshold, unable to be entirely in any room that had more than one exit. Ayla near the door with a hunter's dislike of being cornered. Isla with her elbows on the table as if ready to take it apart and see how it worked. Eryx wherever the sightlines were most interesting. Lysandra with her hands folded, patient as a field waiting for spring. Thane not opposite anyone; opposite everyone.

Eleni unrolled a map that had not been printed so much as argued into existence. Ink walked it in two languages—the one the world used now and the one the world had been taught to forget. Several places had been circled in a different hand. One of those circles was over the Aegean and had three question marks and the word "ZERO" written with the pressure of someone who had wanted to write something else and stopped herself.

"We need structure," Eleni said. "Not to chain you. To keep you from tearing each other apart under the pretense of being free. I propose we write down—now—what we will not do and what we must. The Institute will witness. Not judge. Craft. Record. Say the thing later the way it happened, not the way we want it remembered."

"What we will not do," Naia repeated. "Fine. I will start." She put both hands flat on the table. "We will not hand this city to anyone who wants to wear it as a crown. Not the Orb. Not men with weapons. Not us. I am not interested in being queen of rubble."

"Add: we will not pretend any of us is not dangerous," Selene said. "To others. To ourselves."

"We will not break Thane in half to see what is inside," Isla said. She didn't look at him when she said it. She looked at Damien.

Damien looked back and, to his credit, nodded. "We will not break Thane."

Thane closed his eyes for half a second. Then opened them. "We will not break Damien either," he said, deadpan, and because he gave them a good line, they took it, and something in the room unclenched.

"We will not treat knowledge like a dragon treats gold," Zara said, voice level. "We will not hoard it until it becomes useless. But we will not toss it from the backs of floats to impress a crowd either. We will choose what to say and when and to whom."

"We will not forget that the world is watching," Cassian said. "And that it is not wrong to watch."

Eryx scratched a column heading into the margin of the map: WILL NOT. He added a second: MUST.

"Must: return to the Orb at first light," Isla said. "Measure what changed. Map stress. Decide if a second crack can be prevented or is inevitable."

"Must: tell no one with a uniform we do not give a uniform ourselves," Eryx said. "Sorry, Director. I have bad manners around states."

Eleni's mouth curved. "You think I have not watched governments fall in love with artifacts from a distance and ruin them up close?" she said. "We will keep our own counsel."

"Must: stop assuming the Watchers are fools," Zara said. "They are patient. And they are listening."

The word dropped into the room like a coin into a fountain. No one had given them permission to name the enemy aloud tonight. They did not need permission.

"Must," Leo said slowly, surprised by the shape of what his mouth wanted to make, "stay together. I know we can't always be in the same room. But not again—not like Chicago. Not like the observatory. Not like—" He stopped, because there were too many nouns and the room did not have the width to hold them.

"Then write it," Naia said. "Say it. Sign it. Make it cost something if we break it."

Eleni slid a sheet from a folder and put it in the center of the table. She did not plan for rituals. She recognized them when they walked into the room anyway.

"Write," she said to Leo.

He wrote, slowly, the pen scratching like a small animal. We will not act alone when together is possible. He looked up. He did not apologize for the simplicity.

"Sign," Naia said, and signed. The others came after, even Damien, even Thane. When it reached Zara, she signed with her left hand because her right was busy not shaking.

Lysandra took the paper after Thane and set her palm on it gently. "There," she said. "Now it will be harder to burn."

"Very poetic," Eryx said.

"Very literal," Isla murmured. "Paper's different now."

They did not know whether to laugh. So they didn't. They breathed.

A tremor went through the building that had nothing to do with foundations. It was a sympathetic vibration—the kind that passes through a body when a note played far away agrees with the shape of your bones. The lamps fluttered. Kai's head lifted.

"The Orb," he said.

"Not breaking," Isla said. "Resonating. Like… it just learned a word."

"Or a name," Selene said.

"Or a promise," Cassian said.

Eleni looked at them as if taking a photograph she would try to develop for the rest of her life. "You understand what happened downstairs has already happened everywhere else," she said quietly. "It is not contained because we shut the door."

"We're not trying to contain it," Naia said. "We're trying to deserve it."

Thane looked at the door.

"You can go," Damien said, not unkindly, which meant perhaps more than an apology would have. "If you need to."

"I wasn't leaving," Thane said. He did not know until he said it that it was true. "I was counting."

"Counting what?" Eryx asked.

"How many times tonight I wanted to run," Thane said. "And how many times I didn't."

Silence accepted this as payment.

Zara's hidden glyph-burn seared awake, hotter than fire, echoing the secret she had concealed since the Watcher vault she thought briefly—now—and then the pain went from sparking to articulate. She pressed her hand flat on the table. The glyph under her skin flared and dimmed, a heartbeat answering a heartbeat.

She looked at Thane and, for once, did not think about strategy.

"At first light," she said, "we touch it again. Not one by one. Together. If it cracks farther, we will know the cost. If it heals—"

"It won't heal," Isla said, not with despair, with engineering. "Cracks don't heal. They redistribute."

"Good," Zara said. "Then maybe it's time something else carried weight for once."

"What else?" Leo asked.

"The lie," Zara said. "The one we keep telling ourselves about what we are."

"And what are we?" Thane asked, very softly.

"Not kings," Zara said. "Not weapons. Not accidents."

"Then what?" Eryx said, because every myth wants a line to print on a poster.

"Chains," Zara said. "Not to bind each other. To hold together what was broken."

"Bridges," Leo said at the same time.

They looked at each other.

"Both," Eleni said, with the relief of a teacher whose class has finally tripped over the answer with their own feet instead of being dragged. "Language is a net with more than one knot."

The lamps went out.

They didn't scream. A second later the emergency lights on the stairwell hummed to life, red and insufficient.

Downstairs, a pulse moved through the building like a drumbeat learned by a heart older than any human's. It did not ask permission.

Thane heard the voice again. It did not give him orders. It did not say his name. It said, with a patience that functions as a kind of cruelty, *Mine.*

He did not tell them. Not yet. He would. Perhaps. When he understood what word would come after mine in a sentence that could be survived.

♦ ♦ ♦

Night wrapped the canals. The blackout reached for the city and the city reached back. On a rickety balcony, a woman who had not cried since she was twelve let herself cry and did not ask why. On a barge, a boy pressed his ear to the hull and swore he could hear whales. In a police boat, two officers who no longer trusted their radios performed the old ritual of human cooperation: they looked at each other and decided to be brave.

On a line near a school, laundry snapped like flags.

On a table in a room full of lamps that were not on, a sheet of paper cooled with twelve names on it and the weight of a palm that had blessed it with the promise of being a harder thing to burn.

In a vault that was not a vault, light crawled across an Orb that had forgotten a great many things and remembered one, and the crack that crossed it did not heal and did not widen and did not sleep.

♦ ♦ ♦

At the window, Zara watched the lights move and not move and let the burn in her palm speak to her without words. She thought of the vault. Of the mark that had been a secret and felt, tonight, like a mirror. She did not know what it reflected.

At the threshold, Damien kept count of exits and reasons to use them and reasons not to and did not lie to himself about which column was winning.

Leo closed his eyes and felt water press against stone with the eagerness of a tide that has learned the path to a door.

Cassian stood still enough to make thunder impatient.

Ayla rubbed a knot out of her shoulder and cataloged every sound a building makes when it changes its mind about being only a building.

Isla flattened the map with both hands, as if a crease could be persuaded not to exist if you cared enough.

Eryx found a coin under the table and left it there because sometimes you don't take the sign; you let the next person have it.

Lysandra listened to the breath of a room full of people who had never learned how to breathe at the same time and smiled, tiny and real.

Kai hummed the note the Orb had made, under hearing, and it harmonized with the elevator motor in the shaft like two strangers recognizing each other in a station.

Thane looked at his hands and thought, not for the first time and not for the last: If I am a door, who opened me?

Eleni, who had given her life to the care of dead languages and unloved artifacts and had found herself, tonight, midwife to the living, blew out a lamp that had already died and said, to no one and

285

to the building and to a god she did not have a name for, "I'm watching."

Below them, the Orb pulsed once.

The chains did not tighten. They completed.

♦ ♦ ♦

And the world, which had been pretending for centuries not to believe in anything, felt the truth pass through it like a cable taking weight and did not break.

♦ ♦ ♦

# CHAPTER XVII
# THE LABYRINTH BENEATH

Venice, February 24, 2026


The blackout city still whispered above them, its lanterns faint against the dark. But beneath the Institute, where Zara walked with Kai and Isla, only the Codex glowed to mark the path.

Eleni's voice had been firm when she chose them. "Zara, you carry the Codex. Kai, your light may reveal what torches cannot. Isla, you know the bones of stone. The labyrinth belongs to you three."

The descent began in silence.

The spiral staircase twisted into the dark, its stone steps choked with dust and age. A hairline crack shivered across the ceiling; fragments of grit rained into Zara's hair. The Institute groaned around them, the sound too alive to be stone alone. None of them spoke. Not even Isla, who normally muttered under her breath when things got tense.

Zara led, holding the Codex fragment close to her chest like a compass. It pulsed faintly now—just enough to illuminate the crumbling walls with a soft, golden glow.

Kai walked just behind her, his bow ready but lowered, eyes flicking constantly to the edges of the passage. Every so often, he glanced up at the ceiling, as if half expecting it to collapse.

Isla brought up the rear, her hand trailing along the stone wall beside her. "There's something wrong with the stone here," she murmured. "It's not carved. It's grown."

Zara didn't respond. She'd noticed it too.

The crack in the Orb still pulsed in Zara's thoughts, each step into the labyrinth echoing the same wrong rhythm.

The labyrinth wasn't just underground—it was alive with old memory. The walls pulsed faintly as if breathing. Veins of shimmering silver ran through the stone, like starlight trapped in granite.

The path opened into a chamber.

♦ ♦ ♦

Round. Hollow. Carved by something older than tools. The air here was colder, not in temperature, but in weight. As if time moved slower.

The Codex fragment pulsed brighter.

Zara stepped into the chamber's center. Her boots echoed against the black stone floor. Twelve shallow depressions ringed the room, like empty sockets in a great eye.

Glyphs surrounded her.

Etched into the walls, carved into the ceiling—spirals, blades, waves, wings. Some she recognized from the scroll. Others were stranger.

Foreign.

Isla stepped beside her, peering at one of the sigils. "These aren't all Olympian."

Kai raised an eyebrow. "You're saying these came from outside the Pantheon?"

"I'm saying…" Isla traced one symbol with her fingertip. It burned faintly gold beneath her touch. "I don't think Olympus made this place."

A pause.

Zara said nothing, but inside her chest, her pulse quickened.

The Codex agreed. It shimmered again, casting reflections that rippled across the floor like water. The glyphs responded—lighting one by one in a slow, spiraling sequence around the room.

Then the floor vibrated.

Just slightly.

Enough to send fine dust falling from the cracks above them.

"Trap?" Kai asked, arrow notched in a blink.

"Or theatre," Eryx muttered, his grin stretched too tight. The joke fell flat, echoing too loudly in the chamber's suffocating hush.

"No," Zara said slowly. "It's a test."

The central platform rose.

It wasn't fast. It wasn't dramatic. Just a slow elevation—revealing a second spiral, this one carved not into stone, but into glass.

And inside it, suspended by nothing—

A second scroll.

The twin to the one Zara held.

For a long moment, no one moved.

Zara stepped forward first. The scroll hovered just above her reach, held inside the coiled glass spiral like a flame caught in time.

The Codex fragment in her hand pulsed wildly now, syncing with the scroll in the chamber.

"They're calling to each other," she whispered.

Kai didn't lower his bow. "That seems… not great."

"It's not bad either," Isla said. "They're trying to merge."

Zara glanced back at the glass spiral. "They want to become whole again."

She reached up—

And the glyphs on the walls ignited.

Twelve burned bright.

One—at the far edge of the chamber—stayed dark.

A missing seal.

Or a broken one.

The floor beneath them hummed with sudden power. The spiral glowed red-hot—then white-hot—then fell dark again as the scroll within it dropped.

Zara caught it in both hands.

◆ ◆ ◆

The moment she touched it, the world cracked.

Not physically.

Not with sound.

But with vision.

A torrent of memory surged through her.

A battlefield—sky split by lightning.

Twelve figures surrounded by enemies made of shadow and ash.

One turned against them.

One—

Zara staggered.

Kai was at her side instantly. "What happened?"

"I saw it again," she said. "The same vision as before. But clearer this time."

Isla's face was pale. "Was it him?"

Zara nodded. "The one they sealed away."

"Who?" Kai asked softly.

The word didn't land.

It lingered—uneasy, unanswered.

Zara looked down at the scrolls, then back at the dark glyph.

"Not a god," she whispered. "Something worse."

Kai's brows lifted. "Worse than a forgotten god?"

Zara didn't answer. She turned the two scrolls in her hands—now vibrating in perfect sync. When she brought them near each other, a golden line formed between them. Glyphs danced across it—symbols neither ancient Greek nor modern. Something older.

"The Codex was split," she murmured. "Not just broken. Torn. These are pieces of something meant to stay buried."

"They were sealed away," Isla whispered. "And we're unsealing them."

Zara looked up. "Maybe that's why someone betrayed them."

Kai frowned. "Who?"

Zara didn't respond.

Because deep inside her, something already knew.

A sound echoed through the chamber.

Not from the labyrinth behind them.

From beneath.

The floor glowed again.

Not gold.

Not white.

But black.

The dark glyph.

It had awakened.

The spiral that had stayed dormant now shimmered with a strange iridescent light—obsidian and oil and flame.

Zara backed away. "It's reacting to the merge."

The black glyph rose from the floor like smoke given shape—curling into a jagged symbol that throbbed with power.

Twelve.

One.

Thirteen.

The air dropped ten degrees in an instant. Isla shivered. "That's not Codex."

"No," Zara said. "That's Watcher."

Kai pulled an arrow to his cheek. "So is this when we run?"

Too late.

The ground split down the middle of the chamber.

The glyph ruptured.

And from the rift… came light.

Not golden. Not divine.

Watcher flame—blue and black, alive and dead, burning in silence.

From the crack, a figure began to rise.

It rose like breath from a dead world.

The flame had no heat. It moved like water and shadow, drifting upward from the shattered glyph in thin coils of midnight blue.

For a long breath, none of them spoke. Dust still hung in the air, each mote catching the Codex's glow as if the chamber itself waited for their answer.

The dust didn't just fall—it swirled, twisting into shapes that seemed almost human: chained silhouettes, drowned cities, fragments of lives the labyrinth had devoured. The vision left them frozen, breaths held, until Zara forced herself to move again.

The figure emerged slowly—first shoulders, then a head. It wasn't fully formed. More outline than body. A silhouette of fire given shape by hatred long sealed.

Zara stumbled back.

The scrolls in her hands pulsed again—hard. Violent. As if trying to reject the presence now entering the room.

Kai's arrow loosed.

It sailed through the air like a comet.

It passed straight through the figure's chest.

No resistance.

No sound.

The flames rippled.

Then reformed.

"I don't think it's solid," Kai muttered, already nocking another arrow.

"It's not meant to be," Isla said. "It's a projection. A memory. Maybe worse."

The figure looked up.

No eyes.

No face.

Just light, flickering across where humanity should have been.

Zara took a shaky breath. "It's watching us."

The figure stepped forward.

The floor didn't crack beneath its feet—it shimmered. The glyphs in the chamber glowed in response, flickering like old memories trying to resist being remembered.

Zara held the twin scrolls close to her chest. "It's reacting to these."

The figure stopped.

Then, slowly, it raised its arm.

The flame coiled along its limb, threading up toward the ceiling. It didn't strike. It didn't scream.

It drew.

Not a weapon.

A symbol.

In fire.

One line. Then another.

A spiral. A chain. A triangle. A broken circle.

The chamber trembled.

"What is that?" Isla breathed.

Zara's voice came low. "A name."

Glyphs burst across the walls. The Codex symbols flared in agony—flickering, fading, returning, then blinking out entirely.

The fire on the figure's arm completed the final line.

The symbol hovered in the air.
And beneath it, a single word formed.
HEIR.

♦ ♦ ♦

Isla's face paled. "It's looking for someone."
"No," Zara said. "It's claiming someone."
Kai shifted slightly. "Claiming what?"
Zara stared into the fire.
"Us."
The fire flared brighter.
Then snapped into stillness.
The figure lifted its head again.
Then turned—to Zara.
She didn't move.
The scrolls in her hands felt heavier now, like they were being pulled toward the flame. Not physically, but spiritually. Like the bond that once sealed this place wanted to reopen.
The figure raised its other arm.
The chain on the symbol above it cracked.
Zara stepped back. "It's trying to unbind the seal."
Kai loosed another arrow—this one wrapped in silver wire.
It struck.
And for the first time—
The figure flinched.
Only slightly.
But it staggered.
And the glyph above it pulsed red.
Zara seized the moment.
She dropped to her knees and slammed both scrolls into the floor of the chamber—pressing them against the mirrored glyphs etched into the center stone.
"Help me!" she shouted.
Isla didn't hesitate.
She moved beside Zara, placing her hand over the nearest seal.
Kai fired again—buying them seconds.
Zara felt the scrolls respond.

The glyphs surged with light—gold and silver, merging into white.

The flame figure roared—not with sound, but with pressure. The air bent inward, heatless and crushing.

Zara forced her voice through the weight. "We were never supposed to open it—this whole place was a warning. A lock. And we're holding the key."

"Then let's shut the door," Isla growled.

Zara slammed the scrolls together.

The chamber exploded in light.

It wasn't fire.

It wasn't magic.

It was memory—weaponized.

Twelve glyphs blazed to life. The missing one sparked. The Watcher's mark shrieked in resistance.

The figure reeled.

It twisted violently in the air, flames flaring, arms outstretched.

Then it shattered.

No scream. No final word.

Only silence.

◆ ◆ ◆

The light faded.

Smoke hung low in the chamber.

Zara's breath came in gasps.

She looked down.

The scrolls were fused now—no longer separate artifacts, but one.

A single scroll.

Whole again.

The Codex Fragment was complete.

But it trembled.

Like a heartbeat forced into rhythm.

◆ ◆ ◆

Isla stared at the restored Codex. "What did we just do?"

Zara didn't answer.

Kai stepped beside them, bow lowered. "Did we win?"

Zara looked up slowly.

The glyphs were still glowing.

All of them.

Even the broken one.

"I don't think this was a victory," she said. "I think it was… a signal."

Isla frowned. "To who?"

Zara stood.

And pointed at the far wall—where new words were carving themselves into the stone, letter by glowing letter.

WE ARE WATCHING.

WE REMEMBER.

THE HEIR WALKS.

◆ ◆ ◆

Kai exhaled slowly. "I'm really starting to hate cryptic walls."

Zara tucked the scroll into her satchel.

"We need to go," she said quietly.

Isla hesitated. "Shouldn't we destroy it?"

Zara shook her head. "You can't destroy what was sealed in blood and prophecy. All you can do is carry it… and hope you're strong enough not to fall."

Isla looked at her sideways. "That supposed to be comforting?"

"No."

They turned back toward the tunnel, toward the spiraling stairway that led them above.

But as they crossed the threshold—

The flames ignited again.

Not in heat. Not in fury.

In warning.

The same symbol blazed across the ceiling one last time.

Twelve.

One.

Thirteen.

They didn't speak as they climbed the winding stair.

The chamber's echo still hummed beneath their skin. Every step away from the Watcher's glyph felt like stepping through molasses—thick, resistant. The Codex Fragment burned faintly inside

Zara's satchel, not with heat, but with memory. It pulsed in time with her heartbeat, and each throb whispered in a language too old for words.

When they reached the upper level of the ruins, the sky had already begun to change.

Night hadn't fallen yet, but it was close.

The clouds above the observatory spiraled unnaturally, a slow vortex of gray and silver that rotated with glacial patience.

Isla glanced upward and stopped walking. "That's new."

Kai followed her gaze. "Weather pattern?"

"No," Isla said. "That's not weather. That's… echo."

Zara pulled the scroll from her satchel.

The Codex gleamed—duller than before, as if what it had done below had cost it something. Some part of itself.

Or of her.

Kai moved beside her. "So, we have the fragment. We didn't die. But I don't feel like we're closer to answers."

Zara stared at the horizon. "Maybe we're not supposed to have answers yet. Maybe we're just supposed to carry the questions long enough to understand them."

"Cryptic," Isla muttered. "You're starting to sound like the Codex."

Zara gave a small, tight smile. "Let's hope that's not contagious."

They moved toward the outer ridge of the observatory where the glyphs had first begun appearing.

The outer stone was fractured now, as if the structure itself had been reacting to what lay beneath. The old mosaics that once told stories of Athena's wisdom were charred black around the edges, as though burned by truths too dangerous to speak aloud.

Then Zara stopped walking.

At the base of the last wall, a new glyph had appeared.

No flame.

Just a carved mark—like it had always been there, waiting to be uncovered.

It wasn't a glyph they recognized.

Three spirals.

One inverted triangle.

And beneath them: a broken chain.

Kai frowned. "That wasn't here before."

"No," Zara said. "It followed us."

Isla drew closer. "It's etched into the foundation. It's older than the stone."

Kai pulled a small blade from his belt and traced the air over it. "Then how did it get there now?"

Zara didn't answer.

The Codex fragment in her hand trembled.

Then the glyph on the wall pulsed—

Once.

A wave of pressure pushed outward. Not physical—but temporal.

Zara staggered.

And suddenly—

She was elsewhere.

A city in ruins.

But not like the vision before.

This one… was alive.

Fire ran through the streets, not with destruction, but with purpose. Each flame marked with glyphs. Some Zara recognized—Poseidon, Athena, Hades. Others felt stranger, older. Lost.

Figures moved through the smoke—twelve of them. Each bearing power. And at their center stood another.

A man wrapped in gold and shadow. He bore no emblem. No glyph.

Only chains wrapped around his forearms, carved into his flesh like iron shackles. They glowed faintly, pulsing with the rhythm of Olympus itself.

He lifted a hand—

And the city stilled.

Zara blinked.

The memory shifted—

And the man turned.

His eyes locked with hers.

But he wasn't seeing her.

He was seeing through her.

As if the vision was a window, and she had opened it too far.

He lifted one chained hand—and pointed.

Not at the city.

At her.

Zara gasped, stumbling back into the present. Her knees hit stone.

Kai rushed to her. "Zara!"

"I saw him," she breathed. "I think I saw… the Thirteenth."

Isla's breath caught. "You mean—"

"No. Not just him. The others were with him. All twelve. And they weren't fighting him. Not yet."

Kai knelt beside her. "What did he do?"

Zara met his eyes. "He pointed at me."

Kai said nothing.

But his silence weighed more than words.

The glyph on the wall cracked.

Not loudly—but decisively.

A single fracture ran down the center of the symbol. The inverted triangle split slightly. The spirals began to unwind.

Zara stood slowly. "It's breaking."

Isla stared. "I thought we sealed it."

"We did," Zara said. "But I don't think we were the only ones watching."

A breeze stirred around them.

Then stopped.

The Codex fragment pulsed again.

And Zara heard it.

Not aloud.

Inside.

A whisper carried through memory.

He waits beneath.

The heir must choose.

Zara's fingers tightened around the scroll. "It's not over."

Kai shook his head. "It never is."

Then—another sound.

A hum.

Subtle. Soft. Building.

They turned as one.

The ground around the observatory was vibrating. Loose stones rattled. Dust lifted in faint spirals.

From the far edge of the mountain, just beyond the crumbled threshold of the ruins—a flame ignited.

No torch.

No magic.

Just fire.

Blue.

Cold.

Watcher flame.

Kai lifted his bow again. "We're not alone."

Isla drew her charm blade. "Can we fight it?"

Zara stared at the flame. "It's not here to fight."

"Then what's it here for?"

"To watch."

The flame didn't move.

But the space around it warped—slightly. Like heatwaves bending the air.

Then it flickered—

And the glyph from below reappeared. Etched into the grass in lines of fire.

Not just the seal.

But something new.

A trail.

Leading down the other side of the mountain.

Kai frowned. "That wasn't here before."

"It is now," Zara said. "It's guiding us."

"Toward what?" Isla asked.

Zara didn't answer.

She just looked at the Codex scroll—now fully whole, glowing faintly in her hands.

Then back at the fire-glyph trail.

And whispered, "The next seal."

♦ ♦ ♦

The trail of fire did not burn.

It shimmered.

A line of blue flame, coiling like a serpent down the far side of the mountain, fading in and out as it twisted through stone and moss and root. Each time it flickered, the Codex scroll pulsed in Zara's hands—faint golden light meeting ghostly blue, like two languages struggling to remember how to speak to each other.

Kai paced a few steps ahead. "I don't like being led like this."

Isla crouched beside the nearest glyph, tracing it lightly with a charm-stone. "It's not just guiding. It's reacting. I think it knows we're following."

"That's somehow worse."

Zara didn't respond. Her mind was still ringing from the vision. The man with the chains. The way he'd pointed—not at her, but through her. Like he wasn't just seeing her, but everything inside her.

Every ancestor.

Every glyph.

Every lie Olympus had buried.

She clutched the Codex scroll tighter and stepped forward.

The path obeyed.

The fire unraveled ahead of them, drawing a gentle arc into a sharp descent—toward the forest below the ruins. The mountain swallowed the trail, and the mist thickened.

"I don't think we're meant to make it to the bottom," Kai muttered.

"No," Isla said. "We're meant to get lost."

They didn't speak much after that.

The further they followed the trail, the less the world seemed to behave.

Gravity tilted. Shadows stretched in the wrong directions. The air changed—no longer cold, but silent. As if sound itself had been left behind somewhere higher up the mountain.

Even birds refused to sing here.

And then the fire stopped.

No fade. No flicker.

Just gone.

They stood in a clearing surrounded by stone pillars, half-collapsed and covered in ivy. At the center was a circle—another spiral, carved into the earth.

Zara felt it before she saw it.

The pull.

Like a tether being yanked from behind her ribs.

She stepped into the circle, and the world shuddered.

For a moment, everything blurred.

Not her vision.

Reality.

The air shimmered. The ground rippled. Glyphs flickered around the edges of her sight, like something ancient was trying to claw its way into the present.

Then she saw it.

Not with her eyes, but with memory.

A door, buried beneath the stone.

Round. Metallic. Covered in rusted sigils that weren't part of the Codex. Or Olympus.

But they recognized her.

Each one lit up as she approached.

Kai called out. "Zara—what are you doing?"

"I think it's showing me," she murmured. "Where to go next."

Isla stepped into the circle beside her. "Where is next, exactly?"

Zara swallowed. "Below."

The ground cracked.

Not open—but downward.

Like a drain had been pulled.

The spiral pattern collapsed in on itself, and a shaft of blue light opened beneath their feet. Not flame. Not magic. Something deeper.

Memory given weight.

They fell.

Not far. Just enough.

The ground rose to meet them.

♦ ♦ ♦

And suddenly they were standing in a cavern lit by bioluminescent stone. Glyphs marked the walls like burns—some glowing, some dark. The floor was glassy and uneven, reflecting their shapes back at them in warped patterns.

Kai drew his bow. "Tell me we didn't just walk into another trap."

"We didn't," Zara said, already moving toward the far side of the chamber. "We walked into the past."

On the far wall, a mural waited.

Not painted.

Carved.

It showed thirteen figures.

Twelve in a circle.

One in shadow, above them all, marked with chains.

At the base of the carving were three words.

The first word cracked through the cavern—SEAL—and the walls themselves split, molten light bleeding from the stone as if Olympus had just chained the world again.

The second thundered—SACRIFICE—and from the dust rose the faint image of a figure bound in chains, hands reaching as though from beneath the sea.

The last word struck—SILENCE—and in an instant all sound vanished: the drip of water, the rasp of their breathing, even the hammer of their hearts. Then, just as sudden, the glyph burned back into stillness.

Isla touched the stone. "This wasn't a prison. It was a covenant."

Zara nodded. "They didn't lock him away to destroy him. They locked him away to protect something else."

Kai stared. "Protect what?"

She turned to face them.

"Us."

The Codex scroll pulsed in her hands.

Then flared.

Words unfolded across its surface—glyphs flowing like molten gold. A message that hadn't been there before.

WHEN THE SEALS BREAK

THE FLAME WILL RISE

AND THE TRUE GOD WILL SPEAK

Zara's voice came soft. "This wasn't just prophecy. It was warning. And invitation."

"To who?" Kai asked.

Zara met his eyes.

"To the heir."

Kai stepped back slightly. "Which heir?"

"I don't know," Zara said. "But it's not me."

Isla looked between them. "If the Codex is whole again… what happens now?"

Then, from the other side of the rift—

A voice.

Whispered.

Fragmented.

Familiar.

"Are you ready… child?"

Zara flinched.

The voice wasn't talking to her.

It was talking to someone else.

But she had heard it before—in the dream, in the memory.

Kai stepped beside her. "Who was that?"

Zara shook her head.

And then the rift collapsed.

The glyph vanished.

And silence returned.

♦ ♦ ♦

They stood there for a long moment, listening to nothing.

Then Zara tucked the Codex scroll back into her satchel.

Kai slung his bow over his shoulder. Isla didn't sheath her blade.

No one said it aloud, but they all understood the same truth:

They had come looking for answers.

What they found were pieces.

Pieces of something bigger. Older. Still waking.

And somewhere—beyond the Codex, beyond Olympus, beyond even Aetherion—

Someone was listening.

♦ ♦ ♦

**Hellenic Institute of Mythology**

Athens, Greece                                    Venice, Italy

Mr. Ginn,

It has come to our attention that your first volume is now     nearing completion. We extend our congratulations on preserving the integrity of the fragments entrusted to you.

We also wish to inform you that additional materials have recently been recovered and catalogued. These codices have been removed from their excavation site and are presently in secure transport to our **Athens Authentication and Preservation facility**. Until such time as they undergo full examination and verification, no claims of authenticity can be made.

Given your ongoing work, and your intention to continue publishing further volumes, we assure you that once these fragments are formally authenticated, we will make them available for your use and for the benefit of your readers.

Respectfully,

Dr. Eleni Makris
Director, Hellenic Institute of Mythology
(on behalf of the Institute's Codex Review Committee)

# CHAPTER XVIII
# THE FEAST OF GHOSTS

Venice, February 26, 2026

Venice always hid behind its masks, but within the Institute , light gathered for a feast that should not have been possible. They had slept little since the labyrinth, haunted by the Codex's echoes.

Now Eleni summoned them all, every heir, to dine in the depths.

♦ ♦ ♦

The wind howled down the corridor, low and mournful—like a voice stretched thin over centuries of silence.

Zara moved first.

Zara still felt the image of the Orb's fracture burning in her mind, its shadow-thrum echoing beneath every step. The memory of its crack haunted the silence as much as the Codex itself.

The Codex fragment in her grip still pulsed from the last glyph, warm and reluctant. She held it tightly, her boots crunching over ancient bone dust as they passed into the deepest chamber yet. Behind her, Isla's flame-charm cast a flickering glow across the crumbled frescoes and fractured pillars.

Isla whispered, almost to herself, "Stone shouldn't remember like this…" Her voice cracked, as if the ghosts had pressed the words out of her.

Kai brought up the rear, bow drawn, scanning every alcove with a hawk's vigilance.

"This place smells like death," Isla muttered.

"It is death," Zara replied. "Ritual death. Look."

She pointed toward the walls—lined with cracked stone masks, each carved in anguished expression. Not artistic. Not theatrical. Realistic.

Isla drew closer. "These aren't for show."

"No," Zara said. "They're funerary masks. But not for honoring the dead."

Kai stepped forward, reading the glyphs carved around the doorframe. "They're warnings."

"Or seals," Zara murmured. "This whole complex—it's not a temple. It's a tomb."

Behind them, the entrance flickered—then closed. Not physically. But the light beyond it dimmed, like a veil had been drawn across the mountain itself.

They were sealed in.

♦ ♦ ♦

Kai exhaled slowly. "Typical."

The central chamber was circular, massive, and sunken. Dozens of concentric steps spiraled down toward a dais in the center. It looked like an altar, but there was no statue. No idol. Only a scorched indentation—like something had once been bound there in flame.

"Not Olympus," Isla whispered. "This was never theirs."

Zara scanned the murals.

The walls here were older. Cruder. No signs of Greek influence. The figures depicted were masked, draped in robes, their faces smudged or scratched out by centuries of erosion or intention.

One image remained intact: a ring of twelve standing around a thirteenth—chained and bowed. No faces. Only glyphs.

Each one different.

Each one burning.

"The original feast," Zara said. "Before the myths. Before the gods as we knew them."

Kai's voice was quiet. "Before Olympus rewrote the truth."

The air grew colder as they descended.

When they reached the center, Zara felt it—not physically, but like a presence watching from inside her skin.

Isla removed a metallic disk from her pouch and laid it flat on the stone. It unfolded—three rings of etched metal expanding outward into a full circle. A portable glyph scanner, keyed to the Codex.

"It should read the echo imprint here," she said, adjusting the dials. "Unless it's too degraded."

Zara knelt beside it and unrolled both fragments of the Codex. The moment they touched the altar, the etched surface glowed.

Not gold.

Not red.

But violet.

A deep, eerie violet that shimmered with shadows beneath its light.

Kai tensed.

The glyphs rose from the stone like mist.

And then—

A scream.

Not from a person.

From the walls.

It wasn't sound—it was memory. Pain. Sacrifice.

The chamber shifted around them.

The masks on the walls blinked open—empty sockets now filled with faint, flickering light.

And the thirteenth glyph in the mural above the altar pulsed.

Zara stood.

"It's a ritual echo," she said. "A memory imprint from the original sealing."

Kai drew an arrow. "Which means someone—or something—might still be watching."

Isla didn't respond. She was staring up at the ceiling.

"The masks," she whispered. "They're not just funerary."

"What are they?"

Isla pointed.

Around the rim of the ceiling was a spiral constellation of masks—twelve in total—each with a different emblem above its brow.

A trident. A torch. A bow. A thunderbolt.

Zara stepped back, her voice low.

"They're the original heirs."

A sound echoed from beneath the dais. A low, resonant hum—like chains dragging across stone. The floor trembled.

Kai stepped between the girls and the altar. "We need to decide now—do we keep going, or get out while we can?"

Zara looked down at the Codex. The violet glow was growing stronger, and the symbols between the two fragments had begun to align—forming one long, continuous passage.

"We can't stop now," she said. "This is where the truth is buried."

Isla's voice was softer. "Then we better be ready to face it."

The moment the words left her mouth, the dais cracked.

A burst of violet fire exploded upward—not heat, but memory. Images flashed through the chamber, fragments of time reawakened:

A masked figure raising a golden blade.

A chained being thrashing beneath a stormlit sky.

Twelve voices chanting a final decree.

One hand pulling away.

A betrayal.

The images vanished.

The chamber went still.

Then the voice came.

Not spoken. Not heard.

But carved—line by line—into the very air.

"Twelve sealed one."

"One broke free."

"The feast begins again."

♦ ♦ ♦

The Codex fragments burned white-hot. Zara dropped them—too late. The glyphs leapt from the pages and circled the room like fireflies.

308

Kai loosed an arrow into the center of the altar, but it shattered mid-air—caught in some unseen force.

For a long breath, none of them moved. The chamber itself seemed to pause, as if waiting for one of them to speak first. Dust drifted in the Codex's glow, each mote bright as an ember in the silence.

Kai swallowed hard, but even he couldn't summon a joke. Isla's hands clenched white around her satchel, the Codex's glow painting her face like a mask she couldn't remove.

A spiral formed on the floor.

Another gate.

But this time—no figure stepped through.

Instead, twelve cloaked forms flickered into being around the rim of the chamber—silent, unmoving, masked.

Ghosts.

The echoes lingered, shadows settling like dust before the next vision stirred.

But not dead.

Shadows.

Sentinels.

Bound by a vow older than Olympus.

Each one bore a different glyph at their chest.

The same glyphs the heirs now carried in secret.

Isla stepped forward, face pale. "They're not Watchers."

"No," Zara said. "They're echoes."

"Of us," Kai whispered.

The twelve figures turned—slowly—inward, toward the altar.

Then, one by one, they looked up.

At the three of them.

And the thirteenth glyph—the one blackened and cracked—shuddered.

The air inside the chamber shifted—no breeze, no sound. Just presence. Thick, pressing down on their lungs like memory given weight.

Zara stepped back toward the altar, the Codex fragments now floating inches from the stone. The violet glow was gone, replaced by something darker. Deeper. A cold that hummed with resonance.

Kai scanned the shadow-forms surrounding them—twelve masked echoes, flickering and silent. They hadn't moved. Not yet. But he could feel their awareness. Not like watching… more like remembering.

"They're echoes," Isla said again, voice taut. "But they're not just visions. They're waiting."

"For what?" Kai asked.

Zara didn't answer. Her gaze was locked on the thirteenth glyph embedded above the dais—fractured, charred, and trembling faintly. It hadn't lit up like the others. But something pulsed beneath the blackened surface. Something old.

Then she saw it.

Just beneath the mural. A second glyph. Smaller. Carved not by chisel, but flame.

The Forbidden Seal.

The same burn pattern as before—black and gold and red. Shadow bleeding into light. A glyph outside all known systems. Not Codex. Not Watcher. Not divine.

She whispered, "It's here too."

Kai followed her gaze. "The one from the observatory."

Zara nodded. "It wasn't a warning."

"A trigger," Isla said, stepping beside them. "Or a lock."

Zara's voice dropped to a whisper. "And we just opened it."

One of the echoes moved.

Not with steps. With intention. Its form shimmered—like oil rippling on water. Its mask cracked slightly, and a flicker of glyph-light poured from within. At its chest, the symbol of Demeter burned faintly—wheat entwined with a scythe.

Then another stepped forward. Hermes. Then another. Hephaestus. Slowly, all twelve echoes turned toward the altar. Toward the three of them.

Isla activated her scanner again. "These aren't random projections."

Zara shook her head. "They're patterns. Glyph-bound. They're… rehearsing the ritual."

Kai's voice was tight. "And what happens at the end of that ritual?"

Zara looked up at the thirteenth glyph—fractured, smoldering. "Someone is betrayed."

As if in answer, the echoes raised their arms.

Each held something now. A piece of the Codex. Not scrolls, but fragments—tablets, bone, fire, steel—each one unique.

Zara inhaled sharply. "The original Codex wasn't a book."

"It was a vault," Isla said.

Kai squinted. "A vault for what?"

Zara didn't want to say it.

Because the answer was already pressing at the back of her mind, clawing for escape. She clutched the two scrolls tighter. The fragments they carried weren't just knowledge—they were keys.

"Power," she said. "Divine power."

"But not for mortals," Isla added. "Not even for heirs."

"For one," Zara whispered. "The Thirteenth."

The masked echoes stepped in unison, encircling the altar. The chamber dimmed again—not from lack of light, but from something deeper. A draining. The mural above began to change.

The twelve glyphs pulsed.

The thirteenth began to glow.

Red. Then gold. Then black.

A symbol re-formed in its center.

The triangle.

The golden flame.

The shattered chain.

Zara took an involuntary step back. "No. That's not part of the Codex."

"I know that glyph," Isla said grimly. "Watcher."

"No," Zara breathed. "It's worse."

Kai's voice cut through the tension. "Incoming."

The altar cracked.

Flame burst upward—but not fire. Memory again. This time, it wasn't ritual. It was conflict.

They saw it as if living it:

A god chained in a throne of obsidian.

Twelve shadows pressing their palms to a seal.

One pulling away.

Breaking the pact.

Betraying the others.

Then—the world split.

The vision shattered.

The echoes vanished.

♦ ♦ ♦

The chamber went still.

Zara was the first to speak. "We just saw the sealing."

Isla nodded slowly. "And the betrayal."

Kai's face was grim. "So who broke the Codex?"

Zara turned back to the fractured thirteenth glyph, her voice low.

"Someone who was supposed to protect it."

Kai frowned. "A god?"

Isla stepped beside them, her tone sharpened. "Or an heir."

Zara didn't respond.

Not because she didn't know.

But because deep inside her… something already did.

The Codex scrolls had changed. The glyphs that once glowed gold now flickered in multiple colors—echoing the Forbidden Seal's hues. Red. Gold. Black.

They were evolving.

Zara's mind reeled. "The fragments… they're reacting to what we're seeing. To what we're learning."

Kai adjusted his grip on his bow. "So the more we uncover, the more unstable they become?"

Zara didn't answer. But she knew.

This wasn't just about unlocking ancient secrets anymore.

It was about releasing them.

The altar cracked again.

But this time—it didn't emit memory.

It opened.

Stone slid apart in jagged, unnatural lines. Not mechanical. Not magical.

Glyph-born.

From the center rose a single object: a dark obsidian box etched with a spiral on each face.

Zara reached for it.

Kai grabbed her arm. "Don't."

Isla didn't speak. Her eyes were wide. Fixed on the box.

It was pulsing.

Not with power.

With heartbeat.

Zara opened it.

Inside lay a third scroll. Smaller. Wrapped in what looked like shadow silk. No light escaped from its surface. But when Zara reached for it—glyphs burned across her fingers.

They weren't hers.

They weren't any she recognized.

"Do you feel that?" she asked.

Isla nodded. "It's… speaking."

"Not in words."

"Emotion," Zara said. "It's grieving."

Kai frowned. "Grieving what?"

Zara looked up at the mural again.

The thirteenth figure was now fully illuminated. No longer cracked.

No longer sealed.

"The god without a name," she whispered.

Kai's jaw clenched. "The one they sealed?"

Zara nodded. "And we just cracked the lock."

◆ ◆ ◆

The mural cracked.

Not just symbolically—stone gave way, shearing down the center like a wound torn through time. Dust spiraled around them in silent whorls. From the fracture, a dull hum emerged—not sound exactly, but pressure. As if the chamber itself were holding its breath.

Zara stepped back, scrolls tight in her arms. "The pact was never completed."

Kai glanced at the glowing Codex fragments. "You think this chamber was the site?"

Isla scanned the walls again, stepping cautiously toward the dais. "No. This was the interruption. This is where it was broken."

313

Zara looked up at the now-complete mural. The twelve figures ringed the center—glyphs on their palms, marks glowing. But the thirteenth…

It was still obscured.

Not by shadow.

By absence.

As if the wall refused to depict what had been there.

From the crack in the wall, a shape began to emerge—slowly, uncertainly. Not a figure. A room. Another one. Hidden behind the dais, sealed by glyphlight and time.

They weren't alone.

Kai stepped between the others, bow ready. "Movement inside."

Zara shook her head. "No… it's memory again."

And yet—this memory bled into reality. The hidden room wasn't just appearing—it was returning, like something drawn from another time, syncing with the present.

The glyphs responded.

Lines of silver and gold etched across the floor and into the secret chamber, connecting altar to glyph, scroll to seal. And as the circuit completed—

They saw them.

The original twelve.

Not masks this time.

Faces.

Younger than expected. Human. Divine.

And at the center: the thirteenth. Back turned. Cloaked in midnight shadow, skin humming with gold-veined power.

His presence hurt to look at.

Not because of darkness.

But because of recognition.

"Do you see it?" Isla whispered.

Zara's breath hitched. "It's not just history."

Kai didn't speak. His eyes were fixed on the one in the center. The Thirteenth. He didn't move like a villain. Didn't leer or threaten. He stood calm. Resigned. Powerful—but heavy, like someone carrying more than just fate.

The twelve stepped back from him—some in fear, some in sorrow.

Then the pact began.

The memory played out in near-silence. The glyphs on the twelve began to glow, burning brighter, their lights forming a ring around the Thirteenth.

Chains of light descended from the air, interlocking across the chamber. One by one, they moved into position.

Until one paused.

Zara's eyes widened. "She didn't go through with it."

"Who?" Isla asked.

Zara pointed. "That one." She stepped closer. "I know that face."

Kai frowned. "From where?"

Zara didn't answer. Her thoughts raced.

She had seen that face before.

The Thirteenth turned his head.

The memory froze.

And the figure looked directly at them.

Not past. Not echo.

Now.

His eyes were golden flame rimmed with void.

"Run," Zara said.

◆ ◆ ◆

The room responded before the others could.

The memory collapsed inward.

A wave of glyphlight exploded from the hidden chamber, forcing the heirs back. The scrolls sparked in Zara's arms, glyphs flaring hot with rejection. Isla raised a defensive charm. Kai stepped in front of them both.

The Thirteenth stepped forward.

Not in body.

But presence.

His image burned across the air—searing like an afterimage against a lightning strike. His voice wasn't heard. It was felt, a reverberation through blood and bone.

Twelve betrayed.

One broke.

Thirteen waits.

Zara screamed, clutching her head.

Isla dropped to a knee. "It's in the glyphs—it's rewriting them!"

Kai fired instinctively, the arrow passing through the projection—but it slowed. Warped. Dissolved into flame.

The Thirteenth lifted one hand.

The Codex scrolls fled.

They shot out of Zara's arms, spiraling midair before colliding—forming a single, writhing spiral of flame and scripture. From it, a new symbol burned:

A broken ring.

A locked door.

A shattered pact.

The projection faded.

◆ ◆ ◆

Zara collapsed, panting.

The scrolls dropped, smoking, now etched with new symbols neither Greek nor divine.

Kai rushed to her. "Zara—"

"I'm okay," she whispered, eyes wide. "I saw him."

"Who is he?" Isla asked.

Zara's voice broke. "He's the one who was betrayed."

The chamber began to fall apart—not crumbling, but unraveling. The glyphwork collapsed in waves, collapsing as though whatever energy had been sustaining this place had been spent. The walls flared, symbols liquefying into molten gold and dripping into the floor.

The mural fractured completely.

The thirteen were gone.

In their place   one figure alone. Watching.

Waiting.

The Codex seal flashed once more.

Then died.

The escape tunnel behind the altar opened of its own accord.

No invitation. Just necessity.

Kai didn't hesitate. He pulled Zara to her feet. "Time to go."

Isla snatched the scrolls. They were still hot.

Still pulsing.

But intact.

Barely.

As they ran, the sound of collapsing glyphs chased them—a chorus of divine unraveling. They didn't look back.

Only forward.

Toward whatever remained.

The tunnel was too smooth to be natural.

As they descended into the earth, Zara couldn't stop noticing the precision of the walls—how the stone hadn't been carved so much as melted into shape. Glyphwork faintly marked the curves, but not in the style of the Codex. These were older, rougher, like echoes of a language forgotten even by the gods.

Behind them, the chamber collapsed in silence.

Not a single tremor followed.

Almost as if the temple had never existed.

◆ ◆ ◆

"Tell me again this is a good idea," Kai muttered, bow ready.

"It's not," Isla replied, her voice low. "But it's the only one we've got."

Zara's fingers still burned from the glyphlight. She couldn't tell if the sensation was pain or memory. The scrolls pulsed faintly inside her satchel. They felt heavier now—not in weight, but in consequence.

"Where do you think it leads?" Isla asked.

Zara hesitated. "Somewhere that remembers."

After what felt like an eternity, the tunnel opened into a chamber.

Not vast. Not decorative.

Functional.

Ancient.

The room's walls were lined with metallic plates etched with spiral patterns. One wall bore a single mirror—tall, thin, and framed by twelve glowing points of light. The floor beneath it cracked with faint lightning pulses.

The mirror shimmered when they stepped closer.

Not reflection.

Response.

It knew they were here.

"This isn't Olympus," Zara whispered.

"No," Kai agreed. "This is before Olympus."

Isla approached the mirror. "Do you see that?"

Within the glass, a scene flickered—grainy and colorless, but real.

A battle.

Twelve figures standing atop a broken mountain, the sky above them torn open by shadow and flame. Chains coiled through the air like snakes, and in the center, a thirteenth figure stood—arms out, not in surrender, but in command.

Beneath him: a fractured seal.

Isla reached toward the mirror.

Zara grabbed her wrist. "Don't."

"I'm not touching it," Isla said. "I think it's showing us what it wants to show."

Kai stared at the glowing points surrounding the frame. "These are… places. I recognize them. That one—" he pointed to a northern mark— "that's Kyoto."

Zara's heart skipped. "And that's Alexandria."

Isla looked to the left. "And that's Santorini."

They weren't just glyphs.

They were the awakening sites.

Zara stepped back, chills running up her spine.

"The mirror is tracking us."

"No," Kai said. "Not tracking."

"Testing," Isla said.

The points pulsed in time with the Codex scrolls.

Zara unlatched her satchel.

The moment the scrolls were revealed, the mirror pulsed. Light from the frame surged inward, forming lines—one to each location, then all toward the center of the mirror.

And the thirteenth point ignited.

Not one they recognized.

A blank space.

Unmarked.

Unclaimed.

Isla's breath caught. "There's another site."

Zara turned sharply. "But there are only twelve heirs."

"Are we sure about that?" Isla asked.

They stared at the thirteenth point. Its glyph was different from the others—black and gold and red. A hybrid mark. Familiar, but twisted.

Zara's pulse quickened. "That's the same pattern from the seal upstairs."

Kai turned to her. "The one that reacted to the merge?"

Zara nodded. "And the one that wasn't part of the Codex."

The mirror changed again.

The battlefield vanished.

In its place: a throne.

Not majestic.

Cold.

Angular.

Surrounded by Watchers with no faces.

Only glyphs.

The central figure rose from the throne. Flame wrapped around him like a second skin.

He wore no crown.

But everyone bowed.

Even the gods.

Zara's mouth went dry.

"That's not Olympus," she whispered.

"No," Isla said. "That's... something else."

Kai stepped forward. "It's not prophecy, is it?"

Zara shook her head. "It's memory. Or vision. Maybe both."

They stared in silence.

Then, one by one, the twelve points faded—until only the thirteenth remained.

The mirror spoke.

Not with voice.

With glyphs.

Words burned into the air above the glass.

One was betrayed.

One betrayed.

One remains.

Then the glass cracked.

From top to bottom.

The thirteenth glyph pulsed once—and then shattered.

The room began to darken.

Not from shadow.

From drainage.

As if the light was being pulled into something deeper.

Zara backed away. "Something's wrong."

The mirror collapsed into dust.

◆ ◆ ◆

Where it stood—now only the thirteenth mark remained, etched into the floor, still glowing.

"We need to go," Kai said.

Zara stared at the mark. "This wasn't built for us."

"No," Isla agreed. "This was built to lure us."

A tremor rolled through the chamber.

Real this time.

Glyphs across the ceiling flickered and failed.

The Codex scrolls snapped shut, locking themselves.

And from behind—the tunnel collapsed.

One way forward.

Zara turned to the sealed wall where the mirror had been.

New glyphs formed.

A doorway.

Or a warning.

Maybe both.

They didn't speak.

They ran.

◆ ◆ ◆

The next chamber wasn't ancient.

It was recent.

Built into the earth like a bunker, covered in technology grafted to stone—machine cables intertwined with roots, glass screens flickering with broken static, as if someone had tried to make sense of what should have stayed myth.

Kai's bow was up again. "This doesn't belong."

"No," Zara whispered. "But it's real."

They passed through metal corridors that smelled of ozone and rust. Sensors blinked overhead—then died as they moved beneath them.

They weren't just in a ruin anymore.

They were in a facility.

At the end of the corridor, a single door waited—circular, like a vault.

Its face bore no markings.

But Zara felt something pull in her chest.

The Codex scrolls vibrated violently.

"They don't want us here," Isla said.

Zara shook her head. "They don't want him here."

"Who?"

Zara looked down at the thirteenth mark now faintly etched on her palm—the one she hadn't told the others about. The one that had burned itself into her skin the moment the scrolls merged.

She didn't speak.

Because she already knew.

As they approached the vault door, it split apart—no mechanism, no noise.

Just opened.

Inside was only silence.

Rows of empty containment rings.

Shattered seals on the walls.

In the center, a single chair.

Not a throne.

Not a weapon.

Just a seat.

Worn.

Waiting.

Zara stepped forward slowly.

The Codex fragments flared.

Above the chair, glyphs began to burn.

They were not from Olympus.

They were Watcher script.

But not just that.

It was his mark.

The god without a name.

The chamber didn't just house memories.

It housed a warning.

A record.

A prophecy written in reverse.

Not of the future.

But of what had already begun.

Zara turned to the others.

"We were never meant to find this," she said.

"But we did," Kai said.

Isla stepped beside her. "And now we know."

Zara nodded, quietly.

"Now we choose."

♦ ♦ ♦

## INTERLUDE IV
# THE MARK OF THIRTEEN

Venice, February 28, 2026

Stormlight shifted above the ruin, but deep beneath the mountain, another flame waited.

It begins again.

That was the thought that pierced the silence first—not spoken, not even formed by tongue or breath.

Just a truth rising from the deep.

Beneath the ruins of a mountain that no map remembers, the chamber pulsed with black light. Twelve obelisks ringed the space, cracked and weeping shadows. Their glyphs, once sharp and radiant, were now dulled—worn down by time or guilt. Perhaps both.

The silence stretched, as if the chamber itself was holding its breath.

And at the center of it all: a flame that was not fire.

It did not burn.

It waited.

The Watchers stood at the perimeter, faces hidden by veils of oil-black silk, each one marked by a single mirrored glyph etched above the heart.

His hand hovered, trembling—not from doubt, but from recognition.

They did not speak.

They did not move.

One veil quivered against no wind. When it spoke, the voice was jagged as broken glass: "It does not whisper. It laughs." The others did not answer.

Only the figure in the center dared break the stillness.

She stepped forward, hood lowered, hands bare. Her skin shimmered with veins of gold that pulsed in sync with the chamber. Her presence pulled the shadows inward—as if the chamber knew her name even before she'd given it.

She called herself many things.

But here, in this sacred ruin?

She was The Voice Beneath the Flame.

The ritual was old. Older than Olympus. Older than the gods who claimed the Codex as theirs.

And now—it must be finished.

She raised her hand toward the silent flame.

The chamber answered first—a low note thrummed through the stone; the notfire indented inward, as if taking its first breath in centuries.

"Mark the turning," she whispered.

Glyphs ignited beneath her feet, not in a circle—but a spiral. Thirteen interlocking turns. At each point, an echo flared: not light, not memory, but will.

"The heirs have gathered," she said. "The seals begin to crack."

No one answered.

So she continued.

"The vault has been breached. The scrolls are no longer dormant. The Codex awakens."

Still silence.

Then—movement.

One of the obelisks groaned.

A crack split down its center, revealing a glyph that hadn't glowed in centuries.

The Seal of Aphrodite.

But it was not pink or rose gold. It was black.

Wreathed in shadow.

Beneath it, the mark of Thirteen coiled into place like a brand.

The Voice knelt.

She placed a hand over the mark and closed her eyes.

"I see you," she said softly. "Even now, your path unfolds."

Elsewhere.

A boy stood before a cracked mirror in a Venetian alley, rain sliding down his face.

He didn't see his reflection.

Only flame.

Not the kind that burns.

The kind that whispers.

You do not belong to them.

You never did.

His breath caught.

In his palm, a glyph glowed—just faintly.

But not the one they believed.

Not Aphrodite's. Something else.

Older.

Watcher-born.

Back in the chamber, the Voice straightened.

She didn't smile. She wasn't built for joy anymore.

But she did nod.

"The mark has passed," she said. "The first step has been taken."

♦ ♦ ♦

The Watchers around her stepped forward in unison, thirteen cloaks brushing the stone. Each one removed a single item from within their robes—mirror shards.

Each shard bore a piece of a glyph.

And when they arranged them in the center of the spiral, they began to glow—not individually, but as a constellation. Fractured light formed a symbol no Codex had ever recorded.

A triangle of mirrors.

A golden flame.

A chain—breaking.

The same glyph Zara had seen.

♦ ♦ ♦

The glyph of the Watchers.

"Soon," the Voice said, "the false order will fall."

She walked to the edge of the spiral.

"The gods lied. They sealed him because they feared him. Because he remembered what they chose to forget."

The shadows pulsed in agreement.

"The heirs believe they are fulfilling prophecy. But prophecy is just a cage dressed in starlight. We gave it to them. We shaped their dreams."

One of the Watchers stepped forward.

"What of the thirteenth?"

The Voice turned slowly.

"His glyph has changed."

The watcher didn't flinch.

"And the others?"

"Still dreaming of glory," she said. "Still clutching their fractured truths. Still believing Olympus deserves to rise again."

Her tone darkened.

"But Olympus was never meant to rise. It was meant to be judged."

The chamber darkened as the ritual reached its end.

Above them, through the cracks in the ancient ceiling, a sliver of moonlight fell upon the spiral.

And there, in its center, a new mark formed.

Not flame. Not chain. Not mirror.

But an eye.

Unblinking.

Burning.

Watching.

He dreamed of fire.

Not warmth. Not destruction.

Judgment.

It curled through his veins like memory, pulling apart the lies he didn't know he'd been told. He stood in a chamber of flame— not burning, but breathing—and in its center was a crown. No jewels. No throne. Just a ring of broken glyphs and a mirrored band.

He had seen it before.

But only in pieces.

And now—it called him by name.

◆ ◆ ◆

Except it wasn't his name. Not the one Zara or Kai used. Not even the one he'd whispered to himself in the dark.

This name had no sound.

Only weight.

Thane.

He turned.

The figure in the dream stood taller than any of the others. Robed in shadow. Crownless—but only for now. Its face was obscured by a veil of smoke, but the eyes beneath shimmered with liquid gold.

"You see it now," the figure said.

Thane didn't answer.

"You've always felt it. Haven't you? That you don't belong to them. That your power doesn't match your god."

The voice was velvet. Soft. Patient.

"Because you were never meant to be Aphrodite's heir."

Thane's breath caught.

The room trembled.

And something inside him… cracked.

Far away, in the ruin beneath the mountain, Maelis opened her eyes.

The Watchers around her kept their positions, forming a ring around the mirrored glyph. None of them spoke—but one leaned forward slightly, as if sensing what had just shifted.

"His mind opens," Maelis said quietly. "He's beginning to remember."

"Should we guide him further?" the watcher asked.

Maelis shook her head. "Not yet. The dream must unfold naturally. He must choose."

The flame behind her pulsed once.

Not in agreement.

Not in dissent.

Just presence.

Watching.

Back in the dream, Thane was moving now.

Through visions he couldn't control.

A battlefield.

A broken chain.

A girl screaming his name—and then forgetting it.

Twelve glyphs pulsing in time.

A mirror shattering into three.

A scroll covered in golden lines, too bright to read.

And at the center of it all—

Him.

But not him as he was.

Him… becoming.

"Do you know who you are?" the voice asked.

Thane looked down at his hands.

They were burning.

But not in pain. In purpose.

And for the first time in his life, he didn't want to put the fire out.

He saw a memory that wasn't his.

A boy kneeling before a cracked altar.

A woman with eyes like embers placing a mirrored glyph against his chest.

"You were born of fire and shadow," she said.

"Not to serve. To remake."

The boy nodded.

But as he rose— his reflection changed.

One moment he was the boy.

The next—he was the crown.

The chain.

The thirteenth.

In the waking world, Thane stirred in his sleep.

◆ ◆ ◆

Zara didn't notice.

They were camped on the rooftop of a half-collapsed tower just outside the Venetian ruin, everyone asleep except her.

She was watching the stars.

Or what passed for them.

Stormlight moved in strange patterns tonight.

And in her palm, the burn from the glyph still glowed faintly—
no longer painful, but insistent.

Like something was waiting.

♦ ♦ ♦

# PART V – THE STORM BREAKS

# CHAPTER XIX

# THE BETRAYER'S SHADOW

Venice, February 27, 2026

The city lay silent above, but deep below, the waters stirred in ancient unrest.

The air changed before they saw anything.

Zara stopped at the top of the stairwell, boots wet with seawater, and tasted the shift in the air. It wasn't just colder—it was older. Like something had been waiting too long to be found.

Behind her, Kai paused mid-step. "What is that smell?"

"Salt," Isla said. "But wrong."

The stairwell ended in a narrow arch of crumbling stone. Just beyond, water shimmered in shallow pools along the floor, illuminated by strands of soft white algae that pulsed faintly with bioluminescence.

They weren't in the labyrinth anymore.

This place breathed.

◆ ◆ ◆

"Are we… beneath Venice?" Kai asked.

Zara nodded. "Deep beneath. Too deep."

The path ahead opened into a collapsed chapel. Pillars lay broken like bones across the floor. The ceiling was missing, but no light came from above—only shadows dripped down, long and shivering.

Isla's whisper trembled against the cavern walls. "Stone shouldn't bleed shadows like this…"

And the Codex fragment in Zara's bag began to hum again.

Not just hum.

Resist.

She slowed her steps.

The thirteenth glyph on her palm flared beneath her glove—sharp and sudden.

Zara winced. "It knows we're here."

They reached the center of the chapel.

Here, the mosaic tiles still held fragments of design. A starburst. A chain. A face half-buried in stone.

The walls were lined with ruined statues—some recognizable, some monstrous.

One bore Athena's helm.

One had Poseidon's trident—cracked in half.

One statue stood taller than the rest.

Faceless. Head bowed. Hands held out—not in welcome, but in judgment.

Cassian's breath caught. He had seen that posture before—in the storm's flash on the tower, in the vault's chain. Not a statue, but a shadow waiting for recognition.

Its chest bore no glyph.

Only a deep burn.

Kai stepped back. "That wasn't made by time."

"No," Isla said. "That's a wound."

Zara stared at the broken stone. "That's where the thirteenth seal was carved."

Kai frowned. "The Watchers?"

Zara shook her head. "Before them."

A faint tremor rippled beneath their feet.

The water around the statue glowed faintly—and a crack opened in the floor.

Not violently.

Like an invitation.

Steps descended into the dark.

This wasn't supposed to exist.

But neither were they.

The steps were carved from obsidian. Smooth, precise. Lined with traces of gold that didn't reflect light but drank it.

Zara led the way, her hand hovering near the Codex satchel.

The deeper they went, the more the air grew still—not heavy, not stale.

Held.

Like the whole space was waiting for a breath that hadn't come in centuries.

The tunnel finally ended in a narrow stone gate.

Its arch bore no glyphs. No words. Just a carved circle, blackened at the edges as if once burned.

Zara raised her hand to it.

The thirteenth glyph on her palm flared again—brighter this time.

The gate opened.

The room beyond was not a room.

It was a city.

♦ ♦ ♦

Below the surface of the earth, inside the broken shell of an inverted cathedral, lay streets submerged in black water. Cracked bridges arched over canals that glowed faintly from glyphs etched into their undersides.

Buildings leaned against one another—twisted and broken like the aftermath of a storm.

And above it all, at the center of the dome, hung a chain.

Not attached to anything.

Just floating.

Massive.

Shattered at three points, but still pulsing.

Kai whispered, "What... is this?"

Zara stepped forward.

"The city that shouldn't exist."

The water didn't rise.

It simply existed—shallow in some places, deep in others, rippling despite the stillness of the air.

Zara felt every movement echo through the glyph in her palm.

The city wasn't empty.

It was aware.

And watching.

Cassian slowed, boots scuffing against the stone, and let the others pull a few steps ahead. His gaze traced the black water, following its ripples like he was reading a code written in motion.

"Places like this don't sleep," he said quietly.

Kai glanced back. "You've been here before?"

Cassian didn't answer right away. "Not here." A pause. "But I've seen what wakes up when the wrong person walks in."

His tone wasn't warning. It was certainty. And when he caught Zara's eye, it was like he already knew which of them the city had been waiting for.

They crossed the first bridge slowly, boots ringing softly against the stone. No birds. No insects. No sound but their breath.

At the far edge of the bridge stood a gate with no wall.

Just stone pillars in the shape of open hands, fingers bent toward the center as if trying to close.

Beyond it, a structure half-submerged: a temple with thirteen pillars.

One shattered.

Zara stopped cold.

She knew that shape.

So did Kai.

"That's the same temple from the mirror," he said. "The one in the throne vision."

Kai's voice cut the silence, brittle with disbelief. "This isn't archaeology anymore—it's myth breaking through stone."

♦ ♦ ♦

Isla's jaw clenched. "And it's real."

Inside the temple, the glyphs were arranged in a spiral around a central basin. Water pooled within it, clear as glass.

Reflected in the water were twelve faces.

Not their own.

Others.

Heirs from another time.

Each face flickered when Zara stepped forward.

But the thirteenth never appeared.

The water shimmered.

Zara knelt beside it and held out her palm.

The glyph pulsed.

Once.

Twice.

Then the water blackened.

A voice filled the air—not sound, but glyphlight.

It scrawled across the walls, burning into the stone with a gold-red shimmer.

The seal is broken.

The chain remembers.

The pact is undone.

♦ ♦ ♦

Zara stood. "The city was a prison."

Kai looked around. "And now it's a warning."

Isla turned slowly. "Then where's the prisoner?"

Something shifted in the far dark.

Not movement.

Absence.

Like a piece of the city had blinked out.

Zara backed away from the basin.

The floor beneath them shivered.

Not with magic.

With footsteps.

Something was waking.

Not ancient.

Not god.

Something worse.

The footsteps stopped.

But nothing came through the mist.

The city exhaled.

And the water moved.

Not from wind. Not from current.

From will.

It parted along the canal behind them, revealing a line of jagged stone that hadn't been visible a moment before. Glyphs glimmered in the cracks—old, unfinished. Like a sentence never completed.

Kai took a step toward it. "It's showing us something."

"No," Zara said. "It's testing us."

The path led to a shrine.

Circular. Open-roofed. Surrounded by thirteen half-statues—each shaped in divine likeness, each partially destroyed.

Zara recognized Athena. Hephaestus. Poseidon.

But one statue in the center had no identifiable features.

It was nothing but flame—scorched into the stone.

It bled shadows into the shrine floor.

And at its feet: another scroll.

Tightly sealed. Black wax. The seal bore the same mark as Zara's palm.

The glyph she hadn't told them about.

Yet.

Isla knelt beside the scroll. "It's humming."

"Don't touch it," Zara said quickly.

Kai gave her a look. "Since when do you hesitate?"

"Since it started matching me."

She peeled off her glove.

The thirteenth glyph glowed dimly, not gold—black-red like dying embers.

It pulsed in time with the scroll.

Isla's voice lowered. "That's… not normal."

Zara exhaled. "It showed up when I touched the last fragment in the Watcher vault. I didn't tell you. I wasn't sure what it meant."

Kai stepped closer. "And now?"

"I still don't know," she whispered. "But I think this city does."

She reached for the scroll.

The moment she touched it, the statues flared.

Twelve glyphs burned to life—each over a divine heir.

And then one more.

Not on a statue.

On Zara.

The thirteenth lit her chest like a brand.

She screamed—once—before falling to her knees.

Kai caught her just in time.

Zara wasn't unconscious.

But she wasn't here.

The temple faded from her sight.

And in its place: a battlefield of memory.

Ash. Flame. Chains falling from the sky like divine punishment.

Twelve figures surrounded a thirteenth.

But the thirteenth was not bound.

He was begging.

They wouldn't listen.

One by one, they sealed him away.

Not because he betrayed them.

But because he questioned them.

Because he remembered something they wanted forgotten.

And because they feared him.

Zara opened her eyes with a gasp.

The shrine was silent again.

The scroll was gone.

So was the thirteenth statue.

Only the ashes remained.

♦ ♦ ♦

Kai whispered, "What did you see?"

Zara didn't answer.

Because in her hand—burned into her skin—was the seal from the vision.

A triangle. A chain. A spiral.

All in shadow.

They didn't speak again until they reached the far edge of the sunken city.

There, rising from the water like the remains of a divine skeleton, stood a tower half-submerged. Its roof was broken. Its stairs led downward—again.

Kai squinted. "That doesn't make sense. We're already beneath the city."

Zara's voice was low. "This place doesn't follow rules."

Isla nodded. "We keep going."

The descent was different this time.

No glyphs.

No light.

Only stone slick with centuries of grief.

The air pressed tighter with every step.

Zara's heart beat in time with the glyph on her palm.

And something behind her eyes began to ache.

Like memory trying to claw its way out.

At the base of the tower, they found a chamber.

Circular again—but this time, made entirely of mirror.

Cracked. Dust-covered. But still reflective.

Zara stepped inside and froze.

Each reflection showed her.

But not her now.

Versions.

One in armor. One bleeding. One alone.

One… chained.

She stepped back—right into Kai.

"I see it too," he whispered.

Isla hadn't entered. She stood at the edge, hand on the wall.

"It's a mirror vault. Watcher-level containment. These weren't meant for memories. They were meant for truths."

Zara turned. "What kind of truths?"

Isla didn't answer.

Because the mirrors began to speak.

Not sound.

Not light.

Glyphs.

Each mirror scrawled a phrase across its surface—one after another.

You will betray them.

You will be betrayed.

One line broke.

One seal shattered.

One flame still burns.

Zara looked to Kai. He was watching her—not afraid, not angry.

Just… waiting.

"I don't know what it means," she said.

But even as she spoke, something inside her disagreed.

Because the glyph in her palm had stopped pulsing.

And begun to burn.

She stumbled out of the chamber.

Isla steadied her. "We need to go."

"No," Zara said. "We need to understand."

Kai touched her shoulder. "Not here. Not now."

Zara nodded reluctantly.

But as they turned away from the mirrors, one last glyph flared behind them.

Not in gold.

In blue.

A name etched into the glass.

Thane.

Zara froze.

Kai turned back. "What was that?"

Isla whispered, "I saw it too."

Zara whispered, "He wasn't in the city."

Kai narrowed his eyes. "But he left a mark."

Zara didn't respond.

Because deep inside her chest, something was beginning to crack.

The mark on the mirror hadn't been random.

It was calling.

Zara lingered at the edge of the chamber, eyes fixed on the glowing glyph that had spelled Thane's name. It shimmered once more, then faded—leaving behind the faint impression of a spiral, etched just deeply enough into the glass to suggest permanence.

Kai stood beside her. "He never came down here. We would've known."

"No," Zara murmured. "But something tied to him did."

She didn't realize her hand had started to shake until Isla caught her wrist.

"Your glyph," she said. "It's glowing again."

Zara peeled back her glove. The mark on her palm had darkened—no longer red and black, but edged with gold-white lines, as though it had started to absorb the symbols around it.

"The city is syncing with you," Isla whispered.

"Or I'm syncing with it," Zara said, voice flat.

Kai scanned the chamber again. "This place is collapsing memory, time, and intent into one thing. I don't think it was meant to last. We're pushing it past its limit."

"No," Zara said. "We haven't even reached the center."

◆ ◆ ◆

The next chamber was deeper.

The water reached their knees now—warm, almost thick, like it had memory of its own. It clung to their legs, rippled even without motion. The walls curved inward here, forming a spiral tunnel, descending in slow, deliberate rotations that narrowed with each pass.

As they stepped deeper, something began to change.

The architecture wasn't Venetian anymore.

It wasn't Roman. Or Greek.

It was… Other.

Walls bled into roots. Ceilings shimmered like sky. Every few steps, a glyph would ignite for a heartbeat and vanish again—flickers of divine code stitched into the stone.

The Codex scrolls began to hum in Zara's bag.

Then: her mark burned.

They reached a room with no doors.

Only mirrors.

Dozens of them, cracked and half-melted, arranged in a circle like a crown of thorns.

In the center stood a pedestal.

Upon it: a third Codex fragment.

Zara didn't move.

She knew, without knowing how, that touching it would complete something.

Or unleash something.

Kai stepped forward. "This might be the last one."

"No," Isla said. "There are more. But this is the keystone."

Zara stared at the glyphs burned across the pedestal.

Seal the traitor.

Forget the name.

Erase the fire.

Bind the truth.

But one phrase was fresher. Burned in newer lines.

The fire returns.

Zara reached out.

The moment her fingers touched the scroll, all light vanished.

She wasn't in the chamber anymore.

She stood in an infinite mirror.

Reflections of herself spun out in every direction—some older, some broken, some dressed in armor, in chains, in white robes of judgment.

But one stood still.

A version of herself with burning eyes and a gold-black glyph glowing from her chest.

This version spoke—not aloud, but directly into her bones.

"You are the gate," it said.

"You are the memory."

"You are the lie."

Zara recoiled. "What am I supposed to remember?"

The other her didn't answer.

It burned away.

The city reappeared.

Zara was on her knees.

The scroll had vanished.

So had the mirrors.

The chamber now bore a symbol scorched into every wall.

A triangle. A spiral. A broken crown.

Isla looked down at her. "You dropped."

Kai added, "The scroll dissolved into light."

Zara stood slowly. "Because it's inside now."

She touched her chest. "It's all inside."

◆ ◆ ◆

As they stepped into the final corridor of the sunken city, Zara's glyph lit the walls like a torch.

Each glyph they passed told part of the same story.

But now they could read it.

Twelve lights forged a pact.

One questioned the cost.

Twelve struck him down.

They buried the truth.

And the flame remained.

Waiting.

Watching.

Remembering.

◆ ◆ ◆

Kai whispered, "This was never about the gods losing their power."

Zara nodded. "It was about hiding what they did to keep it."

Isla stopped walking.

A new mural loomed.

It showed a figure in flames.

Not bound.

Not banished.

Ascending.

Zara's voice trembled. "The gods feared something they couldn't kill."

"And now," Isla said, "we've woken it up."

The city trembled.

This time, not with footsteps.

With breath.

The air shuddered like something massive had inhaled—just once.

Zara turned.

All thirteen glyphs had ignited across the ceiling above them.

Each flared in turn.

One by one.

Until only one remained.

Hers.

Then, slowly—

It lit.

And everything began to move.

The floor peeled away like mist, revealing stairs that led nowhere—and yet down.

Bridges unspooled from the air.

Chambers folded into themselves, realigning toward a central axis.

The city wasn't decaying.

It was reforming.

For them.

For her.

Zara stumbled back.

Kai grabbed her arm.

"Zara—what is this?"

Isla said, "It's a ritual chamber."

"No," Zara whispered. "It's a throne room."

At the center of it all, an altar rose.

No body.

No god.

Just flame.

Hovering. Watching.

Shaped like a figure not yet born.

Zara's glyph flared so violently she cried out.

The flame pulsed in answer.

And the city went still.

The altar flared.

Not like fire. Like memory catching light.

A crown-shaped glyph emerged in the center—spinning slowly in place, formed of gold lines and shadow sparks. It hovered above the platform like it was waiting for a name.

Zara stepped forward despite herself.

Each step echoed—not in sound, but in resonance. Like the city was responding. Like it knew her.

Kai whispered, "Zara—wait."

But it was too late.

The altar reached for her.

Not physically.

In glyphs.

Lines unspooled from the base of the floating crown—curling through the air like threads of smoke and lightning. They danced toward Zara, weaving a pattern around her body. Her glyph pulsed in rhythm.

Then—connection.

A flash behind her eyes.

A memory that wasn't hers.

Thirteen seats.

Twelve filled.

One empty.

A voice rang out—not in words, but in purpose.

We buried the truth.

We forged a lie.

But the flame remembers.

Zara gasped.

She fell to her knees at the edge of the altar as the crown glyph spun faster, unraveling glyphs into the air. The chamber's walls lit with lines of myth no one had read in millennia. The very city began to bend inward, its domes and canals folding toward the altar like petals drawn to heat.

Kai caught her before she collapsed.

"She's syncing again," he said through gritted teeth.

Isla was already reaching into her pouch. "I can break the link."

"No," Zara rasped. "Don't."

Her voice sounded distant, like it came from beneath water.

"I have to see."

She stood—somehow—within the vision again.

But this one was different.

It wasn't memory.

It was future.

The twelve stood in a circle.

But they weren't the heirs.

They were older. Wiser. Weathered.

The original pantheon. But distorted.

And in the center—one stood alone.

Unnamed.

His face was flame.

And in his hand: the Codex.

Whole.

He raised it like a verdict.

And the twelve turned away.

One by one.

Until only one remained.

She stepped forward, hand outstretched.

But before she could reach him—

She was pulled back.

By chains of light.

The thirteenth screamed.

And vanished.

Zara collapsed.

For real this time.

The altar dimmed.

The crown glyph dropped to the floor with a soft ring.

But it didn't shatter.

It pulsed.

Waiting.

Isla knelt beside her. "Zara? Come on—come back."

Zara's eyes fluttered open.

She looked at the crown glyph on the ground and whispered, "It wasn't always his."

Kai frowned. "What?"

"The thirteenth seat. It didn't belong to him. He inherited it. Because the one who came before—vanished."

Isla whispered, "Then that means…"

Zara nodded slowly.

"There was a fourteenth."

◆ ◆ ◆

The chamber began to tremble.

This time—not breath.

But warning.

The glyphs around them shimmered violently, as if rejecting the knowledge spoken aloud. Lines warped. Stones cracked.

And then—

A voice.

Not flame. Not wrath.

But hollow.

You see too much.

You remember too well.

You are not yet ready.

The city recoiled.

Water surged back into the lower corridors, flooding the mirror chambers and erasing the glyphs from the walls. The spiral staircase leading upward began to collapse behind them—stone folding in on itself as if retreating from the truth.

Kai shouted, "We have to go—now!"

Zara snatched the fallen glyph crown and clutched it to her chest.

The moment she touched it, her own glyph flared again.

Too bright.

Isla blinked. "You're glowing—your whole body."

Zara stood—unsteady.

"It's reacting to what's coming."

They ran.

♦ ♦ ♦

Through flooded chambers, collapsing sanctuaries, and glyphs that flickered like dying stars. The city wasn't just falling—it was folding. Erasing. Making sure that what they'd seen couldn't be found again.

But it didn't stop them.

Not this time.

Not yet.

They reached the outer corridor—the same one they entered from. But the way was different now. The canals were still, glass-flat. The domes had gone dark. The city was watching, not resisting.

And on the far edge of the water…

A figure stood.

Not cloaked.

Not masked.

Just still.

Tall. Hooded. Its face was empty—no features, just reflective surface.

Like a mirror.

Kai raised his bow.

Zara stopped him. "No."

The figure didn't move.

Didn't speak.

But her glyph pulsed again.

And the figure's chest flared—briefly—with the same golden spiral.

Zara stepped forward, only a few paces.

"Who are you?"

No answer.

Just a whisper across her mind—not words, but the weight of them.

I am the echo.

I am the memory.

I am the first to fall.

And then—it vanished.

The city froze.

Every glyph blinked out.

Every ripple ceased.

And for one breathless moment, it was as if the entire world had stopped.

They emerged from the ruins just as dawn broke over Venice.

The gondola was still there—half-sunk, but waiting.

None of them spoke.

Zara looked back only once.

And on the stone behind her, etched into the marble of the exit archway:

The Codex Remembers.

♦ ♦ ♦

Later that night, when she tried to sleep, Zara dreamed of the altar again.

But this time, the throne wasn't empty.

It burned.

And in the fire—

347

A reflection.
Of her.

# *Codex Fragment*

## *The Mark of Thirteen*

Twelve marks burn with the fire of
thrones.
A thirteenth coils in shadowlight,
unseen yet near.
It crowns not with laurel, nor
lightning, nor love —
but with a mirror of what was broken.
The chain completes where it should
not,
and the hand that takes it wears no
name.
Beware the throne that waits
uncounted,
for it remembers
more than gods
allow.

**Institute Archive Reference – Document 447-B**
Fragment recovered from a collapsed archive vault in Delphi.
Initial translation is unstable; the language shows irregularities not seen in other Olympian codices.
Further verification required before authentication.
— *Filed by Dr. Eleni Makris, Senior Archivist*

# CHAPTER XX
## THE WATCHERS' HUNT

Venice, March 1, 2026

The darkened city leaned too close, its towers warped like listening faces. Beneath it, the heirs moved as one, though trust was already fracturing.

The wind off the black water still carried the echo of what they'd seen.

The glyph had faded, but the feeling it left behind hadn't.

Zara didn't speak. Neither did Leo. Even Kai's usual half-smirk was gone, replaced by the rigid focus of someone cataloging every shadow.

Isla's whisper trembled against the cavern.

They crossed the cracked causeway in silence, boots scuffing stone slick with seawater. Above them, the City That Shouldn't Exist seemed to breathe—every flicker of lantern-light in its leaning towers too deliberate to be the wind.

Selene's voice finally broke the stillness. "We weren't supposed to be seen."

◆ ◆ ◆

Her words came out low, but they cut through the night like a blade.

Thane was at the rear, his pace measured, his gaze on the horizon instead of the group. If anyone noticed the way he kept glancing toward the blind corners of the city wall, no one said it aloud.

Zara clutched the Codex fragment against her chest. Even wrapped in leather, it thrummed faintly, as though remembering what had just happened. She could still see the black spiral in her mind, the shadow that had watched them without moving.

Leo slowed to match her stride. "When we get back to the tower, you tell me exactly what you saw."

She hesitated. "Some things… don't belong in the open."

Before Leo could press, a whisper rolled along the stones—soft, wrong, like dry leaves across glass.

Every heir turned.

Nothing moved.

Then Kai muttered, "We're being herded."

From somewhere beyond the seawall, a pulse of light flared—quick, sharp, and gone. It was followed by the scrape of stone on stone.

"Not here," Thane said suddenly, his voice sharper than the others had ever heard it. "We move now."

There was no debate. They broke into a run, scattering across the causeway's uneven spans, every step sounding too loud against the waiting dark.

By the time they reached the inner gates, the air felt heavier, like the city itself was leaning in to listen.

The main thoroughfare was a narrow channel of shadow between towers that leaned so close they almost touched. Balconies drooped above them, warped by salt and time, their railings twisted into spirals that mimicked the glyph they had seen.

Naia paused to study one of them, her eyes narrowing. "These weren't built this way."

"Keep moving," Selene urged.

They did, but not quickly enough.

A flicker of motion rippled across the rooftops. Kai caught it first—his bow came up, an arrow nocked without a sound. "Two o'clock. They're tracking us."

"How many?" Leo asked.

Kai's jaw tightened. "Enough."

The shapes above them moved like liquid shadow, their forms indistinct but fast. Every leap between rooftops was too far for any normal human to make.

"Watchers," Selene said under her breath.

The group quickened their pace, the uneven stones of the street forcing them into single file. The deeper they went, the more the city felt wrong—walls that curved too sharply, doors built for giants, windows set high where no light could reach.

Thane drifted toward the rear again, his head tilting as though listening for something the rest couldn't hear. His steps slowed.

Zara glanced back at him. "Thane—"

"I'll catch up," he said without looking at her.

The words were casual, but they carried the weight of something else—something he wasn't saying.

They broke into a wider square at the heart of the city. The cobblestones here were black and smooth, worn down as if countless feet had passed this way—but no one lived here now.

In the center stood a fountain, long dry, carved into the shape of twelve figures standing in a ring. All but one had their faces worn away.

The thirteenth pedestal stood empty.

◆ ◆ ◆

Zara felt her grip on the Codex fragment tighten. She could almost hear it—an echo of the humming from before, low and insistent.

Leo stepped forward, studying the empty pedestal. "This is deliberate. Someone erased them."

Selene shook her head. "Or someone never wanted them here in the first place."

From above came the sound of something landing—soft but heavy.

The Watchers dropped into the square.

◆ ◆ ◆

They weren't cloaked this time. The figures were tall, their armor black as obsidian, segmented like insect carapaces. Each helm bore a different sigil—none that Zara recognized from the Codex.

One stepped forward, its voice like glass dragged over stone. "Return what you took."

No one moved.

Kai's arrow was already drawn. "Try and take it."

The Watcher's head tilted. "You are not ready to know whose hand shapes your fate."

Leo stepped up beside Kai, trident in hand. "Then maybe you should stop talking in riddles."

The Watcher ignored him, its gaze settling on Thane. "You… are closer than you think."

The others turned to look at him, but Thane's expression was unreadable.

The first strike came without warning. A bolt of black light shot from the Watcher's palm, hitting the fountain and shattering half the circle of figures.

The heirs scattered. Kai's arrows hissed through the air; Leo's trident sparked as it met a Watcher's blade. The Watcher twisted with inhuman precision, its segmented armor folding inward before snapping open again—its forearm reshaping into a curved blade that hissed with black heat. Leo barely ducked in time, the strike shearing a groove into the stone behind him.

Isla pulled a hammer from nowhere, flames licking along the head as she swung.

Zara ducked behind the fountain, the Codex fragment still in her grip. She knew she couldn't let it fall into Watcher hands.

A figure moved beside her—not one of the heirs. Thane. He crouched low, his voice barely above a whisper. "If I take this, I can lead them away."

Zara stared at him. "You think I'd just—"

"They're not here for all of us. They're here for this." He nodded toward the scroll.

She hesitated. Every instinct screamed don't. But the Watchers were pressing in, and if they all fell here—

Thane's hand closed over hers, steady, almost reassuring. "Trust me."

The words struck her like the fissure in the Orb—wrong in their certainty, echoing a fracture that had never healed.

Against every ounce of judgment she had, she let go.

Thane was gone before she could second-guess the choice.

♦ ♦ ♦

He slipped between two Watchers, his movements fluid, purposeful, drawing them away from the fountain.

It worked.

Half the Watchers peeled off after him, their pursuit silent but relentless.

The rest pressed harder against the others.

Zara rose, flinging a handful of light from her palm—a flare of pure glyphfire that drove the remaining Watchers back just long enough for Leo to shatter their formation.

"Move!" Kai shouted.

They did. Through a side street, over a collapsed archway, into a warren of alleys so narrow they had to go single-file again.

The city swallowed them whole.

♦ ♦ ♦

When they finally stopped to breathe, the only sounds were the wind and the faint creak of distant towers.

"Where's Thane?" Isla demanded.

No one answered.

Zara didn't say it, but she felt it—the Codex fragment was gone. And with it, Thane.

♦ ♦ ♦

The alleys twisted like a living thing.

Every turn narrowed until their shoulders brushed damp stone, then widened into sudden open pockets littered with broken statuary and shattered columns. Lanterns flickered overhead, hanging from ropes strung between the leaning towers, but the flames burned the wrong color—cold blue, like light stolen from the moon.

No one spoke.

Zara led, every muscle wired tight. The loss of the Codex fragment felt like a missing limb. She could still sense it—faint, distant, as if it were moving further with every breath she took.

Leo kept glancing back. "We should circle. Find him."

"We can't outpace Watchers if we double back," Selene said. Her voice was clipped, but not unkind. "If Thane's alive, he knows where to find us."

Kai's tone was sharper. "If he's alive."

That hung in the air longer than it should have.

A sudden rattle overhead made them all freeze.

Something moved across the rooftops. Quick. Four-footed. The scrape of claws against tile.

Zara signaled with her hand—low, open palm—before sliding into the shadow beneath a collapsed balcony. The others followed, silent.

The thing above them stopped moving.

A breath.

Two.

Then—gone.

"Not Watchers," Isla whispered.

"That's not better," Kai muttered.

They pressed on, each turn of the alley feeling more like a throat closing around them. The city wasn't just abandoned—it was waiting. Zara could feel it, in the way the air seemed heavier the deeper they went, and in the faint tremor underfoot, like something vast and hidden was breathing beneath the streets.

Finally, they spilled into another square. This one was ringed by statues, all eroded into facelessness, their hands outstretched toward the center where a single black obelisk jutted from the cobblestones.

Kai's voice cut the quiet, brittle with disbelief.

It was humming.

Not loudly, but enough for the Codex glyphs along Zara's skin to prickle in answer.

Leo frowned. "That sound—"

"It's the same pitch as the fragment," Zara said before she could stop herself.

Kai's head whipped toward her. "You can still feel it?"

She nodded reluctantly. "Distant. But yes."

Selene's gaze flicked around the square. "If that thing's amplifying the pull, then it's not for us. It's for them."

The words had barely left her mouth when the shadows shifted.

Four Watchers stepped into the square from different alleys, their movements precise, their helms reflecting the obelisk's cold light.

The group formed a quick ring, backs to each other. Kai's bow came up, Leo's trident spun in a tight arc, Isla's hammer flared with molten heat.

One Watcher advanced. Its voice rasped like rusted chains. "The one who runs cannot outrun us forever."

Zara's pulse quickened. "Where is he?"

The Watcher tilted its head. "Closer to truth than you dare tread."

No one moved. Then Kai's arrow hissed through the space between them, striking the Watcher's helm and rebounding in a spray of sparks.

The square exploded into motion.

Leo lunged, trident sweeping low to hook one Watcher's legs before driving the butt of the weapon into its chest. Isla's hammer met another with a ringing impact that sent a shockwave through the air. Selene's shadows writhed into form, gripping a third Watcher's blade mid-swing.

Zara ducked toward the obelisk, palm flat against the stone. Glyphlight flared across its surface—different from the Codex, but similar enough to send a shiver down her spine.

It showed her something.

Thane, running. The fragment clutched in his hand. The streets ahead of him shifting, closing, as if the city itself were steering him.

Then—gone.

The vision shattered with the crack of stone as the obelisk splintered under a Watcher's strike. Zara stumbled back, the hum cut off, her connection to the fragment severed again.

Kai's voice snapped her focus back. "We need to move!"

Leo had already broken their line, clearing a path toward a narrow archway at the edge of the square. "Go!"

They ran.

♦ ♦ ♦

Through the arch, into another warren of sloping streets. The sound of pursuit followed—measured, relentless.

Zara risked a glance over her shoulder. The Watchers weren't rushing. They didn't need to. They knew the city better than the heirs ever could.

Her lungs burned by the time they spilled into a slanted courtyard, its far side opening onto a long, descending staircase carved into the cliff. The black water churned far below.

Kai skidded to a halt. "They want us to go down."

"We don't have a choice," Selene said, glancing back at the narrow entry. "Unless you want to fight six of them at once."

The decision made itself. They descended, the steps slick and uneven, half-crumbling into the sea spray.

Halfway down, Zara felt it again. The faintest pull of the fragment—closer now.

Her heart thudded. "He's below us."

Leo shot her a sharp look. "Thane?"

She nodded.

◆ ◆ ◆

They reached the base of the stairs where a half-collapsed dock jutted into the water. And there—at the far end—stood Thane.

The fragment was in his hand. The Watchers were not.

But his expression was unreadable, his posture too still.

The wind shifted, carrying his voice just enough for them to hear.

"You shouldn't have followed me."

The waves slammed against the dock's pylons, sending spray up through the gaps in the warped planks. The air down here was colder, sharper, as though it carried something older than the sea.

Zara slowed first. The others followed, instinctively spreading in a loose arc around Thane.

He didn't move.

The Codex fragment rested in his right hand, the leather wrappings darkened by seawater. Glyphlight pulsed faintly along its edges, in time with the beat of Zara's own heart.

"We came to get you," Leo said, voice low but carrying over the wind.

Thane's gaze flicked to him. "No. You came to take this."

358

Kai stepped forward, bow still in his grip but pointed down. "We came because the Watchers want you dead. And maybe because we thought you weren't stupid enough to run off alone with the one thing they've been chasing for centuries."

Thane's lips curved—not quite a smile. "Maybe I'm not running from them."

The words landed heavy.

"Then what?" Isla asked, eyes narrowing.

He didn't answer. Instead, he lifted the fragment slightly, turning it so the glyphlight reflected off the black water. The light shimmered, bending in ways that made the horizon ripple.

Zara's voice was tight. "You're playing with something you don't understand."

"That's where you're wrong," Thane said. He stepped toward the edge of the dock, staring down into the waves. "I understand it better than any of you. Because I've seen what's on the other side of the chains."

Selene's shadow seemed to recoil from the words. "What chains?"

Thane looked over his shoulder, his expression sharper now. "You've felt it, haven't you? The thing that watches when you hold a fragment. The one your Codex doesn't name."

Zara's throat tightened. "That's not for you to—"

"It's for all of us," he cut in. "Only none of you want to admit it. There's something bigger than Olympus, older than the gods you claim as blood. And it's been waiting for a very long time."

The dock groaned under a sudden shift of weight. A Watcher dropped onto the far end, armor gleaming wet. Then another. And another.

Kai cursed under his breath. "We don't have time for this."

But Thane didn't move. "You think they're here for me? They're here for him."

The way he said it—him—sent a chill straight down Zara's spine.

The nearest Watcher advanced, its helm tilting toward Thane. "You've come far enough."

Thane's fingers tightened on the fragment. "Not far enough."

And then—he stepped off the dock.

Zara lunged, but too late. He hit the water without a splash, the surface swallowing him as though it had been waiting.

The Watchers froze, their heads turning in eerie unison toward the black water. Then, without a word, they followed—sliding into the sea like predators returning home.

The dock fell silent except for the waves.

♦ ♦ ♦

Leo swore, spinning toward Zara. "What did he mean, 'him'?"

She shook her head, heart pounding. "I don't know. But I think he's gone where we can't follow."

Kai scanned the shoreline. "This whole city is built like a maze. If there's a way back to him, it's not through the water—it's through whatever's beneath it."

Selene's voice was barely audible. "And that means going deeper into the city."

No one liked that idea. But they all knew there wasn't another choice.

♦ ♦ ♦

They turned back toward the stairs.

The climb up was slower, the air heavier. Every step felt like it was leading them not away from danger, but toward something far worse.

At the top, they cut through a narrow street they hadn't taken before. The buildings leaned even closer here, their upper stories connected by bridges of black stone. Every window was dark, but Zara couldn't shake the feeling that they were being watched from behind the glass.

Halfway down the street, Leo stopped. "You hear that?"

At first, Zara didn't. Then—faint, like a heartbeat—thud. Thud.

It was coming from below.

They followed it to a recessed archway that led into a stairwell spiraling down into darkness. The steps were slick, the walls damp with condensation that gleamed under the thin strips of glyphlight leaking from Zara's palm.

360

The sound grew louder as they descended, until it was no longer a heartbeat—it was a drum. Slow. Deliberate. Each beat echoed through their bones.

The stair ended in a vast chamber. The walls were lined with towering pillars, each carved with a different glyph. In the center stood a dais, and on it—a map.

Or what looked like one.

It wasn't parchment, but a slab of translucent stone. Glyphlight swirled within it, constantly shifting to form the outlines of continents… but not as they were now.

Isla stepped closer, brow furrowing. "That's… wrong."

"It's old," Selene corrected. "Before the continents split."

Zara's breath caught. The shapes matched what she'd seen once before—in a fragment's vision.

Kai traced a finger above the surface. "Why would the Watchers have this?"

Leo answered without looking away. "Maybe because they know what broke it apart."

The map shifted again—this time showing the continents drifting, the ocean swelling between them. At the center of it all, a black spiral opened, swallowing light.

Zara's stomach dropped. She knew that spiral.

And she knew whose mark it was.

Selene's voice was just a whisper. "The one Thane meant."

Zara looked at her, then back at the map. "We need to find him before he finds the rest of the fragments."

◆ ◆ ◆

At the top of the stairs, they slipped into a narrow street they hadn't taken before. The towers leaned even closer here, their upper levels bridged by spans of black stone, their windows nothing but unbroken panes of darkness. Every one of them felt like an eye.

A whisper of wind curled between the bridges above, carrying a faint creak like timber under strain—but the sound came from stone. A fine mist of dust drifted down, sifting through the dim light, and for a heartbeat Zara swore the nearest balcony had shifted closer.

Halfway down the street, Leo stopped dead. "You hear that?"

At first, Zara heard nothing. Then—thud. Thud. A deep, deliberate rhythm, faint but steady, like the echo of a distant heartbeat.

"It's below us," Selene murmured.

They followed the sound to a recessed archway where a stairwell curled downward into black. Moisture slicked the stone walls, catching the thin spill of glyphlight leaking from Zara's palm. The deeper they went, the more the beat filled the air, not a heartbeat anymore but a drum—slow, patient, impossible to mistake for anything natural.

The stair ended in a cavernous chamber. Pillars rose into the dark, each carved with glyphs no Codex page had ever shown them. The air here tasted metallic, tinged with something ancient.

In the center stood a low dais, and on it—a map.

It wasn't parchment. It was a slab of translucent stone, taller than Zara's waist, with light swirling inside it like smoke caught in amber. Shapes shifted within the glow until they resolved into a single outline: a world of continents joined together, wrong and yet… familiar.

Isla's voice was low. "That's not Earth."

"It's Earth," Selene corrected, stepping closer. "Before it broke apart."

Zara's pulse quickened. She had seen this shape once before, in the visions the fragment forced on her.

Kai hovered over the slab, tracing the air above the ancient coastlines.

Leo's answer was grim. "Maybe because they know what shattered it."

The continents began to drift apart in the light, slow at first, then faster. Seas swelled between them. And at the center of the sundered world, a black spiral unfurled—swallowing the glow until everything else was gone.

Zara's breath caught. She knew that spiral.

Selene's eyes met hers, the realization unspoken but certain. "The one Thane meant."

Zara couldn't look away from the spiral. "We have to find him… before he finds the rest of the fragments."

CHAPTER XXI

# THE FIRE AT THE GATES

Venice, March 2, 2026

Venice had not slept, and neither had the heirs. The storm above was only the shadow of the one hunting them below.

The spiral still burned behind Zara's eyes long after they left the map chamber.

She pushed it down the way she always did—with motion, with math. Numbers didn't lie. Numbers didn't care who you were or what hunted you. Twelve steps between turns. Nine to the broken lintel. Fourteen to the fork that shouldn't exist. Count, measure, repeat. Numbers steadied the mind.

Kai's voice was brittle, disbelief pressed thin. "This isn't pursuit—it's execution."

The alleys closed in around them until even the sea wind came thin and metallic. Their shoulders brushed walls veined with salt, slick as frost. Overhead, narrow bridges knitted tower to tower like black stone sinew, drawing the city into one vast, watchful body.

Isla's whisper bled into the silence. "The stone remembers their steps. We're not the first they've hunted here."

"They're moving with us," Kai breathed.

Zara didn't ask how he knew. He was the Sun's heir—he felt arcs, trajectories, the geometry of motion—the same way she felt codes. She could sense it too, in the places light didn't touch: the

363

slip of shadow that wasn't just shadow, the faint skitter timed perfectly between footfalls.

Selene lifted a hand, palm outward. Stop.

They froze.

Silence thickened—the held-breath kind, the count-to-three kind. From somewhere high above, a bead of grit rolled across stone, then another. Not random. A rhythm, like a cheap clock trying to pretend it was a heart.

Naia's voice stayed low. "This city's architecture is wrong."

Leo's trident dipped slightly, bronze catching the ghost-blue of Zara's glyphlight. "Define wrong."

"Those spans weren't engineered to hold their loads," Naia said, chin tilting toward a bridge. "And yet they do."

"Magic beats math," Kai muttered.

"Math is just magic you can repeat," Zara countered. "Move."

They moved.

A balcony groaned overhead, the metal whining in a pitch just above human comfort. Zara's gaze snapped upward. Two Watchers crouched there—one flat to the stone, the other rising with the slow, deliberate articulation of something that had practiced mimicry until it was art. Armor unfolded with insect precision, plates locking into place with a whisper.

Kai's bow came up.

"Don't," Selene hissed without turning. "Loose an arrow here, and the flanks collapse."

"We have flanks?" Leo asked.

"We are the flanks," Selene said.

The pace quickened. Boots splashed through shallow tide pools, sending ripples through warped reflections—reflections that weren't quite right. Too many limbs. Faces stretched sideways. Eyes where mouths should be. Zara told herself it was the angle.

The street ended without warning in a chasm—not the ragged tear of a quake, but an intentional cut. A mouth in the city's stone.

The wind rising from it bit at their skin, carrying that same drumbeat they'd heard in the map chamber—faster now, breathless, as if whatever made it had broken into a run.

Leo swore quietly. "We're not going back."

Behind them came the whisper-click of claws on stone. One set. Then two. Then more. The Watchers had closed.

The ocean's salt was sharper here, undercut with a metallic tang that raised goosebumps along Zara's arms. This place was older than any of them had guessed—and far more dangerous.

Isla flicked soot from her cheek with the back of her hand. "There's no crossing."

"No crossing," Leo agreed. "Not without a bridge."

"Not without a miracle," Kai said, shoulders tight.

Zara dropped to a knee at the edge, running fingers over stone cold enough to sting. Her glyphs tingled faintly—the hum of old magic, deep beneath the city's bones.

"Wait," she whispered.

They did.

From far below came a slow, deliberate thrum—the city's heartbeat, deep and resonant. It wrapped around them, through them, vibrating in their chests.

Selene's eyes narrowed. "The drum."

Naia's gaze sharpened. "It's calling us."

The spiral in Zara's mind coiled tighter, tugging her toward the abyss.

"We have to cross," she said. "No other way."

Kai's eyes swept the walls. "I could rig something—"

"No time," Leo cut in. "They're close."

From the far side of the chasm, two Watchers stepped into view. Armor gleamed wet, their helms tilting in perfect sync.

Zara swallowed. "On my mark."

Eyes met eyes—a silent agreement. This wasn't about winning. This was survival.

She stepped forward.

The bridge wasn't there—and then it was. A span of black glass unfurled across the gap, glistening like oil under a dead sun.

Zara's boots touched first. The surface was slick but unyielding. One by one, the others followed, weight settling carefully onto the conjured path.

The city's silence deepened, thick and expectant.

Kai's bow tracked every shadow. Selene's darkness clung close, trailing her like smoke. Isla's hammer radiated a low heat, pushing back the bite of the wind rising from the depths.

Behind them, the Watchers advanced—armor reshaping mid-stride, weapons morphing from spear to blade to hook. Each movement was precise, practiced, a ritual in motion.

"Keep moving," Zara murmured. "No stopping."

Halfway across, the drumbeat deepened, a second pulse folding beneath the first—slower, heavier, like the measured heartbeat of something vast beneath their feet.

Selene's gaze flicked up. "There's more than one."

The city was awake.

A stone fell from a ledge above, striking the glass with a sharp clang. The Watchers' heads snapped toward the sound.

Kai loosed an arrow. It hissed through the air, struck a helm, and skittered off in a spray of sparks. The Watcher didn't falter. Its forearm split and reformed into a curved blade wreathed in black fire.

Leo barely dodged the slash. The blade carved a smoking groove into the glass.

Isla swung her hammer, molten heat flaring as the Watcher twisted aside. The sizzle of steam filled the gap between heartbeats.

Zara ducked low, glyphfire pooling in her palm. The spiral in her mind urged her forward, faster, deeper.

The fight was vicious, the Watchers adapting with every strike. Weapons shifted seamlessly, each parry answered with a counter too quick for mortal reflexes.

Then—the far edge appeared.

The heirs broke into a run, the glass dissolving behind them like smoke in wind. They hit solid ground together, breaths ragged.

The drumbeat faded, but the weight of the city's gaze lingered.

Ahead stood a gate—a towering slab of black stone carved with glyphs older than Olympus itself. Each symbol pulsed faintly, as if the stone itself breathed.

Zara's glyphs flared in recognition. She stepped forward, palm brushing the cool surface. The gate shivered under her touch.

"We're close," she whispered.

The others closed in, weapons ready.

The Watchers were not far behind.

The gate loomed before them, its glyphs shifting in the faint light—not random, but breathing, the strokes curling and straightening as though remembering how to move.

Zara's fingers traced one of the symbols. The stone was cold, but beneath the surface, a heat pulsed in rhythm with the beat she still felt in her bones.

Leo stood to her right, trident angled down but ready. "The Watchers guard this for a reason. We're trespassing."

Selene's shadow unfurled around her, stretching across the stones like a living veil. "Trespass or not, the pull has been leading us here since we stepped into this city. We see it through."

The faint scrape of armor on stone echoed down the alley behind them. The Watchers weren't rushing. They didn't need to.

Kai scanned the gate's edges, searching for seams. "No hinges, no latch. This isn't meant to open from this side."

Naia's eyes narrowed as she studied the curling wards that framed the door. "These are protective bindings. Old ones. Opening it will require a precise invocation… and the right key."

Isla hefted her hammer, the head glowing with faint molten light. "Anything I can break?"

"Not without unleashing something worse," Naia said. "These glyphs are woven into the stone's memory. Damage them, and the wards unravel. If they're holding something in—"

"—we'd be letting it out," Leo finished.

The loss of the fragment still pulsed in their chests, Thane's shadow lingering heavier than the storm. Trust had cracked, and nothing felt whole.

Zara glanced at the Codex fragment strapped against her chest. "The fragments opened the map chamber. They might open this too."

Leo's brow furrowed. "If the Watchers are behind us, and you start feeding power into this thing—"

"They'll come faster," Selene said. "Which means we open it faster."

The footsteps behind them grew louder, measured and inhuman.

Zara pulled the fragment free, unwrapping the damp leather until the glyphs along its edge caught the cold light. They pulsed once—faint, like something far away trying to hear her—then steadied.

She began to chant. The words were ancient, carrying the cadence of tides and storms. Glyphfire threaded from her palms into the carvings on the gate, sparking along the grooves like veins of molten gold.

Cassian's gaze tracked the storm above, his palm tight with restless sparks. "Even the sky feels hunted," he muttered.

The gate shuddered.

The wards flared bright, then dimmed, resisting.

The Watchers stepped into view at the far end of the street. Four of them, their helms turning in eerie unison toward the gate's light.

"Hold them," Zara said without looking back.

Kai's bowstring sang. An arrow hissed through the space between them and struck a helm dead center, forcing the Watcher to pause. Leo moved in to block the next one, trident clashing against segmented steel. Isla met a third with a hammer swing that rang like a struck bell.

Zara poured more glyphfire into the wards. The symbols flickered, then began to spin slowly in place, turning like gears aligning. The stone groaned, dust falling in thin streams.

A deep rumble vibrated up through the street as the two halves of the gate split along a seam so fine it hadn't been visible moments before. Cold air spilled from the widening gap, carrying the scent of deep water and something older than the gods themselves.

"Inside!" Selene called.

The heirs broke for the opening, slipping past Zara as she held the channel steady. She was the last to step through, and the gate slammed shut behind her with the finality of a sealed tomb.

The chamber beyond swallowed them whole.

The air was thick, heavy enough to taste. Glyphs older than Olympus were etched into towering pillars that circled the room, their lines worn but still faintly glowing. At the center sat a basin of black water—so still it looked solid.

Zara felt it before she heard it: the basin was breathing.

They moved closer, weapons loose but ready. The water didn't ripple. Instead, shadows seemed to shift inside it, as though something moved beneath the surface but refused to break it.

Naia crouched beside it, her reflection blurring the moment it formed. "This isn't water. Not exactly."

"It's a mirror," Selene said, voice low. "But not for this world."

Zara's glyphs tingled. "It's connected to the fragments."

The surface rippled once, slow and deliberate, and then faces emerged—pale, distorted, silent. Mouths opened in screams that made no sound. Hands reached, stopped just short of breaking through.

Isla's flames flared in response. "Spirits."

"Warnings," Leo said, stepping closer.

One of the faces locked eyes with Zara. It was gone in the next heartbeat, replaced by another—older, its gaze heavy with something that felt like recognition.

Behind them, something moved.

The Watchers stepped from the chamber's shadows, their armor gleaming in the basin's faint light.

One advanced, helm tilting slightly. "You have reached the heart of the city."

Zara turned to face it. "We seek understanding."

"Understanding," the Watcher said, "has a price."

The chamber trembled, dust trickling from the high arches above.

Leo tightened his grip on the trident. "And what's the cost?"

The Watcher didn't answer. Instead, its head turned toward the basin.

From the water, a shape rose.

It was tall, robed in shadow, its helm carved with glyphs none of them recognized. Where its eyes should have been, there was only darkness. When it spoke, the voice seemed to come from the stone itself.

"I am the keeper of balance," it said. "And the harbinger of choice."

The spiral in Zara's mind clenched like a fist.

"What choice?" she asked.

"The fate of gods and mortals alike," the figure replied. "The reckoning draws near. The chains weaken."

A ripple of unease passed through the heirs.

The keeper raised a hand. Glyphlight flared in the basin, and the still water shifted, showing not faces this time, but scenes—temples burning, oceans swallowing cities, skies torn in two.

"This is what comes if the wrong hands unite the fragments," it said.

Selene stepped forward. "And if the right hands do?"

The vision shifted. Cities rebuilt. A sky unbroken. A peace that looked impossible in the shadow of what they had seen before.

"The path is narrow," the keeper said. "And not all who walk it will reach its end."

The Watchers closed their ring around the basin.

"Choose," the keeper said. "The fragments call to many. Only one path will keep the balance."

Zara's pulse thundered in her ears. She thought of Thane, of the spiral that burned when she held the fragment, of the map in the chamber above. She thought of the way the city seemed to move for him.

"We don't have all the pieces yet," she said.

"Then the choosing will be harder," the keeper replied.

The basin stilled. The glyphlight dimmed. The Watchers stepped back into the shadows, leaving the keeper alone in the circle.

"You will be tested," it said. "Here, in the heart of what was lost. Pass, and the way forward will open. Fail, and the city will keep you."

The silence that followed was heavier than the words.

Zara stepped forward. "We'll face it. Together."

The keeper inclined its head once, then dissolved back into the black water.

The chamber exhaled—a long, slow sigh.

Somewhere deep below, the drumbeat started again.

The drumbeat was slower now, but heavier—each pulse like a hand pressing against Zara's chest from the inside. It didn't just echo through the chamber; it crawled up the pillars, winding around the carved glyphs like a living thread.

Beneath her glove, the old glyph burn flared faintly, as if remembering the Thirteenth's mark. She didn't dare show it.

No one spoke. The heirs stood in a loose circle around the basin, weapons lowered but not at rest. They had crossed cities, bridges, and blood-soaked ground to reach this place, but for the first time since entering the Watchers' city, motion felt like a mistake.

The air held weight. Waiting weight.

A low scrape cut through the silence—a deliberate sound, not stone shifting under its own age. Selene's gaze tracked it to the far shadows where the pillars broke into archways. The Watchers were there. Not dozens. Hundreds. Silent, layered in darkness, helms glinting with that cold, wet sheen.

They didn't advance. They didn't need to. The basin had become the true center, and the Watchers ringed it like a living wall.

Kai's bowstring was drawn but loose, his eyes flicking between Zara and the shadowed mass beyond the pillars. "They're waiting for something."

"They're waiting for us to fail," Selene said. Her shadow licked out across the floor, touching the edge of the basin's reflection. It recoiled instantly, like a living thing burned.

Naia's fingers traced one of the pillar glyphs, her brow furrowed. "These markings… they're not just a record. They're instructions. But they're fragmented—like the city itself."

Zara stepped closer to see. "Fragmented how?"

"Like they were broken on purpose," Naia said. "Pieces removed so no one could understand the whole unless…"

"…unless they had the missing parts," Zara finished, her voice low. Her mind flashed to the Codex, to the etched spiral that burned behind her eyelids when she closed them.

Leo's trident tip rang softly as it tapped the stone floor. "Then the keeper wasn't just warning us. This is the test."

The basin shifted again—not a ripple, but a deepening of the black, as though the water sank away into an even darker well. Shapes emerged in its depth. At first they looked like more trapped spirits, but then Zara's breath caught.

They were the heirs.

Not as they stood now, but fractured—each one in motion, fighting alone against shadow. Selene dragged down by black chains. Leo on one knee, trident broken. Kai loosing arrow after arrow into an enemy that wouldn't fall. Naia screaming without sound. Isla's hammer cooling to dull iron in her hands.

And Zara—standing in a circle of light, alone.

The image was wrong in a way that gnawed at her, as if it wasn't prophecy or memory, but something worse: inevitability.

Kai broke the tension. "I've had enough of their games."

The moment he stepped toward the basin, the drumbeat spiked—three quick pulses, like the city's heart had skipped.

The keeper's voice returned, not from the water this time, but from everywhere at once.

"Prove you are worthy of what you seek."

The black surface exploded upward.

Water—if it was water—rushed from the basin in a spiraling column, wrapping the pillars, sealing the archways. The Watchers didn't move. They simply watched as the liquid hardened into walls of black glass, cutting the heirs off from one another.

♦ ♦ ♦

Zara

Zara spun, but the others were gone. No sound, no movement beyond her own. Just the drumbeat.

Her spiral flared, burning gold against the dark.

She stood in a perfect circle of smooth black stone, the basin gone, the pillars gone, the city gone. Only the glyphlight from her own hands kept the dark from swallowing her whole.

The voice came again, softer now. "Show us who you are when the path breaks."

The floor shifted under her feet. Shapes rose from it—Watchers, but wrong. Their armor was cracked, faces uncovered, and where their eyes should have been was only that endless spiral, spinning.

Zara's pulse climbed, but she set her stance. Numbers didn't lie. She counted their steps, measured their angles, fed the data into the pattern in her mind.

The first lunged. Her glyphfire met its blade with a shriek of metal on magic. Sparks lit the spiral in its eyes before it dissolved back into the stone.

One down. Eleven to go.

♦ ♦ ♦

Leo

The darkness pressed cold and wet against his skin. He was waist-deep in water, but it didn't ripple when he moved. The trident felt heavier here, like the ocean itself was holding it back.

From below, pale hands reached up. Not to grab him—worse. To pull the trident down. He saw faces in the water, warriors wearing his father's crest, their mouths moving in soundless curses.

"You let the storm take you," one mouthed.

He tightened his grip and wrenched the weapon free, lightning flaring along its length. The water hissed. The hands retreated—but he knew they would be back.

♦ ♦ ♦

Selene

Chains. Always chains.

They coiled around her arms and throat, but they weren't forged iron—they were shadow made solid, each link etched with the Watchers' glyph.

She pulled, and they pulled back. Every time she broke one, another tightened somewhere else.

But shadows were hers.

She let go of the fight, let the darkness spread through her fingers, and instead of resisting the chains, she became them. When she stepped forward, they moved with her, breaking and remaking until she was no longer bound—she was crowned.

♦ ♦ ♦

Kai

The bow was steady. His heartbeat was not.

Targets emerged in the dark—first one, then three, then a dozen. All Watchers. All moving faster than any arrow could fly.

He breathed in, slowed the world, let the geometry settle into place. The arrow's arc became the only truth.

One shot. One target down.

Again.

The drumbeat matched his release until he could no longer tell if he was following it or if it was following him.

◆ ◆ ◆

Naia

The ground split, water roaring up to meet her. But it wasn't saltwater—it was the kind that remembers.

She saw her own reflection in its rise, but older. Wiser. Alone.

The wave didn't crash; it stood, holding its own shape, waiting.

Naia stepped forward and placed her hand against it. The water folded around her fingers without wetting them, glyphs spinning just beneath the surface. She whispered the binding words, and the wave bowed before it broke.

◆ ◆ ◆


Isla

The forge was cold. The hammer was cold. Her breath fogged in the still air.

Shapes moved beyond the dying light, all edges and hunger. She struck the anvil once, twice, but the sound was thin.

She closed her eyes. Remembered heat. Remembered her father's forge and the way fire lived when you fed it.

When she opened them, the hammer blazed again, and the dark took a step back.

The walls of black glass shattered all at once.

The heirs stood together again, weapons raised, breathing hard.

Zara remembered a marginal note in Dr. Eleni's files—Venetian ruins often conceal mirror trials; survivors are rare. The memory knifed through her as the fragments fell away.

The keeper emerged from the basin, taller now, the glyphs on its helm burning white.

◆ ◆ ◆

"You have endured the trial," it said. "The path remains open—but narrow." The chamber exhaled—a long, slow sigh

◆ ◆ ◆

The drumbeat softened, fading into the stone until it was only memory.

The Watchers stepped back into the shadows, leaving the basin still and empty.

Zara's spiral dimmed, but it did not fade.

"What's next?" she asked.

The keeper tilted its helm toward the archway that had not been there before. Beyond it was only darkness.

"Next," it said, "you walk where the gods feared to tread."

◆ ◆ ◆

The archway yawned before them, taller than the gate they had forced open, its edges carved in patterns that resisted the eye— every time Zara tried to follow one, it bent away into something else. The darkness beyond wasn't absence; it was presence, thick and slow, as if it might reach back and touch whoever stared too long.

No one moved at first.

It was Selene who broke the stillness, stepping until her shadow kissed the threshold. The air there was different—colder, sharper, carrying a metallic tang like the taste of lightning before a strike. She glanced back over her shoulder. "If we stop here, every-thing we've done to get here means nothing."

Leo's grip tightened on his trident. "I wasn't planning on stop-ping."

The Watchers still lined the chamber's edge, motionless, their helms glinting faintly in the guttering glyphlight. They did not fol-low, but Zara could feel their attention like the weight of deep wa-ter. She didn't trust the stillness; still water only meant the current ran somewhere unseen.

The keeper had already dissolved back into the basin, leaving no ripple to prove it had been there at all. But the echo of its voice clung to the stone: The path remains open—but narrow.

375

Naia stepped forward, her gaze sweeping the archway's carvings. "These wards… they're not meant to keep something out." She paused, voice lower. "They're to keep something in."

Kai let out a humorless breath. "So we're volunteering to go inside the thing the Watchers don't leave unguarded. Great."

Zara's spiral pulsed once—a golden coil tightening in her mind—and she knew with the cold certainty of math that Naia was right. This wasn't the next chamber in the city. This was below it.

She swallowed. "We move together. No one outpaces the others."

They crossed the threshold.

The darkness didn't swallow them all at once. It layered, thickening around their ankles like fog before climbing to their waists, their chests, their throats. Glyphlight dimmed against it, as though each step leeched a little more color from the world.

Somewhere far behind, the drumbeat started again.

They kept walking. The floor shifted from cut stone to something older—slabs shot through with veins of dull silver that hummed underfoot. Zara felt each vibration in her teeth.

"Feels like walking on a heartbeat," Isla muttered. Her hammer gave off only the faintest glow now, like embers under ash.

The tunnel widened into a long gallery, its walls etched with reliefs so eroded they seemed half-forgotten by the stone itself. Figures in crowns stood above oceans on fire; winged shapes fell through shattered skies. Between each scene, the same symbol repeated—not a god's glyph, but a spiral so old it made Zara's own burn hotter in response.

Leo slowed beside one, running his fingers over the groove. "These are warnings. Someone carved the end of the world into these walls."

"They're not warnings," Selene said quietly. "They're records."

A faint whisper rode the air. Not words, but the sound of words—too far away to hear clearly, too close to ignore. It threaded through the gallery like smoke, curling into their ears no matter how they turned their heads.

Zara glanced back. The archway was gone.

Her throat tightened. "No turning back."

The gallery ended in a set of descending steps, shallow and wide, as if made for something much larger than them. A pale blue glow pulsed faintly from below, rhythmic—three quick beats, pause, three quick beats.

Kai exhaled sharply. "That's the same pattern from the trial."

"No," Zara said. "It's faster."

They descended. The steps grew damper, the air cooler, until the faint tang of salt sharpened into the smell of a tide pool just before a storm. Somewhere ahead, water moved—not waves, not current, but the deliberate shift of something alive.

The final step opened onto a vast platform jutting out over black water. The glow came from far below, pulsing in time with the drumbeat. Beyond the platform, the cavern stretched into a darkness so complete it resisted even Isla's hammer-light.

Naia's breath caught. "This… isn't part of the city. The city was built around it."

Zara stepped to the platform's edge. The spiral in her mind ached now, pulling toward the water. She didn't know how she knew, but she knew—somewhere down there lay another fragment.

And something else.

The drumbeat deepened, resonating up through the soles of their boots.

From the darkness across the cavern, two points of light appeared. Then two more. Then dozens. Cold, silver, unblinking. They were too high above the water to be reflections.

Kai nocked an arrow. "Tell me those aren't—"

"They're watching," Selene finished.

The lights blinked out, all at once.

The cavern exhaled.

Something in the water moved.

The spiral inside Zara's head flared so bright she had to close her eyes. In the dark behind her eyelids, she saw not the cavern, not the city, but the map in the Codex—lines shifting, corridors rearranging themselves, converging here.

The keeper's voice came from nowhere and everywhere at once.

"Walk further, and the path will close behind you."

When Zara opened her eyes, the blue glow below was rising, slow and deliberate, lighting the water from within. Shadows broke across its surface—long, thin shapes gliding just beneath.

Leo's jaw set. "Too late to turn back now."

Zara took a breath, the air heavy with salt and the weight of choice.

"Then we keep going," she said.

Together, they stepped to the edge as the light beneath the water grew brighter… and the darkness above them began to move.

◆ ◆ ◆

Within the spiral chamber, Maelis stood at the edge of the ritual.

She held a mirror shard in one hand. It didn't reflect her face—only Thane's.

Still dreaming.

Still drifting.

"He resists," a watcher murmured.

"No," Maelis said. "He chooses."

Back in the dream, Thane stood before the flame.

It opened like a flower made of shadow and light.

Inside was a voice. Not the same as before.

This one belonged to her.

"You are not theirs," she whispered. "You never were."

Thane's fists clenched.

"Then what am I?"

She stepped forward.

And in the flicker of flame, he saw her—just for a second.

Golden eyes. A burn over one brow. Hair like liquid coal.

"You are the Thirteenth."

She pressed the mirrored glyph to his chest.

It didn't burn.

It fit.

The spiral flared behind them.

The vision fractured.

Thane woke with a gasp.

The sky above him was black with storm.

In his hand, the glyph pulsed—mirror-bright and watching.

And somewhere deep in the shadows beneath the ruin—

Maelis smiled.

♦ ♦ ♦

Thane didn't sleep again.

Not really.

He drifted.

Between flame and silence. Between what he remembered and what had been planted in its place.

Every time he closed his eyes, the same image returned:

A spiral that was also a lock.

A crown made of shattered mirrors.

And Maelis—watching.

Not commanding.

Inviting.

Beneath him, the city groaned.

Venice wasn't just sinking—it was whispering.

He could hear it now.

The ruined sanctum they'd uncovered was older than the canals, older than the stone.

The others didn't feel it.

But Thane did.

Like a hook in his blood.

A crack sounded behind his thoughts.

A ripple through his dreamself.

Then a whisper:

"Come to me."

In the forgotten chamber, Maelis walked the spiral once more.

Twelve Watchers stood still. The thirteenth was absent.

Her voice echoed across the mirrored glyph floor, each word bending light and shadow:

"What was written shall be unwritten.

What was sealed shall be sung.

And he—he shall choose not Olympus.

But judgment."

She reached the center of the spiral and dropped a single drop of her own blood onto the glyph.

It shimmered. Then flared.

From the dark: his reflection.

Not Thane as he was.

Thane as he would be.

Crowned. Unchained. Alone.

She knelt.

Her eyes burned, but not with power. With memory.

"I never wanted this for you," she said quietly.

"But I could not stop it."

Thane walked the alley alone.

The others were camped, debating the ruins.

He told them he needed air.

That was true.

But it wasn't the whole truth.

His hand was clenched in his pocket. The mirrored shard pulsed against his skin.

He didn't know when he'd taken it.

But he couldn't let it go.

A whisper guided him.

Not through the streets.

Through the seams.

He stepped between shadows and suddenly he was there—

In the chamber.

Not in body.

But in will.

Maelis turned.

And smiled.

It was not cruel.

It was grieving.

"You came."

He looked around, unsure if he stood or floated.

"Where is this?"

"A memory," she said. "And a promise. One the gods broke."

Thane's chest ached. "Why me?"

"Because you remember," she said. "Even if they forced you to forget."

She walked toward him.

"Do you want the truth?"

He didn't answer.

She extended her hand.

And in it—a crown of shadowlight.

Thirteen points.

One flame.

No chain.

"Will you wear what was denied you?" she asked.

"Not as heir."

"As Watcher."

Thane reached—

And stopped.

"…If I say yes," he whispered, "what happens to them?"

Maelis's voice softened.

"They keep believing."

He trembled.

But he took the crown.

And when he did, the mirror glyph in his hand melted into his skin.

Far above, Zara stirred.

The glyph burn on her palm had gone cold.

Dead.

And she didn't know why, but it made her want to weep.

In the spiral chamber, Maelis whispered the final words:

"The pact is made."

"The flame is chosen."

"The thirteenth mark… awakens."

And far beneath the Codex—

A fourteenth glyph cracked.

◆ ◆ ◆

# *Codex Fragment*

## *The Lightning That remembers*

Lightning does not strike —
it remembers.
Each bolt a name, each echo a chain.
The heir of storms is both beacon and
target,
bearing the crown that calls the
tempest home.
When thunder walks, the past awakens.
Follow the fire that scars the sky,
for it marks the place where gods
still breathe.

# CHAPTER XXII

# The Gods' Silence

Venice, February 28, 2026

Darkness still pressed against the surface, but below, the Gate of Ash stirred.

The light beneath the black water swelled, rolling in slow, deliberate pulses that threw shifting ripples against the cavern walls. Every beat of it vibrated through the soles of Zara's boots, as if the stone itself shared the rhythm of some vast, unseen heart.

The darkness above them moved again.

It wasn't wind.

It wasn't alive in the way flesh and blood were alive.

It was slower, heavier—a vast canopy shifting, as if an ocean's worth of shadow had decided to lean closer.

No one spoke.

Leo angled his trident upward, the bronze tips catching what little light the rising glow offered. "Anyone want to tell me what that is?"

No answer came.

Because they all knew.

Watchers didn't blink.

But something was blinking up there—whole swaths of darkness closing and opening, each time revealing the faintest suggestion of eyes. Not silver now, but deep blue, the color of midnight tide.

Zara's spiral flared in her mind, not in warning, but in recognition.

Whatever was above them was tied to the same geometry that had pulled her down here.

A shiver passed through her—not fear, but the same bone-deep recognition she'd felt in Cambridge when the spiral first woke. It was as if the geometry itself leaned forward, curious, waiting to see if she would step where it wanted her to. Somewhere, far beyond the black water and the breathing dark, the pattern answered her back.

Kai shifted, bow drawn but not aimed. "If those are eyes, then we're already inside its gaze."

"They're not just eyes," Selene said, her voice a blade's edge in the dim. "They're wards. Living wards."

The pulse from the depths quickened—three beats, pause, three beats. The same cadence from the trial chamber, but heavier now, the air thick with it.

The blue glow rose higher, and for the first time they saw what swam beneath.

Long, skeletal shapes slid through the water, each one impossibly thin but stretching longer than the platform itself. They wove around one another in perfect spirals, tails and heads never touching, bodies refracting the light into razor fragments.

Naia's breath hitched. "That's... not any sea creature I know."

"Because it's not from the sea," Isla murmured. Her hammer gave off only the faintest ember-glow now, a pale defiance against the cold rising from the water.

Zara stepped to the platform's edge, the pull of the spiral inside her skull nearly dragging her forward. The Codex fragment pressed against her ribs like it wanted out.

She closed her eyes.

The map shifted in the dark behind her eyelids—corridors folding in on themselves, gates unsealing, lines converging here. The pull was absolute.

When she opened her eyes, the skeletal shapes had stopped moving. They hung in the water like suspended ink, heads tilted upward toward the platform.

They were listening.

The keeper's voice came from everywhere and nowhere. "Walk further, and the path will close behind you."

"Too late for that," Leo muttered.

Selene's shadow curled at her feet, then stretched toward the water as if reaching for its own reflection. It stopped just short of the surface, shivering.

"They don't want us here," she said.

"Or," Kai countered, "they're waiting for us to prove we should be."

A deep, grinding noise rolled through the cavern. Across the black water, something began to rise—not from the depths, but from the far wall itself. Stone split along hidden seams, slabs pulling apart to reveal a gateway as tall as a watchtower.

And behind that gateway burned light.

Not glyphlight. Not fire. Something between the two—molten gold shot through with threads of shadow, churning like a storm in a forge.

Isla took a step forward, her eyes locked on it. "That's not just an exit."

Naia's voice was low, urgent. "That's the Gate of Ash."

Isla inhaled sharply. The stench was the same as the Santorini caverns—the tang of molten stone and iron sweat. Her forge answered even here.

Zara frowned. "You know it?"

"I've read the fragments," Naia said, not looking away from the blaze. "The Gate was built to keep a fire that could burn gods contained. If it's open…"

She didn't finish.

The skeletal shapes in the water stirred, curling tighter, forming spirals that mirrored the one in Zara's mind. The glow beneath them dimmed, as if they were drawing it into themselves.

The grinding from the far side stopped. The Gate of Ash stood fully revealed, its surface a lattice of blackened metal and burning light. Even from here, the heat licked at their faces.

The keeper's voice returned, heavier now. "Only those who carry the fire may pass."

In the shifting heat, Zara thought she saw something in the lattice beyond Isla—twelve faint shapes, their glyphs lit not with gold, but with a pale, fractured light. One of them bore the curved motif of Aphrodite's crown, but splintered into shadow. She blinked, and the vision was gone.

Every gaze shifted to Isla.

Her hammer's ember-light flared—then guttered.

"I'm not ready," she said, her tone flat with the kind of honesty that leaves no space for argument.

"You're not alone," Leo told her. "None of us are."

"Then we go together," Zara said. Her glyphs tingled against her skin, resonating with the burning light across the water. "But that means crossing."

As if in answer, the skeletal shapes moved again—not toward them, but downward. The glow from below followed them into the depths, and the water stilled.

Kai scanned the drop. "That's not exactly a bridge."

Naia shook her head. "It's a test. The Gate won't let us cross unless we give it what it's asking for."

"And what's that?" Selene asked.

Naia met her gaze. "A spark."

Zara turned to Isla. "You can do this."

Leo stepped up beside her, his voice low but steady. "Hey—remember the docks in Chicago? First leap's always the hardest. After that, you just keep moving."

Isla's jaw tightened. "I can try."

She stepped forward, toes to the platform's edge. The hammer in her hands began to glow again, faint at first, then brighter, threads of molten gold chasing each other along the metal's grooves. She raised it high.

The air shifted.

The water below rippled without wind. From the depths, a column of light surged upward, meeting the hammer's glow in a burst that threw heat across the platform. The skeletal shapes reappeared, spiraling around the light like living filigree.

When the flare faded, a path stretched across the water—narrow, black, and steaming.

The Gate of Ash burned brighter.

Zara exhaled. "Move."

They crossed single file, weapons ready, every step echoing against the cavern walls. The path trembled underfoot, heat seeping through their boots. Behind them, the darkness above shifted again, following.

Halfway across, a sharp hiss broke the air.

The skeletal shapes dove beneath the path, vanishing into the black. The heat under their feet surged, and thin cracks began to form along the edges, glowing from within.

"Hurry," Naia urged.

They broke into a run.

The Gate loomed closer, its lattice shifting as if aware of their approach. Figures began to take shape in the fire—not Watchers, not gods, but something between, their outlines fluid, their faces hidden.

By the time they reached the far side, the path behind them had already crumbled into steam.

The skeletal shapes resurfaced, curling protectively around the remaining shards before sinking again.

The Gate's fire roared.

Zara felt the spiral inside her head thrum in time with it. The Codex fragment burned against her skin.

The keeper's voice came once more.
"You may enter—but the fire will test you."

The fire in the Gate did not flicker. It churned.

Molten light rolled and folded over itself like waves in a storm, threaded with veins of black that pulsed in rhythm with the unseen heart of the cavern. The lattice of charred metal framing it was not fixed—it shifted subtly, expanding and contracting with each thrum, like the ribs of something alive.

Zara's palm itched where her glyphs burned faintly. The Codex fragment pressed harder into her side, as though it had been waiting for this exact moment.

Behind them, the platform was gone—only steam rose where the crossing had been. The skeletal shapes in the water were nowhere to be seen, though their absence felt intentional, as if they were now part of the Gate itself.

Selene's eyes narrowed. "It's not just heat coming off that thing."

Naia nodded once. "It's alive."

"Alive?" Kai asked, keeping his bow low but ready. "Please tell me you mean in the symbolic, ancient, very-much-not-trying-to-kill-us way."

"No," Naia said simply. "It's breathing."

The heat grew thicker with every step they took toward it. By the time they reached the Gate's shadow, sweat had already begun to bead at Zara's temples. Isla seemed unaffected, though the glow in her hammer had deepened, as if feeding on the proximity.

The voice came again—the keeper, but lower, resonating from the ground itself.

"The fire tests all who enter. Those unworthy will burn before the first step is taken."

The lattice shifted, widening to reveal a corridor of molten light beyond. The floor within was black stone shot through with faint veins of gold, like cooled lava still remembering the heat.

Leo angled his trident toward the threshold. "So… do we just walk in?"

"That's never how this works," Selene muttered.

They crossed the threshold together.

The moment the first boot hit the black stone, the world changed.

The air was fire—not burning them outright, but pressing close, testing their limits. Every breath felt like drawing molten metal into their lungs. The corridor ahead was long, its walls alive with movement, glyphs crawling and rearranging like insects across the surface.

"Stay in the center," Naia said quickly. "The edges are unstable."

"How unstable?" Kai asked.

She didn't answer—because the wall nearest him shifted suddenly, a hand of pure flame lashing out. He twisted away, the arrow he had half-drawn already loosed. It passed through the hand without slowing, but the flame recoiled, hissing.

"They're watching us," Zara said. She didn't mean the flames.

The corridor ended in a wide chamber.

The fire here was not contained to the walls. It fell from the ceiling in sheets, poured from cracks in the floor, spun upward in twisting columns. In the center stood a circular platform of black stone, suspended over a pit so deep the firelight could not reach its bottom.

Bridges of obsidian extended from the platform to the chamber's edges—twelve of them.

One for each heir.

The keeper's voice rose, echoing without origin. "The fire knows your truths. Step where you belong."

The heirs froze.

"What does that mean?" Leo asked, scanning the bridges.

Naia's eyes were fixed on the nearest one, where faint waves of heat shimmered above the surface. "They're not all safe."

"Safe?" Kai said. "Pretty sure none of them are safe."

Zara stepped forward, the spiral in her mind tugging her toward one of the bridges on the far side. The gold veins in its surface pulsed faintly, matching her glyphlight.

"I think… it's calling us," she said.

One by one, they moved.

Kai's steps carried him to a bridge lined with etched suns, each one radiating faint warmth.

Selene found herself facing a span shrouded in flickering shadow, the flames along its edge bending away from her as if in recognition.

Naia's bridge glistened as if wet, though no water could survive in the heat of the chamber. Steam curled up with each of her steps.

Leo's bridge roared faintly beneath his boots, lightning-like threads running along its sides.

Isla's was a path of deep crimson, each step sparking faint embers that clung to her hammer.

Zara's bridge was etched with spirals—not hers, but older, their curves broken and mended again.

When they reached the center platform, the fire changed.

It rose higher, encircling them without touching, a wall of living heat. Shapes began to form within the flames—not Watchers, not gods, but figures of molten gold and black glass. Each one held a weapon shaped from the same fire that birthed them.

Twelve in all.

"They're… us," Kai said quietly.

He was right. The figures were mirrors—twisted reflections of the heirs, their weapons burning brighter, their eyes lit from within by the same fire that filled the Gate.

The keeper's voice returned, quieter now, but carrying more weight.

"To carry the fire, you must face the fire."

The mirrored figures moved.

For a heartbeat, none of them moved. Breath rattled in chests, eyes flicked between allies and reflections, the silence louder than the storm above. Fear pressed, but so did resolve.

Zara's stepped forward first, spiral glyphs flaring along its arms. Its movements were hers, but faster, sharper—no hesitation. Her first strike met its counter in a burst of heat that drove her back two steps.

To her left, Isla's double swung a blazing hammer that sent shards of molten stone flying. She met the blow with her own, the two weapons ringing like struck bells.

Kai's twin loosed arrows of pure flame, each one arcing unnaturally toward him. He rolled, returned fire, and watched as the arrow burned out before it could land.

Selene's shadow-double struck without warning, chains of fire lashing out to bind her arms. She twisted free, her own shadows burning where they touched the chains.

Naia faced a figure that moved like water, its flames rippling rather than flaring. Every strike she made was absorbed, every defense tested.

Leo's double fought like the sea in a storm—relentless, surging forward with each clash, the trident's tips white-hot.

The battle was relentless.

Every blow from the doubles carried more heat, every clash feeding the fire in the chamber. The bridges behind them began to crumble, one by one, dropping into the pit with no sound.

"This is the test," Naia shouted over the roar. "It's not about killing them—it's about surviving them."

"Then we survive," Zara said through clenched teeth.

Her spiral flared again, burning gold against the heat. She let the pattern guide her—not matching the double's speed, but changing her rhythm, stepping out of the mirrored dance entirely.

The shift worked. Her next strike landed clean, spiraling glyph-fire unraveling part of the double's form. The fire recoiled, but did not vanish.

Across the platform, Isla roared, driving her hammer into the stone. The shockwave rippled outward, breaking her double's stance. Kai's arrow found its mark a moment later, punching through the figure's chest in a burst of molten spray.

Selene's shadows twined around the chains of fire, pulling them apart link by link until the double dissolved into smoke. Naia whispered a binding, and her rippling opponent froze, then shattered.

Leo's trident caught the light of the Gate itself, a surge of gold-and-bronze fire running down its length. His final strike sent his double spinning into the pit, where it vanished in a plume of steam.

One by one, the doubles fell.

When the last burst of flame faded, the fire around the platform pulled back, lowering until it was just a faint wall at the chamber's edges.

The keeper's voice returned.

"You have carried the fire—for now. But the fire will carry you, too. Remember that."

The bridges were gone. Only a single path forward remained—a narrow causeway of black stone leading deeper into the Gate.

Zara's pulse was still high, the heat still in her blood. She glanced at the others.

"We keep moving," she said.

No one argued.

They stepped onto the causeway together, the roar of the Gate fading behind them, the darkness ahead already shifting.

The causeway narrowed after the first dozen steps, its edges breaking away into the chasm below.

Here, the heat changed. It no longer pressed against their skin like the breath of a forge; instead, it sank inward, lodging deep in bone and muscle, as if the Gate had left its brand inside them.

Zara kept her focus on the spiral burning in her mind. It pulled forward, steady, unwavering, even as the air grew heavier.

"Feels… different," Leo murmured.

Selene's gaze flicked to the walls—if they could be called walls. They were not stone but black glass, warped and streaked as if frozen mid-melt. Shapes shifted beneath the surface: skeletal coils, half-seen faces, flashes of glyphs older than Olympus.

"They're watching," she said. "Not the Watchers. Something else."

Naia slowed, fingertips brushing the glass. The surface pulsed faintly under her touch. "Memory. This whole place is a memory."

"Whose?" Kai asked.

The glass shivered—once, sharply—and Naia pulled her hand back. "Not one you want to share a mind with."

The causeway ended in a wide lip of stone overlooking a descent so sheer the glow from below barely reached them. The drop was not total darkness; pale blue fissures cracked through the walls far beneath, lighting what looked like a spiral staircase carved into the hollow of the chasm.

Except the staircase was moving.

Not rising, not falling—rotating. Slowly.

"Tell me that's not what it looks like," Isla said, stepping closer.

"It's a descent spiral," Zara confirmed. "But it's alive."

And it was. The steps shifted with a muscle-like ripple, edges flexing before settling back into shape. Each movement came with a deep bass thrum that rattled in their teeth.

Selene's mouth tightened. "We have to get down there."

"How?" Kai asked. "We can't jump. And if that thing's moving, climbing's a good way to lose a leg."

The keeper's voice returned, faint but close—as though it stood directly behind them.

"Step with the spiral, or be unmade by it."

They didn't debate. There was no point.

One by one, they leapt from the lip to the first curve of the living staircase. The heat flared instantly through their boots, and Zara felt the spiral in her mind sync with the rhythm beneath her feet—a subtle pull forward when the step flexed, a warning twist when it shifted too far.

The descent began.

The staircase rotated in deliberate arcs, carrying them downward along the inner wall of the chasm. Sometimes the pale blue fissures in the glass revealed more than light—flashes of enormous shapes coiled deeper still, slow and patient, their forms too large to comprehend.

At one turn, Kai leaned too close to a fissure. His breath caught.

"What did you see?" Zara asked without looking back.

"An eye," he said. "Bigger than the platform in the Gate. And it was looking at me."

No one commented.

Halfway down, the first shift came.

The staircase convulsed, a tremor racing ahead of them. Segments collapsed into the wall and reappeared further down, faster than stone should move. The spiral in Zara's mind screamed a warning.

"Run!" she shouted.

They sprinted, boots slamming on hot stone, each step timed to the shifting rhythm. Twice, Isla's hammer struck the surface to anchor her balance. Naia nearly slipped when the step under her rolled forward like the deck of a ship, but Leo caught her arm and pulled her upright.

The thrum grew louder, closer to a roar.

They leapt the last collapsing section together, landing hard on a broader platform far below.

Here, the heat was gone.

The air was cold, the kind that clung to bone. Breath misted instantly. The only light came from a wide fissure ahead, spilling that same pale blue glow into the chamber.

Through it, Zara could see a massive door—not metal, not stone, but something that looked like frozen water shot through with veins of light. Glyphs swam across its surface like fish beneath ice.

Naia stepped forward, awe softening her voice. "This isn't part of the Gate. This is older."

"Older than Olympus?" Selene asked.

Naia nodded once. "Much."

The Codex fragment in Zara's ribs pulsed once in answer, and an image—unbidden, unwelcome—flashed in her mind. Not Olympus as the world knew it, but a broken continent sealed beneath an endless tide, its heart chained by spirals like these. A prison, not a city. And something within it still listening.

They approached the door cautiously. The cold deepened with every step, but beneath it was something else—a vibration that matched the spiral in Zara's skull, the same geometry that had pulled her through the city, the trial, the Gate.

When she laid her hand on the surface, the glyphs froze in place.

The Codex fragment against her ribs flared hot.

"This is what it's been leading to," she said.

Leo's trident angled toward the dark around them. "And what's on the other side?"

Before she could answer, the fissure-light dimmed—not from within the door, but from something passing in front of it.

The first figure emerged from the shadows to their right.

It wasn't a Watcher.

It wore no armor, only a skin of black glass that reflected the pale blue glow like shards of a broken mirror. Its limbs were too long, its movements smooth in ways that felt wrong for a thing made of solid matter. The face was nothing but a spiral carved into the surface, glowing faintly.

Another appeared behind it. Then a third.

"Twelve," Kai said, voice flat. "Always twelve."

Selene's shadow stretched toward the nearest one, but recoiled when it touched the surface. "They're not shadow or flame. They're… void."

The lead figure tilted its head. The spiral on its face spun once, slow and deliberate.

When it spoke, the voice was a chorus—layered, shifting pitch mid-word.

"The path you walk does not end at the Gate. Beyond lies the Hollow. The Hollow does not forgive."

Kai's knuckles whitened on his bowstring. He hated the silence more than the fire.

No one moved.

"The fire lets you pass. We do not."

The figures advanced.

The first blow came fast—a slicing arm that elongated mid-swing, forcing Leo to parry with the trident. The impact rang like striking glass with a tuning fork, a vibration running up his arm.

Isla swung her hammer into the second figure's chest. It cracked but did not break, the fracture sealing almost instantly with a hiss.

"They heal," she warned.

"Then hit harder," Kai said, loosing an arrow. The shaft sank into a spiral-glyph and stuck there, the glow dimming for half a breath before returning.

Zara's spiral burned hotter. She could feel the pattern in their movements—not random, but a looping rhythm, each strike part of a cycle.

"Break the cycle!" she called.

They shifted tactics.

Instead of meeting strikes head-on, they disrupted them mid-arc, forcing the void-figures to reset. Selene tangled one's legs with her shadow and pulled just as Isla's hammer came down, shattering the joint completely. This time, the fracture didn't seal.

Naia summoned a sheet of water from the air—impossible in the cold—and slammed it into another's spiral-face. The glow sputtered.

Leo drove his trident into the same gap twice, splitting the crack wider.

One by one, the void-figures faltered, their glass bodies losing cohesion. The last collapsed in a spray of black shards that vanished before they touched the floor.

Silence returned.

The pale blue light brightened again, flowing across the door's surface until the glyphs began to turn, aligning with the spiral in Zara's mind.

The keeper's voice returned, softer now, as though spoken from far above.

"Beyond this threshold lies the Hollow Descent. Once taken, it cannot be reversed."

Naia's voice was hushed, reverent. 'The Hollow remembers us, even if we don't remember it.'

Zara's breath clouded the air. "We go together."

One by one, they placed their hands on the door.

The ice-like surface rippled outward from their touch, the glyphs locking into place with a sound like stone grinding underwater.

With a deep, resonant sigh, the door began to open.

What lay beyond was not fire, nor ice, nor shadow—but a vast, spiraling chasm that seemed to descend forever, lit only by a distant, pulsing light far below.

The spiral in Zara's mind pulsed back in answer.

They stepped through.

The door closed behind them without a sound.

The silence was absolute.

Not the stillness of an empty room, but the kind that swallows the memory of sound itself.

Their footsteps landed too softly, as if the stone absorbed them before they could echo.

The spiral stretched downward in perfect arcs, each step broad enough for three to walk abreast, each edge dropping into nothing. Far below, that pulsing light throbbed—slower now, almost a heartbeat in hibernation.

Kai leaned over the inner edge, his breath ghosting into the dark. "That's… a long way down."

"No edges to catch you if you fall," Naia said, tracing the outer wall. Her voice was hushed, not by fear, but by reverence. "The descent is meant to be walked, not survived by accident."

Selene's shadow bled along the wall, curling into its cracks like ink in water. "Then we walk."

They moved in tight formation, Zara in the lead, her spiral sense tugging them along the safest rhythm. The Hollow seemed to shift around them—not changing shape, but subtly bending perspective, so each glance back revealed a different curve than the one they'd just taken.

"Anyone else notice the steps are… warmer?"

Isla nodded, the haft of her hammer leaving faint steam when it brushed the stone. "Heat's building as we go down."

The warmth was slow at first, creeping in under the chill, but within minutes, it became undeniable. The air thickened, carrying the faint tang of ash—old ash, long settled, stirred again.

Half a tier down, the wall fractured into alcoves. Inside each, a single object rested: a helm, a blade, a fragment of armor. All burned black, all etched with spirals.

Naia paused at one alcove, her fingers hovering over a shattered bracer. "These aren't offerings."

"They're warnings," Selene finished.

Zara's spiral tightened. The pattern told her the Hollow had claimed these before. Claimed, and kept.

The further they descended, the louder the pulse from below became—not in volume, but in pressure, pressing at their chests and temples.

It was not the rhythm of a heart. It was the slow, deliberate cadence of something vast at rest, measuring their steps as if weighing their worth against the ages it had already endured.

Isla exhaled through her teeth. "Feels like it's breathing on us."

"It's breathing with us," Zara said before she could stop herself. And she was right—the pulse matched their steps now, adjusting when they slowed, quickening when they pushed forward.

Kai's bow hand flexed. "Not creepy at all."

At the third curve, the light from below flared, bright enough to throw moving shadows across the walls. But nothing moved on the spiral.

Not at first.

Then, from below, a whisper rose—dry, like sand shifting over glass. It came in threads, weaving into words only when the Hollow carried them close.

"One fire is not enough."

The voice didn't belong to the keeper. This one was older. Rougher.

Isla's hammer flared, molten heat spilling across the steps in a brief, defiant glow. "If it's looking for more fire, it's going to be disappointed."

The whisper came again.

"More fire… or more ashes."

Something stirred in the light below.

It wasn't one thing—it was dozens, maybe hundreds, moving in concentric spirals of their own. Each was no bigger than a man, but their movements were precise, their heads turning upward in unison.

Zara's stomach knotted. They weren't Watchers. They weren't the glass-bodied sentinels from before. These looked almost human—until they stepped into the glow and the light slid straight through them, as if their bodies were made of smoke trapped in skin.

Selene's shadow coiled tight around her boots. "They're waiting for us to come to them."

"And if we stop here?" Kai asked.

Leo's gaze never left the moving shapes. "Then they come to us."

The whisper rose to a hiss. The figures began to climb—not on the steps, but up the air between them, their limbs folding at wrong angles to find invisible purchase.

"Down," Zara ordered.

They quickened their pace, steps landing in perfect rhythm with the spiral's pull. The climbing shapes mirrored them, matching speed, never breaking formation.

Naia drew water from the air, letting it swirl at her fingertips in a silent readiness. Isla kept her hammer loose but high.

The light below grew brighter still, spilling up the spiral like a tide about to break.

They reached the next tier—and stopped.

The spiral ahead had collapsed. The steps dangled in midair, their ends smoothed to glass, edges glowing faintly from heat. The drop was open and absolute, nothing between them and the pulsing light far below.

"Options?" Kai asked.

"Make one," Isla said, stepping forward.

She slammed the hammer down. The impact rang like a struck bell, molten lines spiderwebbing outward until a new span formed—narrow, steaming, but solid.

"Move," she said.

They crossed fast.

Halfway across, the climbing figures reached their level. The first lunged—its body flickering into a smear of smoke and then back into shape mid-air.

Zara's glyphfire met it head-on, the impact sending it twisting away in a scream like wind through a crack.

Leo caught another on his trident's prongs and hurled it into the abyss. No sound followed its fall.

By the time they reached solid spiral again, the shapes had halted their climb, fading back into the lower glow as if satisfied to let them pass.

The heat spiked. The air shimmered.

They rounded the last visible curve—and the Hollow opened into a vast, circular platform suspended over the source of the light. The platform's surface was carved with a spiral so vast it could be seen only from above, every groove filled with molten gold.

At its center stood an altar of black glass, its surface rippling faintly as if it were liquid pretending to be solid.

The Codex fragment at Zara's side flared hotter than it ever had before. Her spiral pulsed so hard she had to steady herself against the heat of it.

Naia's voice was barely audible. "This is it."

Before anyone could move closer, the molten grooves brightened—not from the light below, but from within the platform itself. The spiral began to turn, slow and deliberate, pulling the air into its center.

The whisper returned, louder, clearer.

"Bring the fire to the Hollow… or be burned away."

All eyes turned to Isla.

She stepped forward, hammer blazing now in full flame, and set it on the altar. The black glass hissed—then melted around the metal, drawing the fire in like a breath.

The platform trembled.

The light below surged upward, swallowing the edges of the spiral.

Zara's mind went white with heat and geometry. She saw the path forward—not through stone, not through shadow, but through light itself.

She turned to the others. "When it opens, we run. No looking back."

"Carrying the fire is only the first choice," the whisper rasped, curling into the edges of her thoughts. "The last choice will be what you burn with it."

The spiral's center split, revealing a narrow drop churning with molten gold and threads of shadow.

The Hollow exhaled—and they jumped.

INTERLUDE V
# THE HIDDEN THRONE

Venice, March 2, 2026

In the deepest trench beneath the city-that-shouldn't-exist, where the walls curved away into a dark so total it felt carved from absence, twelve pillars rose from the stone.

Between them, the air bent—not from heat or cold, but from the weight of something that had no right to fit inside a mortal world.

The Watchers moved in silence.

No scrape of boot. No rustle of cloth. They simply existed where they were needed, drifting from pillar to pillar like fragments of shadow that had learned the shape of men. Even silence had texture here—dense, heavy, almost damp against the skin.

Their masks gleamed faintly—not with the silver of the hunt, but with a new glow: thin lines of midnight-blue tracing spirals that pulsed in time with something unseen.

At the center of the pillars stood a throne.

It was not built. It had been grown—stone coaxed upward into twisting roots, branches, and spines, as if a single seed of darkness had been planted here long ago and left to feed on centuries of silence. The seat was wide enough for two men, but the shadow pooled there claimed the space alone.

Maelis sat as if the throne had been waiting for her since the first crack in Olympus.

Her hair spilled in dark, metallic strands that caught the faint light like oil. The crown she wore was not gold or iron but a circlet of fractured glass, each shard etched with spirals so small they seemed to crawl when looked at directly.

In her hands rested the Mirror-Glyph—a disk of black metal, polished to such a depth that it reflected not the chamber, but another place entirely: a bleeding horizon, a city drowning in firelight, and above it, the shadow of something vast and wingless, blocking out the stars.

She was watching the heirs. Each reflection split into dozens, as though the mirror remembered futures more clearly than the present

Not as they were now, but as they would be. The Mirror-Glyph showed no present. Only futures. Only endings.

From the shadows between the pillars, Thane stepped forward.

The blue light from the mask spirals caught in his eyes—though his mask was gone, tucked under one arm. His face was pale, too pale, as though whatever breath the Silence had left him with had been weighed and measured before being returned.

"They've taken the threads," he said.

Maelis didn't look up from the Mirror-Glyph. "And so the wheel turns."

"They shouldn't have been allowed to leave with them," Thane pressed. His voice was even, but a tremor curled beneath it—not fear, but the kind of tension that comes from seeing too far ahead. "Each thread binds them tighter to the fire. To him."

"That is the point," Maelis said. She finally looked at him, and the air between them seemed to fold. "A tether is a chain only if you cannot see where it leads."

Thane's jaw tightened. "And where does it lead?"

Her smile was faint. "To the place where gods kneel."

From the far side of the chamber, another voice emerged— dry, deep, and threaded with amusement. "You speak as though the gods will remember how."

A Watcher stepped into the glow. Not masked. Not mortal. The spirals burned openly in his skin, as though carved into his flesh with light. He leaned on a spear longer than he was tall, its head forged from the same black metal as the Mirror-Glyph.

Maelis inclined her head. "Varos."

"Your hidden throne grows restless," Varos said, glancing to the pillars. "It feels the threads in motion. It feels the heirs drawing closer to the place-that-isn't."

His words scraped like stone grinding, old as the pillars themselves.

Thane looked between them. "Then we stop them before they—"

"No." Maelis' voice cut clean. "We let them come."

Varos tilted his head. "You want them to find it?"

His spear hummed faintly, resonant with the chamber, as though the stone itself disliked his question.

"I want them to open it," she said. "The heirs believe they seek the gods' return. In truth, they are carving the key to the gate that holds him."

At that, the shadows in the chamber seemed to shift, as if the name unspoken had weight enough to bend them. The throne itself seemed to hum at the thought of something vast and buried—The One Beneath, the presence every Watcher's oath was built to serve. The cold at the base of Thane's skull deepened, spirals tightening like chains around his mind.

Thane stepped closer, his shadow stretching long across the floor. "And when the gate opens?"

Maelis held his gaze for a long moment, then turned the Mirror-Glyph so he could see.

For an instant, he saw the heirs—all twelve—standing in a place lit by fire and storm, the ground beneath them splitting to reveal chains so massive they could only hold a god. The chains trembled, each link taller than a tower.

One by one, the chains began to break.

Thane flinched back from the image.

"They'll never trust me again," he said. It was almost a confession.

Maelis rose from the throne, her crown catching the light in a hundred fractured shards. "Trust is a mortal leash. You will cut it when the time comes. Until then, you will walk with them, bleed with them, and when they open the gate…"

She reached out, placing the Mirror-Glyph in his hands. It was colder than it looked.

"…you will decide whether you stand beside me—or against the god who will offer you his throne."

The shadows around the pillars shifted again, drawing tighter, like walls closing in. Somewhere far above, the Hollow's surface groaned, as though the entire city-that-shouldn't-exist had felt the weight of her words.

Thane looked down at the mirror. The firelit horizon within it wavered, showing not chains now, but a single spiral burning black against gold. His glyph.

And for the first time, he didn't look away.

The shadowlight dimmed as Maelis leaned back into the throne, her crown catching stray threads of the unseen glow. For a long breath, she said nothing—letting the silence coil tight enough that even the Watchers lining the walls seemed unsure if they were still meant to breathe.

Varos shifted his weight. "You risk too much letting him stand here."

The old Watcher's voice carried the grit of centuries. "He's untested. The Spiral will not—"

Maelis' hand rose in a casual flick, not to silence him, but to invite him to continue.

Varos hesitated, then: "The heirs fracture easily enough without your hand guiding one away."

Her smile was thin, the kind that suggested amusement without warmth. "You speak as if the fracture is my creation." Varos' masked head tilted toward Thane. "Half-flame, half-chain," he said, voice flat with disdain. "Not forged, not chosen. Something else."

Her gaze shifted to Thane, holding him there without force. "Tell me—when you look at them, do you feel whole?"

Thane didn't answer. Not yet. The question wasn't a trap, but neither was it harmless.

Varos stepped forward, eyes on Maelis, not Thane. "And if he walks out of here still theirs?"

Maelis rose. Every Watcher in the chamber straightened as though gravity had changed. "Then he walks out knowing more than he did before—and knowing that knowledge does not require loyalty." She descended the steps toward Thane, each one measured. "Do you understand, heir of Aphrodite? I have no interest in pulling you from them today."

The words were easy. Almost too easy.

"But," she continued, circling just far enough to keep him in her periphery, "there will come a moment when they will not understand you. When the pattern you follow will run counter to the path they demand you take. And in that moment, you will want a place to stand that is not theirs."

Her tone made it sound like a promise, not a threat.

Thane met her eyes. "And you think that place is here."

Maelis tilted her head, as though considering. "Perhaps. Or perhaps it's nowhere. But nowhere is a dangerous thing to stand in alone."

A ripple of unease moved through the chamber.
Even Varos did not interrupt this time.

She stopped just short of him, close enough that the crown's light caught faint silver in her hair. "When the silence between you and your so-called allies becomes louder than their words, remember that the shadows have always listened."

The way she said it, it didn't feel like an invitation. It felt like inevitability.

She stepped back toward the throne without another word. The Watchers shifted, their ranks parting, as if the moment between them had been a ceremony in itself.

Varos spoke again, quieter. "He will leave with questions."

Maelis lowered herself into the seat. "Good." She glanced toward Thane one last time. "Questions keep the mind turning. Answers end things."

♦ ♦ ♦

# PART VI – THE RECKONING

# CHAPTER XXIII
# THE BREAKING STORM

Venice, March 3, 2026

The storm broke like a war drum over the lagoon. Lightning crawled spiderwise across a sky the color of bruised steel, and thunder rolled through the Hellenic Institute's foundations until ancient glass rattled in its frames.

Alleyways echoed with fleeing footsteps, costumed revelers abandoning their silks to the rising water.

Naia lifted her chin, crown-mark burning faintly, her voice sharp against the panic: "Hold your composure. Fear is what they want."

Zara kept the Codex tight to her ribs and pretended her hands did not shake. The blackout city whispered above them—lantern light skimming the canals like shaken gold—yet down here the corridors breathed their own weather. Stone exhaled cold. Dust drifted in veils. Somewhere deeper, chains murmured in the walls as if the building remembered its makers and the weight of their vows.

"They're not circling anymore," Cassian said. His voice had roughened since Venice, like someone had taught a storm to speak. "They're closing."

Dr. Eleni Makris stood at the landing with a torch held high. Firelight cut her profile severe, scholar's lines sharpened into commander's edges. "You have minutes," she said. "Not hours. We hold here or we do not hold at all."

Thane lingered in the mouth of the stair, half in shadow, pale hair damp against his forehead. He had spoken little since the map chamber—the one moment he reached for Zara's hand, and she felt the Codex shiver as if recognizing its own betrayer. He met her gaze now and looked away first.

Isla brushed her fingers to the wall. "The stone's wrong," she whispered. "Like it's bracing."

"Bracing for what?" Kai's tone was all brittle glass. He had slept less than any of them. "The next lie?"

Zara's glove hid the faint flare beneath her palm. The burn had quieted after the council in shadow—Interlude V writ across her memory like a warning—but here, on this day, it quickened again, a coal beneath leather. She forced her fingers to still.

"Positions," Eleni said. "If they breach, they'll drive you toward the water. Don't give them a straight line."

◆ ◆ ◆

They moved. The Institute's main hall opened like a nave, statues marching along the walls, their faces eroded into expressions the sculptors had never intended. Rain hammered the skylight in a thousand thin fists. Through that glass, the storm bared its teeth.

Watchers did not announce themselves. They unmade the space around them and let your eyes figure it out too late. The first mask appeared at the far end of the hall, balanced on a body that did not move like a body should. The porcelain face was smooth except for the hairline fissures running away from where a mouth might have been—old cracks, the way ice remembers a winter from two years ago.

"There," Eryx said, faster than his breath. He had a messenger's poise and a knife he spun on reflex. "And there."

More masks. Along the balcony. In the archway that led back toward the labyrinth. Their heads tilted in the same insect-precise motion, clicks stuttering in the ribs of the building.

"Remember what we practiced," Eleni said. "You do not meet shadow with more shadow."

Zara had cataloged the Watchers the way she did texts: movement rules, silence rules, the way frost bled from their claws and ate warmth out of air. None of that mattered when they came for you. Then all you remembered was the absence of breath.

"On me," Cassian said, and stepped into the center of the hall as if the weather had asked him to. Lightning laced the skylight. The storm tasted him and leaned closer.

"Cass—" Leo began, salt at the edges of his voice, but Selene shook her head once. Not yet.

The first Watcher dropped from the balcony, soundless and wrong. It landed in a crouch that bent the joints the wrong way. When it looked up, the mask had no eyes. It didn't need them.

"Now," Eleni said.

The hall erupted. Lightning cracked through glass and answered Cassian's raised hand. Isla's sparks leapt like metal remembering heat. Leo's breath pulled the canal until water shouldered the doors but did not break them. Naia's power moved in the hush between motions, a net cast of control and expectation. Kai drew light itself to a bowstring and loosed—an arrow that burned like an idea you couldn't unthink once you'd heard it.

Zara did not throw. She placed. Knowledge was a weapon you positioned—the way you set a stone that could not be unseated. She lifted the Codex. Glyphs ran across its face like fish under ice. "Here," she said, and the word meant more than place. "Hold."

The Watcher collided with Cassian's lightning. Porcelain webbed with cracks. Frost skittered across the stones, reaching for ankles. Eryx darted through and cut the tendons of a shadow that should not have had them; it buckled like smoke made to remember bone.

Lightning crawled too far, biting into Cassian's skin, burning deeper than mortal flesh should endure.
His knees buckled, but Selene's gaze found his, dark and steady. "You are not alone," she whispered, and her voice steadied the storm.
Chains of lightning coiled around his arms like sigils of Zeus, a mantle not chosen but claimed.
The storm did not consume him. It crowned him.

They should have felt invincible; the storm was theirs. Instead, every surge uncovered more masks waiting in the edges, attention humming without sound.

♦ ♦ ♦

In the lull that wasn't a lull, Kai's voice came thin and sharp. "This isn't pursuit—it's execution."

"They won't stop at us," Naia said. Even now, she was composed enough to sound like a lesson. "They'll take the Institute for what it holds. And then the city."

"Then we don't give them ground," Isla said. The sparks had steadied around her hands into rings, forge-light tamed by will. "This place taught us. It deserves to stand."

"Places don't stand," Damien growled. "People do." The burn along his knuckles whitened as his grip tightened. Ares' drum still lived somewhere behind his pulse; Zara could hear it if she listened too long.

Another mask tipped. The gesture read like a smile if you'd never seen one. They moved.

Zara set her feet. "Chain," she said, and felt it gather—threads tightening through her chest, pulling through others as if each of them were a bead and the world had decided to string them together. It hurt a little. It always did when they were this close and this afraid.

The chain answered. She felt Kai's disbelief sand its edge to something meaner. She felt Leo's protectiveness and the taste of salt where it met fear. She felt Selene's quiet, which was never empty; hers was the kind that made rooms listen. She felt Cassian's storm like a hand on her shoulder saying stand.

She did.

♦ ♦ ♦

The Watchers hit them in a wave. Porcelain shattered in white petals. Shadows reformed. Frost bloomed. Lightning wove a cage across the skylight, and for a second the whole hall was bright enough to show you the dust that had been waiting since Rome fell.

"Left!" Eryx called.

"Right," Isla said, because she could hear the stone and it had already told her where to put her feet.

Zara should have been thinking of angles and reading patterns across the fray. Instead she kept seeing a hand over hers, pale as a mirror's back, and the way the Orb had cracked like something inside it wanted out. She blinked hard and the picture didn't go away.

"Zara!" Kai's shout barely reached through the thunder. "Now!"

She moved. The Codex flared. Symbols lifted off the page as if refusing gravity, spiraling around her wrist in obedient Orbit. She threw—not a blast but a geometry, a shape the world would rather be. The Watcher stepping toward her walked straight into an argument older than language; it folded along lines it had never noticed.

Something laughed above them without making a sound in air. It vibrated through stone. The skylight flickered. For a heartbeat the storm drew back like breath held too long.

"Why did it stop?" Leo said.

"It didn't," Cassian answered. "It's listening."

◆ ◆ ◆

Eleni was already moving them, the lines of defense redrawn three times in as many minutes. "Back," she said, her voice the only thing not knocked off its axis. "We hold the crossing by the archive doors. If they take the stairs, they take the Institute."

They fell back in a wedge—Cassian center, Zara slightly behind with Codex, Isla and Leo flanking, Naia laying constraints across the floor that made motion feel like it had to be polite to pass. Selene watched the shadows, not with fear but with the kind of attention surgeons pay to anatomy.

"Thane," Cassian said without looking back, "left."

He did not answer. He was already where he had been told to be. He had always been good at that. Obedient, even when he wanted anything but. Zara felt him like a cold current through the chain, moving parallel and apart.

A Watcher dropped from the balcony. Another crawled out from under the stair with no space to have hidden in. A third unfolded at the end of the hall and walked toward them as if the world should step aside; things did, and Zara hated that.

411

"Do not break the line," Eleni said. "No matter what you see."

It would have been easier if the Watchers only wore the faces of masks. The ones that were older had learned to borrow other shapes. One of them turned its head, and Zara saw her mother for the half of a breath it took to blink, the tilt of her chin exactly right. It was a mercy that anger came faster than grief. She steadied.

"Hold," Cassian said again, low. Lightning traced his knuckles and did not burn him. It never did.

◆ ◆ ◆

The first breach came as a whisper. Frost slid across the floor and set the old runner to glass. Boots skidded. Naia caught Leo's elbow before the fall could pull the line. "Not today," she said, and her voice made it true.

Watchers struck. Light answered. The chain tightened until it hurt enough to be something you could lean against. Eryx dove and rolled, a knife flashing across another porcelain throat. It should not have mattered—those throats did not carry anything like breath—but it did. The mask split and the body rethought itself into smoke.

"Stone shouldn't bleed shadows," Isla said. "And yet—"

"And yet," Kai said, drawing and loosing without looking away from whatever needed dying next. "We live in a world built on and yet."

Zara moved as the Codex told her to move. She did not need to understand the theory of the shape to build it. Not today. Shapes had always loved her if she gave them room. They obliged her now. She set another pattern into air and the Watcher that had pretended to be her mother broke like a puppet cut from its strings.

A fissure snapped down the center of the skylight. Wind screamed through the gap and flung rain into the hall in sheets. Lightning came with it, not a strike so much as a spill; it poured over Cassian's shoulders like a cape he had not asked to wear.

"Cassian," Selene said. She spoke his name like a warning and a permission both.

He stepped forward one pace. Storm-fronts have edges; you can stand on them if you know how. He had learned. The air around him steadied in the way a hand steadies before it closes.

♦ ♦ ♦

They could have held there for hours if holding were the same as winning. The Watchers learned them by the minute. The next wave did not try to break the line. It went for the doors—three at once—seeking a shape of the building they had not yet defended.

"No," Dr. Makris said, almost to herself, and ran. For a heartbeat the Director of the Institute did not look like a scholar. She looked like someone who knew where to put her body to stop a fall that would break the world. She slammed the first door with both hands as if she could convince wood to be more than wood; for her, sometimes, it listened.

"Go!" Cassian called. "Zara—"

"Already," she said. She tore glyphs from the Codex and set them like nails through the second threshold, a ward woven from language that had been used more often in oaths than in prayers. The door groaned as if grateful.

Isla's hammer became a bright idea given weight. She struck the floor once and the stone remembered how to be unbroken. Cracks crawled backward as if ashamed they had ever occurred. The third door sealed with a sound like a breath being taken and not released.

The Watchers hissed without sound. You learned to hear it anyway.

"You can't keep us," a voice said from no place. "You can delay."

Zara did not waste words on the air. "Delay is a kind of victory."

"Only if you have somewhere to go," the voice answered, and the walls rang with it. "Do you?"

♦ ♦ ♦

They had not discussed leaving. They had only discussed not failing here. But the question sat there now, and it asked them who they were trying to be.

413

"Bellamy Tower," Eleni said, the words scraping her throat. "We hold, then we move. The Tower will buy you days the Institute cannot."

Dr. Eleni Makris' command cut through the storm. "Enough. The Institute was never built to fight a war.
Bellamy Tower is older, chained with Olympian wards. It will hold when this cannot."
Naia's tone was sharp. "So we run?"
Damien spat. "We fight here!"
Eleni's eyes blazed. "We survive. That is how wars are won."

Leo exhaled—a sound like a wave deciding against a break. "Then we get them their days."

"We do not make corridors," Naia said, already calculating angles and people as if they were debts owed and paid. "We make crossings."

"I can buy you a minute," Cassian said. He sounded like someone looking over the edge of a thing and deciding that, yes, he would jump; he just wished someone else had asked first. "Maybe two."

"We need five," Eryx said.

"We'll take the two," Eleni said. "We'll steal the three."

Zara's palm burned, a flare sharp enough to bring water to her eyes. She curled her fingers to hide it. Not now. Not when the line depended on the part of her that had not yet admitted what it had touched.

Thane looked at her then—eyes the color glass has before it remembers a color—and for an instant she saw a boy who had never learned how to be anything but beloved. It passed. He looked away.

◆ ◆ ◆

The last wave came with the storm itself. The skylight surrendered and the glass came down in a shiver of clear knives. Rain entered as if it owned the hall. The Watchers crossed the threshold like a fact.

Cassian lifted his hand. Lightning braided down his arm and did not stop at the palm; it laced his chest, his shoulders, the line of his jaw. He became a place weather recognized.

414

"This is going to hurt," he said, to no one and to all of them.

"We've been hurt," Selene said. "Do it."

Zara had thought storms were chaos. She was wrong. They were systems too complex to be polite. And if you could find the right pressure point, you could make them choose. Cassian found it now. The thunder did not break; it held. The light did not scatter; it focused.

He stepped forward. The world stepped back.

Lightning stitched itself into a circle around them—a perimeter drawn in white fire. Watchers lunged for it and learned what happens to things that forgot light had teeth. The air smelled of rain and the first moment after a match dies.

For a heartbeat, silence. The storm itself seemed to hold its breath.

The heirs looked at one another, shock written in every face.

Isla whispered, "Stone shouldn't remember like this…"

Eryx attempted a joke, but it faltered into nothing.

Lysandra closed her eyes. "No earth beneath us. Only water. Only emptiness."

"Move!" Elenis' voice had the command of a captain and the fear of someone who knows the cost of courage. "Go!"

They ran. Not away—through. Leo's water shouldered Watchers off the staircase and back into the hall. Isla set the steps to remembering how to hold weight at speed. Eryx went first, because messengers always do, and because someone had to find where the next danger started. Naia kept them tight without touching them at all.

Zara went with the Codex held flat to her chest, as if it were a shield and not a book that had learned to pretend. She did not look back until the edge of the stairs made it safe to do so.

Cassian stood in the circle he had made, the storm running through him like music through an instrument. Lightning climbed him and did not burn. It lit his eyes from behind. For an instant, she saw what leadership looks like before the person wearing it accepts the name.

For a heartbeat, silence. Even the storm listened.

"Cass!" Leo shouted.

He moved then, a single clean step backward, the circle drawing with him. The Watchers pressed, porcelain catching the light
and shattering in white blossoms. Their laughter sounded like ice
cracking on a river you were too late to get off.

By the time they hit the lower corridor, the water had already
found it. Venice always arrives first by canal. Cold flooded their ankles. The floor declined in a way that made escape feel like a bad
plan written in a hurry.

"Left," Isla said, hand to wall. "It's older that way."

"Older is better?" Kai asked.

"Older remembers," Isla said. "New breaks."

They cut left. The corridor narrowed, then opened abruptly to
a small courtyard roofed in glass that had not yet surrendered. A
single door faced the canal, barred in iron that had rusted honestly.

Eryx threw the bar. "Crossing," he said, and held the door as
Leo tasted the water and made it fall lower than it wanted.

Dr. Makris counted heads faster than Zara could name them.
"All right," she said, "go—"

A shadow stepped in front of the door and became a Watcher
with a face it wore badly. The porcelain had been painted to smile.
The paint had run.

"I'm tired of this one," Damien said, and met it without grace.
War is not a dance; it is a decision. He made it. The rusted sword
he carried since Antarctica met the Watcher's arm with a sound like
two bad ideas colliding. The porcelain split. The body did too.

"Two minutes," Cassian said from behind them. He was walking backward, the circle holding, the storm making room as if the
sky were a door he knew how to open and close. "Make them
count."

Zara counted. Not the seconds—she trusted Eryx for those.
She counted choices. When they reached Bellamy Tower, they
would need more than courage. They would need the parts of
themselves they did not like and the ones they saved for after. She
was not sure she had either left.

Her palm burned again. The glyph that was not hers wanted to
be. She did not allow it.

◆ ◆ ◆

They made the door. The iron shrieked the way old courage does when you ask it to matter again. The canal lay beyond, black as a pupil blown wide. Gondolas had left; the city had learned to be elsewhere.

"We can't all cross at once," Naia said. Calm. Always calm. "Pairs. Eryx and Dr. Makris first."

"No," Dr. Makris said, the word steady. "I'll last."

"You're the one the Institute needs," Zara said before she decided to. "You go."

"The Institute needs you," Dr. Makris said, and in that moment Zara almost believed it. "Go."

Eryx vaulted down, caught the post, and made the gondola behave like it had always been intended to do this. Dr. Makris followed, a scholar lowering herself into a craft built for the slow miracle of cities made of water.

"Next," Leo said.

They moved in pairs. Leo with Naia. Isla with Kai. Selene alone because sometimes quiet needs room. Damien with the sword he had not bothered to clean, because war has rules he no longer respected.

Zara turned for the stairs. Cassian was almost to them. The circle was thinner now; lightning frays if you ask too much of it. Watchers pressed at the edge and learned, and learned, and learned.

It crowned him.

"Go," he said.

"I can hold—"

"Not your job." He said it gently and without options. "Go."

There was a man in the Codex who had written a treatise on the virtues of obedience. He had been killed by his own soldiers. Zara thought about that and decided to argue later. She went.

◆ ◆ ◆

The gondola rocked. The canal slapped its sides like an indifferent god. Leo steadied the water with a palm over the surface; it thickened under them the way custard does when you get it right.

"Where is Thane?" Kai asked, sudden, like the question had been stalking him through the last twenty minutes and had finally caught his heel.

417

Zara looked back. Thane stood in the stair mouth, pale as poured milk, the storm gilding his hair as if it had chosen him too. His hand rested against the jamb. For an instant she thought he would step forward, take his place in the circle beside Cassian and be the boy he had practiced being his whole life. He did not. He lowered his gaze and moved along the wall, seeking shadow as if looking for a mirror to tell him he still had a face.

"He's here," Selene said. It did not help.

Eryx raised a hand. "Last ferry."

Cassian broke the circle. He did not let it die; he folded it into his palm and brought it with him like a secret he had decided to keep. The Watchers poured forward and struck the place he had just been. Lightning met them anyway, late and sufficient.

They shoved off. The gondola slid into rain. The Institute receded behind them, a throat cleared after a scream.

"Bellamy Tower," Eleni said, not as a suggestion. "We regroup there. We learn there. We live there." She did not add for now. She did not have to.

◆ ◆ ◆

The lagoon did not calm. Storms do not end because you have decided to be brave somewhere else. Lightning stitched the sky in white sutures. Thunder laid its body over the city and would not move. Masks watched from bridges and did not follow, not yet; patience is a hunt too.

Zara drew the Codex into her lap as if it needed warmth. She thumbed the edge until the book chose a page. Glyphs lifted and hovered, pale as fish under ice. Her palm ached in time to a rhythm she did not want to name. She curled her fingers to cage it.

Cassian sat opposite, hair wet, eyes bright with the kind of light you cannot pretend isn't there. He did not look like a leader. He looked like someone a storm had chosen and who wished it had asked for an appointment first. She liked him for that.

"You did it," Leo said softly, as if admitting it too loudly would make the sky take offense.

Cassian shook his head once. "We did it." He met Zara's eyes. "For now."

Across the water, Bellamy Tower shouldered up out of rain like an accusation. It had stood longer than governments and better than men. Chains were carved into its skin the way guilt is carved into memory. They did not glow. Zara did not trust that.

Thunder rolled again, closer, then farther, like something pacing. The city shivered, every pier a rib.

Zara looked back at the Institute, at the broken skylight, at the hall where lightning still stitched itself into a circle because that is what circles do when you ask them to hold. She thought of the Orb, cracked. The map, older than continents. The crown of glass the shadows had taught themselves to wear. Her palm burned.

"The storm has broken," Cassian said, very quiet, as if speaking to the water more than to them. "And nothing will hold it back again."

♦ ♦ ♦

# Letter from William Ginn to the Hellenic Institute

*To the Esteemed Hellenic Institute,*

I wish to extend my deepest gratitude for your guidance and collaboration throughout this endeavor. Your tireless preservation of ancient histories, your willingness to share fragments and whispers, and your scholarly patience in answering my endless questions have been invaluable in shaping this first volume.

I am pleased to tell you that **Book I is nearly complete**. Yet, as you well know, one book can never contain the full weight of these stories. The storm has broken, but the echoes of Olympus are far from finished. More codices lie hidden, more glyphs remain to be uncovered, and more voices call to be remembered.

This is only the beginning. I look forward to continuing our partnership as we bring forth the volumes yet to come.

With respect and gratitude,
**William Ginn**

CHAPTER XXIV

# THE BATTLE AT BELLAMY TOWER

March 4, 2026

Lightning licked the steel ribs of Bellamy Tower, then bit down, turning its glass-and-girder skeleton into a white-hot x-ray of a giant in pain. Thunder hit a second later—too slow to be honest, too loud to be normal—rolling down the canyon of shuttered high-rises like a warning drum. Rain came at a forty-five-degree slant, needling skin, pooling in gutters, rattling against busted traffic lights that blinked red to no one.

Zara reached the plaza first.

She slid behind a toppled bike rack, breathing in through her nose, out through her mouth, counting beats. Three in, three out. Triple time. The storm had been keeping it since dusk. Her braid was a soaked rope down her back, curls escaping to stick like inked commas along her cheekbones. The notebook under her jacket was already damp around the edges, but the pages with tonight's sketches—angles, trajectories, fractures—were dry. She'd planned for that much.

Bellamy Tower leaned into the wind like a listening thing. On clear days its façade mirrored the sky and pretended to be harmless. Every sheet of glass was slicked in rain, but the rivulets didn't fall straight. They curved. They gathered in arcs that met each other on the panes like fingerprints. Spirals. Imperfect, but close enough to make Zara's gut twitch before her mind caught up.

Not a picture. A behavior.

She pushed the thought away before it could bloom. Confirmation bias. Pattern-hunting. She'd burn out if she chased every echo now.

"Zara!"

Leo's voice came ragged through the noise. He sprinted across the plaza, hoodie dark with rain, a streak of soot still like a thumbprint along his jaw from somewhere they barely escaped ten minutes ago. The trident mark along his forearm pulsed under the wet fabric like a heartbeat that didn't belong to him. Water swelled at his heels with every step, as if the city's entire river system had been strung to his tendons.

He dropped beside her, shoulder to shoulder, breathing hard. "Any sign?"

"Three," she said, eyes not leaving the tower's revolving doors. The lobby lights beyond were on but dim, swimming through glass like a drowned star. "One inside. Two above. They're not rushing. They're waiting for us to choose."

Leo's mouth flattened—no surprise, just irritation. "Of course they are."

A shadow detached from the base of a sculpture across the plaza and crossed the rain in three soundless strides. Selene arrived without panting, without apology. The crescent on her wrist glowed like a coal under skin. Her braid was a black blade down the center of her back, and the Veil blade at her hip shimmered in the storm like metal that had forgotten to be only metal. She stood with one hand resting on the hilt and one palm out flat to the air, as if feeling for something in it.

"They're threaded through the building," she said. "Thin. Like spider-silk stretched between floors."

"Tripwires?" Leo asked.

"Leashes," Selene murmured. "Not ours. Like the bindings they use in the Underworld—thin as silk, strong as vows."

A chord rose up behind them like someone plucked the storm itself. Kai emerged with his case across his back, hair plastered to his forehead, eyes brighter than the lobby lights. The sun-ring on his arm was dimmed by rain and night, but not dead. He took in the tower, the angles, the broken benches, the way the rain insisted on whorls, and his jaw tightened almost imperceptibly.

"Tell me this wasn't the plan," he said.

"It wasn't the plan," Zara said. "It's the field."

"Feels like a trap."

"It's both."

Another figure thundered up the steps, less shadow than blunt force. Damien's boots hit water and threw it. He rolled his shoulders as if trying to break out of them, spear slung casually but ready. The red-hot thread that lived inside the weapon made the rain hiss when it ran along the shaft.

"I don't care if it's a trap," he said. "Just point me at the thing I'm supposed to break."

"Not a thing," Zara said, and finally looked up into the tower's glass belly. Her fingers moved in the air, drawing lines no one but she could see. The rain cut through them and made them real for a second, threads of a web. "A choice."

Isla arrived last, lugging a battered canvas bag that clanged like a toolbox and a forge fell in love. Soot streaks made constellations along her forearms. She blinked rain out of her lashes and pushed her goggles up to her hairline, leaving a clean crescent above her eyebrows like a reverse moon.

"I hate this building," she said simply, setting the bag down with a care that undercut the words.

"You hate every building," Damien said.

"I hate lazy engineering," Isla said. "And this tower cheats. It looks like weight and grace, but the stress lines are wrong. Like someone taught it to lie."

"Someone did," Selene said.

Lightning cracked close enough to rattle the fillings out of a sinner's teeth. The reverberation rolled up Zara's bones and nested under her sternum, an echo against the counted beats in her head. Three in. Three out.

Inside the lobby, the rotating doors made a slow, stately spin no one had started. The security desk lamp flickered three times and steadied. Elevator numbers blinked in a pattern that wasn't a pattern if you didn't know how to listen: 1—4—7—10. Every third floor.

Leo rubbed water out of his eyes with the heel of his hand. "We going to talk this to death or—"

"We're not here to die," Zara said, too sharp. She eased her voice down. "We go in together. No splits. If they separate us, we lose the board."

"And if they want us to go in together?" Kai asked.

"Then we make going in together our choice." Zara's gaze didn't move. "They don't get to name it for us."

Damien smirked without humor. "That's the most Athena thing I've ever heard."

"It's the smartest thing on the table," Isla muttered, already unbuckling the bag. She pulled out a compact cylinder and flipped two levers. The thing shook like it remembered being a part of a volcano. "I can weld the lower doors if we need to bottleneck. But if they go phase through like Naples, it won't hold."

"It'll hold long enough to make them choose a shape," Zara said. "I don't need forever. I need a second of truth."

The rain changed. It didn't slow; it changed. The sound softened by a shade. The needles became threads. The plaza's standing water stopped shivering for a heartbeat and then resumed. Selene's head tilted the smallest degree.

"They're here," she said.

A figure was already in the revolving door—no footfalls, no approach, just there, as if the storm had condensed into shape. Cloak black, glazed ceramic mask white. No fogging on the glass where breath should be. It let the door carry it into the lobby and then stopped, facing out, a mannequin with intent. Two more shapes slipped along the interior mezzanine like someone had painted them into the shadow lines.

Leo's palms sparked with cold electricity that wasn't lightning and wasn't not. Water rose from the plaza like wasps.

"On my signal," Zara said.

The Watcher in the lobby lifted its right hand and placed its palm flat against the glass. Five black finger marks bloomed on the pane. Another lightning flash made the white of its mask too white, like bone fresh from a cut.

♦ ♦ ♦

Isla pulled her cylinder's pin. "Say the word."

Zara didn't speak. She stood. She stepped out from the bike rack. The rain stung her scalp, slid into the collar of her jacket, sketched cold lines down her spine. She walked toward the doors with her hands open and empty.

"What are you doing?" Kai hissed.

"Setting the field," she said.

The Watcher's head cocked a quarter turn, birdlike, like it was trying to make out a sound.

Zara stopped at the threshold, just outside the revolving door's arc. Close enough to see her reflection ghosted over the mask. She lifted one hand and placed her palm on the glass where its hand had been.

The temperature dropped like someone opened a door to winter. The pane thrummed under her skin, not with heat, but with attention.

"Three floors," she said without looking away. "One, four, seven, then ten. That's their path. If we try to skip, they'll fold the building until we can't."

"Fold?" Leo asked.

"Like a map," she said. "Like a throat."

Damien's spear made a low, impatient sound, or maybe it was Damien.

"On your call, Ath—Zara," he amended, catching himself.

She almost smiled. Almost. "On mine."

The Watcher moved first. Not a lunge. A step backward. Hands lowering, palms open. It retreated like a waiter clearing a table. The revolving door pivoted, slow as ceremony, and Zara stepped into it.

Leo swore and followed, shadowing her panel. Selene slipped in behind him. Kai next, jaw set, fingers flexing in invisible scales. Damien's shoulder brushed the glass with a scrape like a growl. Isla came last, cylinder tucked like a heart under her arm.

The lobby smelled like wet marble and toner. The security desk lamp hummed at a pitch humans didn't make. Zara's shoes left crescent moons on the tile.

The Watcher had not moved far. Ten feet back, centered, balanced, empty, like the room was arranged around it. Another waited at the base of the escalators, hand resting on the rail like it remembered pretending to be human.

Zara lifted her right hand, palm open, fingers slightly spread. Wait.

Leo's mouth was a line, but he obeyed. The water gathered at his heels went still, a dog lying down.

The Watcher at the desk lifted its right hand in response. Palms mirrored. Fingers spread.

Selene's voice was a whisper that didn't want to be one. "Like a call-and-response."

"Like code," Zara said.

The elevator chimed. No door opened. The number flicked from 1 to 4.

Damien's spear kissed the floor. "Say when."

Zara inhaled. One, two, three. Exhaled. One, two, three. Triple time.

She stepped to the left, exactly three tiles, and the Watcher did the same, exactly three tiles. She raised her hand, lowered it. It raised, lowered.

"Zara." Kai's tone was a string tuned too tight. "We are dancing with the thing that almost killed us in Naples—and it's leading."

"It didn't," she said. "It tested us. It left you breathing."

"You call that mercy?"

"I call that a rule," she said.

The desk lamp flickered. Three beats. On, off, on. Off.

"Now," Zara said.

Isla slammed the cylinder onto the tile and rolled it toward the revolving door. It lodged in the gap and erupted, a flower of white-hot filaments lacing across the glass. The lower panels glowed, sagged, then stiffened as the weave fused to the steel frame. The door was still a door, but not one that would revolve quick.

The Watcher didn't flinch. The mezzanine shadows shifted like ink remembering gravity.

Zara pointed at the elevator bank. "If we jump ahead, they'll fold the building around us—walls swallowing halls until there's no way back out. We go where they're telling us to go—but we choose how we get there."

Damien barked a laugh. "You know that sounds like pretending."

"Pretend smarter," she said. "Selene—left flank. If they phase, cut the shadow not the shape. Kai—you are light on call. Not all the time. On my count only or they'll learn the rhythm. Leo—keep the water out of our feet and in their noses."

"My favorite place for it," Leo muttered.

"Isla."

"I heard it," Isla said, already pulling from her bag. "I brought gifts."

She tossed each of them a disk the size of a coin. On contact with a palm, each disk buzzed and flashed a pattern of lines that resolved, then vanished. For a second the same pattern flickered in the air between all six of them—six filaments crossing, knotting, the smallest version of a larger thing.

A spiral.

Zara felt it in her chest before her eyes logged it—a loop that wasn't a loop, a path that didn't close but rose. It half-remembered the shape of something she'd seen once before, burned into the edge of her vision.

"Keep those," Isla said. "If someone's grip goes cold, we'll know."

The elevator chimed again. The door on the far right slid open to reveal an empty car. It wasn't lit, and yet they could see inside, as if it had learned to drink light instead of reflect it.

"After you," Damien said to no one visible.

"I'll take point," Zara said.

"You always do," Leo said.

She met his eyes and saw fear there, and trust, and the thin wire of something like anger threaded between. At the Watchers.

At the storm. At the fact that every time they walked into a place like this, the world asked them to be older than they were.

"Stay on the floor lines," Zara said. "Don't step in the seams."

They moved.

The Watcher did not move with them. It watched.

Inside the elevator, the walls were mirrored steel. Seven reflections of six people and a choice. The doors slid shut without a sound, cutting the storm down to a memory.

For a heartbeat, none of them spoke. The car hummed with a pressure that wasn't motion but judgment, as if the tower itself were listening. Rain was only a memory now, pressed into their clothes, but the storm still drummed in their chests.

The panel had no buttons.

"Cool," Damien said. "Love this."

Zara lifted her palm to the seam where doors met. Cold thrummed under her skin like a held breath. She tapped three times. Tap, tap, tap. Waited. The car did not jolt; the floor simply began to rise, soundless, frictionless, like they had been falling this entire time and the world had finally decided to let them stop.

"On four," Zara said.

"On four what?" Leo asked.

"Floor."

"Right."

"Zara," Selene said quietly.

"What do you see?" Zara asked, not turning.

"In the metal," Selene said. "Not our reflections. Other ones. Like… like someone's rehearsing us from the wrong side."

"Don't look at them," Zara said.

"Too late," Kai murmured.

The panel where numbers should have been blinked to life at last. The same number the lobby had promised—4—cold and certain.

♦ ♦ ♦

The car slowed. The door seam shivered. The storm on the other side wasn't as loud here. Different air. Different rules.

"Remember," Zara said. "If they make you move, make them move first."

Leo snorted under his breath. "The most Athena thing."

"Shut up and live," she said.

Cold air spilled into the car—not the wet chill of the storm below, but something dry, stale, faintly metallic, as if the floor had been sealed for years and was only now tasting the night again. The light was wrong. It didn't fall from above but seeped from the walls themselves, a dim pearlescent shimmer that clung to surfaces without ever touching the floor.

The carpet, if it could be called that, was a faded slate blue with an intricate repeating pattern—whorls again, compressed so small they almost looked like dots until Zara's eyes adjusted.

She stepped out first, boots whispering on the weave, scanning left and right. The corridor stretched long in both directions, curving slightly, so that perspective lines met not in the distance, but in a suggestion of enclosure—like the floor itself was a loop.

Leo came next, water rolling in a thin halo around his feet, refusing to sink into the carpet. Selene followed, her blade low but angled to catch the wall's glow. Kai's gaze flicked up and down the corridor, fingers twitching as if plucking unseen strings. Damien's spear gave off a low hiss, metal reacting to something in the air. Isla was last, letting the elevator doors close behind her, tucking her welding cylinder back into her bag.

The doors sealed without sound. No indicator light above them. No call button. The car was gone the instant it left their sight.

"This place smells… old," Kai murmured.

"It's watching," Selene said, not bothering to lower her voice.

Zara crouched, pressing two fingers to the carpet. The whorls beneath her touch were slightly raised—woven in, not printed. She traced one. The loops bent subtly, almost imperceptibly, toward the left corridor.

"They want us to go that way," she said.

"Then we go right," Damien replied without hesitation.

"That's what they'll expect you to think," Zara said, standing. "They leave breadcrumbs either way. The trick is knowing which ones rot."

Leo adjusted his hood. "Then let's pick one before this place folds itself."

They chose left.

The corridor's glow deepened with each step, the light thickening like fog trapped behind glass. Their shadows didn't follow naturally—Selene's was longer than it should be, stretching ahead of her feet, while Kai's seemed to walk a step behind.

Every twenty paces, they passed a closed door, each identical: matte black, flush with the wall, no handle. The whorls in the carpet always bunched tighter before a door, then loosened again after.

By the fifth door, Isla spoke without looking up. "These aren't rooms."

"Storage?" Damien asked.

"Containment," Isla said. "These walls are too thick. You'd lose square footage building them like this unless you were keeping something inside... or outside."

Selene brushed a hand over the seam of the next door. Her fingertips came back dusted with frost. "Not rooms. Cells."

The corridor curved tighter. Somewhere ahead, a faint ticking began—steady, mechanical, inhuman.

Zara slowed her pace, counting under her breath. The ticking was in threes. Not a clock's heartbeat, but a metronome's.

They turned another bend—and the hallway ended in a wide hexagonal chamber. The whorls in the carpet radiated outward from a central dais, where a glass column rose floor to ceiling, filled with a liquid so dark it looked like shadow given weight. Inside the column, suspended like an insect in amber, was a Watcher.

Its mask was cracked down the center, porcelain flaked to reveal something darker beneath. The cloak around its body floated in the liquid, edges unraveling like smoke. The fingers of one hand curled loosely, the other pressed flat to the glass.

"Dead?" Leo asked.

"Not in the ways that count," Selene said.

The ticking grew louder here, and Zara saw its source—six thin metal rods extending from the base of the column to the floor around it, vibrating in sequence. The pattern matched the elevator floors: 1, 4, 7, 10.

Isla crouched, examining the rods. "Vibration sensors. Might also be conduits."

Zara circled the column once, careful not to step between the rods. The Watcher's mask followed her, a hair's breadth of movement with each step.

"It's tracking you," Kai said quietly.

"No," Zara said. "It's measuring me."

Damien tapped the butt of his spear against the floor. "Do we break it?"

Zara hesitated. The spiral in the carpet beneath her feet seemed to rise—not physically, but in her perception—like a coil ready to unwind.

"They want us to," she said finally. "That's the test. Will we act before we know the cost?"

The rods hummed faster, the sequence shifting: 1, 7, 4, 10.

Selene's head snapped toward the far wall. "We're not alone."

Three Watchers emerged from alcoves they hadn't noticed before, moving in perfect silence. No masks this time—their faces were shadow voids, depthless, rimmed in a faint glow that made the absence sharper. They spread out, forming a half-circle around the group.

Leo raised his hands; water surged up in a defensive arc. Kai unslung his case, fingers brushing strings that caught light from nowhere. Damien stepped forward, spear angled like a promise.

Zara lifted her palm. "Hold."

The Watchers stopped three paces out. One extended a hand toward the glass column, palm open. The suspended Watcher's mask tilted fractionally, and the cracked seam widened with a faint sound like splitting ice.

The rods hit a new sequence: 10, 1, 4, 7.

◆ ◆ ◆

"They're shifting the map," Zara realized.

Kai's eyes darted between the rods and the newcomers. "Then we're already off their path."

"Good," Damien muttered.

The Watchers moved. Not forward—sideways, as if sliding across invisible rails. They closed the circle without stepping closer, the gaps between them narrowing until the only open space was directly behind the group… toward the right-hand corridor they hadn't taken.

"They're herding us," Leo said.

"Then we don't go where they want," Isla replied.

The hum of the rods deepened into a bass note that vibrated in their teeth. The whorls in the carpet seemed to pulse in time, edges blurring.

Zara made the call. "Break the pattern."

Kai struck a chord that shattered the hum for half a heartbeat. Selene lunged at the nearest Watcher, blade slashing low—not at its legs, but at the shadow where they should have been. The Watcher's form jerked, edges fuzzing.

Damien's spear hit the floor, sending a line of molten red racing toward the glass column. The liquid inside churned, the suspended Watcher twisting slowly, mask tilting up.

Leo flung both hands forward. Water shot under the Watchers' feet, freezing instantly into jagged ice that locked them in place.

Isla slammed a magnetic disk onto one of the rods. It sparked, hummed off-key, and the sequence stuttered—1, 4… 4… 7.

The Watchers reacted at once. The ice shattered. The hum doubled. The column's liquid boiled.

"Move!" Zara ordered.

They didn't retreat down the right corridor as expected. Instead, Zara vaulted over a rod, landing inside the spiral pattern around the column. The air thickened instantly, pressing against her skin like underwater pressure.

"Zara!" Kai shouted.

"Trust me!" she called back.

She placed both palms on the glass, meeting the cracked mask's gaze. The temperature plunged. The whorls in the carpet aligned under her boots.

And for a moment, she saw—not the Watcher, but through it.

Corridors folding like paper. Floors stacked out of order. A path winding upward to the tenth floor… and something waiting there, larger than the building could contain.

She stumbled back, lungs burning. "We take their path. All of it. But we choose the steps."

No one argued. Not after the way her voice shook.

The Watchers froze as if given a silent command. The rods hummed back to their original sequence—1, 4, 7, 10.

"Go," Zara said, already moving toward the far exit.

This time, the Watchers let them pass.

The stairwell was narrow, the walls closing in like the building had decided stairs were a mistake halfway through construction. The air was stale, but beneath it lingered a trace of the storm from below—faint salt, faint static. Zara counted the steps. Always counting. Forty-two between floors four and five, then the wall on the landing rippled like heat haze before opening onto another flight.

They weren't supposed to be here.

Leo noticed first. "These aren't the same stairs."

"They're stairs," Damien grunted. "One foot, then the other."

"No," Leo said, voice tight. "They're repeating. The same crack in the railing. The same rust blotch."

Selene brushed the wall with her fingertips. Frost clung there, delicate filigree. "They're folding us."

"Then we're not getting to seven this way," Kai said.

"We are," Zara said. "We just stop thinking of it as up."

She turned sideways, pressed her palm to the frost, and stepped through as though the wall were smoke. It wasn't—cold hit her skin like the plunge into winter sea—but it gave, flexing around her until she fell forward into a hallway that had no right to be on the seventh floor.

The others followed, one by one. Damien swore under his breath as the cold bit him; Kai emerged blinking, Isla shuddering like she'd walked through an ice forge. The space they entered was larger than it had any reason to be—an open floor with no partitions, lit from nowhere and everywhere.

The carpet whorls here were different. Broader, overlapping, creating whirlpools of pattern that seemed to spin if you looked too long. At the far end of the floor stood four Watchers in a perfect row. No masks, no cloaks—just humanoid silhouettes carved out of negative space, edges bleeding shadow into the air.

"They're not moving," Leo said.

"They don't have to," Zara replied.

She started forward, and the whorls responded. Under her feet, the loops elongated, reorienting so that every step fell exactly on a curve. The Watchers mirrored the motion—not physically, but in the way the space shifted around them, the air thickening between loops.

"They're setting a rhythm," Kai murmured.

"And if we step wrong?" Isla asked.

"Then we lose the board," Zara said, her voice calm but clipped. "Selene—shadow watch. Damien—don't hit anything unless I say. Leo—keep water in play but low. Kai—stay ready to break rhythm on my mark."

They advanced, each step careful. The whorls seemed to breathe with them, a slow expansion and contraction. The Watchers didn't advance, but their silhouettes swelled, stretching taller, wider, as if the building were feeding them mass.

Halfway across, Selene hissed. "Movement above."

Zara didn't look up—she could feel it. The ceiling wasn't solid; it was shadow given the pretense of a surface. Something crawled there, a weightless drag like a spider over silk.

"Don't break pace," Zara said. "It's bait."

The shape above them mirrored her steps exactly, but its limbs were wrong—too long, bending in places human joints wouldn't. The others kept moving, but she could hear the tension in their breaths.

Three steps from the Watchers, the floor buckled—not physically, but in perception. The whorls reversed, spinning inward instead of out. Leo stumbled.

The shadows surged.

Zara snapped her fingers once. "Now!"

Kai struck a chord so sharp it cracked the air. The whorls froze mid-spin, giving them a half-second opening. Damien lunged, spear cutting a red-hot arc through one Watcher's outline. The shadow ripped apart, evaporating into the floor. The others wavered, but didn't fall.

Selene leapt, slicing upward at the crawling ceiling-thing. Her blade caught—not the shape, but its tether to the floor—and the creature dissolved like smoke in wind.

The whorls started spinning again, faster now, the floor pulling at their steps. Zara broke formation, sprinting the last three paces and planting herself dead center between the remaining Watchers.

She didn't attack. She stood, hands open.

The Watchers froze.

"Path to ten," she said.

For the first time, the shadows tilted their heads in unison. The whorls underfoot slowed, then widened, the loops aligning toward a single point at the far wall.

♦ ♦ ♦

A doorway appeared where none had been.

"They're letting us through," Isla said.

"No," Zara said. "They're showing us the way they want us to go."

"Which we're taking?" Leo asked.

Zara met his eyes. "Yes. But on our terms."

They passed through the doorway into a narrow hall. Behind them, the Watchers melted into the carpet, leaving only whorls that slowly faded to stillness.

The hallway narrowed until they had to move single file. It wasn't dark, but the light had no source—it just existed, pressed close to the walls. The floor here was bare steel, cold even through their boots.

Halfway along, the air changed. Thicker. Heavier.

"Smell that?" Damien asked.

Leo nodded. "Salt."

They emerged into a chamber dominated by a circular pit in the floor. The walls were ringed with black glass panels, each show- ing fragments of the outside storm—but out of sync. One showed

435

lightning, another rain slanting the wrong way, another a view of the plaza from before they'd entered.

In the pit, water churned without spilling over. Not sea water—too dark, too heavy. The surface bulged and rippled in slow, deliberate motion.

"It's aware," Leo said.

Something broke the surface—a hand, black as ink, with too-long fingers tipped in glassy claws. It rested on the rim of the pit, testing weight. Another hand followed, then a head rising like it had been sculpted out of the night sky.

Not a Watcher. Bigger. Older.

Zara stepped forward. "We're not here for you."

The thing tilted its head. When it spoke, the voice came from everywhere—walls, floor, water. "Yet you came through my floor."

"We came through a choice," Zara said.

"Choices have a cost."

The pit water surged upward in a column, breaking apart into shapes—familiar shapes. Them. Six figures made of water, perfect down to the tilt of Damien's spear and the curl of Selene's braid.

"Mirror match," Kai muttered. "Because that's not overdone."

The water-versions moved first, surging forward with inhuman speed. Damien's double met his spear with a weapon made of churning liquid, every blow splashing into steam. Selene's mirror darted low, blade cutting shadows. Leo's opponent was relentless, water battering like a tide.

Zara's double didn't attack. It circled, steps perfectly matching hers, eyes—if they could be called that—locked on her face.

"Break the pattern!" Zara shouted.

Kai slammed a discordant note into the air, making the doubles falter for a heartbeat. Isla tossed a small canister into the pit—it exploded in a burst of steam, clouding vision.

Damien drove his spear through his mirror's chest. It collapsed, splashing to the floor, but the water slithered back toward the pit, reforming.

"They'll keep coming!" Leo yelled.

Zara stopped moving. Her double froze.

"They're me," she said, "so they follow my rules."

She stepped forward once. The doubles stepped back. She raised her hand. They lowered theirs.

"Stand down," she said.

The water figures dissolved, draining back into the pit. The dark water stilled, the hands sinking last.

The voice came again. "Tenth floor, then."

♦ ♦ ♦

The far wall split down the center, revealing a short corridor that ended in a single elevator.

The car was waiting, door open. Inside, the walls weren't mirrored steel anymore—they were black glass, faintly reflective, showing them as though from far away.

They stepped in. The doors closed.

This time there was no sense of movement—only the feeling of being drawn upward by something that didn't care about physics. Numbers blinked once: 10.

No more sequence. No more choice.

They were going where the building wanted.

The elevator shuddered once—soft, like a breath held too long—then stopped.

No chime. No announcement. Just the faint pressure change that told Zara they had arrived somewhere that wasn't meant to exist.

The doors slid open.

Cold spilled in, not the clean bite of winter air but the kind that had passed through stone cellars and hollow mountains, carrying whispers in its teeth. Beyond the threshold stretched a room so vast it couldn't possibly fit inside the tower's blueprint. The floor was black glass, polished to a mirror, but the reflections didn't match the people standing on it.

"Yeah, that's… wrong," Damien said, his voice low.

In the reflections, their doubles stood further away than they should—like the mirrored world was bigger, deeper. Zara's reflection wasn't looking at her at all; it was staring past her shoulder, lips moving soundlessly.

The walls were curved, ribbed with pale archways that rose into darkness. Between them hung enormous glass panels, each filled with shifting imagery: a battlefield under a blood-red sky, a forest turned to crystal, the drowned spires of a city she didn't recognize.

"This isn't a floor," Kai murmured. "It's a map."

"Or a prophecy," Selene said, her voice gone distant.

The center of the room was empty—no desk, no furniture, nothing but the mirrored floor. The storm outside didn't touch this place, yet the air hummed like it carried lightning in its bones.

Zara took one step forward.

The glass beneath her foot rippled outward, as if the floor were made of water. The ripples reached the room's edges and vanished into the archways. A heartbeat later, the room answered.

Figures stepped through the arches—not Watchers exactly, but something close. Their masks weren't porcelain-white; they were obsidian, veined with faint gold that pulsed like a heartbeat. They moved with the same fluid precision, but each one carried something the others had never shown—blades, staffs, relics shaped from the same gold-veined black stone.

There were twelve of them.

"They know," Leo said quietly. "They know what we are."

The twelve spread into a wide semicircle, their weapons angled downward but ready. The one in the center tilted its head, and the golden veinwork in its mask flared brighter. When it spoke, the voice came not from its mouth but from the mirrored floor under their feet.

"Step forward, heirs."

Damien's spear lifted a fraction. "Not a fan of that tone."

Zara kept her voice steady. "You brought us here. Why?"

The central figure's head turned—not toward her, but toward the reflection of her, still whispering to something unseen.

"To weigh you."

The others shifted. Not in aggression—at least, not yet—but like pieces on a game board ready to change formation.

Kai stepped closer to Zara's shoulder. "Define 'weigh.'"

"Choice measures more than power," the voice said. "It measures shape. The shape you will take when the board is gone."

Leo's trident mark throbbed beneath his sleeve. "And if we refuse the game?"

The gold-veined mask pulsed once. "Then the game plays without you."

Zara glanced at the others. "Form close," she said softly. "If they're twelve, it's not random."

"Us," Isla said. "One for each."

The twelve shadowed figures began to move—not attacking, but circling. Their reflections on the mirrored floor didn't match their real positions, lagging by a heartbeat, like a delayed signal.

Selene's voice was a thread of ice. "The reflections are lying. Don't trust them."

One of the figures broke from the arc, gliding forward. Its weapon was a long, narrow blade with no hilt, edges shimmering like liquid. It approached Zara but didn't strike, simply stopping an arm's length away.

"Athena's heir," the voice murmured, though the mask's mouth never moved. "The board bends for you. Will you bend for it?"

Zara held its gaze—or what she thought was its gaze. "No."

The gold veins in the mask flared once, twice, then dimmed. The figure stepped back into the line. Another came forward, this one toward Leo.

They were testing them—one by one, measuring responses, weighing something Zara couldn't see but could feel tightening like a net.

When the last of the twelve returned to position, the circle closed.

"You have been placed."

The mirrored floor split open beneath them. Not physically— the glass stayed solid—but their reflections fell, vanishing into darkness. The storm sound rushed in through the absence, carrying the scent of rain and stone.

Zara's pulse counted triple time.

"Now what?" Damien asked.

The gold-veined mask tilted. "Now you climb."

The floor beneath their boots hardened again—but the archways had changed. Where there had been twelve, now there was only one, directly opposite where they stood. Beyond it was a stairwell rising into nothing but white light.

Kai exhaled. "Final level."

"Not final," Selene said. "Just next."

Zara nodded once, starting toward the arch. "Stay tight. The storm's not done with us."

The twelve masked figures did not follow. They simply turned inward, their weapons crossing in a silent salute—or warning—as the heirs passed between them into the stairwell.

♦ ♦ ♦

The white light was blinding at first, then softened into the gray wash of stormclouds. The stairwell ended on a narrow exterior platform near the very top of Bellamy Tower, the city sprawled out below in fractured reflections from the wet streets. Lightning flickered somewhere far off, but the storm above the tower's crown seemed unnaturally still, as though holding its breath.

A single figure waited at the far end of the platform.

Not masked. Not shadowed.

The man stood tall, coat whipping in the wind, the pattern on his cuffs glinting faintly gold-veined black. His eyes were fixed on them—sharp, unblinking, like he had been watching the whole climb.

"You've made it," he said, voice carrying without being loud. "Good. It will make the rest… easier."

Zara didn't slow. "And you are?"

His mouth curved—not quite a smile. "The one who set the board."

Leo's fingers twitched near his side, water curling in the gutters. "Then you know how this ends."

The man's gaze swept over them all, lingering a fraction longer on Thane, who stood silent at the back. "I do," he said. "And it isn't here."

The lightning struck then—close, bright enough to white out the city for a heartbeat. When vision cleared, the man was gone, and the far railing was empty save for the faint outline of a spiral burned into the wet metal.

Zara stepped to it, laying her palm over the mark. Cold thrummed beneath the skin. Not Watcher-cold. Older.

She turned back to the others. "We're not done. This was just the opening move."

The storm began again—not wild, but precise, raindrops falling in whorls across the tower's crown.

"The Twelve — Image recovered from the archives of the Hellenic Institute, believed taken by Dr. Eleni Makris during the early gatherings in Venice. Provenance uncertain."

# Chapter XXV
## The Thirteenth Mark

Venice, March 6, 2026

The storm's triple-time heartbeat had not broken, only shifted. It followed them down the Bellamy stair into black glass.

The spiral still burned under Zara's palm.

It was faint to the eye—just a ghost-mark etched into wet steel—but in her skin it was alive, humming in triple time, answering her heartbeat like an echo from somewhere far below. She drew her hand back and the chill lingered, threading into her knuckles, creeping toward the bones.

The storm above the tower's crown had changed. The wild, thrashing rain from earlier was gone. Now it fell in ordered spirals, each drop seeming to follow an invisible path before vanishing into the glass. Not a storm anymore. A diagram.

Behind her, the others shifted in the gray light. Leo scanned the sky like it might try to speak to him in the next breath. Selene's gaze flicked to every shadow, every gutter, her fingers never leaving the hilt of her blade. Damien stood too still, jaw set, as though the wind might take it as a challenge. Isla had her hands buried in the pockets of her soot-streaked coat, but her eyes kept darting to the spiral mark, calculating.

Thane lingered furthest back, just inside the stairwell, half in shadow. Lightning from the distant clouds caught on the wet black of his jacket, but his expression was unreadable.

Zara straightened. "We're not staying here."

"Where?" Leo asked, his voice low.

"Wherever this leads." She glanced at the spiral again. "It's not just a mark. It's a… handoff."

"A what now?" Damien said.

"When one player leaves the board," she said, "and another picks up the move."

Selene's eyes narrowed. "And we're the next move."

The wind changed direction in a single, deliberate turn, like someone had reached into the sky and twisted a dial. The spirals in the rain elongated, stretching toward the city's southern edge. Even through the mist, Zara could see the faint glint of lights—broken, flickering, some moving against the wind.

"That's not random weather," Leo murmured.

"No," Zara agreed. "It's a path."

"Or a lure," Kai said.

"Same thing," Isla muttered. "The trick is knowing who's holding the line."

Zara turned toward the stairwell. "We go."

No one argued. The air in the tower felt heavier now, as though the spiral mark above them had sealed a door they couldn't see. Every footstep echoed in the narrow stair, each beat dampened by the strange stillness clinging to the building. The storm sound faded the deeper they went, replaced by a faint, irregular pulse, like water dripping onto hollow stone.

◆ ◆ ◆

They descended three flights before the pulse grew louder—and changed. It wasn't dripping anymore. It was a heartbeat.

Damien slowed. "Tell me that's not coming from the walls."

Isla touched the steel railing, then pulled her hand back like it had bitten her. "Not the walls. The air."

They reached the landing between floors six and five when the stairwell bent sharply and ended in a solid wall of black glass. It reflected them perfectly—too perfectly. No fogging from their breath, no distortion from the stairwell's narrow light. It felt like staring into a memory of themselves, held still.

"Another mirror trick?" Kai asked.

"No," Selene said. Her voice had a strange weight to it. "This is a gate."

The spiral mark from the platform above shimmered faintly across the reflection's surface, curling into shape as if inked by an unseen hand. It completed itself in one long, unbroken line, and the heartbeat in the air matched its rhythm exactly.

Zara stepped forward until her reflection's eyes were level with hers. "What do you want from us?"

The heartbeat stopped.

The glass shivered—not cracking, but rippling outward from the spiral. When it stilled again, Zara's reflection had changed. The same posture. The same clothes. But her palm, now raised against the glass, carried a second mark burned into the skin—another spiral, smaller, darker, coiled tighter.

The Thirteenth.

She didn't recognize it from the Codex sketches or the Watcher patterns. This was different. Wrong, in a way that tugged at her teeth. It made the air behind her reflection bend, like the space itself was trying to draw inward.

Leo stepped closer, his reflection mirroring him. "What is that?"

"It's not ours," Selene said.

"No," Zara murmured. "It's theirs."

The spiral on the reflection's palm pulsed once, sending a ripple through the glass. The stairwell's air turned heavy, pressing against their lungs. Isla staggered back a step, muttering something under her breath about structural resonance. Damien's spear vibrated in his grip.

Then the spiral began to turn.

Slowly at first, then faster, until it spun like a vortex. The reflections blurred, their features smearing into dark shapes. The glass gave way—not breaking, but opening, peeling back like water under a blade.

The space beyond was impossible to measure—neither room nor hallway, just a long stretch of dim, gold-veined shadow. The air smelled faintly of salt and burned stone.

♦ ♦ ♦

Zara's pulse hit triple time. "Stay behind me."

She stepped through.

The others followed, their footsteps swallowed by the strange surface underfoot. It wasn't floor so much as a thin membrane stretched over something vast and moving. Every step sent out ripples, which vanished into the gold-veined darkness before they could return.

The space narrowed until they were walking single file again. The walls here pulsed with faint light, veins branching like roots or capillaries, converging ahead into a single point.

A voice spoke from that point—low, resonant, neither male nor female, but layered like several voices speaking together.

"The board is wrong."

The air trembled with it. Thane's head lifted sharply at the sound, his eyes fixing on the convergence ahead.

Zara didn't stop. "Wrong how?"

The voice pulsed again, each word matching the heartbeat in the walls. "Twelve where there were thirteen. Thirteen where there will be none."

Kai's fingers flexed against his case. "Not creepy at all."

They reached the convergence, and the space opened into a small chamber. In the center stood a single pedestal, its surface etched with spirals that seemed to shift when not directly looked at. Hovering above it was a fragment of something—stone or metal, it was hard to tell—shaped like a broken crown, its edge jagged, its surface veined with the same gold-thread pattern as the walls.

The spiral mark glowed faintly on one side of the crown piece.

Zara's throat felt dry. "What is this?"

"The Thirteenth Mark," the voice said. "Hidden when Olympus divided its heirs. Buried when the board was reset. Found when the storm split the sky."

♦ ♦ ♦

The crown fragment turned slowly in the air, and for a moment, Zara thought she saw symbols crawling along its edge—glyphs she didn't recognize, each one folding into the next like steps in an unending path.

Isla exhaled, her voice hushed. "It's... a keystone."

Damien frowned. "To what?"

Selene answered without looking away from it. "To whoever wears the rest."

The voice spoke again, softer now. "One already bears it. One will take it. One will refuse."

Zara's eyes flicked to the others—Leo, Kai, Selene, Damien, Isla... and Thane, still standing at the back, his gaze locked on the crown fragment.

No one moved.

The fragment rotated with lazy certainty, like it had all the time in the world and the world would wait.

Zara forced her voice to be even. "If it's a keystone, it completes something."

Completion is the lie they taught you. The board does not complete. It decides.

Damien shifted his grip. "Comfort's not on my shopping list."

"Neither is getting played," Leo said, eyes still on the shard. "Who already bears it?"

Silence. Not empty—listening.

Zara stepped closer to the pedestal. The spirals etched there weren't decorative; they were routes, braiding and unbraiding. Some ended in neat closures. Others broke off like snapped thread. A few didn't end at all—just climbed, disappearing into a nowhere the eye couldn't follow.

"Don't touch it," Selene said softly.

"I'm not going to," Zara said, though the shard had weight in her palm already, phantom-warm, as if memory could pre-burn skin.

The gold-veins in the walls brightened, syncing to the triple-time beat the storm had been keeping since dusk. Isla's eyes flicked between the veins and the shard, mapping unseen stress. "This chamber's balanced on a knife. We act, it tips."

"Then maybe the point is not to act," Kai said.

"That's a kind of act," Thane said.

Everyone looked at him.

He hadn't moved from the back. The white of his Carnevale-schooled smile didn't show; his face was blank in the clean, expensive way that said he was wearing a mask by choosing not to wear one. The Mirror Mask wasn't on him. It never needed to be.

"You seem… interested," Damien said.

"I'm interested in traps," Thane said. "And in the people who make them."

"The board is wrong," the voice repeated, as if their stalling required a refrain. "Fix it."

"How?" Leo demanded. "By crowning a ghost? By crowning one of us?"

"By naming what the gods refused to name."

A low breath slipped between Selene's teeth. "The one they chained in the deep."

The chamber didn't shiver. It braced.

The gold-veins dimmed and then flared like a struck nerve. The shard's spiral mark brightened a shade, and for the first time, something like a texture rippled across its surface—letters, then not letters, then a shape that made the eye slide away rather than read it.

Damien swore under his breath. "Hate that."

Zara's mind pushed through the repulsion. "You said one already bears it."

"Borne unwittingly," the voice said. "Borne because the storm remembers who touches it first."

"Leo?" Kai asked, instinctive.

"Not me," Leo said. "I touch storms, they bite back."

"Selene?" Isla.

Selene didn't answer. She was looking at the false floor of the air—the place all rooms have that's not made of materials but of expectation. Her eyes were glassy, like she was listening to shallow water over stone. "Not me."

All at once the chamber's pressure eased, like it had stopped pretending to be impartial.

Thane looked away from the shard and met Zara's gaze head-on. There was nothing coy in it, nothing flirted or softened. Just a simple, precise admission.

"I touched it," he said.

Silence again. That other kind. The kind that makes the throat want to swallow and keeps it from doing it.

"When?" Leo asked, too quickly.

"On the platform," Thane said. "When you were reading the spiral in the rain, I… brushed it. Reflex."

"Reflex," Damien echoed, dry as iron filings.

"Sometimes the hand moves because the mind wants to know if it still can," Thane said. "Even when the mind is telling it not to."

Zara believed him. Not because she wanted to—she didn't—but because the pattern snapped into place around the admission with that crisp, cruel relief only truth gives. The voice's phrasing. The shard's heat in her palm-that-wasn't. The way the storm had pivoted toward the south after.

She didn't say any of that. She said, "You don't look any more crowned than usual."

A ghost of a smile. "That's the trouble with masks. The best ones don't look like anything."

Isla exhaled through her nose, calculating again. "If he already bears a trace, taking the shard might not kill him."

"Comfort word," Damien said, glancing at the ceiling, like if there were gods worth the name they'd send better choices.

Selene stepped to Thane's side. Not close. Close enough. "If you take it and it isn't yours, it won't just burn you, Thane. It will burn the path off all of us. We'll fall out of the board."

Thane accepted the warning with a small nod. "Then perhaps we let it choose."

He moved as if to step forward.

"Wait," Zara said.

He did.

She turned her attention back to the pedestal, to the braid-work of routes. Two spirals in the pattern had been cut and then mended. Another was new—thread laid atop thread, refusing to choose one depth. She traced that new line in the air and felt everything in the chamber lean.

Choice measures shape.

Her mouth was dry. "We can force-distribute the risk."

"Distribute?" Leo asked.

"Shared contact," Isla realized. "A spread load. If it tries to drop the whole weight on one bearer, it has to move through a conductor. We become that."

"Great," Damien said. "We all get to burn together."

"No," Zara said. "We all get to refuse together if it isn't ours."

Selene nodded once. "It won't like that."

"I don't like the alternatives," Zara said. She lifted her left hand and extended it into the span above the pedestal—close enough that the shard's heat prickled her palm, not touching. "Hands."

Damien snorted. "This where we sing camp songs?"

"Hands," she repeated.

Leo put his palm under hers, fingers not quite touching. Kai added his, then Isla's callused one, then Selene's cold one. Thane waited a heartbeat longer than felt safe and then slid his into the stack, ring finger brushing Zara's wrist, pulse steady as a metronome that had learned to lie.

Nothing in the world happened.

Then everything did.

The shard dipped—not falling, bending, as if the air between their hands and the stone had become irresistible gravity. Heat licked the thin spaces between fingers, searching skin. The gold veins in the walls flared, and the heartbeat in the chamber doubled.

The shard flared.

Pain hit.

Not the clean pain of a burn, not the dull pain of a bruise. A remembering pain. It ran along old burns none of them had, lit up maps under skin that had been drawn before they were born. It found the places the gods had shaped and the places they hadn't quite reached. It tasted all of it and chose.

It tried to settle in Thane.

He didn't flinch.

The heat climbed his veins, seeking a throne under his collarbone, a hinge in the sternum. The Mirror Mask he wasn't wearing pressed against his face from the inside. He could feel the shape of a crown that wasn't a crown at all—it was a yoke, silk-lined and beautiful.

He almost let it.

Zara felt the decision before he made it.

"Refuse," she said, not to him. To the board.

Thane exhaled. A laugh with no humor in it. "No."

The shard hesitated.

A second path opened in the heat—split like a forked river and then like a river thinking better of being a river at all. It moved through Selene. She was ready; the Veil in her blood opened like a door for a guest she did not trust. The shard tasted her shadow and shied away.

It licked Isla's knuckles—spark-metal-static—tested Kai's bright lattice, throbbed once at Leo's tide.

Zara let it test her last.

When it touched her, it didn't burn.

It rang.

Not music—notation. Not words—grammar. The shard's spiral aligned with the one that had been tinting her dreams for weeks, the labyrinth that wasn't a prison but a verb. The sound ran down her bones and bounced back, proof-of-echo. The chamber leaned again, and the shard made its decision.

It didn't seat itself in her chest.

It cut.

A thin seam opened across her palm—blood bright as the gold-veins and just as quick. The shard tilted, accepted one drop, and then another, and the spiral on its face drank the pattern like a hungry thing.

The chamber lightninged.

The pain stopped.

Heat receded, not gone but banked, like a forge waiting.

The shard hovered again, its glow altered—deeper, the spiral within tightened, an iris closing.

"Bound," the voice said. "Not taken. Not worn. Bound."

Zara pulled her hand back. The cut closed too fast, leaving behind a mark that wasn't a burn—a thinner spiral, dark as ink under skin. It looked wrong and right at once, like an extra digit hidden on a hand.

Damien blew out a breath. "That didn't feel like winning."

"Because it wasn't," Selene said quietly. "It was choosing the terms of the next loss."

Thane flexed his fingers, expression unreadable. When he spoke, it was to Zara alone.

"You said distribute the risk," he murmured. "You took more."

"I took the math," she said. "I can carry that."

Something like rue curved his mouth. "And here I thought I was the one who lies for a living."

The shard drifted back over the pedestal, its spiral dimming to a coal-glow.

The chamber changed.

Not physically. Intention. The way air changes when a room's owner walks in.

"The board moves," the voice said. "The Thirteenth sees."

"Sees what?" Leo asked.

The wall directly behind the pedestal peeled back into a window of black glass and then into something more impossible—a view that wasn't a view: not a place, but all the places the spiral could point if it unfurled. A field of thrones in shadow. A city kneeling to a sky that had never known blue. A tower not unlike Bellamy's built of ribs instead of steel. At the center of each, a chair that was not empty so much as refusing to admit it had ever been sat in.

Zara felt nausea roll through her in a slow, cold wave. "Close it."

It did. Not because she commanded it—because it had shown what it was allowed to show.

The heartbeat in the gold-veins slowed. The spiral on the shard cooled to dark.

Selene tilted her head. "Listen."

Footsteps. Above. Many. Not the careful hush of Watchers. Not the liquid tread of a Harbinger.

People.

"Part of the same handoff," Zara said. She turned, blood-wet palm already dry, and pointed to the gold-veined corridor that had brought them in. "We're done here."

♦ ♦ ♦

Damien didn't argue. No one did. They moved together, tighter than they had on the way down. The membrane-floor rippled under their boots as they crossed it, the rhythm of the chamber's heart now matching their stride rather than forcing it.

At the glass gate, the reflection that met them was wrong for a heartbeat—thirteen shapes instead of six, the extra one a silhouette echoed by every mirrored surface since the Cradle. It wasn't any of them, who could it be?

It was a space shaped like a person.

Then it was gone. The glass smoothed. The spiral unwound and rewound into the ordinary lie of reflection, and the stairwell breathed them out into the bowels of Bellamy Tower.

They climbed.

The storm's sound returned in layers: rain, wind, the sub-bass thunder rolling along the city's bones. Mixed into it now—distant shouts. Sirens. A helicopter rotor chopping the air out of tempo with the rain's spiral.

"Public eyes," Kai said, grimacing. "Because this wasn't hard enough."

"Let them look," Damien said. "Maybe if the world watches us bleed, someone will send a bandage."

"Or a moving camera," Thane murmured.

They reached the lobby. The welding lattice Isla had grown across the revolving door still glowed faintly, threads charred but holding. The desks were empty. The elevator numbers blinked wrong again—1, 4, 7, 10, then all at once, like the building was clearing its throat.

Zara checked the plaza through the glass. Not crowds—clusters. Curious citizens pulled by siren-magnet. Police cordons sagging against weather. A news van trying to reverse down a street turned into a river by the storm. On the far side of the plaza, a construction crane turned slowly, though no wind touched it.

Leo made a low sound. "Do you feel that?"

"Feel what?" Isla asked.

"Her," he said.

♦ ♦ ♦

The word landed like a dropped coin in a well. The ripples took a while to come back.

Selene's hand went to her blade. "Maelis?"

Leo shook his head. "The other her."

The air pressure shifted.

The storm did a thing storms didn't do: it parted.

Rain still fell everywhere else. On the plaza, across the slicked glass of the tower, on their faces. But in a line between Bellamy's doors and the far curb, a dry corridor opened, raindrops skimming its edges and then rejoining the spiral as if embarrassed.

At the far end of that corridor stood a woman.

Not Watcher. Not cloaked.

Her dress was the color of storm-apex—not gray, not blue, the particular near-black of a cloud pregnant with lightning. Her hair was silver the way surf is silver, her eyes the color of steel pulled from seawater. She wasn't young, and she wasn't old. She belonged to the first version of both.

Zara knew her without knowing how she knew.

The one who had spoken to Leo in the water first. The echo. The memory. The keeper.

She lifted her hand, palm out, spiral burned there in faint light.

A match to Zara's.

Leo exhaled like someone had cut a rope he hadn't seen around his ribs. "It's her."

"Which makes this a bad idea," Selene said.

"Every good idea starts as a bad one," Isla muttered, but her tools were already in her hands again.

"Stay together," Zara said. "We don't give the camera a picture of us fractured."

She put her palm to the glass and felt the lattice read her mark. The weave shrank back in a hiss, a petal closing, enough for a body to pass. Wind knifed through the gap, sharp and clean. The plaza smell rushed in—ozone, old rain, concrete, the faint metallic tang of the river rising in its banks.

They stepped out.

The woman at the end of the dry corridor didn't move toward them. She waited, the way a shore waits for tide. When they closed half the distance, the spiral on her palm dimmed to match Zara's; when they closed the rest, it went out.

"Hello," she said, as if they were arriving for tea and not from an impossible tower. "At last."

"Name?" Zara asked.

"Call me what the oldest stories called me." The woman's mouth curved. "I am the wave that remembers. Tritonis will do."

There was something in the way she said it—not a title, not a boast, but a marker laid down across centuries.

Leo blinked. "That's—"

"A name hidden in your myths for mine," she said. "Before the Olympians kept their neat lines of succession, I walked the board when it had more than twelve spaces. When there were no pieces—only currents." Her gaze flicked to Zara's palm, then to the rain curling around them. "You carry a mark the sea knew long before the storm learned it."

The spiral on her own hand was older, etched deeper, its lines softened like a stone worn smooth by centuries of tide.

"You have found something that belonged where it was hidden," she said, "and you have not put it on your head."

Her gaze moved to Thane—once, precise, surgical—and then back to Zara. Approval like a razor's kiss.

"The Thirteenth Mark stirs," she said. "The board is almost set."

"Almost," Selene said. "Meaning…?"

"Meaning the chains are moving," Tritonis said. "And you haven't decided whether to wear them or break them." She tilted her head toward the storm, as though listening to something deep beneath it. "If you break them, the board may drown before it can reset. If you wear them… you'll need to remember who tied the first knot."

Thunder rolled like a laugh spoken too softly to admit it's a laugh.

"What happens if we break them?" Damien asked.

Tritonis didn't answer.

She looked up, past them, to the spiral of rain knitting itself tight over Bellamy Tower, and when she spoke again, it was to the storm.

"Bring them north," she said. "Before the Queen of Ash decides to harvest in the south. Her fire does not ebb—it consumes. And she has been patient too long."

The dry corridor collapsed. Rain rejoined itself around them, grateful to be ordinary water again.

Tritonis stepped backward once, twice, and was gone—not invisibly, not like a Watcher, but like a person who knows the exact turn where any city stops being a place and starts being a story.

"North," Leo said.

"North," Zara agreed. "On ours."

♦ ♦ ♦

She turned toward the river and the train lines that stitched the city out from its heart.

The storm shifted its measure, just a hair, like a conductor acknowledging a new tempo.

Triple time, still.

But the downbeat now was theirs.

The storm's triple-time heartbeat followed them into the streets, steady and unyielding.

♦ ♦ ♦

Zara led the way north, her gaze fixed on the gray smear of the river cutting through the city. The train lines were out there somewhere, threading toward the industrial districts and beyond. Every route she plotted bent instinctively away from the plaza, as if Tritonis' warning had already carved itself into her internal map.

She didn't need to look at the spiral in her palm to know it was still there—thinner than the others' marks, but constant. Every step seemed to tighten it, a coil winding toward some unseen release.

The city smelled different after Bellamy Tower. Not just rain and ozone, but something hotter, metallic, as though a forge had been left open to the air. Isla noticed too—her eyes kept scanning the rooftops, following curls of steam that didn't belong to the weather.

"Feels like the city's breathing wrong," she muttered.

"It's not the city," Selene said. "It's what's moving through it."

Damien swung his spear over one shoulder, expression carved from the same granite as the wet sidewalks. "If she's real—this Queen of Ash—then why send us north instead of just telling us to fight her?"

"Because," Thane said, "someone who calls themselves a queen doesn't fight on your schedule. You fight on theirs, or not at all."

Kai's voice came quiet, nearly lost under the slap of their boots. "Or maybe the fight's not the point."

Zara slowed just enough to let him catch up. "Explain."

Kai's fingers drummed against his case, each tap in sync with the storm's off-beat. "Sometimes a piece doesn't move to attack— it moves to force everything else into position. Maybe she's not here for us at all. Maybe we're just the lever."

No one liked that thought, so no one argued with it.

They crossed an intersection where the traffic lights blinked in patterns that didn't match any cycle Zara knew. 7, 4, 1, blank. Then again. She filed it away, not because she understood it, but because the board understood her.

The blocks thinned into an industrial zone—brick warehouses, skeletal cranes, shipping containers stacked like toy blocks abandoned mid-play. The storm gathered thicker overhead, the spirals tightening. Somewhere to the east, a siren wailed three long notes before cutting off.

Leo stopped abruptly. "Hear that?"

"What?" Isla asked.

He tilted his head, eyes narrowing. "Not the storm. Under it."

They listened.

At first, it was nothing—just the wind snagging between warehouse ribs. Then the sound found shape: a dry, rolling hiss, like paper burning in a sealed jar.

Selene's knuckles whitened around her blade. "Ash."

The word carried weight now.

The hiss grew into a whispering rush, accompanied by a faint peppering sound against the rooftops. Tiny black flecks began to drift down through the rain. Where they touched the puddles, the water dimmed, clouded, as if swallowing soot.

Zara caught one on her palm. It didn't smear like ash should— it kept its shape, a perfect fragment of something that had once been sharp. It was warm, too, despite the rain.

"That's not from a fire," Isla said, stepping close to see. "That's from a breaking."

"What's breaking?" Damien asked.

Isla didn't answer.

The storm above them flickered with heat lightning, no thunder following. The air tightened, pressing against their eardrums.

Then, in the gap between warehouses, Zara saw it: a tall, slow-falling column of black dust spiraling upward against the rain's spiral, as though defying the sky itself. At its base, something glowed faint red—dull, banked heat rather than open flame.

"That's her," Leo said. He didn't sound certain, but his voice held the gravity of someone whose blood recognized a tide it couldn't stop.

Zara didn't let herself look at it for more than a heartbeat. The Queen of Ash wasn't theirs to face—not yet. Tritonis' order had been clear enough. Still, the sight lodged behind her eyes, an image her mind would keep turning over like a dangerous coin.

They moved faster, keeping the column to their backs. The air grew cooler again, the black flecks thinning, though the metallic tang lingered.

At the far end of the district, the rail yard emerged through the mist—a sprawl of parallel tracks and rusting switch towers, half-flooded from the storm. A handful of trains stood silent under the gray, their windows dark.

"Which line?" Kai asked.

"The one that still believes it's moving," Zara said.

They found it three rows in: a freight train that hummed faintly, the vibration running through the rails like an old song. The doors on one container stood half-open, revealing crates strapped tight with worn rope.

"Think we can ride it out?" Damien asked.

"Long enough to put distance between us and her," Zara said.

They climbed in, boots thudding on the steel floor. The air inside was stale but dry, a brief reprieve from the rain. Isla moved to the door and pulled it almost closed, leaving a thin gap to watch the yard.

Through it, Zara could see the spirals in the rain adjusting again—widening, shifting their focus. The triple-time beat didn't change, but the accent had moved, like the downbeat was now elsewhere.

The train jolted. Somewhere ahead, an engine growled to life.

"That's not us," Leo said.

"No," Zara agreed. "That's the board."

The train began to move, slow at first, then gathering speed. The city slid past in wet, blurred shapes.

No one spoke for a long stretch. The rhythm of the wheels joined the storm's beat, creating an uneasy polyrhythm that seemed to measure more than distance.

Finally, Selene broke the silence. "When she said 'chains,' what did you think she meant?"

"Not iron," Zara said. "Something harder to see. Harder to cut."

Thane leaned back against the crate behind him, his expression unreadable. "Obligations," he said. "Oaths. The kind you make before you know what they cost."

"Or before you know who wrote them," Leo added.

The train clattered over a switch, the sound sharp in the stillness. Zara let the conversation settle into the hum of motion, her mind turning over the possibilities. Chains could be anything. Could be anyone.

Outside, the storm kept pace, spirals unbroken, as though it had been waiting for them to move.

They were still on the board.

But something else had just been set in motion.

The train settled into its rhythm—steel on steel, the muted roar of rain against the container roof, the occasional flicker of passing light slipping through the narrow gap in the door.

Zara leaned her shoulder against the wall, not resting so much as keeping herself steady. The spiral in her palm had gone quiet, but not dormant. It felt like a sealed envelope in her blood—waiting for the right hands to open it.

Across from her, Thane sat with his long legs stretched out, one boot braced against a crate. His eyes tracked the slow sway of the hanging straps overhead. He hadn't spoken since they'd boarded, and the silence around him was the kind that made others measure their words.

Leo was the first to break it. "We can't just ride this out forever."

"No," Zara agreed. "But we can ride it far enough that she—" She didn't say the Queen of Ash. Saying the name felt like leaving a door open. "—loses our scent."

Damien's voice was flat. "You think she's hunting us."

"I think she's watching the board. And we just moved a piece she's been waiting on."

Selene shifted her grip on the blade resting across her knees. "Then she'll follow the move, not us. Unless we're the move."

The words lodged in the cramped air. None of them liked the symmetry.

Kai slid the latch on his case open just enough to check the contents. "She didn't look like someone who follows. She looked like someone who waits for you to cross her threshold, then locks the door behind you."

"Which is why," Isla said, "we keep to our own paths. No thresholds. No invitations."

Zara nodded once, but the truth was heavier. Tritonis hadn't told them to avoid the Queen of Ash. She'd told them to get north before she harvested. That meant the queen's reach extended farther than they wanted to believe.

The train swayed, and a sharp metallic scent rolled through the container—stronger than the rust and oil that clung to freight cars. Isla caught it first. "That's not the yard."

Zara moved to the narrow opening and peered out.

The rail line was passing over a bridge now, the swollen river flashing below in the stormlight. On the far bank, the skeletal remains of an old signal tower leaned at an unnatural angle. Something glowed inside it—faint, pale gold, like a lantern behind warped glass.

Leo joined her at the gap. "That's not normal track equipment."

"No," she said. "It's a relay."

"For who?" Damien asked.

Zara didn't answer. She didn't have to.

The glow pulsed once, and the spiral in her palm answered— one slow turn, like a key testing a lock. She pulled back from the door.

"They're still tracking us," she said.

Thane's gaze finally shifted to her. "The board never stops tracking its own pieces."

"Then we get off," Leo said.

Damien frowned. "In the middle of nowhere?"

"Better nowhere than somewhere they expect," Leo shot back.

Zara weighed it. The relay could mean anything—Watcher tech, Harbinger signal, something older. But the longer they stayed on the train, the easier it would be for whoever built it to predict their next move.

She gave a short nod. "Next low stretch, we jump."

♦ ♦ ♦

It didn't take long. The train began to cut through a shallow embankment where the land rose to meet the tracks. Rainwater sheeted down the slope, making the ground slick, but better that, than rock.

"Go," Zara said.

One by one, they slipped through the narrow opening, landing in wet grass and mud. The train didn't slow. Within moments, its tail-lights vanished into the dark, leaving only the hiss of the storm.

They moved quickly, keeping the embankment between themselves and the line. The land beyond was a patchwork of fallow fields and scattered trees, the horizon blurred by rain. In the distance, a faint orange glow marked a cluster of lights—too dim for a city, too steady for lightning.

"Shelter?" Kai asked.

"Maybe," Zara said. "Or a beacon."

Isla adjusted the strap on her satchel. "We won't know which until we're too close to turn back."

They headed toward it anyway.

◆ ◆ ◆

The glow resolved into a collection of weathered buildings—an abandoned grain co-op, by the look of it. The main structure was a squat concrete silo, its rusted chute hanging like a broken limb. Smaller outbuildings leaned into one another, their windows boarded or gone entirely. The light came from inside the silo, filtering through cracks in the concrete.

Selene stopped at the edge of the clearing. "We're not alone."

Zara followed her gaze. Tracks in the mud—boot prints, deep and fresh, cutting toward the silo's service door. Too many to count, and not all the same tread.

Leo exhaled through his nose. "Watchers?"

"Or worse," Damien said.

The rain slackened just enough to let another sound through—the faint, deliberate creak of hinges. The silo's service door eased open, and a figure stepped into the light.

He was tall, gaunt, wearing a rain-slick coat that might once have been black. His face was shadowed by the brim of a hat pulled low, but the spiral burned on the back of his left hand in the same wrong-dark as Zara's new mark.

Her pulse tightened.

"Travelers," the man said, his voice carrying easily over the distance without raising in volume. "The road ahead is closed. You'll find better shelter inside."

Zara didn't move. "Who closes it?"

"The ones you're running from," he said. "And the ones you're running toward."

Kai murmured under his breath, "That's comforting."

The man's gaze slid over each of them in turn, pausing for just a fraction longer on Thane before returning to Zara. "You've already taken the Mark. That means you're on the list whether you stand in the rain or under a roof."

Zara's fingers twitched toward her blade. "Whose list?"

He smiled faintly. "The same board you think you're playing."

That was enough. Zara took a single step forward, closing the gap between her and the others without entering his reach. "We don't take shelter in someone else's move."

"Every square belongs to someone," he said. "Best to pick one with walls."

Before she could answer, the glow inside the silo flared—and with it came a whisper, not in the air, but in the marrow.

Bound, it said. The chain waits for the next link.

The man's smile widened, not in triumph, but in recognition. "You hear it. Good. That means you're ready to choose."

A gust of wind slammed the service door against the wall, revealing more figures inside—three, maybe four, all wearing the same rain-slick coats, all marked with the dark spiral. They didn't advance. They didn't need to.

Zara took one last look at the man, memorizing the way the rain slid from his hat brim without touching the skin beneath. Then she turned away.

"North," she said.

No one questioned it.

They skirted the clearing, keeping to the treeline until the glow of the silo was swallowed by the storm.

♦ ♦ ♦

When it was gone, the spiral in her palm cooled again, but the words it had carried did not.

She didn't know if that link was them—or the Queen of Ash— or something worse. But she knew the board was already moving to close the distance.

And north felt farther away than it had an hour ago.

♦ ♦ ♦

# CHAPTER XXVI
# THE CHAIN WEAKENS

Venice, March 14, 2026

The rain hadn't stopped, but it had changed again. The spiral tempo that had carried them out of Bellamy was breaking, threads loosening, the storm's shape shifting in the sky above like a net being rewoven.

They moved fast, staying close enough to feel each other's motion in the dark. Bellamy Tower receded behind them, its crown lost in cloud, but the pulse of its gold-veined heart still seemed to throb in Zara's palm. The spiral-mark under her skin burned faintly, not in pain—more like the warmth of something that remembered her.

No one spoke until they reached the edge of the river. The water was swollen from the storm, brown and slick with the churn of debris. On the far bank, the northern rail line rose on steel legs, a thin promise of escape.

"Bridge is out," Damien said, scanning the skeletal remains of a truss downstream.

"We don't need the bridge," Leo replied, eyes tracking the water's flow. "We can—"

He stopped.

The rest of them saw it too.

Across the river's mouth, a new structure had grown where no map, no memory, no sane geometry said it should be. It was a chain—no, several chains, thick as subway tunnels, arcing from bank to bank. Each link was the length of a boxcar, black iron slick with rain, and yet it caught the lightning overhead in pale gold flashes.

Isla went very still. "That's Hephaestus' forge pattern."

"Yours?" Kai asked.

She shook her head. "No. But whoever made it… knew how."

The nearest link hummed with a tone too low to be sound, a pressure in the chest that matched the beat Zara had felt in the tower's gold-veins. As the wind shifted, the hum sharpened—becoming distinct notes.

Kai's jaw clenched. "If this was meant to carry us, why does it sound like it's breaking?"

Zara's stomach knotted. "Those aren't notes."

Leo looked at her. "What are they?"

"Glyphs," she said. "It's spelling us."

They stepped closer without meaning to. The rain seemed to thin around the structure, droplets bending away from its mass. As they reached the riverbank, they saw it clearly: etched into the underside of every link was a different symbol.

Kai crouched to see the nearest one. His own glyph blazed there in miniature, carved with the precision of a master scribe.

"They're ours," he said. "All of ours."

Selene's was on the link beside his. Damien's on the next. Zara's, Isla's, Leo's. Even Thane's, near the midpoint, gleamed faintly like it had been polished more recently than the others.

"They're not just showing them," Isla murmured. "They're holding them."

Her hammer hovered above the iron. "Stone shouldn't remember like this. Not unless it wants to."

Damien's voice dropped into the low register he used when talking to weapons. "Meaning if we step onto this thing, it's going to take something."

"Or give something," Thane said quietly. His eyes hadn't left the far side of the chain. "Depends on which way you're walking."

Zara weighed the span between banks. "We can't go around. The southern lines will be under water by now. This is the only path north before the next storm surge hits."

Kai glanced upstream. "And swimming's not an option with that current."

The hum deepened, and the first chain shuddered, settling lower into the water. The links rose like vertebrae from a spine, one after another, until a single continuous path arched toward the far bank.

Leo exhaled. "Feels like an invitation."

Selene's tone was flat. "Or a test."

They stepped onto the first link. The iron was slick but gripped their boots like a living thing. Underfoot, the hum became a steady vibration, and the glyph carved into the link warmed against their soles.

One link in, nothing happened.

The second link was different.

The moment Zara's foot touched it, a thread of heat darted up her leg—not enough to stagger her, but enough to make her gasp. She looked down. The glyph under her boot was hers. It pulsed once, as if recognizing her, and then dimmed.

"I felt that," she said.

"It took something," Leo guessed.

She shook her head slowly. "It measured something."

One by one, they crossed their own links. Each time, the hum shifted, notes disappearing into the larger vibration. By the time they reached the midpoint, the chain was quieter, but the quiet felt heavier, like the absence of a heartbeat.

Halfway across, the world tilted.

It wasn't physical—the chain didn't sway—but the sky above them folded in on itself, clouds forming a perfect ring directly overhead. From the center of that ring, something dropped into the space between rain and water.

Figures.

They landed without sound. Tall, narrow, draped in armor that looked poured rather than forged. No cloaks. No masks. Their faces were featureless, polished obsidian where eyes and mouths should have been. Each carried a hooked staff taller than themselves, the metal at the ends sharpened to a crescent so thin it vanished when turned sideways.

Selene inhaled sharply. "Harbingers."

Damien's knuckles whitened around his spear. "We were supposed to have more time."

There were six of them. Three ahead, three behind. None spoke.

The lead Harbinger stepped forward until its staff hovered inches above the link they stood on. It tapped the metal once. The sound wasn't a clang but a bell-tone that rang in the gut. The glyphs on the chain flared in answer.

Zara felt her spiral-mark burn hotter. "They're not here to fight."

"They're here to pull," Selene said.

The first movement was almost casual—the forward Harbingers sweeping their staves in a slow arc. The space between links widened, not physically but perceptually, as if the distance between one step and the next had been doubled.

Kai swore under his breath. "They're stretching the path."

The rear Harbingers began to move in, their steps deliberate, the hooked ends of their staves grazing the chain. Wherever they touched, the glyphs dimmed.

"We move," Zara ordered.

They did—but the chain was no longer just a path. Each step resisted them, dragging at their legs like they were moving through deep water. The air thickened, heavy with the metallic scent of old storms.

The first clash came when Damien lunged at the nearest Harbinger. His spear met the hooked staff, and the sound was like stone grinding on ice. Sparks leapt between them—not fire but images, flashes of places Zara didn't recognize: a desert under a black sun, a hall of mirrors with no reflections.

The Harbinger didn't flinch. It absorbed the blow and pushed Damien back a full link.

"Not kill," Isla muttered as she swung her hammer at another's staff. "Separate."

The realization hit at the same time the chain beneath them gave a long, slow creak.

They weren't trying to knock them off the chain.

They were trying to pull the chain itself into the water.

The chain shuddered under their boots, a vibration that ran through Zara's bones. The links ahead swayed just enough for the river's black surface to flash up between the gaps. That water wasn't ordinary—she could feel it looking back.

"Keep moving!" she shouted, forcing her own feet forward against the pull.

Leo's hand lashed out to grab her arm as one of the Harbingers twisted its staff in a wide arc. The movement didn't strike her, but the air around the staff bent, and for a heartbeat she saw herself falling—slammed into the water, cold teeth closing around her ankles.

She blinked hard. Still on the chain. Still moving. But her heart rate spiked, a staccato to match the chain's groan.

"They're playing with perception," Kai called, voice sharp over the rain. "Don't look directly at the bend—"

Selene's blade hissed past his shoulder, catching the tip of a staff and knocking it wide. "Tell me that before they try it on me."

Another yank from below—heavier now. The Harbingers weren't moving in for the kill; they were anchoring, leaning their weight into the chain, feeding whatever waited in the water. The links underfoot pulsed in time with something beneath the surface. A heartbeat.

Zara's spiral-mark flared. Not the searing burn from the Bellamy chamber, but a throb that answered the pulse below.

No. Not answering. Calling.

She forced her gaze forward. "We cut the pull before it hits the pivot point."

Damien's jaw tightened. "You're thinking break the chain?"

"I'm thinking break their hold," she said. "The chain stays. We go."

"How?" Isla's hammer glanced off another staff, sparks scattering into nothing. "They're anchored on both sides."

"Not both." Zara's eyes narrowed. "Just ours."

The Harbinger ahead of her tilted its head, like it had heard her thought. Its mask—a dull steel curve over shadow—caught a line of lightning from the storm. In that brief flare she saw the spiral etched into its surface, but fractured, as though cracked from the inside.

It stepped forward, hook sweeping low.

She met it.

Not with her dagger—this time she caught the staff with her bare palm, the mark on her skin flashing dark against the steel. The impact rattled her teeth, but the pull shivered.

And broke.

The Harbinger staggered half a step, just enough for Leo to slam his shoulder into its chest and send it off-balance toward the river. The figure didn't fall—not fully. It dissolved into a spray of shadow and rain, sinking between the links.

The chain under them lifted fractionally.

"One down," Leo panted.

"Keep them breaking," Zara said.

The others adapted fast. Damien stopped trying to drive his spear through and instead hooked it around a staff, twisting and locking until the Harbinger's weight shifted wrong. Isla's hammer struck the chain itself, sending a shockwave down the metal that made the nearest enemy stumble.

Selene was a shadow's shadow—each time a Harbinger raised its staff, she was already inside its reach, cutting at the haft or pressing her blade against the etched spirals until the light guttered and the figure fell away.

But for every one they broke, another rose from the mist curling off the river. Some came in close, their staffs spinning like oars cutting water; others stayed two, three links away, pulling slow and steady, their eyes—if they had eyes—fixed on Zara.

Her mark burned again. The pull below was no longer only in the chain, it was in her veins.

She bit down on a curse. "We need the center clear. Now."

"Center?" Kai demanded. "That's halfway to—"

"Do it!" she snapped.

They surged forward together, cutting a path. The Harbingers pressed harder, the chain pitching like a ship in heavy seas. Twice, Damien caught Isla by the back of her coat when her boots slid on the wet steel; once, Selene's hand locked around Zara's wrist, jerking her away from a hook meant to take her at the knees.

The center of the chain was marked by a single massive link, thicker than the rest, its surface scored by ancient weld lines. When Zara stepped onto it, the pull from the river slammed into her full-force.

She dropped to one knee.

The water below erupted—not in waves, but in forms. Shapes moved just beneath the surface, their outlines barely visible. Not fish. Not human. Something in between, stretched too long, their hands like fins, their faces nothing but mouths.

Every one of them opened at once.

The pull became a drag.

"Zara!" Leo's voice cut through, but distant, muffled like she was already under.

She planted her palm flat on the link.

The spiral burned hot enough to sear her through to bone. The drag slowed—not much, but enough to let air back into her lungs.

"They're bound to this anchor," she said. "If we break it—"

"The chain drops," Isla warned.

Zara's eyes narrowed. "Not if we give it a new anchor."

Selene's gaze flicked to her. "You."

Zara nodded once.

It wasn't a question of willingness; it was a question of calculation. The anchor would take the mark's pull into her instead of the chain. It might burn her hollow, might leave her unable to stand. But it would keep the path.

She pressed harder.

The anchor link screamed—not metal tearing, but something deeper. The sound vibrated the air into fog. The shapes in the water recoiled, thrashing.

The Harbingers moved as one, staffs snapping forward.

"Hold them!" Damien bellowed.

Leo planted himself in front of Zara, trident flashing in a blur, knocking aside hooks. Isla and Kai closed ranks, hammers and bow in sync, each impact throwing sparks and ripples.

Selene stepped back to back with Zara, blade low, her voice tight. "If you're going to do it, do it now."

Zara drew the spiral's shape in her mind—not the clean diagram from the Bellamy tower, but the living one, the one that shifted under stormlight. She wound it around the anchor link, every curve matching the burn in her palm.

The pull lunged.

She let it.

Heat roared up her arm, into her chest, down her spine. The world narrowed to the link under her hand and the rhythm pounding in her ears. The shapes below surged upward—and then collapsed in on themselves, drawn down into the mark until the river smoothed.

The chain stilled.

Zara's vision swam, the world tilting. She pushed herself up— slow, deliberate—and turned to see the Harbingers dissolve like smoke in wind.

The storm above them shifted. The spirals in the rain widened, stretching toward the far bank.

Leo caught her elbow. "You good?"

She nodded once. "Move."

They ran.

The chain ahead rose out of the water and into the shadow of a massive archway—black stone carved with glyphs that twisted when the eye lingered. The air beneath it smelled of salt and lightning.

As they passed under, Zara felt the mark in her palm pulse, once.

◆ ◆ ◆

From somewhere beyond the arch, a voice—not the layered one from Bellamy, but a single, human voice—spoke.

"You're late."

The storm leaned inward first, as though something pulled the weather into a single breath. The shadows thickened at the archway's edge, bending light without consuming it.

The figure stepped out from the shadowed mouth of the arch.

For a second, Zara's mind refused to place them anywhere on the board she knew. Not Watcher. Not Harbinger. No mask, no spiral-mark showing. Just a man—tall, coat hanging open over storm-dark clothes, rain beading on his shoulders without soaking in. His hair was the color of iron in firelight, his eyes the green-gold of tarnished bronze.

And something about him rang wrong. Not in his stance, which was casual, or in his voice, which carried no threat—but in the way the storm behind him seemed to lean closer.

Damien angled his spear toward the newcomer. "Name."

The man's mouth twitched, like he might smile if it didn't take too much effort. "Names have weight. I don't carry mine lightly."

Selene's blade stayed low but ready. "Then give us one you don't mind losing."

He glanced at her, then at Zara. "Call me… Ferrin. For now."

Leo stepped forward. "You were expecting us."

"I was expecting someone," Ferrin said. "The storm told me the board shifted. That always means new pieces in play."

Zara's pulse ticked up. "You talk like you know the game."

Ferrin's gaze lingered on her hand. "I know you just anchored something that was meant to sink. That's not a move made by someone who doesn't understand risk."

"Risk is surviving the next ten minutes," Isla muttered, eyes scanning the shadows beyond him. "We don't have time for riddles."

Ferrin didn't move to block them. "Then go. North is open—for now. But if you keep to the river path, you'll meet more of what you saw on the chain. The Queen of Ash doesn't like losing ground."

Selene's jaw tightened. "We already have a north-bound rendezvous."

Ferrin's brow arched slightly. "With Tritonis."

Zara didn't answer. Neither did Leo.

"I'm not here to stop you," he said, reading the silence. "I'm here to tell you that the next chain you cross won't be steel."

"What will it be?" Kai asked.

Ferrin's eyes went distant, like he was watching the answer happen somewhere far off. "Bone."

A cold ripple moved through Zara's chest. "Whose?"

Ferrin tilted his head toward the black archway behind him. "That depends on whether you're ready to leave yours behind."

Before any of them could respond, the storm shifted again. This time, it wasn't the wide spiral of rain, but a straight-line wind that cut across the river, hard enough to throw spray against the chain they'd just left.

Ferrin's gaze sharpened. "She's coming."

"Who?" Damien demanded.

He didn't answer. He stepped back into the archway's shadow, his outline breaking apart like smoke in reverse. "Move north. And if you see the bone bridge—don't look down."

Then he was gone.

◆ ◆ ◆

Zara's mark throbbed once, hard enough to sting. She swallowed the questions crowding her throat. "You heard him. North."

For a handful of heartbeats, only rain answered them. Their breaths tore ragged through the storm, boots slipping on stone, the silence between thunderclaps heavy with what had not yet appeared.

The path beyond the arch wound upward along the riverbank, the stone slick under their boots. Lightning crawled over the water in slow, deliberate arcs, each one holding just long enough to throw the far shore into relief—towers, broken and leaning; a spire crowned with fire; the dark gap of a collapsed causeway.

By the third flash, Zara realized the spire's fire wasn't burning. It was breathing.

"Tell me that's not—" Isla began.

"It is," Leo said grimly.

The thing on the spire's peak shifted, wings unfolding with a sound like sails snapping in sudden wind. Its body was too long for its frame, its head narrow and ridged, eyes burning with the same gold-thread light they'd seen in the Bellamy shard.

It launched into the air.

Selene's voice was flat. "Harbingers were the opening act."

The creature banked low over the river, the force of its wings flattening the spirals in the rain beneath it. Its gaze locked on them as it swept toward the bank.

Zara's instincts screamed scatter, but there was nowhere to go. The river was on one side, the cliff on the other, the path only wide enough for two abreast.

"Under the ledge!" Damien barked, pointing to a low overhang in the rock.

They dove for it as the creature passed overhead, the air pressure slamming into Zara's ribs. Stone chipped away above them under the force. She pressed her back to the wall, heart hammering.

The creature wheeled in the rain, slower now, circling.

"It's measuring us," Kai said.

"It can measure all it wants," Isla growled, "as long as it doesn't—"

The thing dove again, this time lower.

Zara grabbed the only option she saw. "Move toward the cliff face—now!"

They pressed tighter to the rock as the creature's talons scraped the path where they'd been seconds before. Sparks lit the rain.

Leo's trident was in his hands, his grip white-knuckled. "We can't stay pinned here."

Selene's eyes tracked the thing's arc. "Next pass, we move under it. Force it to overshoot."

They didn't have to wait long. The creature banked wide, then swept in. On Selene's count, they broke cover and ran toward it.

It roared—not with sound, but with a pressure that made the air ripple. Zara's vision blurred at the edges, but she kept moving, the mark on her palm heating in rhythm with its wingbeats.

As it passed over, Damien thrust upward with his spear, catching the membrane of its wing. The tip sliced through, not deep, but enough to send a shudder down its length. It veered hard, struggling to keep its arc.

"Go!" Zara shouted.

They sprinted up the path, not looking back until the cliff widened enough to give them space. By then, the creature had regained its balance and was circling higher, watching.

Zara knew that look. It wasn't retreat. It was patience.

♦ ♦ ♦

The path leveled onto a plateau, the river curling around its edge. In the center stood what looked at first like a cairn of black stone. But as they drew closer, Zara saw it wasn't piled rock—it was carved, the shapes worn but deliberate. Figures. Faces.

And every face was screaming.

Kai slowed, his voice low. "That's not just a marker."

"No," Selene said. "It's a warning."

The creature landed on the far edge of the plateau, wings folding in with precise, deliberate movements. Its head tilted, eyes narrowing.

The storm's spirals tightened above them.

Zara's mark flared so hot she thought it might burn through her skin.

The creature stepped forward once, talons scraping stone. Then it spoke.

Not aloud. In her head.

"Bound, but not claimed. Chosen, but not crowned."

Her breath caught.

"The chain was yours to break. The bridge will be mine to grant."

The storm surged, wind driving rain in horizontal sheets.

Then, without another word, the creature turned, launched skyward, and vanished into the spirals.

Zara stood frozen for a heartbeat longer than she meant to.

Damien's voice broke the silence. "North?"

"North," she said, her voice steady by force. "Before the bridge finds us."

They moved in a line now, no one speaking, the storm pressing them forward. The rain had shifted, no longer random—each drop fell with a strange rhythm, like the ticking of some massive, unseen clock. Zara counted without meaning to. Seven beats between the louder gusts. Seven steps before the wind shifted.

Her palm burned in time with it.

The plateau narrowed again, forcing them single-file. The cliff edge fell away into nothing but mist, the roar of water far below. Somewhere in the distance, she thought she heard the clatter of chains, faint but growing steadier with each step.

Leo slowed. "You hear that?"

Damien's jaw tightened. "Yeah. And I don't like where it's coming from."

Selene was already scanning the sky. "Not sky. Below."

The path bent hard to the right and dropped into a cut in the rock. The sound grew louder. Chain on stone. Chain under strain.

They descended into a half-circle hollow in the cliffside, where the rock gave way to an enormous arch of iron—corroded, bent in places, but still holding. From it stretched a single chain, links the size of shields, disappearing into the mist below. The links were slick with water, every groove worn deep, as if the chain had been moving for centuries.

Zara stepped close enough to feel the hum through her boots.

"This is it," Kai murmured.

"What is?" Isla asked.

"The bridge," Zara said, before she realized she'd spoken.

No one moved for a long moment. The chain swayed once, slow and deliberate. Then the mist parted, just enough for them to see.

Far below, a second arch rose from the opposite cliff face, the other end of the chain anchored there. Between the two, suspended over a chasm that seemed to have no bottom, were the broken remains of a bridge. The stones floated just above the chain, locked in place by invisible force, shifting slightly as if restless.

"That thing back there wasn't bluffing."

The chain gave a sudden jolt, enough to rattle the stones under their feet. The sound of the links grinding echoed up from the chasm, and from somewhere deep inside the mist came another sound—something vast inhaling.

Zara's hand clenched. "We cross now."

"How?" Isla demanded. "That thing isn't exactly OSHA approved."

Leo's trident tapped against the rock once, twice. "One at a time. Fast."

"No," Selene said, her tone cutting through the wind. "All at once. The chain won't take the same pressure twice."

Before anyone could argue, the wind shifted again—and the first stones of the floating bridge began to slide toward them.

Zara didn't think. She just moved.

The others followed, boots striking wet stone, every step making the bridge tremble underfoot. The mist clung to their legs, cold and strangely heavy, like wading through invisible water. Halfway across, the chain groaned deep in its core, and the stones under them shifted hard to the left.

"Don't stop!" Damien shouted.

They ran.

The mist surged, rising around them until the far side vanished from sight. Zara's breath came in short, sharp bursts, her muscles screaming with the effort. The mark in her palm felt like a brand now.

Something moved in the mist to their right—a shape keeping pace with them, just out of sight. Too tall for a man, too fast for anything with human legs.

"Eyes front," Selene snapped.

The far arch loomed out of the white. They were almost there when the chain shuddered violently. The stones beneath Kai's feet dropped several inches, forcing him to lunge forward. Leo caught his arm and hauled him back onto solid footing, the trident clattering against the chain.

The sound was answered.

Not from the mist this time, but from directly ahead.

The far arch erupted in golden light, threads of it spilling upward like molten veins. The heat hit them a second later, a dry, searing wave that made the rain hiss.

In that light, a figure stood.

Not the creature from the plateau.

Something older.

It didn't move toward them, didn't speak. But Zara felt its attention lock on her like a weight. The mark in her palm blazed white-hot, and she knew—without understanding how—that whatever this was, it had been waiting for them. For her.

The wind surged again, nearly knocking them to their knees. The stones shifted underfoot. The mist boiled upward, swallowing the chasm, the chain, even the far arch, until there was nothing but white.

Then the voice came—not in her head this time, but from everywhere at once.

"The bridge is not yours to cross."

The stones gave way beneath them—then stopped.

They weren't falling.

Instead, the chain lurched upward, like something was reeling it in. The mist thinned just enough for Zara to see the links stretching ahead, taut as bowstrings, vanishing into the white.

They ran again, but the rhythm had changed—slower, heavier, as if the air itself had turned to water. Every step fought them, dragging at their legs.

The mist peeled back in sudden shreds, revealing not the far arch they'd seen, but the black rise of a plateau. It loomed from the void like an island in a storm, its surface slick and glistening with rain. The chain led straight onto it, fusing into stone.

And waiting there, silent and still, was the creature from the spirals.

Its wings were folded now, but even at rest they seemed to hold the memory of movement, the arcs of each pinion sharp enough to cut the rain. The gold-thread light in its eyes didn't waver.

No one spoke. They stepped onto the plateau, boots sinking slightly into grooves carved by something ancient. As the mist burned away under the creature's gaze, the center of the plateau revealed itself—what looked like a cairn of black stone. But up close,

Zara saw the truth: it wasn't piled rock at all, but carved figures. Faces. Dozens of them.

Kai's voice was hushed. "These aren't sculptures."

"They're captives," Selene finished, her tone like a knife's edge.

A chill slid up Zara's spine, even as the mark in her palm pulsed hotter. She searched the carved visages, half-expecting—half-dreading—to find someone she knew.

"Keep moving," she ordered, but the words felt thin in the storm-heavy air.

The creature stepped forward, talons scraping stone. Then its voice came—not aloud, but in all their minds at once.

"Bound, but not claimed. Chosen, but not crowned."

Zara's breath caught.

It turned, and they followed its gaze to the far edge of the plateau. There, spanning a gulf so deep the rain never touched bottom, a bridge was forming—not built, but growing. Jagged black stone pushed itself into place one fractured segment at a time, each pulse of new stone stitched together by threads of gold light.

On the far side, barely visible through the sheets of rain, a cloaked figure stood motionless. The storm bent around it, spiraling inward. Lightning didn't strike near it—lightning avoided it.

The pull hit them all at once. Not to the bridge. To that.

The creature screamed overhead—not in warning, but in command. It landed on the first segment of the bridge, and the gold light brightened. The slabs surged forward another few feet, narrowing the gap.

The plateau tilted under their boots. Not a tremor—an intentional shift.

Rain sheeted sideways, the storm spirals above now so tight they looked like a funnel drawing the sky toward the earth. The figure on the far side lifted its head, and though Zara couldn't see its eyes, she felt the weight of its regard like a closing door.

The pull intensified. Cassian caught her arm as her boots slid toward the edge, but his heels were scraping too.

The bridge lurched again, closing the last of the gap. The cloaked figure waited, unmoving.

The plateau gave one final, decisive tilt.

They were moving—not running, not walking, but being drawn—toward the bridge, toward whatever waited beyond.

The gold-thread light between the segments flared, blinding.

And the world dropped away.

# CHAPTER XXVII
# THE SKY THAT SPLIT AGAIN

March 18, 2026

Rain became mist, mist became weight, and then there was only the sensation of falling. Zara's stomach lurched, the brand in her palm flaring until it blotted out everything else. Her fingers clamped down on the arm she'd grabbed—Damien's, she thought, though she couldn't be sure. The roar around her wasn't just wind or water, but something alive, woven through with that same gold-thread hum from the bridge.

A flash—not lightning, but memory—ripped across her vision: a mountain shattered by waves; a crown of stone sinking into the sea; eyes, vast and endless, staring up from beneath black water.

Her boots slammed into something solid. She staggered, knees buckling, and realized they were no longer falling. The mist peeled back in strips, revealing wet stone underfoot—smooth, unnaturally so, as if carved by a hand that did not care for mortal scale.

The others thumped down around her, some half-kneeling, some catching themselves on weapons. Selene dropped lightly, already scanning the dark ahead.

Not the soft dark of a storm—this was total, suffocating black, a place the sky had never touched. The air smelled of metal and ozone, like they'd stepped inside the breath of lightning.

"Where are we?" Kai whispered.

"Below," Selene said, though certainty didn't touch her voice. "Far below."

The gold-eyed figure from the bridge stood twenty paces ahead, exactly where Zara's gaze landed. No mist to blur it now. Its edges were too clean, its stillness too deliberate. Skin shimmered faintly, not from reflected light but from motion beneath—as if threads were shifting in a loom.

"You were told," it said, voice echoing without echo, "the bridge was not yours to cross."

Damien's spear angled forward. "You threw us off it."

"I spared you." The figure's head tilted, studying them like insects. "The bridge was not your trial. This is."

Beneath their feet, the stone thrummed. From the dark ahead came the sound of chains—not rattling, not loose, but tightening.

Zara's mark burned again. This time she didn't fight it. Heat spread up her forearm, climbed behind her eyes. The edges of the world sharpened in ways they shouldn't. She saw a lake of water far ahead, gleaming without wind, its surface broken by slow concentric ripples. She didn't hear something in it.

She felt it waiting.

Leo stepped beside her, trident at a low guard. "We don't have time for riddles. Either help us, or—"

The gold-eyed figure raised a hand. Leo's voice died in his throat, sound cut away like cloth. "There is no help," it said. "Only passage… earned."

The chains hauled tight. Slow, deliberate footsteps answered the pull, each one ringing off stone like a countdown.

Zara didn't need to hear numbers. Her bones already knew it had reached zero.

A shape stepped from the dark—taller than any man, armor the color of deep water under moonlight. No weapon in its hands, but each step cracked the floor as if its presence weighed more than the world around it could bear. Spirals were etched into its plates—faint at first sight, but pulsing in a dim rhythm that synced, horribly, with the rhythm in Zara's palm.

"A Harbinger?" Damien's voice dropped.

"No." Selene's eyes narrowed. "Worse."

The gold-eyed figure regarded the newcomer with something like approval. "The Sentinel of the Deep remembers the chain. It remembers those who cross unbidden."

The Sentinel's gaze swept them and settled on Zara. Her mark flared—not pain, but recognition, the kind that forced breath from lungs.

"Why me?" she asked, before she could stop herself.

The gold-eyed figure's smile was no comfort. "Because your path is not chosen. It is forged."

It dissolved into threads of light that slipped into the floor and were gone, leaving them alone with the Sentinel.

For a heartbeat, no one moved.

The Sentinel took a step. Stone under Zara's boots cracked.

"Move!" Damien barked.

They scattered. The Sentinel's foot slammed into where they'd been; stone spalled up in razor shards. Leo darted left, trident spinning. Isla rushed right, hammer blazing with heat, and swung for the knee joint. The blow rang like an anvil strike.

The Sentinel didn't flinch. It caught the hammer mid-swing; plates of its fingers clamped around the head. Steam hissed where metal met not-metal. Isla yanked. Nothing.

Selene moved like a shadow thrown by a blade. Twin knives flashed into seams between plates; thin black ichor bled and smoked. The Sentinel's free hand lashed out, caught her shoulder, and flung her across the chamber. She hit the wall hard enough to crack it. Shadows surged, cushioned her landing. She rolled to her feet, teeth bared, eyes mercury-cold.

Kai's bowstring sang—high, clear. Arrows of light stitched the Sentinel's joints; each impact forced the plates to adjust. As it shifted, Zara saw it: a chain. Not the one they'd crossed, not an anchoring tether—one single, thick link of the same impossible metal, embedded dead-center in its chest.

"The chain!" she shouted. "Break it!"

Damien drove the spear headlong into the link. Sparks sheared away, showers of gold that turned black before they hit the floor. A pulse—not sound, not wind—slammed them all back. Eryx skidded; Naia caught his elbow and shoved him upright with an economy that said she'd been planning three moves ahead the whole time.

Zara's palm blazed. She didn't think. She reached for the chain. Heat spilled from her brand into the metal like molten light.

The spirals writhed. Unwound.

The Sentinel staggered. Leo drove the trident into the widening gap, dragged, and Isla wrenched her hammer free and brought it down with a shout that shook the chamber.

The link fractured.

The sound wasn't metal breaking. It was like the bridge had been again—the deep, resonant crack of something foundational giving way.

♦ ♦ ♦

The Sentinel froze, then dropped to one knee. The light in its spirals guttered.

"Passage… earned," said the gold-eyed figure's voice, everywhere and nowhere.

The wall beyond the Sentinel split open, revealing a narrow spiral stair. Pale light pulsed up it like breath.

Damien wiped ichor off the spear haft. "Whatever's up there isn't waiting for an invitation."

They climbed. Steps slick beneath them, air chilling with each turn. The light grew until it forced their eyes to water.

They emerged onto a ledge that shouldn't exist—higher than the storm, close enough to touch it. The sky was a whirlpool of black and gold, spirals winding tighter and tighter until the clouds looked less like weather and more like a living throat. Lightning stabbed again and again into the same point far ahead—into a spire of stone rising from the sea like a blade.

"The end of the storm," Kai murmured.

"No," Selene said. "The beginning."

Far below, a river emptied itself into a bay churned to white rage. At its center, the spire waited. Figures moved on it   too small to make out, but arranged in deliberate patterns that spoke of watch and ritual.

Zara's stomach sank.

She knew, without knowing why, that they were being watched.

The mark in her palm cooled, its presence heavier than ever, a coiled weight burrowing bone. She tightened her grip on her bowstring.

"Then we finish this," she said.

The wind pressed at them like a living thing, pulling and shoving in the same heartbeat, carrying the smell of deep salt and something older—stone that had never seen daylight. Spray climbed the cliff face in sudden gusts, striking cold against their cheeks. The storm above twisted tighter, a whirlpool of black and gold that seemed to drag their eyes upward against their will.

They moved single-file along the ridge, boots slipping on rock slick as glass. Every step toward the spire made the world feel narrower, the air sharper. Far below, waves dragged against themselves in spirals, pulled by a rhythm they could not hear but felt in their bones. Even the heirs who had not yet seen their glyphs flare found themselves glancing at their hands as if expecting marks to appear.

"Feels like walking into a mouth," Eryx muttered.
"Not a mouth," Selene said. "A throat."

The wind tried to steal the words and throw them into the sea. It clawed over the cliff face, pulled at cloaks and hair and anything loose enough to own, and roared until even thunder sounded thin. The ledge trembled—not from waves or thunder. The vibration came deeper, slower, like feeling a giant's pulse through stone.

"Tell me that's not the spire," Damien muttered.

"It's not the spire," Selene said. She didn't blink. Rain threaded down her cheek like a silver burn. "It's what's inside."

Lightning took the spire's crown. The afterimage did not fade. Gold veins crawled down the stone, branching in fine fractures, glowing brighter with every heartbeat until they reached the water.

The sea didn't boil. It recoiled.

Waves drew back in a clean circle around the spire, peeling away to reveal a ring of smooth, impossible stone. Not a reef. Not a platform.

A seal.

"That's new," Leo said, and the casual tilt in his voice was at war with his eyes.

"No," Kai said. "That's a seal."

Zara tasted metal. Her glyph cooled to an almost unbearable density, anchoring her wrist. The lines in the storm tightened. Somewhere beneath the roar, a pitch changed—a tone deep enough to rattle ribs.

The ring opened. Not with a crack, not with force. It unscrolled like a scroll, revealing a corridor of dry seabed to the spire's base. Water walls rose on either side, sheer and flexing, lit from below by threads of shifting gold. Shadows moved within those walls—slow titans gliding along the corridor's edge, confident as rulers walking a border.

"Invitation," Eryx breathed.

"Summons," Naia corrected.

Behind them, the light from the stair guttered. Then vanished. The hole they'd climbed out of was just wet stone again.

Forward or nothing.

Shapes descended the spire's face. At first, Zara's brain insisted Watchers; her eyes refused it. Limbs moved with a wrong grace, edges blurred like heat-haze, bodies folding into the spiral-carved grooves. They moved in pairs, each step synchronized not with each other, but with the gold veins crawling the stone. Lightning chased those steps, striking precisely where each pair had been, as if punctuating a ritual.

"They know we're coming," Isla said. The head of her hammer glowed faintly in the stormlight, hair plastered to her temple, jaw set.

"They've been waiting," Selene said.

The wind shoved them toward the ridge. Zara didn't fight it. The ridge was a knife-edge leading down toward the sea; to their left, cliffs dropped into hammering waves. To their right, the stormwall hung so close she could see filaments of lightning braided within it. Once, a shape brushed along that wall—a curve like a leviathan's back, there and gone again, displacing the lightning as if it were kelp.

The hum returned. The same low thrumming she'd felt in the bridge, in the Sentinel's chest, but amplified now, harmonizing with her pulse until she couldn't separate the two. Her mark's spirals turned slowly, in time.

They moved in silence. The only sounds were the hard rasp of leather, the clink of buckles, the scrape of soles. Halfway down, the ridge narrowed further, the abyss on either side widening into a wet cavern of black. The air grew cold enough to sting, and it didn't come from the sky.

Zara looked down.

The ocean floor far below rippled, as if the earth itself drew breath. Gold lines brushed it. For a heartbeat, she saw the suggestion of something coiled there, pressed against the bedrock from beneath.

She tore her eyes away.

At the corridor's mouth, water rose in walls that curved overhead. The surface high above bent under stormlight, turning the whole passage into a cathedral nave. The light in the seabed threads moved in braided patterns—sometimes simple, sometimes complex, sometimes spiraling into forms that made her eyes water if she looked too long.

They stepped onto the golden path. The instant Zara's boot crossed it, her glyph flared, painless and blinding. A note—low, absolute—rolled through her skull like a bell struck underwater. She braced one hand against the water wall.

Faces drifted on the other side. Not human—carvings suggested into motion by lightning. Not carvings—eyes the size of shields sliding past, regarding them without hunger.

The arch at the spire's base was built for giants. Glyphs crusted its lintel—Greek, then not-Greek, then something that predated both. Every time she tried to set the sequence in her head, they changed.

They crossed under.

The air shifted again. Salt fell away. The air smelled of cold stone and old moss; her breath steamed. The walls were layered, each stratum etched with spirals and lines that moved if she looked indirectly, like a pattern woven from light and water.

Zara's palm pulsed—once, twice—then settled into a slower rhythm. Their footsteps echoed too long, fading into the walls like whispers they couldn't quite catch. The air pressed close, heavy with the scent of cold metal. On either side, the carved spirals in the stone seemed to tighten whenever they passed, like the walls themselves were watching.

Damien shifted his grip on the spear. "Anyone else getting the feeling we're the last ones to show up for something that's already started?"

"That's because we are," Naia said without looking back. The faint light from her crown painted the edges of her profile in pale fire. "And we're the ones they've been saving the main act for."

No one laughed.

The corridor opened.

The chamber was too big for eyes. The floor fell away into dark, broken only by a single platform in the center, suspended by chains as thick as trees. The chains ran up and down into dark that wasn't darkness so much as distance.

On the platform stood a figure.

Not the gold-eyed one. Taller. Armor black as drowned stone, drinking the gold glow, its surface carved with spirals. Where a face should have been: a mask of polished stone, featureless except for a single vertical fissure down the center, glowing faintly.

Watchers flanked it. They were clearer here: humanoid frames, oil-slick skin, movements too fluid, weapons that grew from their arms and hands as if bone had decided to become blade. Their masks weren't porcelain now. Their faces were smooth emptiness.

"They were waiting," Selene said.

"No," the masked figure said, voice deep enough to make her ribs hum. "We were called."

Her glyph flared in answer, a yes in a language she hadn't learned but had always known.

"You broke the Sentinel's chain," the figure said. "That was not permission. It was provocation."

Damien lifted his spear. "You want another go—"

"You are not here to fight us."

The Watchers lowered their weapons—but didn't relax. Their attention was a physical thing.

"Then why are we here?" Naia demanded, crown a faint star over rain-plastered hair.

"To see," the figure said.

The platform swayed. Chains above groaned in a language they had been speaking since the first storms. Something rose from the depths below—another chain. It glowed faintly, like sun through black water. Its links were carved with the same spirals Zara had worn into her skin. Every time it shifted, she caught glimpses inside the metal: a ruin of white stone, a drowned throne, a hand gripping a link the size of a tower's base.

Her glyph burned. Harder than on the bridge. Harder than in the Sentinel's chest. Recognition slammed into her so hard her knees buckled.

"The bridge," the figure said, "was threshold. The Sentinel, measure. This is burden."

"And if we break it?" Zara asked.

"What the gods feared wakes," the figure said—not a threat. Not a prophecy. A fact.

The storm outside seemed to fall still, just for a breath.

Kai flexed his fingers on the bow grip. "Maybe we… don't?"

"It has already been decided," the figure said. "The chain will break."

"By us?" Zara asked.

Silence. The fissure down the figure's face brightened. The Watchers stepped back, opening space.

The chain drifted closer until the glow of its spirals turned the chamber gold. The hum rose—not loud, but absolute. Sound bent around it.

"Zara," Leo said quietly. "You're—"

Her brand wasn't just shining. Its spirals turned, drawing the chain's light in. Not light. Pattern. Call and answer.

Around her, the others reacted—small, involuntary.

Damien's spearhead split a hair's breadth with a ping that made him flinch; hairline cracks veined the metal, molten-red for a heart-beat before going black.

Isla hissed and snatched her hand back from the hammer's head. Heat—and something else—ran through it. A bright line crawled across the metal and stayed.

Selene's Veilblade took a breath—she felt it—in and out. The shadows at her back leaned forward like wolves, eager and afraid.

Naia's crown's light thinned. For one single second, Zara saw thirteen points of light haloing it instead of twelve.

Kai's bowstring thrummed without touch. A second tone sang from somewhere beneath the floor in perfect fifth.

Eryx's coin—his favorite drachma—spun loose from his fingers and flew into the air. It touched the chain and turned black, then white, then vanished like a hole had opened in the world just big enough for it to fall through.

Lysandra staggered and braced her staff, eyes gone a green too deep for leaves. Her pupils were rings. She whispered, "Roots," and didn't seem to know she'd said it.

Thane—silent until now, masked with bravado that even this place couldn't peer through—exhaled and reached for his Mirror Mask. The mask refused him. It turned to look at the chain.

The masked figure's head tilted, almost a nod. "Your path is not chosen," it repeated to Zara. "It is forged."

Something cracked overhead. The platform dipped. The wind of the storm shoved into the chamber, dragging rain and salt and lightning with it. Chains wailed.

"Time's up," Eryx said.

From the far side, the dark tore—an opening not of light but absence.

Through it stepped something that made the Sentinel look small.

It wore the shape of a man only because the chamber demanded a shape. Its body was lattice: stormcloud and shadow braided with veins of living gold. Lightning crowned its head, never dimming. Its eyes were pits of whirling dark that weren't emptiness so much as gravity.

The chain strained. Its spirals tightened. Its glow flared and guttered.

The masked figure turned toward the new presence and went to one knee.

Watchers bowed their heads as if in relief.

The storm-and-shadow thing spoke.

"Break it."

No one moved.

The word was a pressure—the kind that pushes behind the eyes and under the nails. It went through bone into the floor. Zara tasted iron.

The masked figure reached.

"Stop!" Damien's shout knifed through the hum. He planted himself between the figure and the chain, spear leveled. His hands shook—not with fear. With force countering force. "We don't even know what's in there!"

Lightning flickered in the storm-thing's eyes. It regarded Damien the way you consider a wave that insists it is a wall.

"You will," it said.

The walls groaned. One of the massive chains above snapped taut, slamming the platform downward a foot. Eryx staggered. Naia caught him without looking, gaze never leaving the storm-thing.

"We move," Selene said through her teeth. "Or we drown standing."

"We're not leaving it," Damien said.

"You think you can carry that?" Naia's voice was ice. "You can't even name it."

The storm-thing raised its arm. The chamber answered. Gold veins brightened, arcing down into the chain. The spirals carved in each link seized, then spun faster, engraving deeper as if the metal were being rewritten while they watched.

Zara's palm seared. The mark's motion synced with the chain's until there was no boundary between them. The hum rose until it wasn't sound. It was the only thing there was.

The chain will break, said a voice that might have been the storm-thing's or might have been hers.

Leo caught her wrist. "Don't."

"It's already happening," she whispered.

Another chain above screamed tight. The platform pitched toward the central link. Water crashed through gaps high in the walls and fell in sheets. The Watchers didn't move. They watched, heads tilting in eerie unison like carrion birds waiting for a cliff to finish its work.

The masked figure stepped aside from Damien, gesturing to Zara as if introducing her to something at court. "It knows you. It will answer you."

"I don't—" she started.

The storm-thing flicked its hand. A bolt of gold lightning struck her brand.

She screamed.

Not from pain.

From memory.

A city of white stone collapsing into the sea.

A crown sinking through black water.

Hands—hers?—locking around a chain thicker than a mountain's spine.

Eyes, tidal and endless, opening in a place where light doesn't reach and never has.

"Zara!" Kai's voice was a tether she yanked on blindly. "Stay with us!"

The storm-thing's voice filled her head, a whisper that rolled like surf. You are the key that was not made. The link that was not forged by their hands.

Another chain above snapped tighter. The platform dropped again. The floor groaned the way trees do before they crack.

"We're running out of floor!" Damien shouted over the hum.

Zara's focus narrowed to the central link. Instinct told her to step back. Something older pulled her forward.

She stepped.

Leo moved with her, trident leveled at the storm-thing. "If she touches that and dies, I make sure you understand why that's a problem."

The fissure in the masked figure's face pulsed. "If she touches it, there will be no next."

Zara reached. Her fingers brushed the chain.

Heat roared up her arm like molten glass poured into her veins. In the same instant, the chain's spirals locked into motion, dragging her mind through them. She saw a desert wind uncovering a buried ring of stone, each grain of sand flaring gold before vanishing into shadow. She saw streets flooded not by rain but by the slow, deliberate rise of a tide that ignored every shore. She heard voices layered over each other—hers among them—speaking a prophecy in a language older than stone.

Salt water filled her mouth. The air turned to iron. Her mark spun faster until it was no longer a mark but a door, and something on the other side had noticed her.

The world split.

Not with sound. With pressure. It stomped through her body, through the platform, through the storm. Every hair on her arms stood. The chain's gold went white, then black, then a color that had never had a name because no one survived long enough to name it.

The sky above tore. Not clouds. Not weather. A seam opened. Through it, not stars—

Water.

An ocean suspended over the world, rolling in silent swells. Lightning threaded it, muted, like veins in a sleeping giant's eyelids.

Something moved beneath that water. Not a silhouette so much as a curvature so large her brain refused to call it a body.

The storm-thing stepped back. For the first time, its voice softened. "It wakes."

The central link buckled. A hairline crack knifed through it. The sound wasn't metal. It was a continent shifting in its sleep.

Energy blew outward, invisible and absolute, throwing the heirs off their feet. The Watchers rocked like weeds in wind.

The link held.

Barely.

The wound in the sky began to knit. The ocean drifted back into dark. The storm-thing's edges frayed into mist. Lightning still crowned it, but the gold in its veins burned lower.

"This is not done," it said. "The next mark will fall."

Then it was gone—drawn backward as if hooked, vanishing into a space that hadn't been there a breath earlier.

Silence crashed down so hard the ring in Zara's ears felt like a scream.

They lay in a scatter across tilted stone and chained air.

Zara pushed herself upright. Her mark still glowed, but its spin slowed. In the chain, the dark vein through the link remained—a hairline fracture that would never be anything else again.

Leo limped to her, blood slicking his temple. "What was that?"

"The beginning," she said. Her voice sounded like it belonged to someone older.

Selene's gaze darted the perimeter. "Then choose quickly if we intend to be here for the end."

A Watcher stepped forward and inclined its head to Zara. It spoke without a mouth.

"Passage… earned."

A narrow bridge of stone extruded from nowhere and locked onto the platform's edge with a sound like a seal being pressed into wax. It led not back toward the sea, but deeper—into a tunnel whose walls were veined with faint gold that pulsed out of rhythm with the storm.

No one wanted to touch it.

Zara did.

She glanced back. Small costs glittered the floor.

Damien's spearhead was cracked so thin you could've threaded hair through it. His jaw clenched. He didn't look at it.

Isla wrapped scorched cloth around her palm; a thin bright line had etched across the hammer's face and refused to cool.

Selene flexed her fingers once; the Veilblade trembled and then went still, like something in it had woken up and gone back to waiting.

Naia's crown flickered. For a heartbeat, thirteen lights burned. Then twelve.

Eryx stood very still where his coin had been, empty palm closed as if he could trap absence.

Kai pressed two fingers to the bow's grip. The instrument hummed to him like a living throat.

Lysandra stared at the chain as if it stared back. When she blinked, soil—dark and wet—had smudged her lashes.

Thane slid the Mirror Mask back under his cloak and made a joke with his mouth that his eyes didn't believe.

"Move," Zara said. Her voice came out steady. "Before it changes its mind."

One of the Watchers moved as she passed, its head tilting to follow the spiral in her palm. It didn't reach for her—just watched, the tilt slow, precise, deliberate. For the first time since she'd seen them, Zara thought she heard something from behind their masks: not a voice, but a single, drawn breath.

It let her go.

"That one knows you," Selene murmured as they crossed the first span of stone.

"No," Zara said. "It remembers me.

She stepped onto the bridge.

The tunnel swallowed them. The platform and its chain fell away behind, and with it the watchful stillness of the Watchers.

Gold veins pulsed slow in the tunnel walls. The light was not light; it was a map written in motion. Occasionally the pattern brushed Zara's mark and a phantom image slid under her eyelids: a ruin's steps; a hand she almost recognized; a throne cracking down the center.

The path bent. The hum changed pitch. Somewhere ahead, air thinned.

They climbed.

At a turn, the tunnel widened to a balcony cut into the spire's throat. Wind shoved through. Below, the water-walls had collapsed; the sea had returned, slamming into the spire's base hard enough to throw spray like shattered glass. Above, the storm had swallowed its own wound. The sky spun on, pretending it had never opened.

They stood as a group, not touching.

Zara lifted her hand.

Her brand had cooled to the temperature of her skin. The spirals moved barely. For a second, quiet seemed possible.

A sound touched the back of her teeth.

Not thunder.

A word.

Not in a language her mouth could form, but her bones understood it.

The gold veins in the tunnel flared, then went dark.

Zara's legs folded as if a string had been cut. Leo caught her shoulder. The world whitened—not with pain. With vision.

She saw a desert split by a fault like a smile. A ring of stone surfaced beneath dunes that had forgotten its name. Far below it, a second chain turned, lazy and patient, and a single link crawled with hairline dark the way an old burn stirs in the cold.

She saw a tower she knew rising over a river she loved, its glass bright with rain. The sky above it thinned, and for one insane instant there was water where there should be stars.

She saw a throne carved of night itself. No one sat on it.

She saw a hand reaching for its arm.

Her own.

The vision snapped.

The tunnel's light returned, dimmer than before. The hum settled into a rhythm that did not match her pulse anymore. Her breath came sharp and fast in air that had grown too thin.

Leo's voice was a square of solidity. "Zara. Hey."

"I'm here," she said. It felt like a lie the world would forgive her for.

"What did you see?" Selene asked, softly.

"Another chain," Zara said, and didn't add the rest.

"Where?" Naia asked.

Zara didn't answer.

She didn't have to.

The storm found them and spoke in a voice that wasn't wind.

Thirteen.

The word did not come from one mouth. It cracked from the chain itself, from the storm above, and from the glyph sealing Zara's palm. The chamber shook with it.

The word rattled stone dust from the ceiling.

The tunnel jerked, a convulsion in the spire's throat. Gold veins around them pulsed once—hard—like a heart trying to beat through a band of iron.

♦ ♦ ♦

Somewhere beyond the horizon, in a place no map dared mark, a second chain stirred.

Somewhere closer, in a city that had learned to live with storms, the sky thinned to water for the space of one held breath.

And beneath a throne of night, something old turned its face toward the waking world and smiled.

The mark in Zara's palm burned cold.

The storm closed behind them, the sound thinning to a low, endless hum.

Every step away from the spire felt heavier, like they were walking against a tide no one else could see.

Zara kept her eyes forward. She didn't dare look back. The chain was gone, the Watchers still, but the weight in her palm had not eased. If anything, it was sharper—pressing inward instead of out.

She flexed her fingers. The mark shifted.

Not a burn. Not the familiar hum. It moved, like something alive beneath her skin. The spirals realigned, sliding into a pattern she had never seen before—angular, deliberate, a shape that seemed to press itself into her memory even as it formed.

Selene's voice was soft, but it carried in the thinning wind. "What is it?"

Zara swallowed. She had seen this shape once already—in the vision the chain had forced into her mind. Etched into a black crown, resting on the brow of a man she had never met.

A man who had smiled at her as if they had known each other for years.

And in that smile, she had understood: he knew her name.

The mark flared once, blinding white, and the storm swallowed the rest.

The mark burned one word into her mind, in a language she did not know—yet understood completely.

499

**Hellenic Institute of Mythology**
Internal Memorandum — For Author's File Copy
Mr. Ginn,
We write briefly to confirm receipt of your most recent cor-
respondence. Please note: new fragments have been re-
ported from a private collection in the Aegean. The authenticity of these remains unverified, and the condition is fragile.
You are advised to exercise patience until our archivists
can complete a full translation and stabilization effort. If
verified, the material may alter existing assumptions regarding sequence and content.
Further notice will follow.

Prof. Alexandros Stavros
Codex Authentication Unit
Hellenic Institute of Mythology
*(Filed copy: 491 — catalog reference only)*

# THE AWAKENING ISN'T OVER

Venice, March 19, 2026

The air still smelled like lightning.

Zara braced her palms against the slick stone, breath ragged in her ears. The roar of the storm had gone, leaving behind a silence so heavy it felt like a weight pressing against her skin.

The mark in her palm had cooled, but the weight of it was heavier than ever. Not pain exactly—more like an extra heartbeat that didn't belong to her. It pulsed once, twice, and for a moment she couldn't tell if it was hers or… something else.

A thin mist threaded through the ruins, curling around broken pillars and jagged archways. Every stone seemed sharper in the muted light, edges glinting faintly as if they'd been traced by some unseen hand. She caught the shimmer of gold—just for an instant—sketched along the worn carvings. Glyphs, she realized. Not carved, not painted, but written in light.

The pattern was unfamiliar, yet some part of her recognized it—as if the shape had been burned into her mind long before she'd ever opened her eyes to the world.

"Everyone okay?" Leo's voice broke the stillness, low and hoarse.

He stood a few steps away, trident angled toward the ground, dark hair plastered to his forehead. His gaze swept the group in a soldier's count. One, two, three… twelve. All here. His shoulders loosened a fraction.

"I've been better," Damien muttered, rolling one ankle and wincing. He caught Zara's eye and managed a crooked half-smile. "Still breathing. Mostly."

Ayla had already moved to the perimeter, bow in hand. The arrow she'd notched pointed down, but her shoulders were set like stone. Her eyes flicked over every crack in the wall, every shadow that lingered too long.

Selene stood apart, head tilted slightly as if listening for something beneath the silence. Her hair hung wet and dark down her back, her fingers brushing the edge of her weapon—not ready to fight, but never far from it.

No one spoke. They didn't have to. Every one of them could feel it. The quiet wasn't empty—it was waiting.

A distant crunch echoed from somewhere deeper in the ruins. The kind of sound you could convince yourself was just stone shifting. But it came again, too evenly spaced.

Footsteps.

Leo's grip on his trident tightened. "Stay sharp."

Zara's heart thudded, but her mind was already tracking exit points. She angled her body toward the jagged gap in the far wall. "We move. Now."

They started across the courtyard, boots slipping on moss-slick stone. The mist curled tighter around them, the air thinning with every step.

Halfway across, the fog in front of them shifted—not like wind, but like something moving through it. Slowly, deliberately, the haze pulled back.

A figure stood in the opening.

It was tall, thin, draped in a darkness that didn't belong to the mist. Where its face should have been, there was only the faint suggestion of a mask—featureless, pale, and wrong.

The mark in Zara's palm went ice-cold. She swore she felt its gaze slide over it, as if the thing could read her bones.

The Watcher didn't move. Didn't breathe. It just looked at them—no, through them.

In that silence, Zara felt the weight of centuries pressing in—like the thing standing before them had watched empires rise and fall and found them all equally unworthy.

Then, as slowly as it had appeared, it stepped backward into the mist and was gone.

◆ ◆ ◆

No one spoke.

They moved faster.

The light shifted as they neared the wall—not brighter, but stranger. The clouds overhead seemed to leak pale fire, washing the ruins in a glow that didn't feel like daylight. The air carried a faint tang of salt, though the sea was miles away.

Zara glanced back once. The mist was reclaiming the courtyard, swallowing the place in patient swirls. She knew, as surely as she knew her own name, that if they returned tomorrow, it wouldn't be here.

Beyond the wall, the path twisted downward, a narrow track choked with roots and shattered stone. They followed it in silence.

Eryx muttered something under his breath—too low to catch—but his eyes darted constantly to the shadows. Even the ever-joking Hermes heir wasn't smiling.

"Was that—" Thane started, but cut himself off.

"Don't," Naia said sharply. Her expression was calm, almost too calm, the way it got when she was hiding something.

Zara wanted to ask, but the mark in her palm pulsed again, and she let the question die.

They reached the treeline just as the wind changed. It came low and steady, carrying the scent of wet earth and something metallic. A hum followed—a vibration at the base of Zara's skull, like the echo of a bell only she could hear.

She froze.

The others felt it too. She saw it in the way Cassian's jaw tightened, in the way Lysandra's hand hovered just above the ground as if feeling for a pulse.

The hum faded, leaving only the rustle of leaves. But something had shifted.

They were no longer alone.

503

The forest closed around them, dark and damp. Every step was a whisper of crushed leaves, every breath loud in the close air. Shadows moved in ways that didn't match the wind.

Zara's mind catalogued distances, angles, obstacles. She tried not to think about the fact that the Watcher could be anywhere. That it could be walking beside them right now, just beyond the reach of their sight.

"Almost there," Leo murmured, though she wasn't sure who he was trying to convince.

They broke into a clearing, and the sudden space felt almost violent after the tight press of the trees. The sky above was a smear of pale gray, the air tasting of rain that hadn't fallen yet.

The path forked here—one trail sloping toward the valley, the other disappearing into the high ridges.

No one moved toward either.

Zara didn't know why, but the choice felt heavier than it should have.

Damien shifted his weight, looking at her. "Which way?"

She opened her mouth to answer—

—and the mark in her palm flared so cold it hurt.

Somewhere, far off but too close all the same, came the echo of a voice she'd never heard but somehow recognized.

It's not over.

She snapped her head toward the sound, but there was nothing there. Only the others, watching her, waiting.

Zara tightened her grip on her weapon. "Downhill," she said finally. "We move fast."

They did.

As they descended, the forest seemed to press in tighter, the air thickening until every breath felt stolen. The trees leaned over the path, their branches clawing at the gray light.

Somewhere behind them, a twig snapped.

No one looked back.

But Zara's palm burned again, and she knew without turning that the Watcher was still there.

The path narrowed until it was barely more than a deer track. Brambles clutched at their boots, snagging fabric and skin.

Overhead, the branches knitted so tightly that the gray light broke into fragments, scattering across their faces like shards of glass.

The forest felt wrong now. Not just dangerous—wrong. The air had a weight to it, as if it carried the memory of something it wanted them to feel.

Zara didn't like the way it whispered when the wind touched it.

Kai kept glancing over his shoulder, bow still unstrung but held tight. His usual warmth was gone, replaced by a quiet, fixed focus. "We're being tracked," he murmured, low enough that only those closest to him could hear.

"By the Watcher?" Leo asked without looking back.

Kai's eyes didn't shift. "By more than one."

That drew a ripple through the group—small motions, a tightening of shoulders, the quick flex of fingers over weapons.

Thane's gaze flicked toward the trees, his expression unreadable. For a heartbeat, Zara thought she saw something almost like recognition pass over his features, but it was gone before she could pin it down.

They didn't slow.

The descent steepened. Moss-covered stone jutted from the earth like the vertebrae of some long-dead beast, and their boots slid on the damp leaves. Naia moved ahead, picking a path with deliberate precision. Her voice was calm when she spoke, but there was no softness in it. "We reach the river before full dark. If we don't, we keep moving."

No one argued.

The first drops of rain began to fall, thin and cold. They hissed against the leaves, each one a sharp pinprick of sound in the stillness.

It should have been a relief. It wasn't.

Because the rain didn't mask the footsteps.

Zara heard them clearly now—three sets, maybe four, matching their pace but never overtaking. They were careful, practiced, their rhythm too steady to be chance.

Selene slowed slightly until she was level with Zara. "They're close."

"I know."

"What's the call?"

Zara hesitated. Every part of her wanted to turn and face whatever was there. But the mark in her palm pulsed cold again, and she thought of the featureless mask in the mist. "We keep moving. They want us to stop."

Selene nodded once, but her grip on her blade tightened.

The forest broke suddenly, spilling them onto a ridge high above a black, winding river. The water churned far below, white froth flashing like teeth. The path here was little more than a crumbling ledge, and one wrong step would drop them into the current.

"This is the fastest way," Naia said, scanning the ridgeline.

"It's also the one where they can pin us," Damien muttered.

"Then don't get pinned," Ayla replied.

Halfway across, the world seemed to hold its breath.

The rain stopped. The wind died. Even the river's roar dulled to a muted hum, as though someone had thrown a shroud over the sound.

Zara's skin prickled. She didn't have to turn to know they'd stepped onto the ridge behind them.

Leo's voice was low, steady. "Eyes forward. Keep moving."

They obeyed. Step by step, breath by breath, until the ledge widened again and the trees opened onto a narrow slope leading toward the valley floor.

They didn't stop until the ground leveled, the river now only a faint rush behind them. The air smelled of wet stone and the faintest trace of smoke.

Lysandra crouched, touching the earth with two fingers. "This isn't from us."

◆ ◆ ◆

Zara looked down. The soil beneath her boots was damp but warm, as though it had been scorched from beneath.

"Someone lit this path," Lysandra continued. "Not recently. But not long ago."

They followed the faint burn trail until it faded into untouched forest. By then, the light had shifted—darker now, tinged with violet.

Zara realized she hadn't seen the Watcher again since the mist, but the feeling of being watched had never left.

By the time they reached the valley, the rain had started again. It was heavier now, pattering against their hoods and cloaks, soaking through to skin.

The ruins of an old stone bridge rose ahead, half-swallowed by the riverbank. Ivy and moss claimed its arches, but the carvings were still visible beneath—a pattern of interlocking spirals and jagged lines.

Eryx stepped closer, frowning. "These aren't mortal."

"No," Zara said quietly. "They're not."

The mark in her palm flared—not cold this time, but hot, bright, the kind of heat that lingered after lightning struck too close. She gritted her teeth, swallowing the sharp rush of pain.

A shadow fell across the bridge. Not from the trees, and not from the fading light.

It moved slowly, stretching long over the wet stone, even though there was nothing there to cast it.

The air tightened.

Zara's hand went to her weapon. She didn't speak. She didn't need to. Every one of them felt it.

The shadow rippled once, twice—then split into three.

They moved toward the group.

Leo stepped forward, trident raised, water pooling at his feet. "You've followed us long enough."

The shadows didn't stop.

Ayla's bow was already up. Damien drew steel. Selene stepped to Zara's side, the cold air around her deepening.

The first shadow reached the edge of the bridge and lifted—up, out, forming into a shape that was almost human. A blank mask turned toward them, and behind it, the black swirl of nothing.

The Watcher.

Two more rose behind it.

The mark in Zara's palm flared like a star.

She didn't remember deciding to move, but suddenly she was stepping forward, weapon drawn, voice steady despite the rush in her veins. "You want us? Come and try."

The Watcher tilted its head, as if studying her. Then it spoke—not with sound, but with something colder, something that slid straight into her mind.

*Not yet.*

The world seemed to sway around her. She blinked—and the bridge was empty again.

Only the rain remained.

♦ ♦ ♦

They didn't speak of it as they crossed into the valley.

But Zara knew what the others were thinking.

The Watchers had found them. And they weren't done.

By the time the first lights of the village came into view, the rain had washed most of the dirt and blood from their faces. From the outside, they might have looked like travelers returning from nothing more than a hard climb.

But their eyes told a different story.

Naia was the first to speak as they neared the outskirts. "We rest here. One night. Then we move."

"Move where?" Damien asked.

Naia's gaze flicked toward Zara, then away. "Where we're needed."

Zara didn't answer. She couldn't.

Because somewhere in the back of her mind—behind the exhaustion, behind the cold—she could still hear the voice.

*Not yet.*

It wasn't a warning. It was a promise.

The voice still echoed in Zara's mind as the village gates came into view. *Not yet.* Two words that pressed into her bones like the weight of a blade held just above the skin.

She kept her eyes forward. The others were silent, but the air between them was thick with unspoken thoughts. Each one of them had felt the Watchers, seen the masks in the mist or on the bridge. None of them knew why they were still alive.

The village was small—no more than two dozen stone cottages crouched against the valley wall. Lanterns glowed in the windows, halos in the rain. Smoke curled from chimneys, sharp with the scent of pine pitch. It should have been comforting.

It wasn't.

Because the silence wasn't right. No voices. No movement in the windows. No dogs barking at strangers. Just the creak of wet wood and the hiss of rain.

Naia slowed first. "Something's wrong."

They fanned out automatically, scanning the narrow street. Water pooled in the ruts between cobblestones, reflecting the light in warped ripples. The first door Zara passed hung slightly open, swaying on its hinges.

Inside—nothing. No furniture overturned, no signs of struggle. Just… absence.

Leo stepped to her side, trident low. "Where is everyone?"

Zara shook her head. Her palm burned faintly again, and she let her sleeve fall over it. "Not here."

They moved deeper into the village. Every house was the same—quiet, untouched, but abandoned. Tools left on workbenches, meals half-prepared. Like everyone had simply stepped outside and never returned.

It was the stillness that hollowed her out. Not the absence of people, but the absence of time—as if the village itself had been plucked from the flow of the world and left here, waiting for something to find it.

Selene's voice was low, almost reluctant. "This feels like the catacombs."

That was enough to make even Damien glance over his shoulder.

A movement at the edge of Zara's vision drew her gaze. Across the square, near the old well, stood a figure in a dark hood. Rain rolled off its shoulders in rivulets, but the hood never shifted. It didn't move. Didn't even seem to breathe.

She blinked.

It was gone.

"Watcher?" Ayla asked, already lifting her bow.

Zara swallowed hard. "Or something else."

Naia's eyes narrowed. "We're not staying here."

They were turning to leave when a sound drifted through the rain—soft, measured, and wrong. A chime. Low and resonant, like the toll of a bell deep underwater. It pulsed once, twice, and with each note, Zara felt the mark in her palm answer.

Then she heard the whisper again, clearer now.

Not yet.

But this time, it wasn't alone.

We're waiting.

The words coiled through her like smoke, curling into the corners of her thoughts where fear could take root. Whoever—whatever—spoke them wasn't threatening. They didn't need to.

Her breath caught. That voice—different from the first—was warmer, coaxing. Almost kind. But beneath it was a pull, like hands reaching from the dark.

◆ ◆ ◆

The others shifted uneasily, glancing at her.

"You heard that too," she said.

Cassian's jaw tightened. "Every word."

The rain thickened, hammering the rooftops. Somewhere beyond the ridge, thunder rolled—not the jagged crack of a storm, but a long, steady rumble. The sound of something vast moving.

Naia didn't wait. "We leave. Now."

They didn't argue.

By the time they reached the far side of the valley, night had closed in completely. The path turned to mud under their boots, sucking at every step. Wind tore at their cloaks, carrying with it the scent of salt again. Too strong for a mountain valley.

Leo stopped dead, scanning the darkness. "That's the sea."

"That's impossible," Damien said. "We're days from the coast."

Zara's stomach turned. She didn't need to see it to know the truth. Somewhere ahead, the world was bending. She could feel it in the glyph's steady burn.

A crack of white split the horizon—lightning, but not from the clouds. It came from below, from the ground itself. For a heartbeat, the mountains ahead were lit in stark relief, and she thought she saw… arches. Towering, broken, half-swallowed by the earth. The same interlocking spirals as the bridge, etched in gold.

When the light faded, the afterimage stayed burned into her vision.

No one spoke until the wind dropped again.

Finally, Naia's voice came quiet, certain. "That wasn't for us."

Zara looked at her. "Then who?"

Naia didn't answer.

They kept moving.

♦ ♦ ♦

The path narrowed again, funnelling between sheer walls of black stone. Moss dripped from ledges overhead, each drop echoing like a clock's tick in the stillness. Every sound seemed too loud—boots in mud, breath in the cold air, the faint creak of leather.

Then, just as suddenly, the sound stopped.

Not lessened.

Stopped.

Even the rain was gone.

Zara froze, every instinct screaming. The air was too still. Too heavy.

A shadow peeled itself from the wall ahead.

It wasn't a Watcher.

It was taller, its form less human, edges fraying into smoke. Where a mask might have been, there was only a void—an absence that seemed to drink the light.

The mark in her palm flared, not with cold or heat, but something sharper. Recognition.

It leaned forward, and a dozen voices spoke at once.

The storm has only begun.

Then it was gone.

The air rushed back. Rain fell. The world moved again.

The others stared at her, weapons half-raised. No one asked what it was. They didn't need to.

Some truths were better left unspoken.

511

♦ ♦ ♦

They walked until the first faint blush of dawn touched the clouds. By then, the valley was far behind, the village a memory they wouldn't speak of. The road stretched ahead, winding into a mist that swallowed the horizon.

They would keep moving. They had no choice.

But Zara knew, as the wind shifted and the mark in her palm pulsed one final time, that whatever awaited them in the next valley, the next city, the next shadow—it was already watching.

…not like a storm breaking, but like a tide—slow, inevitable, drowning everything until the sky itself split again.

♦ ♦ ♦

And with that split, the world exhaled. Lamps flickered awake in cities that had forgotten light. Screens blinked, radios crackled, circuits hummed as grids long silent shuddered back to life. Power returned in jagged waves—not as it had been, but as if the storm itself had chosen what to restore. After months of silence, the dark was broken. The waiting was over. But in the corners of that returning light, shadows were already rising, biding their time, waiting for their chance.

## The Story Continues in Book II:
### *The Rising Shadows*

*But in shadows, even blood may betray its own.*

# ACKNOWLEDGEMENTS

No book is written alone, and though this story carries the voices of gods and shadows, its path has been lit by very real people.

To those who walked with me through the storm — my family and closest friends — your faith has been the chain that held fast. Without your belief, this journey would never have reached the page.

To the early readers and encouragers who reminded me this was more than myth — you gave me courage to share it with the world.

To the storytellers who came before, whose legends and epics whispered through the years — this book stands on the echoes you left behind.

And finally, to you, the reader — may these pages remind you that myths are never just stories. They are truths waiting for their time.

# ABOUT THE AUTHOR

William Ginn writes stories where myth and modernity collide, where gods we thought forgotten still whisper in the shadows of our world. Blood of the Immortals: The Last Prophecy is his debut epic — the first step in a thirteen-book saga reimagining the legacy of Olympus for a new generation.

William's mind is always turning — whether shaping another creation for the page or exploring ideas that refuse to rest. To him, stories are not simply written; they are uncovered, fragments of worlds waiting to be remembered. He believes every myth is a memory awaiting its time — and that stories, like storms, are never truly silent.

# Join the Awakened

The storm has only begun. The heirs have risen, but shadows still move. If you are reading these words, you are already part of the journey.

Two paths await you:

www.jointheawakened.com

Enter the Codex · Unlock hidden lore · Explore maps · Decipher glyphs · Follow the prophecy

www.bloodoftheimmortals.com

Meet the heirs · Discover their stories · Explore the series roadmap · Step into the world beyond the storm

Follow the storm across the realms:

Instagram · TikTok · Facebook · X

# Coming in Book II:
## *The Rising Shadows*

The heirs believed the storm was only the beginning. But storms end. Shadows spread.

In Venice, whispers stir the canals, calling one heir by name.

In Kyoto, the sun falters, and a bow is raised against the light.

And in the halls beneath Olympus itself, chains tremble—

and a choice is made that will fracture them all.

*The Rising Shadows* will test the heirs not with storms,

but with silence, betrayal,

and a war no weapon can fight.

Shadows rise. Loyalties break.

Not all will return.

www.ingramcontent.com/pod-product-compliance
Lightning Source LLC
Chambersburg PA
CBHW070242140726
47909CB00019B/1861